CW01500359

Introduction

This work is a snapshot of one part in Operation Market Garden, an air assault into The Netherlands to capture a series of bridges that would lead around the West Wall and into the heart of Germany. If all had gone well, Montgomery's 21st Army Group probably would have beaten the Russians to Berlin and ended the war before Christmas 1944. This epic battle has been told many times from an overall view and has been the subject of many debates as to why the operation failed. This will not be repeated here. Instead, I offer a worm's eye view of a small specialized group of men who did everything that was asked of them and more; losing twenty-four men during their time in The Netherlands.

Compiled from personal accounts, war diaries, reports and a selected bibliography, this is the story of the U.S. 326th Engineer Battalion during the nine days of Operation Market Garden. A story that focuses around all of the bridges in the fifteen mile stretch of highway with which the 101st Airborne Division was entrusted. Around these bridges is where the majority of the action occurred for the members of the 326th Engineer Battalion. Probably the most famous of their actions centers around the Bailey bridge at Zon. However, as you will read, this was not the only bridge that the battalion focused on during the battle.

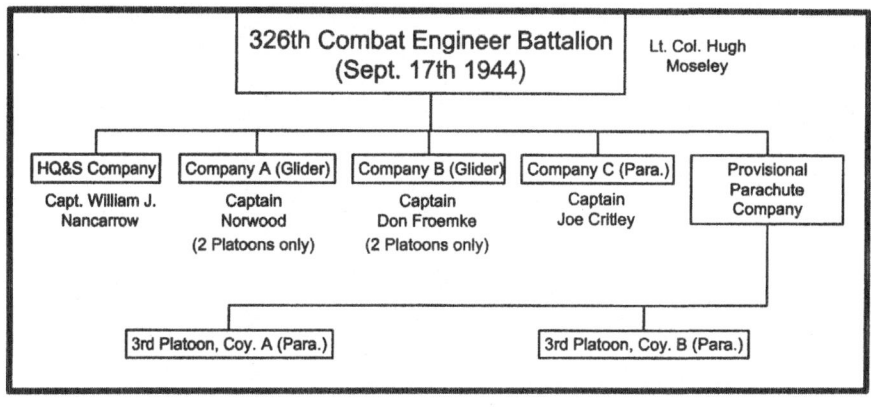

A Brief History

A 326th Engineer Regiment was raised with the 101st Infantry Division during the Great War, but never saw action. It was disbanded in December 1918 and then reconstituted in June 1921 as a reserve unit in Milwaukee, Wisconsin. The reserve regiment was broken up in March 1942 and its elements reorganized and re-designated as the 326th Engineer Battalion (Combat) and the 890th Engineer Battalion, Aviation. Throughout all of this the 326th remained assigned to the 101st Infantry Division. It was withdrawn from the Organized Reserves in August 1942 and in January 1943, the 307th Engineer Battalion (Combat) of the 82nd Airborne Division split into two and the half that was left formed the engineer battalion for the 101st Airborne Division.[1]

Now named the 326th Airborne Engineer Battalion (Combat), it was organized as a Headquarters And Service Company, one parachute (`C') and two glider companies (`A' & `B'). Each glider company consisted of two glider platoons (1st and 2nd) and one parachute platoon (3rd). The three companies were to support the parachute infantry and the two glider infantry regiments. This was different from their counterparts in the 307th who by the time of Operation Market Garden, had one glider and three parachute companies to support the one glider and three parachute infantry regiments of their division.[2]

The 326th arrived in England in September 1943 and their first combat operation was landing in Normandy during the invasion. They fought for five weeks during which their CO, Colonel F.A. Stanlley, was killed in action. He was replaced by Lieutenant Colonel Hugh Moseley and on 12th July 1944 the battalion was taken out of the line and returned to England where they regrouped and waited for the next mission. August was spent planning operations that never came to light so by the time that Operation Market Garden was launched, the 326th was ready to go.[3]

Left: Lt-Col. Hugh-Moseley
Right: Company `B' officers in England. L-R, 2/Lt Mason, 1/Lt. Don Froemke, Capt. Rogers (KIA in June), 1/Lt Hiltunen

Bridging Hell's Highway

The U.S. 326th Engineer Battalion During Operation Market Garden

John Sliz

MGES-5 Bridging Hell's Highway: The U.S. 326th Engineer Battalion During Operation Market Garden Edition 1.1 July 2011
ISBN 978-0-9783838-6-2
Editor-in-Chief: Laura Sliz
Editor: Thomas Shackleton
Consultant: Phillip Purdy
All Maps, Charts and Drawings by John Sliz

Thank you to Philip Reinders, Frans Wilbrink, Peter Dekkers and J. van Eerdt.

It is my best intention to honor the men of the 326th Engineer Battalion by accurately recording their accomplishments. If you think that I have misquoted anyone, gotten anything wrong or have more information please let me know via my website www.stormboatkings.ca

About The Author

John Sliz became fascinated with Operation Market Garden after he read, `A Bridge Too Far' at the age of nine. A visit to Arnhem in the summer of 2001 only added fuel to the fire, eventually resulting in the publication of his first book, `The Storm Boat Kings'. While researching this book and waiting for its publication, he wrote a small booklet on the engineer equipment that was used during the operation. `Engineer Assault Boats In Canadian Service' was published in December 2006.

Since then he has written the first five books of the Market Garden Engineer Series. They are: `The Wrong Side Of The River', `Assault Boats On the Waal', `Basic Function', `Engineers At The Bridge' and the book that you are currently reading. Also, `Non-Bailey Bridging In Canadian Service' was recently published by Service Publications.

He currently lives in Toronto, Ontario and is busy working on book #6 in the series.

For more information please visit: www.stormboatkings.ca

Contents

Maps

Charts And Drawings

Glossary

AA	Anti-aircraft
Abn	Airborne
ADS	Advanced Dressing Station
Bn.	Battalion
CO	Commanding officer
CP	Command Post
Comns	Communication
Coy	Company
Cpl.	Corporal
CRE	Commander Royal Engineers
Cwt	Hundredweight
Div	Division
DUKW	An amphibious truck
DZ	Drop zone
Est	Establish
GIR	Glider Infantry Regiment
HQ	Headquarters
Hrs	Hours
Indp	Independent
KGr	Kampfgruppe or combat team
L/Cpl	Lance Corporal
Lt	Lieutenant
LZ	Landing zone
MC	Military Cross
MG	Machine Gun
MMG	Medium machine gun
MT	Motor Transport
NCO	Non-commissioned officer
O-Group	A meeting of commanders.
O.P.	Observation Post
Op	Operation
PIR	Parachute Infantry Regiment
POW	Prisoner Of War
QM	Quarter-master
RAP	Regimental Aid Post
RAF	Royal Air Force
RAMC	Royal Army Medical Corps
Recce	Reconnaissance
RE/R.E.	Royal Engineers
RV	Rendezvous
2i/c 2IC	Second in command
SP	Self-propelled gun
T/5, T5	Technician 5th Grade. Same grade as a Corporal.
USAAF	United States Army Air Force
Wrls	Wireless
X	Cross. Usually means crossroads

Operation Market Garden

For the operation, the 101st Airborne Division's objectives were to secure the bridges over all of the waterways from the towns of Zon to Veghel and the capture of the city of Eindhoven. They would be the first link in the three airborne division chain that ended at Arnhem; a link that was spread across a long corridor with the three parachute infantry regiments each taking a section of it. This meant that the engineer battalion would also be spread along the division's entire area of operation – over fifteen miles - as they supported each of the three parachute infantry regiments. Added to this problem, only the parachute element of the battalion would land on the first day, thus stretching these resources even further. As a result the two parachute platoons of `A' and `B' companies that had been detached to form a provisional company for D-day would remain that way for this operation as well. To confuse matters, both platoons were called 3rd Platoon. To summarize: the Provision Company consisted of 3rd Platoon, Company `A' and 3rd Platoon, Company `B'. This left each glider company with a headquarters and two platoons, totalling four officers and ninety-one enlisted men each, who would

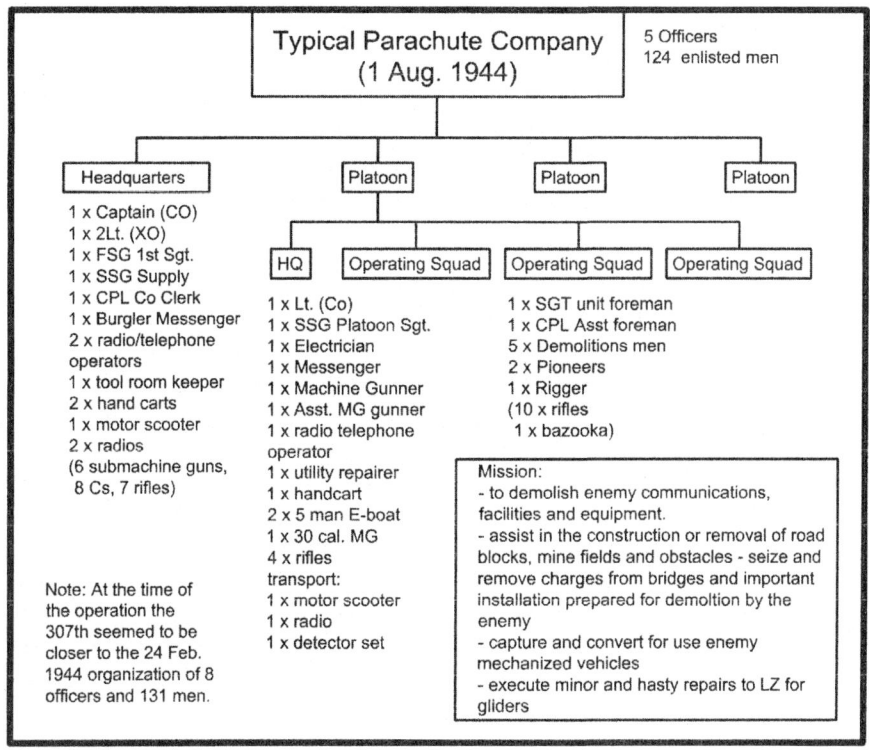

| Typical Parachute Company (1 Aug. 1944) | 5 Officers
124 enlisted men |

Headquarters

1 x Captain (CO)
1 x 2Lt. (XO)
1 x FSG 1st Sgt.
1 x SSG Supply
1 x CPL Co Clerk
1 x Burgler Messenger
2 x radio/telephone operators
1 x tool room keeper
2 x hand carts
1 x motor scooter
2 x radios
(6 submachine guns, 8 Cs, 7 rifles)

Note: At the time of the operation the 307th seemed to be closer to the 24 Feb. 1944 organization of 8 officers and 131 men.

Platoon

HQ

1 x Lt. (Co)
1 x SSG Platoon Sgt.
1 x Electrician
1 x Messenger
1 x Machine Gunner
1 x Asst. MG gunner
1 x radio telephone operator
1 x utility repairer
1 x handcart
2 x 5 man E-boat
1 x 30 cal. MG
4 x rifles
transport:
1 x motor scooter
1 x radio
1 x detector set

Operating Squad

1 x SGT unit foreman
1 x CPL Asst foreman
5 x Demolitions men
2 x Pioneers
1 x Rigger
(10 x rifles
1 x bazooka)

Mission:
- to demolish enemy communications, facilities and equipment.
- assist in the construction or removal of road blocks, mine fields and obstacles - seize and remove charges from bridges and important installation prepared for demolition by the enemy
- capture and convert for use enemy mechanized vehicles
- execute minor and hasty repairs to LZ for gliders

come in during the second lift with the 327th Glider Infantry Regiment.[4]

The mission of Provision Company was to support the 501st PIR as it captured the bridges in and south of Veghel. Third Platoon, Company `A' would land with 1st Battalion on Drop Zone `A1', just west of town to capture the bridge over the Aa River. Third Platoon, Company `B' would assist the 2nd Battalion in securing the bridge across the Zuid Willems Canal, half a mile southeast of Veghel. They would land on Drop Zone `A' south of the canal.

Company `C' was split so they could assist both the 502nd PIR and the 506th PIR with their objectives in the towns of Zon and St. Oedenrode. First Platoon was assigned to the 3rd Battalion of the 506th PIR. From the Drop Zone `C' they were to move south and take Zon and the three bridges over the Wilhemina Canal. Lieutenant Colonel Moseley and his headquarters would land on Drop Zone `B' and proceed to St. Oedenrode with the 2nd Platoon. They were to accompany 1st Battalion, 502nd PIR as they proceeded north from the drop zone to St. Oedenrode and the bridge over the Dommel River. This was a minor bridge which if lost would not pose much of a delay. Third Platoon was attached to Company `H' of the 3rd Battalion, 502nd PIR and would proceed through the Zon Forest towards the bridge south of Best. This bridge was an insurance in case the Zon bridge was lost. [5]

Operation Market Garden was to be the battalion's first major daylight drop and Staff Sergeant Donald T. Pearson of Company `A' parachute platoon was happy for it. He said: *"I believe we were all glad it was a day operation. We had heard of the confusion encountered in the night drop in Normandy."*[6]

As far as the importance of the mission, T5 George Alan Donnenwirth of Company `A' said: *"We had all heard that the war would soon be over if the invasion was successful, the talk was we would be home by Christmas."*[7]

On September 17th, a beautiful sunny day, the parachute element of the battalion boarded the planes at Chilbolten, Aldermaston and Welford Airfields between 1030 and 1100 hours. Third Platoon, Company `A' and 1st Battalion, 501st PIR caught a ride with the 434th Tactical Carrier Group (TCG) as they took off from Aldermaston in forty-five C-47s. Ninety C-47s of the 442nd TCG took off from Chilbolten with 3rd Platoon, Company `B' and 1st Platoon, Company `C' accompanying 3rd Battalion, 501st PIR and 3rd Battalion, 506th PIR. Lastly, twenty-eight C-47s of the

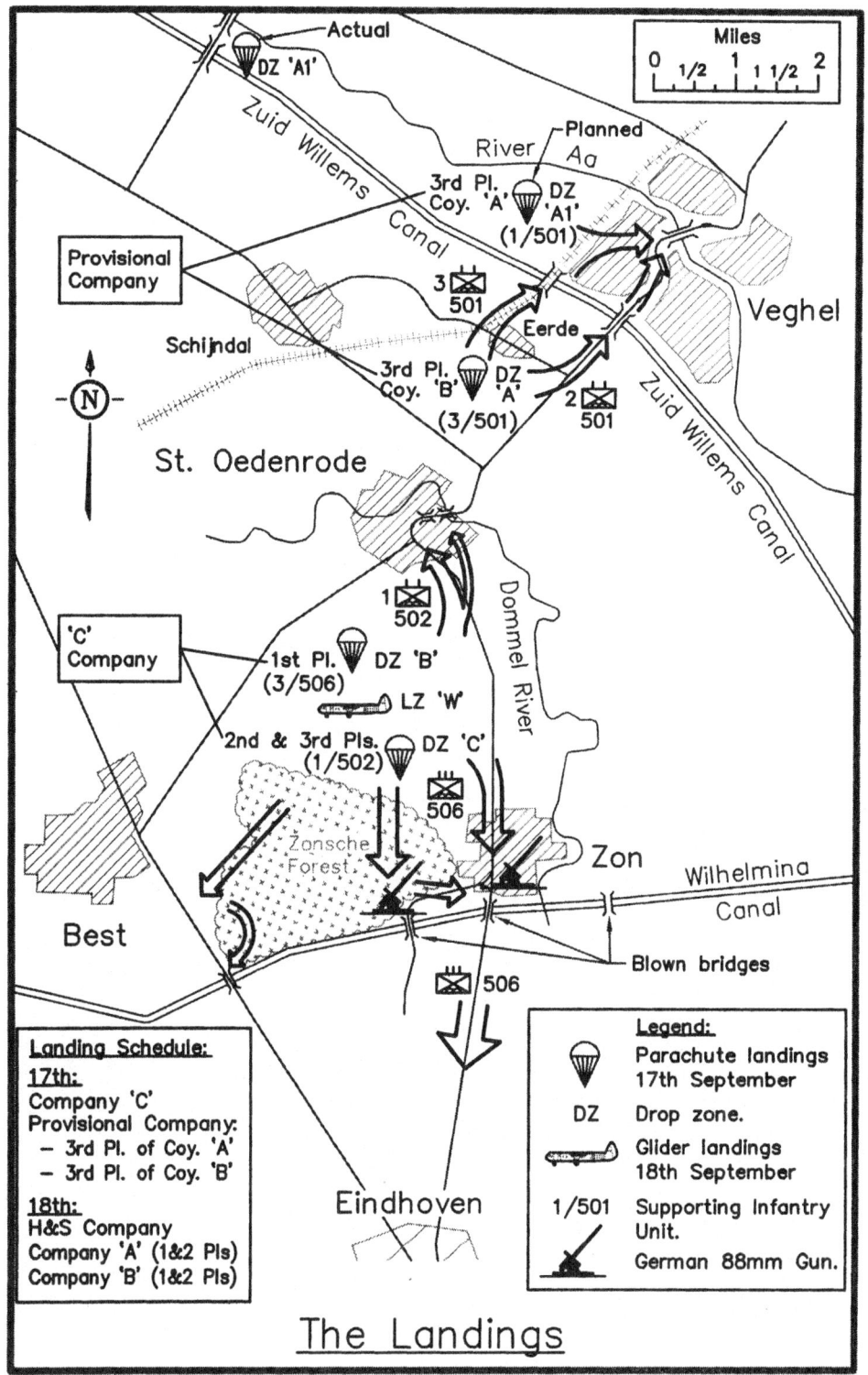

Actual
DZ 'A1'

Miles
0 1/2 1 1 1/2 2

Zuid Willems Canal

Planned
River Aa

3rd Pl.
Coy. 'A'   DZ
          'A1'
       (1/501)

Veghel

Provisional
Company

3 | 501

Schijndal

Eerde

St. Oedenrode

3rd Pl.
Coy. 'B'   DZ
          'A'
       (3/501)

2 | 501

Zuid Willems Canal

-N-

1 | 502

Dommel River

'C'
Company

1st Pl.   DZ 'B'
(3/506)

LZ 'W'

2nd & 3rd Pls.
(1/502)   DZ 'C'

506

Zonsche
Forest

Zon

Wilhelmina
Canal

Best

Blown bridges

506

Landing Schedule:
17th:
Company 'C'
Provisional Company:
 – 3rd Pl. of Coy. 'A'
 – 3rd Pl. of Coy. 'B'
18th:
H&S Company
Company 'A' (1&2 Pls)
Company 'B' (1&2 Pls)

Eindhoven

Legend:
Parachute landings
17th September
DZ   Drop zone.
Glider landings
18th September
1/501   Supporting Infantry
Unit.
German 88mm Gun.

The Landings

435th TCG, of which eight were carrying the majority of Company `C', took off from Welford. [8]

As the slow moving Dakotas made their way to the drop zone, Staff Sergeant Donald T. Pearson was standing in the door of the plane waiting for the signal to jump when he saw two planes of his formation get hit and catch fire. This was his first combat experience so he was anxious and nervous and seeing the planes on fire didn't help his nerves. Small arms fire hit the wing of his plane and the man behind him, Sergeant Field, asked what was causing the noises. *"To save myself from further conversation at such a tense moment I said "backfire".* [9]

Even though four aircraft in their flight were shot down the planes carrying their platoon made it safely over Drop Zone A-1 at 1301. Or at least what they thought was the correct drop zone. Because of an error by the pathfinders marking the wrong field, they landed three miles to the west of the intended drop zone. Despite this 1st Battalion was able to secure its objectives, the town of Veghel which contained the two bridges over the Aa

Above: An aerial view of Veghel taken before the battle. Third Platoon of Company `B' was to strengthen the road bridge (in circle) over canal and build a stronger one beside it. The bridge over the canal to the far left is the railway bridge.

River within the town's limits, within forty-five minutes of landing. However, there was still some resistance that needed to be mopped up.[10]

Upon landing, Sergeant Pearson saw a member of his stick, Private Mendoza, get his front teeth knocked out when he landed. To Pearson's amazement, Mendoza just spit out the teeth and carried on as usual. [11]

Half of the Chilbolton group arrived over LZ `A' at 1311 hours where 3rd Platoon, Company `B' jumped with 3rd Battalion, 501st PIR. By 1515, 2nd Battalion had secured the road and railway bridges over the Zuid Willems Canal southwest of Veghel.

Since the existing lift bridge over the canal was too narrow for heavy tanks to use, 3rd Platoon, Company `B' was assigned to build a second bridge that would be able to handle 70 ton tanks and other heavy traffic. The new bridge was to be a few feet southeast from the existing span, which they were to also reinforce, and a defense line was set up on the west bank of the canal. [12]

By 1600 hours the 1st Battalion had mopped up the rear echelon troops in Veghel. The 501st had taken all of its objectives within hours of landing at a cost of ten jump casualties and two battle casualties and while doing so took thirty-two prisoners.

Like the other platoon in the Provisional Company, 3rd Platoon, Company `A' had a similar assignment and they started work immediately on reinforcing the existing bridge in town and building a new one beside it. The new bridge would be rated at 70 tons and would be the main bridge that the advance would use. Fortunately, the engineers had help. Pfc Harry Yaworski, *"At the Veghel bridge, three Dutch underground men appeared (with orange arm bands) and began working on a bridge next to the existing one."* [13]

This assistance was provided by members of the underground and teachers from the Veghel Technical School. Their first task was to collect heavy timbers and iron beams. Private Edward P. Carowick was impressed with the Dutch helpers. Private Carowick, *"I recall arc-welding under the bridge. Those three underground guys accomplished a lot in a short time."* In addition to help collecting the building materials, they provided welding equipment. [13]

A German truck was found with railroad ties in it. These could be used for support for the bridge. However, there was a problem. Private Carowick said, *"No one seemed too keen on driving a*

Above: The Stad van Gerwen bridge roughly one kilometer west of Zon. It was blown on September 10th. (Frans Wilbrink)

German truck at night, I recall 'searching the gears' – they were different from anything I had previously driven." [14]

The other half of the group from Chilbolton arrived over DZ 'B' at 1312 hours, delivering 1st Platoon, Company 'C' and 3rd Battalion, 506th PIR. The majority of Company 'C' landed on DZ 'C' at 1326 hours with one officer and two Enlisted Men injured during the landing. These were the only reported casualties.

Once assembled Company Headquarters and 2nd Platoon, Company 'C' followed the 1st Battalion, 502nd Parachute Infantry Regiment on its way to St. Oodenrode, some two miles northeast. The infantry took care of the resistance, capturing St. Oedenrode with its two small bridges over the Dommell River easily. Meanwhile the engineers tried to keep the main road open. T5 Carl F. Kelley: *"We took a little dirt road headed for St. Oedenrode. We got to the main highway and started up the road. There were some trees between us and the town. We could see two fighter planes and watched them coming in."* These were P-51s and they watched them release their rockets, but they couldn't see what they were firing at. When they got to the bend in the road they saw two knocked out German tanks. The lead tank's engine was still running. Kelley was with 'Stub' Clark and Wendell Stackhouse, the barber. He continues, *"There was a dead German in*

Above: The Houtens bridge roughly one kilometer west of Zon. It was blown on September 10th. (Frans Wilbrink)

the hatch and Clark said if we could get the German out of there he could drive the tank off the road. Stackhouse was up on the tank with someone trying to help him pull the German out. Whatever the foot of the dead German touched or hit, it caused an explosion. Private Stackhouse was blown off the tank by the blast, which drove his barber tools through the pocket of his jacket and they protruded through his body. He was dead." Five men were also wounded in the explosion. [15]

Upon landing 3rd Platoon, Company `C' assembled on the field northwest of Zon, Holland, and attached itself to Company "H", 3rd Battalion, 502nd Parachute Infantry Regiment and moved southwest to Best. When they encountered opposition, a platoon of infantry (2nd Platoon under Lieutenant Edward Wierzbowski), a platoon of engineers (3rd Platoon of the engineers under Lieutenant Moore) and a squad of machine guns from Battalion headquarters was sent south towards the bridge while the rest of Company `H' dug-in near the Zon Forest between Best and the drop zone.

Lieutenant Wierzbowski was in charge of the mixed group and their journey was a cautious route through a plantation of young pine trees because the Germans had positioned machine

Above: (The Hooijdonk bridge roughly one kilometer west of Zon. It was blown on September 10th. (Frans Wilbrink)

guns to cover the firebreaks. When they moved into the open ground they came under fire. The unit history states: *"Heavy 20mm fire prevented flanking of enemy roadblock and the combined Infantry-Engineer Unit withdrew and proceeded on its original mission, which was to secure bridge across Wilhelmina Canal."* [16]

Lieutenant Charles Moore recalled, *"Lieutenant Ed Wierzbowski and I walked side by side when we left Best. Frankly, we lost control when we were ordered to move form Best to the bridge just before dark. Moving through the dense pine trees in single file in the dark started the problem. The Germans had fire lanes covered by machine guns which continually cut the line of march. I learned later that many of the men drifted back to battalion headquarters."* [17]

The mixed group pressed on and at approximately 2200 hours came out of the woods east of the bridge and through the darkness made it to a quarter of a mile east of the bridge. Walking along the slippery catwalk of the fenced in dock they made good progress until they came under fire from the Germans on the other side of the canal and were forced to retreat. Lieutenant Moore: *"We got to within fifty yards of the bridge. The bridge*

Above: The main road bridge over the Wilhelmina Canal at Zon taken in 1935. It was blown up by the Germans on the first day. (Frans Wilbrink)

guards stared firing. I withdrew over the top of the canal bank to find some cover."[18]

The mixed group dug in and waited for daylight.

The 2200 men of 506th PIR and 1st Platoon 'C' Company landed on DZ 'C' and within an hour of the jump had assembled at 80% strength. All three sticks of 1st Platoon, Company C came down in a closely bunched group, but they could not locate the bundles that dropped with them. First Battalion had the urgent task of taking the highway bridge and two smaller bridges at Zon, so 45 minutes after the jump they were rushing through the woods towards them. When they got close to Zon they came under fire from two 88mm guns and mortars dug-in near the main bridge. By 1600 hours resistance was broken and as the 1st and 2nd Battalions converged on the bridge, the Germans blew it up. [19]

First Lieutenant Harold E. Young and his platoon were bringing up the rear. He could hear that fighting had broken out. Lieutenant Young: "Within twenty minutes or so I heard an explosion up ahead. Instinctively, I knew that the bridge across the eighty foot wide Wilhelmina Canal had been blown. Within three minutes word was passed back down the line, 'Engineers up front!'" Lieutenant Young and his platoon knew that they had work to do! [20]

After the dust had settled, the central column of the bridge was still intact. Lieutenant Young and his platoon jogged towards what was left of the bridge. There was not much of it. He saw a concrete pier with twenty feet of open water on each side. The infantry was swimming to the pier and then to the south bank. According to David Webster of E Company, 2nd Battalion, 501st PIR, *"A naked figure streaked past, dove into the canal, and swam twenty yards to the other bank, where two waterlogged rowboats were moored."* It was the runner from first platoon named Carson who swam the canal. The whole Company laughed and yelled as Carson paddled back one of the rowboats. They bailed the boat out, crossed and cleared the houses on the other side of canal. [21]

Members of the Dutch resistance told them that the two smaller bridges had been destroyed days earlier. Since the engineers did not have any engineering equipment with them it was a challenge to get a footbridge up and running. Lieutenant Young: *"From two years of training and the Normandy experience my platoon was well trained. We had trained for many kinds of improvisations but not this. The men were sent to find hammers, rails, wood, anything that would help build a bridge. Two boats were found and placed halfway to the pier. Then we made a rickety bridge that worked, provided my men helped steady the infantry as they moved across."* [22]

The engineers worked for one and a half hours building a foot bridge that utilized the center trestle. It wasn't pretty, but it worked. The C.O. of the 506th PIR, Colonel Sink, critiqued their work: *"The bridge unsatisfactory from every point of view, except that it did enable me to put the rest of regiment across, single file."* [23]

Private Webster, describes the crossing, *"...after a long wait, we started over, rushing down the planks one by one, into the arms of an engineer, who caught us and steadied us for the run up the other side. A slow process, the company crossing took almost an hour."* [24]

However, it got the 506th PIR across the canal and towards their objective: Eindhoven.

The entire regiment crossed before midnight. Afterwards, Dutch civilians guided the engineers to a nearby garage where a considerable amount of lumber was being stored by a local contractor. During the night the engineers replaced the rickety bridge with a fairly substantial one, using bigger and better planks from the contractor.

At the end of the first day, the 326th Engineer Battalion was divided into several groups which were – as expected – all close to a bridge. The two 3rd Platoons of the Provisional Company were busy reinforcing the existing bridges and constructing new ones in and south of Veghel. The first two platoons of Company `C' were at the Zon bridge site working on the footbridge or preparing the site for a Bailey Bridge while the 3rd Platoon was pinned down near the bridge south of Best. Of all the five platoons of the 326th that had come in on the first day, Lieutenant Moore and his men were in the worst position. However, things were about to heat up for the other groups. The Germans were about to react. [25]

September 18th

As part of the defense of the railroad bridge over the Zuid Willems Canal, Company `E' of the 501[st] PIR was dug in northwest of the bridge. In front of them was a mist restricting visibility. At 0200 hours approximately two hundred German parachutists approached along the east bank of the canal and overwhelmed them. Company `E' was pushed back to the bridge and 3rd Platoon (Company B) of the Provisional Company who was building a new bridge near the highway bridge was one of the units called upon to assist. Its 2nd Squad was sent along the west bank of the canal and they saw the enemy approaching before they were seen. [26]

The unit's after action report states, *"Company B, Third Platoon The second squad moved along a mile of the west bank of the canal, to the northwest. They ambushed an indeterminate number of the enemy and returned to the bridge."* [27]

Private Edward Carowick fills in what the report doesn't say: *"I think that the ambush was the turning point of that action. Rip Reardon could really throw. He was responsible for most of the casualties when the Germans were ambushed. Most of the men passed their hand grenades to Reardon. He threw them right on target. I heard most of the persons involved state that they could not have been thrown that far but Reardon did it."* [28]

PFC Harry Yaworkski was also there: *"One of our men came upon a German rising out of a ditch and coming toward him. He shot him in the midsection. Our man was never the same guy after that. He didn't know whether the German made a movement to surrender or was coming to shoot him."* [29]

By 0700 hours the attackers had retreated and 2nd Squad's services were no longer required. They went back to the bridge, put down their rifles and picked up their tools for building and collecting materials for a 70 ton, two span trestle bridge. Later, Lieutenant Mason and six men were sent with the 1st Battalion, 501 PIR to provide engineer support if needed. [30]

When dawn broke, Lieutenant Moore and his men were in position to observe the bridge south of Best. Before them was a single span a hundred feet long and south of the bridge were barracks. The good visibility also meant that the Germans could see them as well and, as a result, were now firing at them from their dug-in positions on both banks. In their exposed position all the mixed group could do was to keep their heads down and dig their foxholes deeper. Hope for relief came when firing was heard coming from the direction of Best. Second Battalion had started to attack the town and this worried the Germans at the bridge so much that at 1100 hours the bridge was blown. Once the dust had settled Second Lieutenant James R. Watson of Company `C' snuck forward to have a closer look at what was left of the bridge. His movements were seen and he was shot in the midsection. Medic Jim Oravec crawled out to give him first aid and Lieutenant Wierzbowski helped drag Watson to safety into a large hole a hundred and fifty yards back.

Shortly after a P-47 made a pass strafing everything in the area; including the U.S. paratroopers. Fortunately none of his countrymen were hurt by the overzealous pilot. [31]

By the afternoon the lead elements of the British 2nd Army were linking up with the 101st Airborne Division. British armoured and scout cars under Lieutenant Palmar from the 2nd Household Cavalry Regiment, 30th Corps Recon Battalion, arrived on the road on the other side of the canal, and from the shelter of a building fired its machine guns at the Germans. This inspired the Germans to pull out and shortly after contact was made where medical supplies were obtained for the wounded. Unfortunately it wasn't enough to save some of the wounded, including Second Lieutenant Watson. [32]

There seems to be a difference of opinion as to why the group of eighteen men stayed where they were. Some reports state that they were ordered to stay while others say it was Lieutenant Wierzbowski's decision. Regardless of the reason, they stayed and had to deal with a new problem.

The Germans, who had been trapped in the Zon Forest, were attempting to withdraw through the woods, but because the infantry were pressing from the north the Germans had to retreat by the mixed group. T/5 Laino used his .30 caliber machine gun to cut down several of the enemy. Sergeant Adam Slusher remembers watching him, *"He was just great with that gun. We credited him gunning down seventy-five of the enemy during the period."*[33]

At 1700 hours 2nd Battalion was ordered to attack towards the bridge from the north. Fire from 88mm guns on the far side of the canal forced them to stop. It seems that the Germans didn't pull back that far from the bridge. Second Battalion dug-in north of the bridge, but wasn't in contact or even aware of the mixed group.

All of the fighting in and around Best for a bridge that was only a secondary target may have seemed fruitless, but it was important to the overall situation. Though it wasn't apparent at the time, this growing battle did two important things for the Allies. One: it sucked German troops into the area thus relieving the corridor and two; blocked the route to Eindhoven preventing a strong German counterattack on the city.

During the night, First Lieutenant Otto Laier and Sergeant Tom Betras made a break towards the woods and 502nd PIR to seek medical supplies for the group and to return bridge informa-

Above: A training picture showing a raft made of Kapok floats. The principle was the same when Lt. Young's platoon used steel drums to build their rafts. (Author's collection)

tion to higher headquarters. Unfortunately they were ambushed and the Lieutenant was captured. However, Sergeant Betras managed to evade being captured. [34]

Meanwhile in Zon, Lieutenant Young was also busy, but in a different way. A number of his men had suggested that they build a raft to move jeeps back and forth, but the Lieutenant was undecided so he went to see the battalion C.O. Lieutenant Colonel Hugh Moseley. When he got to General Taylor's headquarters, he overhead the General telling Moseley most emphatically that he wanted jeeps across that canal by noon. Lieutenant Young, *"When Moseley came out I told him what the men had suggested. `Go ahead and do it!' he said. I dog-trotted back to the canal."* He was pleased that his enterprising men were already locating metal barrels to which they only had to make and add wooden bungs. The Lieutenant wondered, *"How many barrels to hold a jeep? Somehow we decided on sixteen. These were assembled and held together in a wooden box with a flat top of boards to hold a jeep. We had some rope and tied it to each end to move the raft back and forth. The raft would hold one jeep and one man had to be on the raft to keep it from tilting too much. It worked and we took many men alone or jeeps across."*[35]

Shortly after the rafting operation began a truck full of wounded stopped on the south bank. The civilian panel body truck was too heavy for the raft so the wounded were unloaded and loaded onto the raft and taken over that way. After this, Lieutenant Young sent his men to find materials to build a bigger and more substantial raft to handle the trucks. By the afternoon they had it operating beside the first raft, but before that happened an interesting situation arose. Lieutenant Young: *"In a parachute outfit the men were always testing the officers, Sgt. Andrew Shlapak, the platoon sergeant, was on the south side. Just about the same time a truck load of wounded pulled up and General Taylor came up. Both wanted to move to the other side. Sgt. Shlapak yelled out, `Shall I take the wounded or the General first?' Taylor was busy reading some reports. I yelled back, `Take the wounded first!' and Taylor simply stepped back, not giving any thought to what was going on."*[36]

Pulling a fully loaded raft back and forth across a canal is hard work and unlike the regular engineer units, they didn't have any portable motors to do the work for them. A local farmer showed up with two horses, but the language was a problem. The farmer wanted the engineers to use his horses, one on each side, but the engineers only thought that he wanted across. Unfortunately, Lieutenant Young and his men didn't realize what the farmer had in mind until he had gone away. Having the horses would have saved them a lot of work.

Meanwhile the 2nd Platoon proceeded to remove the wreckage of the bridge in preparation for a Bailey Bridge, which was coming with the Guards Armoured Division.[37]

The lead elements of 30th Corps, the Household Cavalry Regiment, reached Zon at 1400 hours and were prepared to radio back the details of the bridging required to span the canal. However the US engineers* had found a simpler method. The surprised British were told to ask their engineers to call "Zon 244". The C.O. of the 14th Field Squadron, R.E., John Thomas found a phone booth and called the number. It went through the German-controlled automatic telephone exchange and before he knew it he was getting the information from the engineers at the bridge.[38]

* I believe that John Thomas spoke to the C.O. of 2nd Platoon, but I have no proof or a name. I hope to find out both before the next edition.

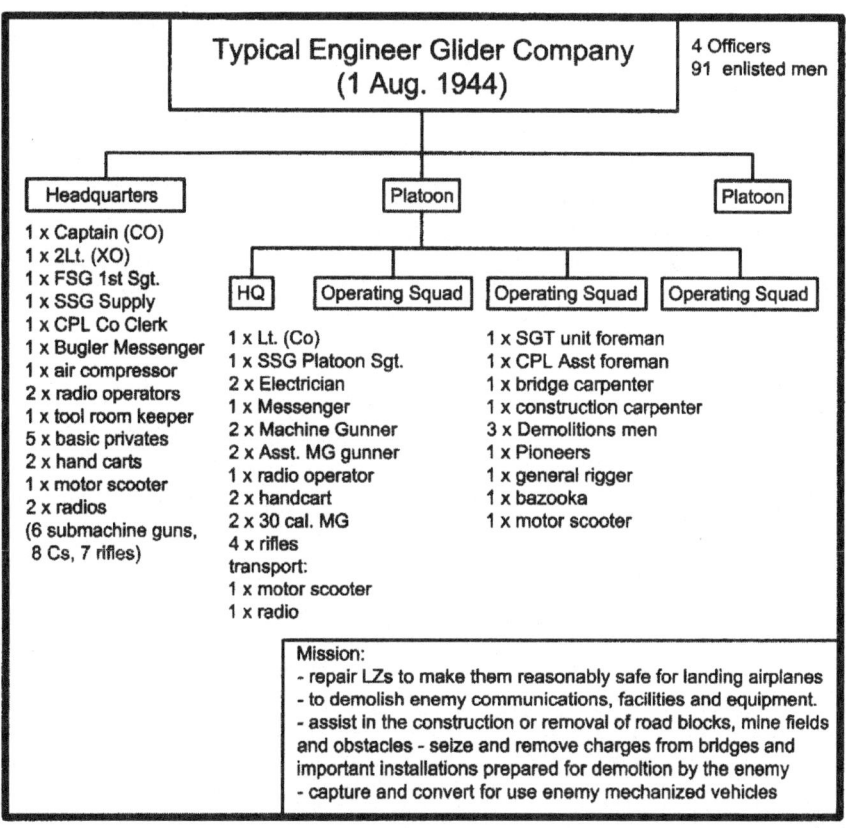

Typical Engineer Glider Company (1 Aug. 1944)	4 Officers 91 enlisted men

Headquarters
- 1 x Captain (CO)
- 1 x 2Lt. (XO)
- 1 x FSG 1st Sgt.
- 1 x SSG Supply
- 1 x CPL Co Clerk
- 1 x Bugler Messenger
- 1 x air compressor
- 2 x radio operators
- 1 x tool room keeper
- 5 x basic privates
- 2 x hand carts
- 1 x motor scooter
- 2 x radios
- (6 submachine guns, 8 Cs, 7 rifles)

Platoon

HQ
- 1 x Lt. (Co)
- 1 x SSG Platoon Sgt.
- 2 x Electrician
- 1 x Messenger
- 2 x Machine Gunner
- 2 x Asst. MG gunner
- 1 x radio operator
- 2 x handcart
- 2 x 30 cal. MG
- 4 x rifles
- transport:
- 1 x motor scooter
- 1 x radio

Operating Squad
- 1 x SGT unit foreman
- 1 x CPL Asst foreman
- 1 x bridge carpenter
- 1 x construction carpenter
- 3 x Demolitions men
- 1 x Pioneers
- 1 x general rigger
- 1 x bazooka
- 1 x motor scooter

Operating Squad

Platoon

Operating Squad

Mission:
- repair LZs to make them reasonably safe for landing airplanes
- to demolish enemy communications, facilities and equipment.
- assist in the construction or removal of road blocks, mine fields and obstacles - seize and remove charges from bridges and important installations prepared for demolition by the enemy
- capture and convert for use enemy mechanized vehicles

Glider Lift

At 1230 hours the planes of 442nd TCG took off from Chilbolten Airfield towing gliders that carried the battalion's Headquarters And Service Company, Company `A' and Company `B'. Inside one of the gliders was T/5 George Adam Donnenwirth. He was thirty-eight at the time and was a Normandy veteran. "I made the trip to Holland by glider with a ton of TNT in a jeep trailer and we almost wrecked our glider on landing, so we were all rightly nervous or just plain scared." [39]

Several of the battalion's gliders were lost en-route. One glider ridden by three Enlisted Men from Headquarters And Service Company broke loose from its tow plane and landed in England. Pfc Arie Van Dort of Headquarters was born in Holland saw another one go down. He said, *"We lost our companion load with trailer when it went down in the English Channel."* [40]

Four miles from the landing zone, immediately to his right, Corporal Courtney H. Boom of Company `B' saw one of his company's glider's wing break off and plummet 500' straight down. On board the unfortunate glider that was piloted by F/O Noel C. McCann was First Lieutenant Ray J. Hiltunen, T/5 Robert J. Le-May and Private Raymond L. Carson. [41]

In a report issued the next day, Captain Ardell C. Tiedeman of the 306th Troop Carrier Squadron stated, *"I was flying directly behind Lt Buckley A. Maynard who was towing F/O Noel C. McCann approximately nine (9) minutes from the target at 1306, 18 Sept 44. F/O McCann was hit by flak and his left wing came off immediately. Right after that the glider seemed to disintegrate in the air. Debris was scattering through the air. I saw no parachute open, and noticed that the remains of the glider were falling straight down."* [42]

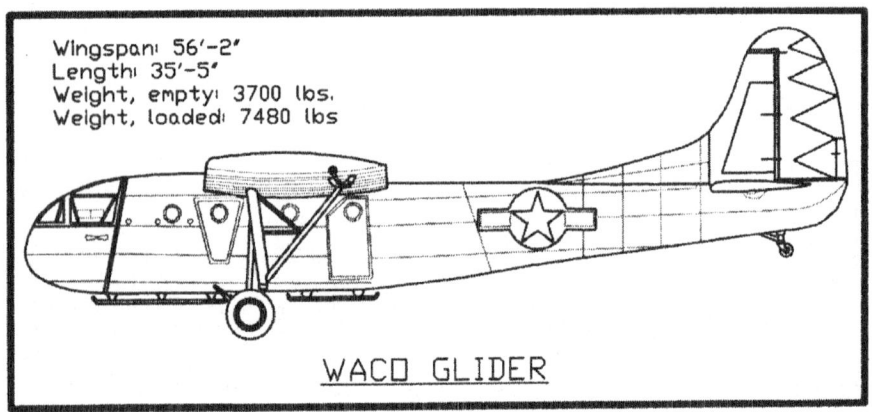

Wingspan: 56'-2"
Length: 35'-5"
Weight, empty: 3700 lbs.
Weight, loaded: 7480 lbs

WACO GLIDER

The first group landed on LZ 'W', one mile northwest of Zon, at approximately 1515 hours and the second group came in around 1600 hours. Once assembled the groups set up a bivouac area half a mile north of Zon and established security for Battalion Command Post.[43]

The commander of the 1st Platoon, Lieutenant Ralph D. Pickens, was given directions to the Zon Bridge by the Dutch. When he got there the platoon laid a hasty mine field south of the Zon bridge.

Two AMM/Clark CA1"Clarker" bulldozer landed as part of Headquarters And Service Company and were used to clear the field of gliders so that other gliders could land. These were the same type as the ones that the 1st British Airborne Division and US 82nd Airborne Division took. They each weighed 4190 pounds and came in a Waco glider. [44]

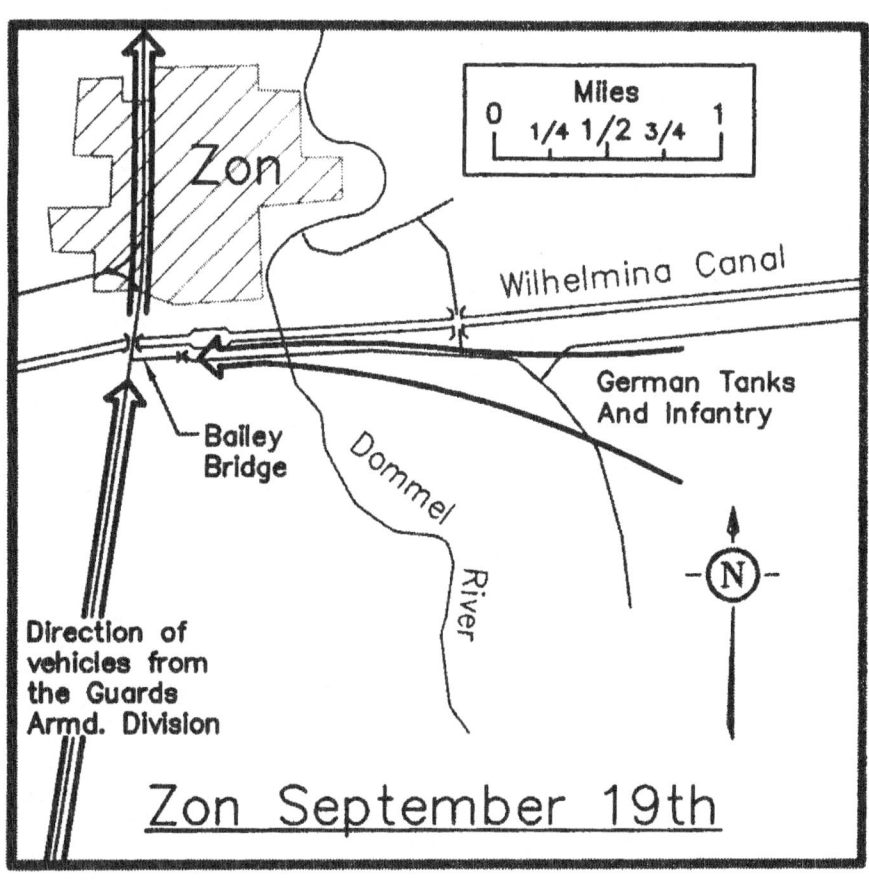

Above: A Sherman tank of the Guards Division crosses the Bailey bridge at Zon on September 19th. (Frans Wilbrink)

The bridging arrived at 1930 and was immediately put to use by the 14th Field Squadron, Royal Engineers, who started to assemble a 110 foot Triple Single Bailey Bridge. According to their recce officer it was a pretty standard bridging job and they should be done early the next morning. There is no indication that any of the engineers from the 326th took part in the building of the bridge. A few members might have, but there is no official record of it.

At 2100 hours both 1st and 2nd platoons of Company 'C' reverted to 326th Airborne Engineer Battalion control and had moved to a bivouac area one-half mile north of Zon, where they joined Battalion glider elements. The H & S Company established security for the Battalion Command Post along with the 1st and 2nd Platoons, from both Company 'A' and Company 'B'. [45]

19th September

At 0615 hours, only fifteen minutes after Major Jones had predicted that the Bailey Bridge would be finished, the first vehicle crossed over the canal. It belonged to the armoured cars of 'B' Squadron, 2nd Household Cavalry Regiment. They were followed by the Sherman tanks of the Grenadier Guards. A half an hour later the column was crossing the bridges south of and in Veghel.

Above: A Sherman tank crosses the improvised bridge built by the 326th engineers at Veghel. To its right is the old lift bridge also their responsibility. (J. van Eerdt)

The improvised bridges had just been finished and the engineers made sure that the tanks and heavier vehicles used it instead of the civilians' bridge, which was only rated at Class 20. They would be responsible for directing traffic as the endless stream of vehicles passed by them.

Finally the 101st had successfully provided a link for the British 2nd Army with the second link of the chain, the 82nd Airborne Division. As the British column passed through their area, the focus was now on defense and the 101st Airborne Division didn't have long to wait to exercise its new role.

At the bridge south of Best, a misty dawn spelled trouble for the mixed group. The Germans assaulted at 0700 hours and came within grenade throwing distance. An enemy grenade exploded on the machine gun of T/5 Vincent Laino, taking out one eye and temporarily blinding the other. By using his sense of touch, Laino was able to locate and hurl back another grenade which landed near his feet, thus saving his own life and those of three of his comrades. Laino would be rewarded a Silver Star. Another grenade landed amongst six wounded and an infantry man named Joe Mann jumped on it, saving the lives of the wounded men at the cost of his own. [46]

Despite the heroics, the Germans overran the mixed group's position, wounding two enlisted men and killing Pfc Jacob R

Northrup. Only nine men were able to fight their way out. The rest surrendered and since the majority of them were wounded they were taken to a German hospital. Soon after, under Lieutenant Laier's direction they talked their captors into surrendering. [47]

Reinforced by 2nd Bn of the 327th GIR and `B' Squadron of the 15/19 Hussars with their Cromwell tanks, the Zon Forest was cleared of Germans by late afternoon. As they probed towards the bridge they were surprised to find the mixed group holding a bunch of prisoners in the hospital.

With the endless stream of traffic going by 1st and 2nd Platoon, Company `C' took up defensive positions in and around Zon. They laid mine fields and mine chains about the Zon bridge. First Platoon had just been relieved by one of the glider engineer platoons, 1st Platoon under Lieutenant Ralph Pickens. Lieutenant Young, *"We demonstrated how to use both rafts with particular attention to the first one which was so rickety but had never failed us. As we left, we watched them put a jeep on the first raft and move it across to the south side. Just as it got to the south side, the jeep went overboard."* [48]

One of the less glamorous, but vital duties of the engineers was to provide water for the division. Because of this it was nec-

Above: A side view of the improvised bridge at Veghel with the lift bridge behind it. (J. van Eerdt)

essary that a water point was established as soon as possible. Run by the eight members of the supply section of the Headquarters & Service Company, the water point was established near the bridge in St. Oedenrode. Security for the water point was provided by 2nd Platoon, Company `B' and 2nd Squad of the 1st Platoon and they had to endure, as their history records, *"Weathered intermittent mortar fire and interdiction fire placed on the nearby bridge by enemy artillery."*[49]

At 1400 hours the Germans attacked St. Oedenrode from the west and 1st and 2nd Platoons, Company `C' were rushed to support 1st Battalion, 502nd PIR. Before they were engaged, the attack was repulsed by the infantry and the platoons returned to Battalion Command Post at 1600 hours.

By late afternoon the 107 Panzer Brigade was concentrated four miles east of the Zon Bridge in the Molenheide woods. Their C.O., Major Freiherr von Maltzahn, managed to get close enough to Zon to observe a constant stream of vehicles crossing the bridge and heading northward. His plan was that the bulk of his armour would act like artillery by firing high explosive shells as six of his tanks (Panthers) and infantry sought out to destroy the bridge. However, like most plans, it sounded good on paper, but the reality was the Germans were having difficulty finding a route for their forty-four ton Panther Tanks, so progress was slow. This, of course, was spotted by a couple of Dutchmen who rode as fast as they could to warn the defenders of the bridge.

This was at 1700 hours and an hour later 1st and 2nd Platoons arrived and were placed a few hundred yards southeast of the Zon bridge to establish a defensive position.[50] The word was that there were five or six panzers with infantry moving along the canal road towards them. The infantry and engineers were dug in and all they could do was to wait for the attack. They heard the large tanks before they saw the lead Panther coming along the canal's tow path. The lead tank fired when it came within view of the bridge. Its shell hit an ammunition truck of the 21st Anti-tank Regiment, Royal Artillery, which exploded and burned furiously. Instantly, the entire area was illuminated by the exploding ammo.[51]

The Germans pressed the attack and Private Lauri W. Hovi, a replacement who had arrived shortly before the operation, was hit. T/5 Paul J. Quaiver, *"At the company area just about 1900 hours, as the sun was going down, hell seemed to break loose in a farmyard which was just across the road. A German tank set a hay stack on fire and was moving around the area firing its weapons. Most of us were in foxholes that the Germans had va-cated and Hovi was hit as he stood outside of his fox hole. He was taken to a convent nearby which was used by the medics and he was dead on arrival."*[52]

The Americans held fast as the German tanks and infantry approached. The main defense was in a school on the north of the canal and the majority of the small arms fire came from there, stopping the German infantry. However, the Panthers still rolled forward towards the bridge, turning their attention towards the school. An anti-tank gun arrived and was able to disable the first tank. The crew jumped out and disappeared. The second tank was knocked out by a bazooka. When this happened, the rest of the attackers retreated. Soon after the 1st Battalion 327th GIR arrived to help the defenders of the bridge. [53]

September 20th

During the night the defenders of the Zon bridge could hear tanks, but most of them figured that they must be their own be-cause they were too close to be Germans. Those who thought that way were wrong. At dawn, a patrol confirmed the enemy's pres-ence southeast of the bridge. The call was put out; everyone who could hold a rifle or not was put into the line. This included all of the engineers in the area. [54]

The second German attack came, but they didn't get as close as the panzers did the day before, choosing instead to shell the vehi-cles on the highway from a distance. This caused a traffic delay until the attack was repulsed. The Germans retreated and at 0630 hours two platoons from Company `C' left their defensive positions following British tanks. The attack was in a southeast direction from the defenses south of Wilhemina Canal. Enemy action was very heavy and during the attack three men were "Killed in Action" and six men were wounded and later evacu-ated. Thirty-four "Prisoners of War" were taken. [55]

Lieutenant Young expands on the day's events. He and his platoon were at battalion headquarters. Lieutenant Young, *"Suddenly, I was told to take my platoon and to report to a glider infantry company commander. I did and he put us on his left flank. My men were in ditches alongside the trees."* Then a runner told him to report to the Captain. *"He told us to synchronize watches and that at a certain time there would be a five minute rolling barrage and then we were to move out with fixed bayonets. I ran back and told my men."* He wondered how he was going to go over the top. *"A whistle blew and that did it. I got up and ran forward and all of my men came out with their bayonets shinning in the sun. The Germans just came out of the holes and surrendered. We moved forward about 500 yards with my main function cutting barbed wire on the fences as I had a pair of linesman's pliers. Now we were really nervous. I saw about six German soldiers in the grass to my left. I yelled to Fritz Balboni and another guy and they swiveled around and blasted those German helmets."* The German helmets turned out to be a big bunch of green cabbages. *"Back at battalion HQ the joke was that the British army was moving east along the highway and Lieutenant Young and his platoon and an infantry company were charging south with fixed bayonets."* [56]

After the German forces in the area was destroyed the battalion was regrouped. First and 2nd Platoons, Company `C' established an outpost line along the river, one-quarter mile east of Zon, from the small bridge east of town, extending north along the river to Wolfswinkle. Further north, part of the Headquarters And Service Company continued to receive mortar fire and interdiction fire at the water supply point. The rest of the company performed supply functions, collecting mines and equipment from the landing zones and delivering them to various units. At Veghel it was status quo for the Provisional Company who continued to direct traffic, guard and maintain the bridge.

First and 2nd platoons, Company `A' patrolled the Wilhelmina Canal, preparing the Dommel bridge for demolitions and maintaining the Bailey bridge at Zon. Meanwhile 1st and 2nd platoons, Company `B' remained as security for the water point near St. Oedenrode bridge. Two details of enlisted men were sent out to establish road blocks at St. Oedenrode and prepare a bridge at Neinsel, Holland for demolitions. No casualties were incurred in spite of the intermittent mortar and artillery fire in the area. [57]

Pearson doesn't remember what day this happened, but it was most likely around this time. Fifteen members of his platoon were dug-in about 1 mile southeast of Veghel. No one was occupying the ground between them and the town. *"There were no continuous lines in that phase of the operation and positions were spaced at wide intervals. Very often the ground outside our perimeter was not visibly occupied by the enemy. A more-or-less peaceful no-mans-land. Dutch civilians in the underground often moved freely between these areas and the ground that could be defined as being held by us. It was common to see a Dutchman*

25

approach our lines on foot or bicycle, rifle strapped to his back, returning from his home outside our held area or from a rescue mission to recover downed American air crews. Therefore, when one night on the outpost a hatless figure with a rifle strapped to his back strode down the road past our position whistling for all he was worth, no one in the position was unduly excited. When he was opposite the first foxhole of the outpost, the occupant of that hole duly challenged him and received a prompt and loud reply "Nederlander". Nothing seemed amiss and he continued down the road towards Veghel past about eight occupied foxholes still whistling loudly. Fortunately, it proved later, when he was opposite

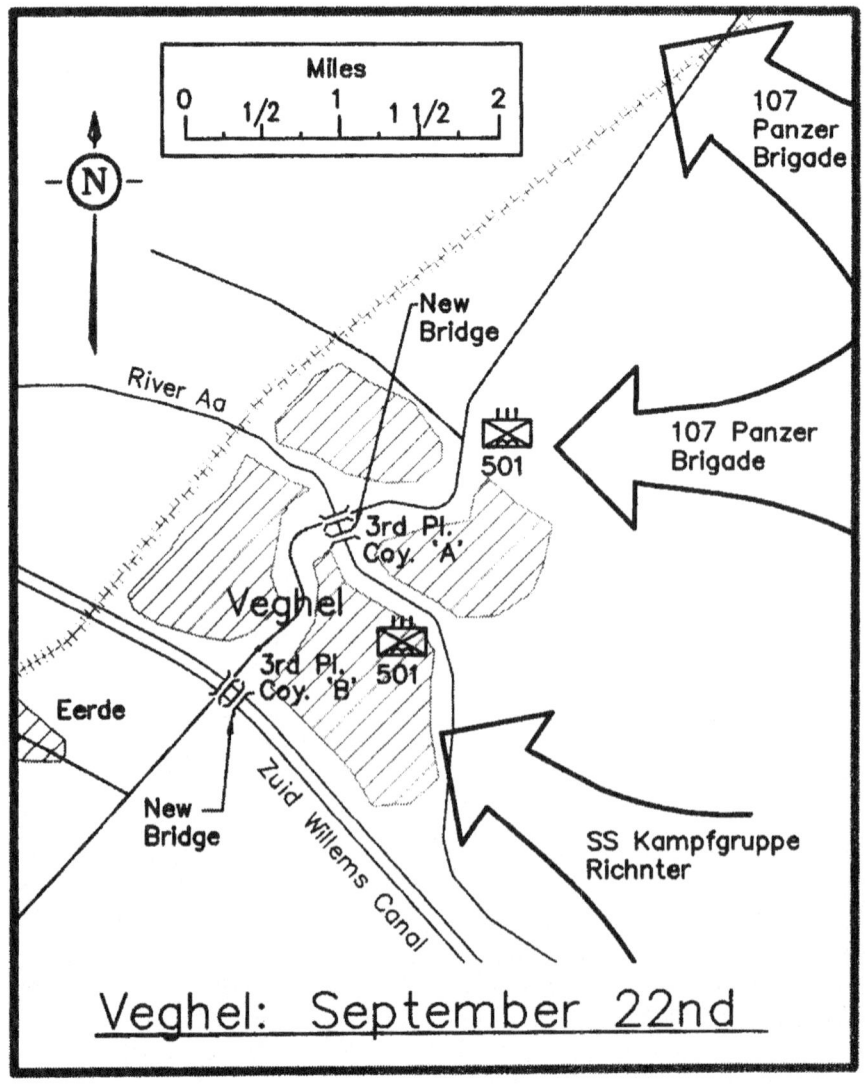

the last hole, one of our men, Private Lucero, being more curious than everyone else, jumped from his hole and approached the striding figure face to face to converse with him. He was real surprised to find himself talking to a fully armed and partially uniformed (no hat) German soldier. The German quite cheerfully surrendered. At this point, when asked where he was going he eventually got it across to us that he wanted to get to his unit across the American held corridor and on the other side of Veghel. His confidence and nonchalance was probably enhanced by a large intake of Schnapps, if our noses served us correctly. We were amazed at his audacity and thankful for Lucero's curiousity. From then on everybody approaching our positions were given face to face scrutiny." [58]

The only real change for the battalion on 21 September was at 1200 hours when 1st and 2nd platoons, Company `C' moved to a defensive position 2000 yards west of Zon to establish a line from the Wilhelmina canal on the south 1500 yards, northeast towards Wolfswinkle. [59]

The next day the third and most significant cut of the highway was by the 107th Panzer Brigade and SS-Hauptsturnfuhrer Richter's Kampfgruppe at Uden and at Veghel. Its goal was to capture Veghel and blow all four bridges to allow time for the Allies cut off north of Veghel to be destroyed. The reports of forty Panthers on the eastern outskirts of Veghel became a reality when the tanks and infantry attacked the town. Staff Sergeant Pearson witnessed a firefight between the Germans and the infantry of the 501st PIR who were in a small brick house and were firing from positions at its corners. *"Outside the house on the side from the enemy there sat an old Dutchman and his wife. Both were calm with a pathetic look of sadness and resignation. It suddenly brought home to me an aspect of war I had not previously considered."* [65]

The paratroopers pinned down the infantry as a squadron of tanks from 44th Royal Tank Regiment and Typhoons attack the Panthers. [60]

As this was happening, one squad from 3rd Platoon, Company `A' was ordered to destroy the bridge across the Zuid Willems Canal two and one-half miles southeast of Veghel. The idea was to prevent the enemy's armour from using that route to attack Veghel. This they did at minimal cost; two Enlisted Men "Slightly Wounded in Action".

To the south, 1st and 2nd platoons, Company `B' established a defensive line south and southwest of St. Oedenrode in conjunc-

tion with elements of the 502nd PIR, southwest of St. Oedenrode.
[61]

On 23rd September the Glider from Headquarters And Service Company, which broke loose in England on invasion day, arrived with the three Enlisted Men from Greenham Commons, England. Master Sgt Harry Shutt Jr., from headquarters was also aboard. He said, *"Unbelievable: After three abortive glider flights. Arrived four days late. Wrecked Glider on landing in Holland, no injuries."* [62]

Like it or not the battalion finally had its Sergeant Major.

Because of another German counterattack, the 2nd Battalion, 501st PIR called for mines and the engineers responded. First Lieutenant Ralph D. Pickens, *"I was assigned to one of the combat teams and had delievered our hasty mine field to the combat team commander. The battle situation was very fluid and he decided not to employ the mines – ordering me to find a safe place in the southern end of town to store them until he determined whether or not to use them."* He did this and then shortly after, *"Captain Tom Norwood, on foot, hailed me down in my jeep and ordered me to return to engineer headquarters and deliver his request for anti-tanks mines. I left to do so and could hear enemy tanks approaching."* [63]

As he and his detail were in the Command Post of the 501st PIR near Veghel, the enemy shelled it with mortar fire, killing T/5 Paul M Hielschen and wounding two men. [64]

At 1430 hours, while the mines were still in route, two panzers with infantry approached a squad of men from 3rd Platoon, Company `A' as they defended a road block on the road by the canal, one and one-half miles southeast of the bridge. During this action, Captain Thomas A. Norwood was seriously wounded and later died as a result of the wounds. [66]

Sergeant Robert L. Salley was carrying mines to the Captain at Veghel and said, *"Captain Nancarrow and I took a load of mines to Captain Norwood at Veghel but he was killed moments before we arrived."* [67]

First Lieutenant. Conrey assumed command after Captain Norwood's death and moved the platoon to the edge of the glider landing field near Best, Holland and maintained an outpost security line along the west edge. [68]

September 24th

Lieutenant Hammond's squad from 3rd Platoon, Company `A' were defending a road block of mines, near Veghel, when they came under enemy fire. Corporal Clampett took a serious hit in the shoulder at the outset of the action. They moved to a nearby barn for cover, and were unable to withdraw. In an attempt to help Lieutenant Hammond and his men withdraw, Lieutenant Plummer crawled along a nearby hedgerow but was seen by the enemy and shot by a machine pistol, wounds from which he later died. Lieutenant Deas assumed command of the Provisional Company of Parachutists after Lieutenant Plummer's death. [69]

Staff Sergeant Pearson saw the Lieutenant get hit and had a different take. *"He had come from Veghel and arrived at the position my group was in moments after we were pinned down by Germans who had infiltrated during the night. He was not immediately aware of the situation and though several of us shouted (from a prone position) for him to hit the ground he did not do so but continued walking to the foremost point of our formation asking aloud, "What's going on? Or words to that effect. In moments he was struck and killed by machine pistol fire."* [70]

The squad was forced to retreat. Pearson, *"I was detailed to make my way back to our lines by an alternate route in order to send help should that unit get pinned down. It was necessary to swim a canal to follow that route and this necessitated my discarding my outer uniform. To make a long story short, after moving through countryside occupied by neither American or German forces clad only in "long Johns" I came upon a farmhouse which was a meeting place for the Dutch underground. They hid me, fed me and subsequently clad me in a gray civilian suit. A young member of the underground was dispatched to our lines and eventually a patrol of the 101st came out and escorted me back, I was instructed to report to regimental intelligence in the center of Veghel and enjoyed myself immensely hitchhiking there in civilian clothes. Each vehicle driver who gave me a lift was quite startled when, who he thought was a Dutchman, talked in New Yorkese. My enjoyment was short lived."* [71]

While still in civilian clothes he was sent to the graves registration unit and helped collect bodies of fallen comrades. Three hours later he was given an uniform and reported back to his unit that evening with the gray suit in hand, happy to have looked like a civilian for a day. [72]

He was also happy to find out that Lieutenant Hammond and the squad also managed to get back to friendly lines.

At 2000 hours on 25 September, the Provisional company was relieved by the 327th GIR and then was attached to the 2nd Battalion where 3rd Platoon, Company `A' provided Security for mortar platoon and 3rd Platoon, Company `B' established security for two Batteries of 907th Field Artillery. Also, Colonel Ballard of the 501st PIR, sent one Officer and two men to contact an infantry outpost in enemy territory and arrange to reinforce this outpost. At 2400 hours, a plan was prepared for placing eleven road blocks. [73]

One squad of second platoon, Company `B' remained on security outpost in bivouac area. Now freed of infantry duties the rest of the platoon was able to perform engineering duties. They joined 1st platoon as they started constructing an air landing strip about 1000 meters south of St. Ooedenrode. This grassy strip was to lie in an east-west direction and was to be marked with flags. [74]

After Operation Market Garden

On 26 September, after the 1st British Airborne Division had been evacuated from the Arnhem area, the battle for the corridor still continued. The plan for placing road blocks was put into effect at 0100 hours. Any of the designated roads were to be blocked, on call from 501st PIR, in case of an enemy tank attack on one of the roads. Each block consisted of a series of mines, tended by two men from 3rd Platoon, Company `B', who were to place blocks on receiving the order.

First and second platoons continued construction on the air strip. [75]

Third Platoon, Company `A' was performing security for mortar platoon when two men were seriously wounded. Sgt Albert J. Engelhardt was in his foxhole when a mortar shell landed close by. Staff Sergeant Pearson, *"Our platoon medic Sam Weiner, who was squatting outside that foxhole conversing with Englehardt sustained a slight shrapnel wound in the hand."* Sergeant Engelhardt died of his wounds. [76]

Second platoon removed a mine field from the St. Oedenrode-Veghel highway.

On 27 September the Headquarters And Service Company moved to bivouac near Battalion Command Post, in Veghel near the forward Division Command Post and set up a new water supply point. Company 'A', joined by the third platoon, which had been relieved from the 501st PIR, also moved there. No enemy tank attack appeared on any of the roads that 3rd Platoon, Company 'B' road block plan was responsible for so they joined the rest of the company at St. Oedenrode where they defended the division's service area. This area had been under intermittent artillery fire during the entire operation of the air strip and one man was killed and one man was seriously wounded. First and 2nd platoons, Company 'B' remained in bivouac on the air strip and repaired vehicular damage to the landing strip.

All was the same until 30 September when Company 'B' joined the rest of the Battalion at Veghel. Finally Company 'C' was withdrawn from their security mission and went into bivouac with the rest of the Battalion. [77]

For the first time since the operation began the entire battalion gathered in one spot. It was probably around this time that the following amusing story took place. Staff Sergeant Pearson: *"One night while on guard I heard one of our men make a dash for the latrine, combat boot buckles (for some reason we had to wear these rather than jump boots) loudly jingling. Within moments he was followed by several others and within the half hour it seemed the entire company was madly dashing for that latrine. All had slipped on their boots but did not buckle them and at the height of the rush it sounded like a wild chorus of sleigh bells. The next morning we all received a ration of rum and paregoric which remedied the situation."* [78]

The battalion was to lose seven more men – all from Company 'B' – before it was pulled out of the line in the fall of 1944. During the Battle of The Bulge the 326th won a Presidential Unit Citation (Army) and a Belgian Croix de Guerre. The 326th Engineer Battalion was deactivated on 30 November 1945 in Germany.

After Word

Even though they contributed so much in so many ways to the battle, the battalion didn't receive a single award. Maybe it was because they were chopped up and had to be in so many places that it was never really seen as one unit. Or maybe it was because they didn't do anything as dramatic as the crossing of the Waal River by their counterpart in the 82nd Airborne Division.

In contrast, the 326th performed a number of smaller tasks admirably. For example, as rickety as the footbridge at Zon was, it still provided a means of getting the infantry across the canal and onto its target. Also built by the battalion were rafts to ferry jeeps and the wounded across the canal. This was all done before they had to switch roles from building to fighting to help repulse the German counterattack on the Zon bridge. There they held ground side by side with the infantry and anyone else who could hold a rifle.

At Veghel two bridges were designed and built by the battalion to insure that 30th Corps' heavier vehicles could cross. If two Bailey bridges were required at these locations then the delay would have been detrimental to the 82nd Airborne Division at Nijmegen.

All of these tasks by themselves don't seem like much, but if any one of them hadn't been done then the effects on the advance would have been felt. The 326th did its job and that allowed others to do theirs. What more do you want from a support unit?

Appendix: Lifts

September 17th
Serial A-4: 45 x C-47, 71st and 72nd Squadrons/ 434 TCG from Aldermaston onto DZ `A-1' at 1301 hours carrying 1st Battalion, 501st PIR and 3rd Platoon, Coy. A, 326th Engineers. Losses: 42-100671, 43-16033, 43-6034 and 43-15491

Serial A-8: 45 x C-47, 304th and 305th Squadrons/ 442 TCG from Chilbolton onto DZ `A' at 1311 hours carrying 3rd Battalion, 501st PIR and 3rd Platoon, Coy. B, 326th Engineers Losses: 43-15111

Serial A-10, 45 x C-47, 303rd and 306th Squadrons/ 442 TCg from Chilbolton onto DZ `B' at 1312 hours carrying 3rd Battalion, 506th PIR and 1st Platoon, Coy C 326th Engineers. Losses: 43-15098 and 42-100874

Serial A-18: 28 x C-47, 77th and 78th Squadrons/ 435 TCG from Welford onto DZ `C' at 1326 hours carrying 1st Battalion, 502nd PIR, Divisional Artillery and 2nd and 3rd Platoons, Coy. C, 326th Engineers. No losses

September 18th
Serial A-41: 40 x Waco, 303rd and 304th Squadrons/ 442 TCG from Chilbolton onto `W' at 1515 hours carrying HQ&SV Coy, 1st and 2nd Platoons, Coy. A, 326th Engineers. No losses

Serial A-53: 40 x Waco, 305th and 306th Squadrons/ 442 TCG from Chilbolton onto `W' at 1600 hours carrying 1st and 2nd Platoons, Coy. B, 326th Engineers and 506 PIR Jeeps. No losses.

Roll Of Honor

Market Garden:

Stackhouse, Pvt. Wendell L., Coy. C, September 17th 1944

Carson, Pvt. Raymond L., Coy. B, September 18th 1944

Hiltunen, 1/Lt. Ray J., Coy. B, September 18th 1944

Le May, T/5 Robert J., Coy. B, September 18th 1944

Watson, 2/Lt. James R., Coy. C, September 18th

Hovi, Pvt. Lauri W., Coy. A, September 19th 1944

Northrup, Pfc. Jacob R., Coy. C, September 19th 1944

Garcia, Pfc. Alberto, Coy. C., September 20th 1944

Hoyt, Pvt. Paul R., Coy. C., September 20th 1944

McGuire, Pfc William J., Coy. C, September 20th 1944

O'Laughin, Sgt. James F., Coy. C, September 20th 1944

Prussman, Pfc. Quentin H., Coy. C, September 20th 1944

Hielscher, T/5 Paul M, Coy. A, September 23rd 1944

Norwood, Capt. Thomas A., Coy. A, September 23rd 1944   [DOW]

Plummer, 1/Lt. William H., Coy. A, September 23rd 1944

Englehardt, Sgt. Albert J., Coy. A, September 25th 1944

Mullen, T/5 Angel D., Coy. A, September 27th 1944

After Market Garden In The Netherlands:

Froemke, Captain Donald H., Coy. B, October 5th 1944

Legg, Pvt. Paul K., Coy. B, October 5th 1944

Werner, Pvt. Richard W., Coy. B, September 5th 1944

Christiano, Pvt. Rocco, Coy. B, October 6th 1944

Portiggia, Pfc Joseph, Coy. B, October 6th 1944

Hunter, Pvt. John J., Coy. B, October 7th 1944   [Silver Star]

Mason, 2/Lt. John M. Jr, Coy. B, October 7th 1944

Notes:

1 – Department of The Army Lineage and Honors 326th Engineer Battalion
2 – US Army Ground Forces TOE WWII
3 – Battalion History Headquarters 326th Airborne Engineer Battalion
4 – Hell's Highway' Sander / Hell's Highway
5 – Battalion History Headquarters 326th Airborne Engineer Battalion
6 – Account: Pearson
7 – Account: Donnenwirth
8 – Then And Now / Battalion History Headquarters 326th Airborne Engineer Battalion
9 – Account: Pearson
10 – Then And Now / Battalion History Headquarters 326th Airborne Engineer Battalion
11 – Account: Pearson
12 – Battalion History Headquarters 326th Airborne Engineer Battalion
13 – p205 Hell's Highway by George Koskimaki
14 – Hell's Highway
15 – p125 Hell's Highway / Battalion History Headquarters 326th Airborne Engineer Bn.
16 – pp107-8 Hell's Highway by Saunders
17 – p136 Hell's Highway by G. Koskimaki
18 – p136 Hell's Highway by G. Koskimaki
19 – Battalion History Headquarters 326th Airborne Engineer Battalion / Then And Now
20 – p 91 Saunders
21 - p77 Parachute Infantry by David Kenyon Webster
22 – pp105-6 Hell's Highway by G. Koskimaki
23 – Band Of Brothers by Ambrose
24 – p77 Parachute Infantry by David Kenyon Webster
25 – Battalion History Headquarters 326th Airborne Engineer Battalion
26 – p209 Hell's Highway / Battalion History Headquarters 326th Airborne Engineer Bn.
27 – Battalion History Headquarters 326th Airborne Engineer Battalion
28 – p209 Hell's Highway by G. Koskimaki
29 – p209 Hell's Highway by G. Koskimaki
30 – Battalion History Headquarters 326th Airborne Engineer Battalion
31 – Battalion History Headquarters 326th Airborne Engineer Battalion
32 – Hell's Highway by T. Saunders
33 – Battalion History Headquarters 326th Airborne Engineer Battalion
34 – Battalion History Headquarters 326th Airborne Engineer Battalion
35 – p106 Hell's Highway by G. Koskimaki
36 – p106 Hell's Highway by G. Koskimaki
37 – Battalion History Headquarters 326th Airborne Engineer Battalion
38 – p358 A Bridge Too Far by Ryan/ Account: Jones
39 – Account: Donnenwirth / After The Battle Then And Now
40 – Hell's Highway by T. Saunders
41 – Unit History
42 – Interrogation Report from Captain TIEDEMAN, Ardell C.
43 – Battalion History Headquarters 326th Airborne Engineer Battalion
44 – After The Battle Then And Now
45 - Battalion History Headquarters 326th Airborne Engineer Battalion
46 – p154 Hell's Highway by G. Koskimaki
47 – p424 A Bridge Too Far by C. Ryan
48 – p107 Hell's Highway by G. Koskimaki
49 - Battalion History Headquarters 326th Airborne Engineer Battalion
50 - Battalion History Headquarters 326th Airborne Engineer Battalion
51 – After The Battle Then And Now
52 – p257 Hell's Highway by G. Koskimaki
53 – After The Battle Then And Now
54 – A Bridge Too Far by C. Ryan
55 - Battalion History Headquarters 326th Airborne Engineer Battalion
56 – p264 Hell's Highway by G. Koskimaki
57 - Battalion History Headquarters 326th Airborne Engineer Battalion
58 – Account: Pearson

59 - Battalion History Headquarters 326th Airborne Engineer Battalion
60 – Hell's Highway by T. Saunders / Hell's Highway by G. Koskimaki /After The Battle Then And Now
61 - Battalion History Headquarters 326th Airborne Engineer Battalion
62 - Battalion History Headquarters 326th Airborne Engineer Battalion
63 – p300 Hell's Highway by G. Koskimaki
64 - Battalion History Headquarters 326th Airborne Engineer Battalion
65 – Account: Pearson
66 - Battalion History Headquarters 326th Airborne Engineer Battalion
67 – p300 Hell's Highway by G. Koskimaki
68 – Account: Pearson
69 – Account Pearson / Hell's Highway by T. Saunders
70 – Account: Pearson
71 – Account: Pearson
72 – Account: Pearson
73 - Battalion History Headquarters 326th Airborne Engineer Battalion
74 - Battalion History Headquarters 326th Airborne Engineer Battalion
75 - Battalion History Headquarters 326th Airborne Engineer Battalion
76 – Account: Pearson
77 - Battalion History Headquarters 326th Airborne Engineer Battalion
78 – Account: Pearson
79 - Department of The Army Lineage and Honors 326th Engineer Battalion

Sources

Primary:
Department of The Army Lineage and Honors 326th Engineer Battalion
Battalion War Diary - Headquarters 326th Airborne Engineer Battalion
Account: Staff Sergeant Donald T. Pearson
Account: Battalion Sergeant Major Harry G. Shutt Jr.
Account: T/5 George Adam Donnenwirth

Secondary:
`United States Army Ground Forces Table Of Organization And Equipment World War II: The Airborne Division 1942-1945 Volume 3/T' by J.J. Hays
`Hell's Highway' by George Koskimaki
`Operation Market Garden Then And Now' by Karel Margry
`Hell's Highway: US 101st Airborne And Guards Armoured Division' by Tim Saunders
`A Bridge Too Far' by C. Ryan
`It Never Snows In September' by Kershaw
`Parachute Infantry: An American Paratrooper memoir of D-day and the fall of the Third Reich' by David Keyon Webster
`The Road To Arnhem: A Screaming Eagle In Holland' by Donald R. Burgett

Index

Printed in Great Britain
by Amazon

48515174R00031

THE RACE FOR MUKALLA

THE RACE FOR MUKALLA

MICHAEL KNIGHTS

PROFILE
EDITIONS

First published in Great Britain in 2024 by
Profile Editions, an imprint of
Profile Books Ltd
29 Cloth Fair
London
ECIA 7JQ
www.profileeditions.com

1 3 5 7 9 10 8 6 4 2

Typeset in Garamond by MacGuru Ltd
Printed and bound in Great Britain by
Clays Ltd, Elcograf S.p.A.

A CIP catalogue record for this book is available from the British Library.

ISBN 978 1 80522 151 7
eISBN 978 1 80522 249 1

FSC
www.fsc.org
MIX
Paper | Supporting
responsible forestry
FSC® C018072

This book is dedicated to the Emiratis who made the ultimate sacrifice during the fighting in Marib governorate since August 2015:

Colonel Jamal Majid Salem Obaid Al Almheiri

Major Mohammed Saeed Rashed Saeed Al Saridi Al Sereidi

Captain Hamood Ali Saleh Saeed Al Ameri

Captain Abdulla Saeed Sheikhan Saeed Al Kalbani

First Lieutenant Saeed Rashed Mubarak Saeed Al Neyadi

First Lieutenant Abdulla Khalifa Matar Khalifa Al Nuaimi

Lieutenant Mohd Khalid Mohd Ibrahim Al Hamedi

Lieutenant Waled Ahmed Ali Khamis Al Khudaim Al Dhanhani

Lieutenant Saeed Ahmed Obaid Bukarrod Al Almarri

Lieutenant Youssef Hassan Youssef Mohammed Al Obeidli

First Warrant Officer Rashed Mohammed Rashed Hadid Al Shehhi

Sergeant Mohd Saeed Mohd Hassan Al Khateri

First Warrant Officer Mohammed Ismaeel Mohammed Yousaf

Corporal Yousaf Abdulla Eissa Bin Jaber Al Ali

Sergeant Khamis Rashed Abdulla Habib Al Abdouli

First Corporal Saad Mohammed Saleh Saad Al Ahbabi

First Warrant Officer Rashed Mohammed Abbas Saleh Al Blooshi

First Sergeant Abdulla Saleh Abdulla Mubarak Al Badri

Corporal Hassan Mohammed Hassan Mohammed Al Teneiji

Sergeant Khalifa Mohammed Saeed Al Yammahi

First Sergeant Salim Rashid Ali Mohammed Al Shehhi

Sergeant Ali Hussain Hassan Abdulla Taher Al Blooshi

First Warrant Officer Sultan Obaid Saif Aboud Al Kaabi

Warrant Officer Obaid Saeed Rashed Saeed Al Mazrouei

Warrant Officer Fahad Ali Mohammed Ahmed

First Warrant Officer Rashed Ali Saeed Al Shehhi Al Shehhi

First Sergeant Nasser Ali Hassan Mohammed Al Blooshi

First Warrant Officer Ahmad Mohd Ali Al Shehhi

First Corporal Adel Saleh Abdulla Al Shehhi

First Corporal Butty Ayel Misfir Ayel Al Ahbabi

First Sergeant Hamed Mohammed Abbas Saleh Al Blooshi

First Sergeant Rashed Nasser Saif Hassan Al Zaabi

Warrant Officer Omar Rashid Ali Al Meqbaali

Sergeant Obaid Saeed Khalifa Al Shamsi Al Shamsi

First Corporal Said Eissa Obaid Al Naqbi

Warrant Officer Abdulla Ahmad Rashid Saeed Al Shimali Al Shemeili

Sergeant Rashed Saeed Rashed Khamis Al Habsi Al Hebsi

First Corporal Sultan Saleh Ali Hussain Saleh Al Shehhi

Sergeant Abdulla Omar Mubarak Salem Al Jaberi

Corporal Mohammed Ali Hassan Ahmed Al Hosani

First Warrant Officer Ali Hassan Mohammed Abdulla Al Shehhi

Sergeant Ali Hussain Ali Abbas Al Blooshi

Corporal Ahmed Ghulam Abdul Kareem Ali

Private First Class Ahmed Hibatan Noor Mohammed Al Blooshi

First Corporal Saood Mohammed Saleh Al Saadi Al Saadi

Corporal Rashed Saeed Mohammed Saeed Al Yammahi

Sergeant Ghalib Amer Saleh Ghalib

First Corporal Waled Mohammed Ali Abdulla Al Yassi

Sergeant Saeed Salem Masood Salem Masood Al Sereidi

Corporal Khalifa Bader Sulaiman Abdulla Joher

Corporal Eissa Ibrahim Hamad Mohammed Gharib Al Bedwawi

First Corporal Shati Saeed Abdulla Al Sayad

First Corporal Khalifa Abdulla Mohammed Ali Saeed Al Sereidi

Sergeant Rashed Mohammed Matar Huzaim Al Al Mesafri

First Corporal Jassem Saeed Abdulla Saeed Al Saeedi

Corporal Sulaiman Jassem Ali Mohammed Hassan Al Blooshi

Corporal Hazza Rashed Mohammed Rashed Al Kaabi

Private First Class Saeed Obaid Fazil Al Ali

CONTENTS

LIST OF MAPS

List of Maps

GLOSSARY

AGM	Air-to-Ground Missile
AM-50	An Iranian anti-materiel rifle capable of penetrating armoured vehicles, used by the Houthis
AQAP	Al-Qaeda in the Arabian Peninsula
ATGM	Anti-Tank Guided Missile
ATO	Air Tasking Order, the pre-written first 72 hours of an air campaign
B-10	A Soviet 82-mm smoothbore recoilless gun used by the Houthis
BMP	The famous Russian infantry fighting vehicle, derived from Boyevaya Mashina Pekhoty
CAOC	Combined Air Operations Centre controlling coalition air operations in Riyadh, Saudi Arabia
chassis	Yemeni parlance for a pick-up truck or sports utility vehicle
CJSOTF	Combined Joint Special Operations Force, a multinational special forces unit
COIN	Counter-insurgency

CSAR	Combat Search and Rescue (pronounced 'see-sar'), the recovery of downed aircrew
CSF	Central Security Forces, a Yemeni paramilitary unit trained by the US but seized by the Houthis
CSS	Council of Sunni Scholars, the religious and judicial reference for the AQAP civilian government in Mukalla in 2015–16
Dushka	A 12.7-mm or 14.5-mm heavy machine gun, derived from the Russian Degtyaryova-Shpagina-Krupnokaliberny (Dshk)
FLIR	Forward-Looking Infrared, a heat-sensing optical device
FLOT	Forward Line of Own Troops, used as a safety measure to show where friendly forces are located
FOB	Forward Operating Base
GBU	General Bomb Unit, the body of a bomb, to which precision-guidance kits may be added
GPC	General People's Congress – the ruling party of Yemen from 1978 to 2011
HBL	Hadrami Bedouin Legion, the last local force built by the Qaiti sultanate with British support before the Communists took over
HDC	Hadramaut Dialogue Council, the AQAP civilian government in Mukalla in 2015–16
HEF	Hadramaut Elite Forces
HESCO barriers	huge sand-filled wire and canvas bags used for military fortifications
HIMARS	High Mobility Artillery Rocket System

IED	Improvised Explosive Device, an explosive mine or booby-trap
IPB	Intelligence Preparation of the Battlefield
IRAM	Improvised Rocket-Assisted Mortar, a simple weapon that can inaccurately lob large warheads over short distances
IRGC	Islamic Revolutionary Guard Corps, the Iranian armed force committed to exporting the Islamic Revolution
ISR	Intelligence, Surveillance and Reconnaissance, military parlance for military sensors
IS-Y	Islamic State in Yemen
JAC	Joint Aviation Command, the UAE's joint helicopter forces
jambiya	Traditional Yemeni curved dagger
jebel	Arabic for mountain
JOC	Joint Operations Command, the UAE's strategic coordination headquarters
JSOC	Joint Special Operations Command, the US's special forces
JTAC	Joint Terminal Attack Controller, a highly trained operative who can direct air and artillery strikes and arrange the movement of aircraft within a set airspace
JTF	Joint Task Force, an organisation that is temporary, fusing together multiple units to perform a mission
K-9	Military dog units, pronounced 'canine'
Katyusha	An unguided rocket, first used by the Russians

KLE	Key Leader Engagement, military parlance for managing relations with the commanders of partner forces or civilian leaders
Kill Box	A numbered grid of territory used to allocate a certain area to specific strike aircraft as their hunting area
kunya	nom-de-guerre
laager	a wagon train (or modern equivalent) set up for all-round defence
LCU	Landing Craft Utility, a smaller landing craft designed to carry troops and vehicles
LRTV	Long-Range Thermal Video, a sensor system
M-ATV	Mine-Resistant Ambush-Protected All-Terrain Vehicle, a lighter MRAP variant optimised for off-road performance
ML-COA	The enemy's assessed most likely course of action (pronounced 'em-el-koa')
MD-COA	The enemy's assessed most dangerous course of action (pronounced 'em-dee-koa')
MRAP	Mine-Resistant Ambush-Protected, a level of armouring intended to protect occupants against small arms fire and mine blasts from below
MRC	Military Regional Command, the geographic military commands used in Yemen
NAI	Named Area of Interest, a defined geographic area in which the intelligence community has strong interest
NEO	Non-combatant Evacuation Operation

OMLT	Operational Mentor and Liaison Team, pronounced 'omelette', an Australian and NATO practice from Afghanistan
PDRY	People's Democratic Republic of Yemen, the post-British, pre-unification state that existed in Aden and much of southern and eastern Yemen between 1967 and 1990
PID	Positive Identification, a means of ensuring the identity of a target
PSO	Political Security Organisation, the main intelligence organisation in Yemen
qat	A chewable leaf that produces a strong caffeine-type narcotic effect
RPG	Rocket-Propelled Grenade, a reloadable or single-use, shoulder-launched, unguided anti-tank or anti-personnel rocket
sangar	A small above-ground fighting position created using stacked-up rocks, often used in mountain terrain where troops cannot dig down into solid rock
SCIF	Secure Compartmented Intelligence Facility
SOC	Special Operations Command, the UAE's special operations military force
TEL	Transporter Erector Launcher, on which a surface-to-surface missile is transported and launched
ZSU	Military parlance for anti-aircraft cannon, pronounced 'shoe', derived from the Russian
VCIED	An IED concealed inside an abandoned vehicle

Glossary

wakil	Arabic for Warrant Officer, a senior non-commissioned officer in the UAE military
YNA	Yemeni National Army

ACKNOWLEDGEMENTS

This book is an almost direct sequel to *25 Days to Aden*, the first military history of the armed forces of the United Arab Emirates (UAE) in the post-2015 war in Yemen. The events in this new book chronicle the concurrent operations that were undertaken in parallel to the Aden campaign, and for many months afterwards, by a different UAE task force responsible for the defence of eastern Yemen against both Al-Qaeda and the Iran-backed Houthi rebels. Unlike the Aden battle, which was concentrated in time and space and which was quite a simple story to tell, the struggle to evict Al-Qaeda from the port city of Mukalla resembled a winding road: the Emirates had first to secure their western flank against the Houthis in the tough mountain battle at Marib, and only then were able to turn their attention south to the liberation of Mukalla. Telling the inspiring story of the Marib and Mukalla campaigns in 2015–16 would require the collective effort of a large number of people, whom I would like to thank here.

The UAE Armed Forces are a learning military and they showed foresight in supporting both *25 Days to Aden* and this new military history. I want to extend my gratitude to the leadership of the armed forces for their strong support for both books. While many Western nations find it hard to keep their secrets, the Emiratis are still good at maintaining operational security. But military history requires access to key persons and records, and the UAE military leadership again adopted a visionary approach in order to accurately record the story of the Marib and Mukalla campaigns so that future generations of UAE soldiers and citizens can commemorate and learn from these operations.

I would like to personally thank the leadership, including the Commander-in-Chief, the Chief of Staff of the Armed Forces, the Commander of Land Forces, the Commander of Air Force and Air Defence, the Commander of the Naval Forces, and the Commander of the Presidential Guard. The UAE Ministry of Foreign Affairs and International Cooperation also deserves my deep gratitude for their continuing support on the diplomatic and international aspects of this history. Following on from the success of *25 Days to Aden*, thank you again for trusting me to tell this new chapter of your nation's military history.

The primary source material for this book are the memories of the participants of the battles of Marib and Mukalla, related to me directly by those men and women. I began to gather these recollections as close as I could after the events, when interviewing Emirati and Yemen troops in Yemen, the UAE and elsewhere in 2017–23. There are too many UAE service-persons to thank individually, and security considerations prevent me from naming serving officers in any case, but I want to collectively thank all the people who told their stories to me. In addition to sharing their history with me, they kept me safe during my periods at the front lines in Yemen and I am eternally grateful to them for their hospitality and protection. I also want to recognise my friend and colleague Alex Almeida for his comradeship on those visits into Yemen and for his unstinting attention to detail as we watched the war unfold. Last but definitely not least, I want to thank all my Yemeni friends in Marib, Mukalla and other parts of Yemen – those who survived and those who did not – for their support for the book. Special thanks go to the two uncles of the book – Jaber L. of the UAE Ministry of Defense and Peter Jones of Profile Publishing.

Above all, *The Race for Mukalla* is about the ultimate sacrifice made by Emiratis in order to free their fellow Arabs from brutal occupation by either Al-Qaeda or the Iran-backed Houthis. There was no time to hesitate, despite the cruel blows suffered by the UAE in the fighting in 2015 in Yemen. Quick decisions were needed if the UAE and Yemeni coalition partners were to stop the Iran-backed Houthis from undertaking a war-winning seizure of Yemen's largest oil and gas fields at Marib; and there was an equally urgent need to remove Al-Qaeda from a city of half a million at Mukalla before they poisoned the minds of the city's youth, as other jihadists were doing in Iraq's Mosul and Syria's Raqqa at the same moment in history. No superpower was coming to help Yemen, yet the UAE commander-in-chief welcomed this chance for Arabs to secure their own region, noting:

> Islam has been hijacked by a small group. Our task is to fix it: it is not the task of the Americans or anyone else, because they are our sons. We need to bring them back to the right way. Islam is our religion and we should correct it.

When called forward in this manner, UAE soldiers, sailors and airmen did not hesitate to do their duty. This book is dedicated to them.

PROLOGUE

Midday, 24 April 2016

Kilometre 162 on the road to Mukalla. Fifty klicks to go.

Azzan stared at the gap in the chain of hills to the convoy's front, where countless millennia of rainfall pouring off the mountains to the sea had carved a 200-metre-wide wadi through the limestone cliffs. It was the final choke point before the coastal plain. That made it the last place where Al-Qaeda could try to block his force of United Arab Emirates (UAE) special forces and their allied Yemeni tribesmen from breaking through to Mukalla, a city of half a million people who had lived under terrorist occupation for the last year.

Azzan's driver Khaled restlessly wriggled his shoulders inside his body armour, stretched out his muscular forearms and let the tension flow out of his fingertips. He had been behind the big, thin steering wheel for 14 hours now. His eyes were stinging after spending half the night driving on treacherous mountain roads with night-vision goggles clamped to his face. There were no more energy drinks left, just crumpled empty cans on the sand-coloured metal dashboard, with its scores of chunky black, red and yellow switches. But this was the end-run: they were almost there.

A serious, intense fellow, Azzan scratched his hot, prickly chin through the thick beard he had grown throughout his year-long mission with the Yemeni tribes. He jammed the binoculars in the glove box, between the notebooks, USB cords and a camouflaged scarf. Azzan had just heard back from the Yemeni general, who could not convince his men – old Yemeni soldiers who thought dying was a young man's game – to put their heads into the lion's mouth one more time.

Azzan and his Emirati special forces would have to lead by example and push on through the pass. Soon Al-Qaeda would recover from the initial 'shock and awe' airstrikes that had started just after midnight. They might put into effect their plans to demolish the ancient trading city of Mukalla if they could not hold on to it.

The clear blue skies above were empty of supporting air power at that exact moment. It was hard to keep the fuel-hungry F-16s, Mirages and F-15s constantly overhead without US refuelling support – which had been denied by Washington. Worse, it was impossible for UAE Apache helicopter gunships to reach him since the Americans had refused to base the choppers on their ships, even though the US Navy vessels were sitting right off the coast and Al-Qaeda was their shared enemy. The Emiratis would have to go it alone.

Azzan ordered his turret gunners to scan the high ground on each of their firing arcs as they passed between the 100-metre-high cliffs. On the far side, he drew up his little force into a triangular 'laager', an old word for a wagon train set up for all-round defence, with their guns facing outwards. Azzan's RG-31 mine-resistant ambush-protected (MRAP) vehicle and three of the larger six-wheel Caiman MRAPs were interspersed with three pick-up trucks full of Yemeni tribal fighters and scouts. Having secured the pass, Azzan planned to hold this position until the old soldiers came up to join them.

Just a few hundred metres away was the permanent outer vehicle checkpoint of Mukalla. A large white metal sunshade covered the *highway. Before the war, it would have been manned by bored, hot soldiers, but it was empty now. This place was a symbol, Azzan knew: if you held it, you held the door to Mukalla. But the enemy knew that too, and suddenly, from every ridge and every direction, Al-Qaeda fighters started to rain down fire on Azzan's men.*

Azzan knew instinctively from his days alongside NATO forces in Afghanistan that he was in a prepared kill zone. A multi-directional attack involving mortars, snipers and heavy machine guns was known as a 'complex attack' in military terminology because it indicated forethought and organisation. Azzan had seen hard fighting against the Taliban and Al-Qaeda in Afghanistan and he had been wondering if these Yemeni Al-Qaeda were made of the same stuff. It seemed they were.

Outside, his Yemeni scouts were bailing out of the flatbeds of their Toyota Hiluxes and finding cover. Azzan's commander-side window now came under accurate fire: suddenly a high-velocity bullet made a milky spider's web of concentric cracks in the layered armoured glass right next to his face. Outside the vehicle, a Yemeni fighter was sniped cleanly between his body armour and his chin, right through the throat.

Azzan tried to think but the repeated sharp cracks on the armoured glass and the metal skin of the MRAP felt like electric shocks in his brain. 'I have to move, return fire; do something!', Azzan told himself through the oppressive wall of noise. If his force stayed passive, they would soon all be dead. He manoeuvred the MRAPs away from the wrecked pick-ups and the Yemeni wounded, to draw the mortar fire off them and to give his gunners better angles on the Al-Qaeda snipers on the ridges above. Azzan cracked open his door momentarily to lob a spread of grenades at the nearest source of fire using his RG-6 rotary-drum grenade launcher.

'Car coming on the main road,' reported in one of his vehicle commanders. In the reporting MRAP, the turret gunner Corporal

Saeed H. looked through the flames and smoke of the burning vehicles and he could see a dirty white Nissan Patrol edging closer. It was Saeed's first enemy contact but he still had the presence of mind to run through his rules of engagement. Even in the midst of this firefight, he knew it could still be a civilian escaping or a resistance vehicle returning to friendly lines.

Despite bullets spanging off his turret, he stared intently at the dusty car. Like a lot of young gunners, Saeed had superb eyesight and as he watched the vehicle's odd progress he could clearly make out the young man driving the car – probably young because older Yemeni tribal men typically had full-grown beards. The Nissan Patrol was not a car you saw a lot in Yemen. None of this looked right. Then, after seeming to pass by the laager to its rear left, the driver veered off the road and headed straight back towards them from behind. Clever.

Everyone scrambled to realign the laager's defensive firepower to the rear. Saeed's driver put his MRAP between the suicide bomber and Azzan's command vehicle. Corporal Saeed hand-cranked his turret traverse as fast as he could. It was a close race. With a second to spare, he thumbed off the safety catch of his heavy machine gun and put a precise grouping of rounds into the driver-side windscreen of the Nissan. He just had time to register the window shattering and a hint of red and then everything went dark.

Above, a watching drone recorded the huge explosion and its concussion wave sending a dust cloud outwards. The Nissan's engine block landed 50 metres away.

As the thick black smoke rose in a mushroom cloud above the laager, Azzan took in the scene of devastation: three burning Yemeni pick-ups; a huge smoking crater; dead Yemenis laying all around; and four intact but battered MRAPs, their tyres and windows scarred by fragmentation and bullet impacts.

Prologue

Remembering ambushes in Afghanistan, Azzan left the radio net clear for those who might need it most – the vehicles closest to the blast. There was a tense silence and he waited with his jaw clenched. The seconds passed agonisingly slowly. Nothing ... Nothing ... Then Saeed's vehicle commander called in, barely able to speak from the acrid smoke and too deafened to hear any reply.

Corporal Saeed looked out from behind his bent and smoking gun shield. His helmet had been ripped up by sharp fragments of the Nissan Patrol. A licence plate was wedged in the anti-RPG cage of his MRAP. He dropped down into the personnel compartment, crouching on the metal gunner's platform between the driver and commander's seats. Everyone was mouthing 'What happened?' and checking each other for wounds. 'You're bleeding,' his commander silently mouthed, pointing to Saeed's arm.

Then, through the damaged windscreen, Saeed saw movement, not far outside the MRAP. 'Enemy!', he shouted, and stood up into the turret to begin gunning again. In the seconds after the suicide car bomb exploded, Al-Qaeda fighters had moved swiftly to close the distance on the smoke-shrouded laager. Veteran fighters, they could be seen skirmishing forward and using tactical hand signals to communicate despite the noise.

As Azzan scanned close by for enemies, a young Yemeni survivor of the bodyguard unit walked dazedly up to his door and placed a bloody hand on the window, one finger missing. Bullets were smacking into the door and window right next to the soldier. Azzan could see death in his eyes. He had been with these Yemenis for a year and they were like sons to him. He had to save the boy.

'Suppressing fire' he called to his gunner and then he clambered through the cramped cabin to the rear door of the MRAP, where the incoming fire was less intense. He took a deep breath and shouldered the heavy door open, pointing his M4 carbine in case of enemies close by, then he jumped out and slammed the door behind him. *Commando-crawling under the vehicle, Azzan pulled the skinny Yemeni down with him, manhandled him to the rear doors and threw him in.*

His driver stared horrified at Azzan, whose face and hands were covered in so much blood that he was sure the commander must have been hit. But no, Azzan was up and scanning all around through the bullet-cracked windows. The enemy was closing in from all directions: 30 metres away, then 15. Soon they would be pulling on the door handles of the MRAP. They were seconds away from the end, Azzan calculated.

Looking out of a window, Azzan could see an older Yemeni tribal fighter with white hair, still firing his rifle. Inside the MRAP, the wounded Yemeni was still brave too: he quietly said to Azzan, 'Don't worry. We'll win.'

Azzan became strangely calm. He knew there would be no retreat. In his heart, he could feel the whole UAE military behind him at that moment, willing him to keep fighting, and he knew the whole of Mukalla was in front of him, needing his force to come and free them. He might die here, but the UAE was not going to fail. Like all the Emiratis serving in Yemen, he was not going to surrender or let himself be captured. If he died, he would be shot in the front, not the back.

Azzan spoke evenly as he issued precise final orders. 'Gunners – expend all remaining ammunition. Full rate of fire, 360 degrees. Everyone – get ready for hand-to-hand fighting. Be prepared to dismount and attack.'

This book preserves for history the true story of Task Force 291, a band of elite forces from the United Arab Emirates (UAE), aided by other Gulf Arab nations. From the outset of the multi-national intervention requested by the Yemeni government in March 2015, their mission was to stop Al-Qaeda and Iran-backed terrorists from taking over the ports, energy sites, and archaeological and cultural wonders of eastern Yemen. The following chapters are an operational recounting of the battles fought in the east of that embattled country in 2015–16, related here by the participants for the first time and meticulously fact-checked.

In 2015–16, a war was raging throughout the Middle East against terrorist armies who aspired to the creation of new countries under their dominion, most famously the Islamic State in Iraq and Syria (ISIS). But this book is not about the parts of that war known to Western television audiences – the destructive struggles for Iraqi and Syrian cities like Mosul and Raqqa. It is about the overlooked simultaneous effort by a Gulf Arab and Yemeni coalition to prevent extremists from taking over the 'birthplace of the Arabs' in oil-rich Marib, and to remove terrorists from the beautiful and bountiful port city of Mukalla, the famed 'Pearl of the Arabian Sea'.

If terrorists like Al-Qaeda or the Iran-backed Houthis could seize and hold these places for years, they could poison the minds of a whole generation of young Yemenis and build extremist states with terrorist armies at the crossroads of the world's greatest sea lanes. With the United States and Europe focused on ISIS, the people of the Middle East received no help from outside, and so they took matters into their own hands. This book tells their story of the war in eastern Yemen for the first time.

The result is a new perspective on the Arab war on terrorism, told by the peoples of the region in their own recollections. To the Yemeni tribes, the members of Al-Qaeda were not alien creatures, as they are often seen in the West. Instead they were a patchwork quilt of fellow Yemenis. Some were brothers and cousins who had gone astray for lack of better options, and who might be returned to the fold. Others were ruthless killers who could never be forgiven and who had to be captured or killed. Nor were the Emirati advisors seen as distant strangers from far-off lands by the Yemeni resistance fighters: they were Arab blood brothers who fought, and often died, shoulder to shoulder with their Yemeni partners. This is a story of Yemeni cities saved from terrorists *and returned intact* to their inhabitants, a stark contrast with the cities of Iraq and Syria, where the international coalition often 'destroyed the city in order to save the city' from the Islamic State.

Most of all, this is a true story of national resilience. On 4 September 2015, the UAE lost 52 dead in a single devastating missile attack – more combat deaths than it would suffer in the rest of the Yemen war. It was, in fact, the first ever mass casualty event in the entire history of the Emirati nation. Above all, this is the story of a nation's most painful sacrifice and how the UAE bounced back from a tragic body blow to fight again and to win, driving its enemies from the battlefields of Marib and Mukalla.

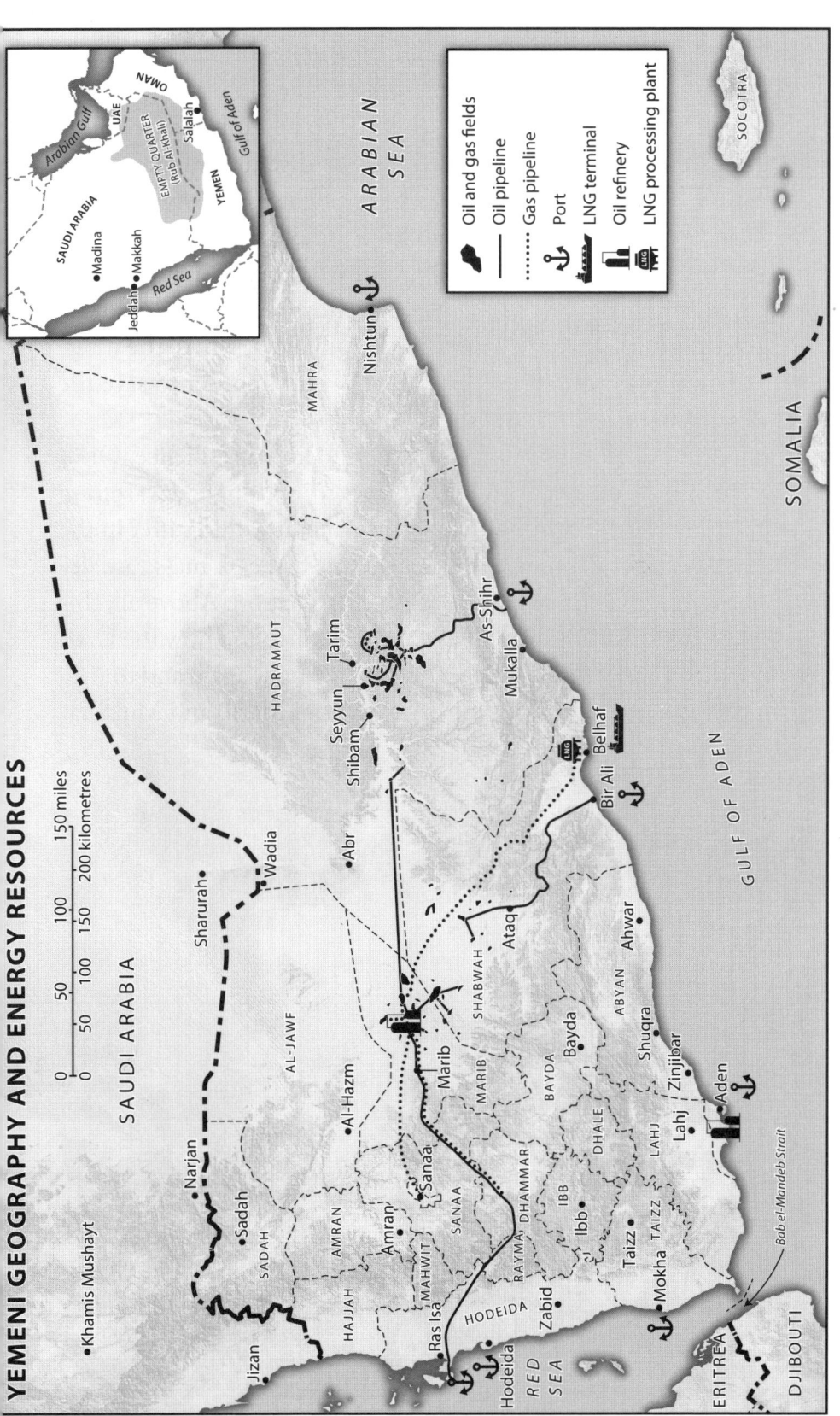

YEMENI GEOGRAPHY AND ENERGY RESOURCES

Legend:
- Oil and gas fields
- Oil pipeline
- Gas pipeline
- Port
- LNG terminal
- Oil refinery
- LNG processing plant

Scale:
0 50 100 150 miles
0 50 100 150 200 kilometres

SAUDI ARABIA

YEMEN

ARABIAN SEA

GULF OF ADEN

RED SEA

SOMALIA

DJIBOUTI

ERITREA

SOCOTRA

Bab el-Mandeb Strait

Inset map labels:
Arabian Gulf
UAE
OMAN
SAUDI ARABIA
EMPTY QUARTER (Rub Al Khali)
YEMEN
Madina
Makkah
Jeddah
Red Sea
Salalah
Gulf of Aden

Place names:
Khamis Mushayt
Jizan
Narjan
Sharurah
Wadia
Abr
Nishtun
MAHRA
HADRAMAUT
Tarim
Seyyun
Shiban
As-Shihr
Mukalla
Belhaf
Bir Ali
Ataq
SHABWAH
Ahwar
Shuqra
Zinjibar
ABYAN
Bayda
BAYDA
MARIB
Marib
AL-JAWF
Al-Hazm
Sadah
SADAH
Narjan
AMRAN
Amran
Sanaa
SANAA
Ras Isa
MAHWIT
HAJJAH
Hodeida
HODEIDA
Zabid
RAYMA
DHAMMAR
IBB
Ibb
DHALE
DHALE
LAHJ
Lahj
Aden
Mokha
TAIZZ
Taizz
Najran
Sadah

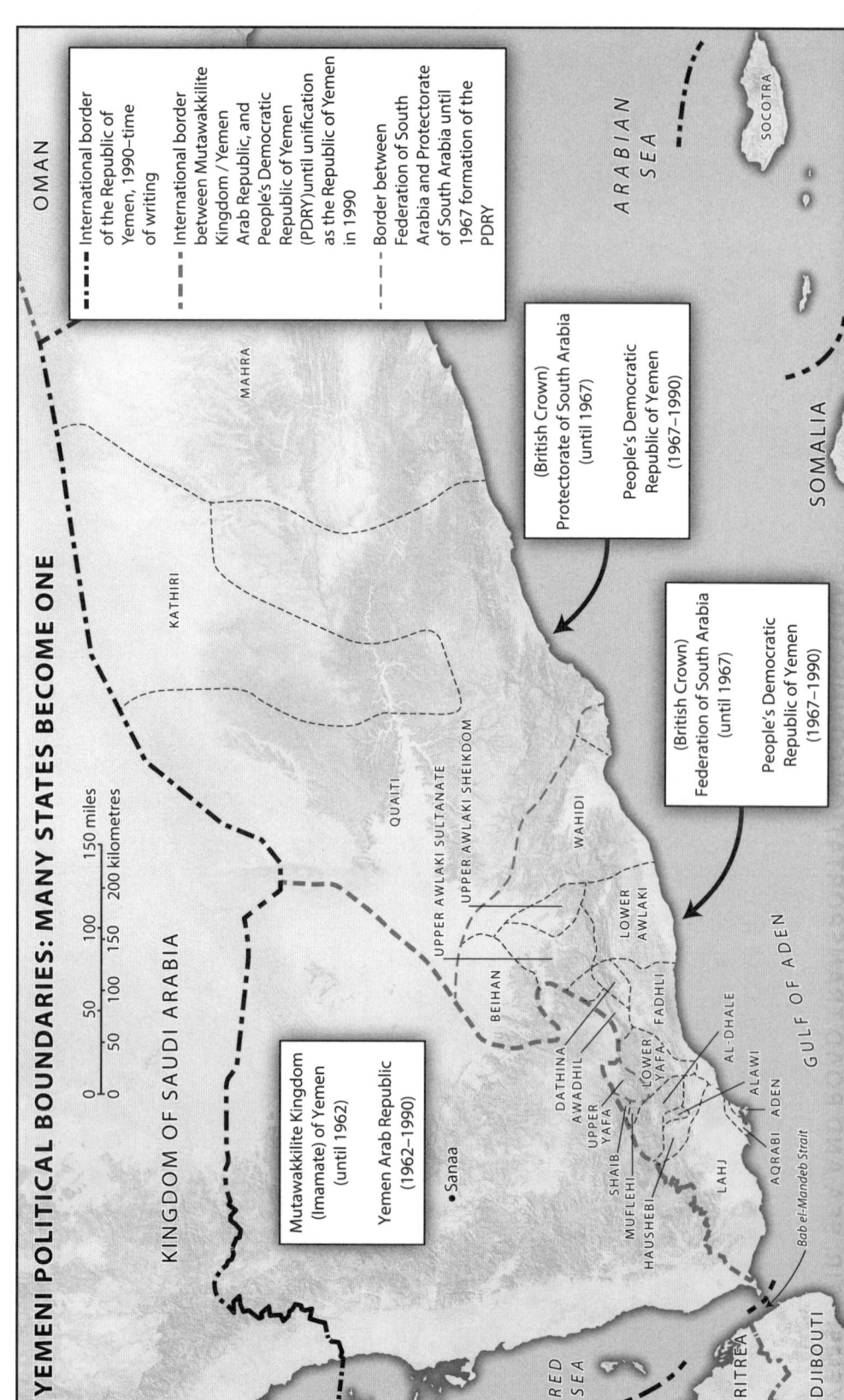

YEMENI POLITICAL BOUNDARIES: MANY STATES BECOME ONE

International border of the Republic of Yemen, 1990–time of writing

International border between Mutawakkilite Kingdom / Yemen Arab Republic, and People's Democratic Republic of Yemen (PDRY) until unification as the Republic of Yemen in 1990

Border between Federation of South Arabia and Protectorate of South Arabia until 1967 formation of the PDRY

OMAN

ARABIAN SEA

SOCOTRA

SOMALIA

(British Crown) Protectorate of South Arabia (until 1967)

People's Democratic Republic of Yemen (1967–1990)

(British Crown) Federation of South Arabia (until 1967)

People's Democratic Republic of Yemen (1967–1990)

MAHRA

KATHIRI

QUAITI

UPPER AWLAKI SULTANATE

UPPER AWLAKI SHEIKDOM

WAHIDI

KINGDOM OF SAUDI ARABIA

LOWER AWLAKI

BEIHAN

0   50   100   150 miles
0 50 100 150 200 kilometres

Mutawakkilite Kingdom (Imamate) of Yemen (until 1962)

Yemen Arab Republic (1962–1990)

• Sanaa

DATHINA

AWADHIL

UPPER YAFA

SHAIB

MUFLEHI

HAUSHEBI

LOWER YAFA

FADHLI

AL-DHALE

ALAWI

AQRABI   ADEN

LAHJ

GULF OF ADEN

RED SEA

ERITREA

DJIBOUTI

Bab el-Mandeb Strait

YEMEN AIR, SEA AND ROAD TRANSPORTATION CONNECTIONS

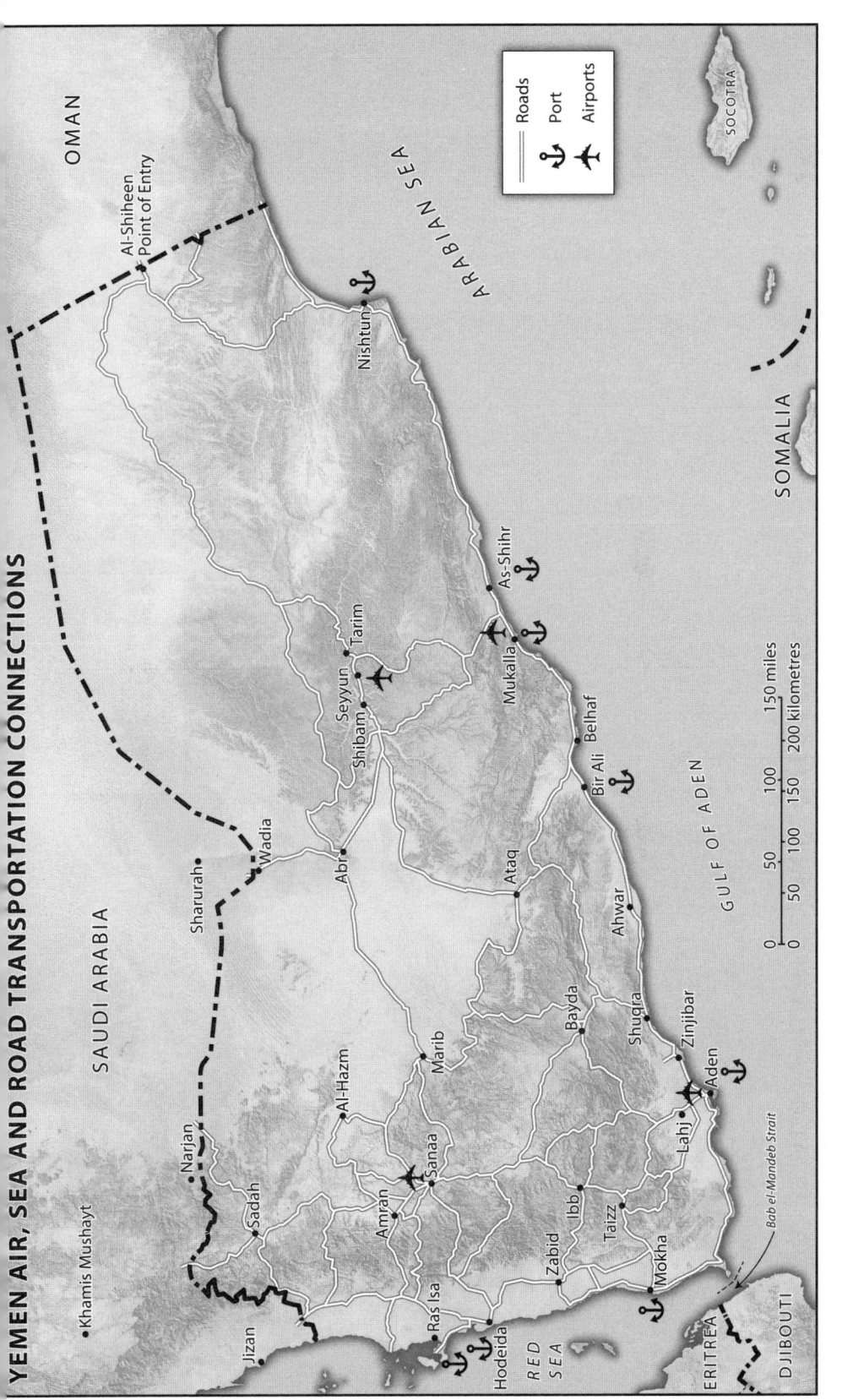

Roads
Port
Airports

OMAN

Al-Shiheen
Point of Entry

SAUDI ARABIA

Khamis Mushayt

Najran

Jizan

Sharurah

Sadah

Wadia

Amran

Al-Hazm

Sanaa

Marib

Abr

Seyyun

Shibam

Tarim

Nishtun

ARABIAN SEA

As-Shihr

Mukalla

Belhaf

Bir Ali

Ataq

Bayda

Ahwar

Shuqra

Zinjibar

Aden

Lahj

Taizz

Ibb

Zabid

Ras Isa

Hodeida

Mokha

GULF OF ADEN

SOCOTRA

SOMALIA

RED SEA

Bab el-Mandeb Strait

ERITREA

DJIBOUTI

0   50   100   150 miles
0   50   100   150   200 kilometres

PART ONE

A WAR WITHIN A WAR

I

AL-QAEDA'S LONG WAR IN YEMEN

Say the name of any country in the world and you will summon up a host of thoughts and feelings about that place. Those ideas and emotions will differ according to the worldview and experiences of the listener. To most people in our modern world, the word Yemen is synonymous with the tragedy of wars, terrorism, poverty and famine. Go to Google and search for images of Yemen and you will be confronted with a screen full of men with guns, ruined houses, destitute civilians and food aid deliveries. In the background of the images will always be children, usually putting on their best face for the camera but who mostly cannot remember a time before the current civil war. Even Yemeni adults would be hard-pressed to remember a time of sustained peace and prosperity.

The images will invariably be captivating. In good times and bad, Yemenis are fiercely attractive people and one of the most photogenic peoples on the planet. They are famously proud, independent, hospitable and individualistic. Today's photojournalists are not the first outsiders to marvel at Yemen's rugged beauty and the swagger of its inhabitants. People from outside the Arab world have been fascinated by Yemen since Roman times, when *Arabia Felix* (blessed Arabia) first became known to Europeans as a mysterious land of handsome people, luxuries and aromatic spices.

Visited by the great seafaring empires – Chinese, Indian, Portuguese and British – Yemeni ports such as Aden, Mokha and Mukalla became known worldwide as centres of trade in frankincense, myrrh, coffee and cinnamon. The opening of the Suez Canal in 1869 placed Yemen's ports astride the newest global trade super-highway, resulting in a century of growth until Aden was among the world's busiest ports, perhaps even rivalling New York as late as the 1950s. At the end of the 20th century, Yemen became fixed in the Western mind as an exotic dream: a place of danger and crushing poverty with more guns than people, a land of curved daggers (the *jambiya*) in the belt and the addictive, chewable leaf, *qat*, in a bulging cheek. Then, as the new millennium of the Gregorian calendar began, Yemen broke into Western consciousness for a new reason: Al-Qaeda's bombing of the destroyer USS *Cole* in Aden's harbour in the year 2000, which killed 17 American sailors.

The word Yemen always had much deeper meaning and significance to the Arabs and to the Muslim world. Al-Yaman (the south, meaning southern Arabia), was the wellspring of the tribes of Arabia and contains some of the oldest permanently inhabited settlements in the world. Indeed, the first Arabian empires existed in Yemen over 2,000 years ago. The Sabeans were the greatest, and their Yemeni capital, Marib, was known in the Roman and European worlds as the seat of the famed Queen of Sheba. As the centuries passed, Yemenis stayed distinct from those Arabs from al-Najd (the uplands) and al-Sham (the north). They held tightly to linguistic, cultural and architectural holdovers from the pre-Islamic past, and their writers for the last thousand years have dwelt on the melancholy of their faded glory. The Marib Dam is perhaps the most famous and oldest archaeological wonder in the Arab world, created around 2,300 years before the birth of the Prophet Muhammad.

The Prophet himself was fond of the Yemenites, saying of them: 'They have the kindest and gentlest hearts of all. Faith is Yemeni, wisdom is Yemeni.' Yet Yemenis were not always gentle; they were fierce warriors too. The tribes of the interior served proudly in the vanguard of the Islamic Conquest of the Arab world in the 7th century of the Christian calendar. The descendants of these fighters spread across the Arabian Peninsula in the form of fierce desert tribes who helped guide the destinies of today's Gulf Arab states. Those who remained in the land known as Yemen guarded the deep deserts of the north-east, the erudite towns of the wadis and the coast, and the mountains and foothills between these places.

Yemen's contributions to the Arab world did not end as modernity dawned. Yemenis remained among the most prolific Arab writers of proverbs, poetry, songs, stories and musical compositions. The uniqueness and beauty of Yemen's architecture became famous across the Arab world. For well over a thousand years, Yemenis have built towering skyscrapers of stone blocks and sun-dried mud bricks. A contrast of earthy browns and painted pastel highlights, the capital Sanaa and cities like Shibam and Zabid have been recognised as cultural heritage sites 'of outstanding value to humanity' by the United Nations Educational, Scientific and Cultural Organisation (UNESCO).

From here, the birthplace of the original Arabs, the Yemenis also spread farther and wider than almost any other Arab people, creating an expansive diaspora tied to the Arab world. This extended network stretches today across the Indian Ocean basin, with branches and trading communities as far afield as Indonesia, Malaysia, the Indian subcontinent and East Africa. Yemeni families also started many of Saudi Arabia's greatest business dynasties of the 20th century and provided the foundation of some Gulf royal families. As colonial powers like Britain faded from view in the latter half of the century, Yemenis looked north, to the Arabian Gulf, for partnership, work and trade. Yet the social connection of these emigrants to Yemen was never forgotten, and Yemen's sights and sounds were fondly memorialised in Arab songs, poetry and stories that echoed around the Arabian Gulf.

Yemen and the global war on terror

Among those who made that journey to the Gulf States was the father of Osama bin Laden, a man named Mohammed bin Awad bin Laden, who was born in Wadi Doan, a massive canyon dotted with oases, honey and frankincense farms, and mud-skyscraper cities. He built Saudi Arabia's largest construction business after travelling from his native Hadramaut province in Yemen to Jeddah (the south-western tip of Saudi Arabia) as a humble porter in the 1920s. His son Osama bin Laden retained this special connection to Yemen and chose the country as the site for Al-Qaeda's first terrorist attack – the bombing of the Gold Mohur Hotel in Aden on 29 December 1992, which killed two civilians but failed to harm the intended target – US military personnel transiting Yemen as part of Operation Restore Hope in Somalia.

In the intervening decade between this strike in 1992 and the 9/11 attacks, Al-Qaeda found Yemen to be an attractive operating location. Unlike faraway Afghanistan, Yemen was adjacent to many important places, located at the southernmost tip of the Arabian Peninsula, bordering Saudi Arabia and Oman, with coastlines on the Red Sea and the Gulf of Aden which allowed easy access to the terrorist sanctuaries in the Horn of Africa and Sudan. As the anti-Soviet jihad in Afghanistan and the subsequent Afghan civil war ended, many Yemeni fighters returned home. Furthermore, to mujaheddin from other Arab countries, Yemen became a place where these 'Arab Afghans' could settle without causing reintegration problems or facing imprisonment in their states of origin. Some of those Yemeni and foreign mujaheddin were then recruited by Yemen's Islah party (a branch of the Muslim Brotherhood) to aid the government forces of President Ali Abdullah Saleh, who had ruled Yemen from 1978 onwards. In 1994, Ali Abdullah needed the mujaheddin's help to support his conquest of southern Yemen, which was trying to break away from his republic after less than four years of ill-considered unification under Saleh. In return, the mujaheddin veterans, including many southern Yemeni tribal fighters, were rewarded with confiscated land and security responsibilities over the occupied south.

The devil's bargain between Saleh's regime and the mujaheddin did not last long. Ali Abdullah was said to be able to 'dance on the heads of snakes', meaning that he was uniquely capable of staying one step ahead of the various factions vying for control of different parts of Yemen. By the late 1990s, he was seeking a new dance partner – the sole remaining superpower, the United States – and offering up jihadists was his inducement to the Americans. Following the deadly bombing of two US embassies in Kenya and Tanzania in 1998 and Bin Laden's declaration of war on the United States, US counter-terrorism officials were actively seeking counter-terrorism partners in the neighbourhood. Two names increasingly brought Yemen to the attention of counter-terrorism agencies.

One was Zain al-Abidin al-Mindhar, a local mujaheddin commander from Yemen's southern governorate of Shabwa. In the late 1990s, he had formed a movement called the Aden-Abyan Islamic Army that was linked to attacks against hotels, churches and Western diplomats and expatriates working in

Yemen. In part to aid Ali Abdullah's courtship of the United States, Mindhar was arrested by Saleh's government in 1998 and eventually executed on 17 October 1999.

The second figure was Al-Qaeda's top maritime attack specialist, the prolific Saudi-Yemeni planner Abdulrahim Mohammed al-Nashiri, who had begun a series of efforts to manoeuvre explosive-packed boats alongside US Navy vessels as they transited south Yemeni ports. One effort – the attempt on 3 January 1999 to bomb the destroyer USS *Sullivans* in Aden harbour with a remote-control explosive-packed speedboat – narrowly failed due to the overloading of the boat, which sank as soon as it was launched. The next effort, the attack on the USS *Cole* in Aden harbour on 12 October 2000, was successful, punching a huge hole into the side of the *Cole* and causing 17 US fatalities.

The *Cole* bombing and the subsequent 9/11 terrorist attacks – in which two of the three hijacker teams were led by Yemenis with Saudi parentage – made Yemen a central battleground in the global war on terror. Ali Abdullah Saleh moved speedily to secure American friendship, being the first Middle Eastern leader to phone the White House to express his sympathy after the 9/11 attacks and inviting US special forces into the country to pursue Al-Qaeda's Yemeni offshoots. On 6 October 2002, when al-Nashiri sought to attack another US warship off the southern Yemeni port of As-Shihr, the UAE intelligence services picked up chatter about a new attack and warned the US, which diverted its vessels away from Yemen. Al-Nashiri then attacked a 'target of opportunity', the French-flagged oil tanker MV *Limburg*, and in doing so was detected by UAE surveillance and was arrested in Dubai in October 2002 and handed over to the US authorities.

In Yemen itself, a US and British special operations task force began to hunt down suspected members of Al-Qaeda and the

Aden-Abyan Islamic Army. Sinan al-Harithi, another Shabwa tribal leader and the operational head of Al-Qaeda's Yemen operations, was killed on 3 November 2002 by an AGM-114 Hellfire missile launched by a US Central Intelligence Agency MV-1Q Predator. The attack against the *Limburg* proved to be the last major operation by Harithi's movement. The new Aden-Abyan Islamic Army leader Khalid Abdal-Nabi surrendered himself to the Yemeni government in October 2003 and aided the capture of the *Limburg* attack planner Mohammed Hamdi al-Ahdal on 25 November. Altogether, 92 Al-Qaeda and Aden-Abyan Islamic Army high-value targets were arrested in 2003. At that moment, the bulk of Al-Qaeda's leadership cadre in Yemen was firmly behind bars in Guantanamo Bay, at various CIA rendition sites around the world, and in Yemen.

The rebirth of Al-Qaeda in Yemen

If Al-Qaeda in Yemen were a horror movie monster, it would be a zombie, soaking up lethal damage and coming back from the dead, again and again. Its first resurrection occurred in the prisons of the Political Security Organisation (PSO), Yemen's feared internal security apparatus. A mix of mujaheddin and Al-Qaeda members had been left to rot in PSO jails after the arrests between 2002 and 2004 and this would provide the launchpad for the rebirth of Al-Qaeda in Yemen. In many ways, a prison is the ultimate terrorist recruitment and networking 'retreat'. It is the one place where the terrorist can sleep secure, knowing that no US drone strike or special forces raid will disturb his sleep. Terrorists are gathered together, not only with their contemporaries but also with numerous non-terrorists, including those unjustly accused of crimes they did not commit and those tortured to force their confessions.

United in shared suffering, isolation and most of all boredom, Al-Qaeda leaders had ample time to bond with other prisoners, talent-spot, demonstrate leadership, recruit and plan for the future. Had such a gathering of high-level terrorists occurred anywhere *but* a prison, it would have been a magnet for US bombs, Tomahawks and Hellfire missiles. Instead, 23 terrorist and criminal suspects were gathered closely together in a tiny cell block in a PSO jail in Sanaa in early 2006, where they formed the new cadre of Al-Qaeda in Yemen and dug an escape tunnel into a mosque courtyard that lay across an alleyway from their solitary barred window. On 3 February 2006, the escapees climbed up out of the tunnel, merged with those leaving the mosque after prayers, and began preparing for their new terrorist campaign.

The leader of the cell block and the escape attempt was Nasir al-Wahayshi (also known by his nom-de-guerre or *kunya*, Abu Basir). Born in 1976 in Mukayris, in Yemen's Abyan governorate, Wahayshi was Yemeni through and through. He was also Al-Qaeda royalty, having spent nearly every day of his life from 1998 to 2001 as the indispensable personal secretary to Osama bin Laden. A religious student in the early 1990s in northern Yemen, Wahayshi had joined Al-Qaeda in Afghanistan in 1998 at the age of 22 and had been alongside Bin Laden every step of the way leading up to the 9/11 attacks. When Al-Qaeda was cornered in the valleys and tunnel systems of Tora Bora in late 2001, Wahayshi's path diverted from Bin Laden's, with Bin Laden going to Pakistan and Wahayshi escaping from Afghanistan to Iran. There the Islamic Republic of Iran's security forces held Wahayshi from 2001 to 2003, before transferring him back to Yemen's PSO at the end of 2003. As a result, Wahayshi had already had two years to ruminate on the future of Al-Qaeda and the lessons of Tora Bora before he landed in Yemen, and then he had three more years to network with the residents of the PSO prison in Sanaa to build a new branch of Al-Qaeda.

Wahayshi and fellow escapees Hamza al-Quaiti and Qassem al-Raimi each brought something special to the construction of the network. Still only 30 years old and in many ways unremarkable-looking, Wahayshi was nonetheless a huge draw for the network. Here was a living link to Osama bin Laden, a born Yemeni, and a patient strategist who was listened to by the 'Al-Qaeda core' leadership in Pakistan and other affiliates in Iraq, Somalia, Asia and Libya. Hamza al-Quaiti was slightly older, born in 1970 in Saudi Arabia to a Yemeni father and a Saudi mother. Quaiti had already been building a new Al-Qaeda network inside the PSO prison system many months before Wahayshi arrived from Iran.

Qassem al-Raimi was the youngest of the three, born in 1978 in Al-Rayma governorate in north-western Yemen. He had been a very young mujaheddin who arrived in Afghanistan too late to join the intense fighting against the Soviets and the subsequent Afghan civil war. He instead applied himself to the development of training camps and syllabuses. After Tora Bora, Raimi returned to Sanaa, the capital of Yemen, where he and his small network of friends were arrested after they plotted to attack foreign embassies and tried to shoot down the US ambassador's helicopter with a surface-to-air missile (in fact, unsuccessfully targeting an oil industry charter flight). In prison, Raimi quickly fell in with Wahayshi and Quaiti. When the three escaped in February 2006, Raimi quickly detached from the other two in order to set up militant training camps in the mountainous Abyan governorate.

The new Al-Qaeda in Yemen organisation was a fusion of the different jihadist communities who were all drawn to the ungoverned spaces of Yemen, where the weak government had only fleeting moments of control in many tribal hinterlands and no control at all in places like central Abyan. Unlike in Iraq and Afghanistan, the US military was not on the ground in Yemen. The stability of Ali Abdullah Saleh's regime still relied on sheikhs, preachers and generals from the local Muslim Brotherhood branch, Islah. These generals ensured that jihadists would never face the full brunt of government and international counter-terrorist efforts.

Yemen would become a safe haven for the defeated remnants of Al-Qaeda from Saudi Arabia, where the kingdom had broken the back of the terrorist group in five years of counter-terrorism work from 2003 to 2008. Fourteen Saudis were repatriated from the US prison at Guantanamo Bay into religious rehabilitation centres in Saudi Arabia in late 2007. Within a year many of them were in Yemen alongside Wahayshi. The most prominent of those recidivists was the 35-year-old Said al-Shihri, another Saudi son of a Yemeni father, who had fought in Afghanistan and Chechnya and who was an enthusiastic advocate of man-carried suicide bombs. Shihri wasted no time after his release in September 2008 in gathering as many Saudi volunteers as he could and crossing over to Yemen to become Wahayshi's deputy and the most senior Saudi in Al-Qaeda in Yemen. Another fateful addition to Wahayshi's Yemeni-based organisation was 25-year-old chemical engineer Ibrahim al-Asiri and his 20-year-old brother Abdullah, who were blocked from flying to join the anti-American jihad in Iraq and instead walked over the border into Yemen to join Al-Qaeda. Both brothers would play dramatic roles in making bombs for the notorious 'external operations' cell of the group that organised terrorist attacks outside Yemen.

Wahayshi's new Al-Qaeda network in Yemen

From the start, Al-Qaeda in Yemen was clearly united under Wahayshi, with Raimi publicly proclaiming Wahayshi's leadership on 21 June 2006, less than four months after the escapees broke out of jail. The Al-Qaeda commanders in Yemen then mounted a series of high-visibility suicide bombings intended to build the international profile of the group and draw in recruits. Four suicide car bombs were launched on 14 September 2006 against oil facilities in Marib and the As-Shihr oil export terminal in southern Hadramaut. Then a car bombing on 2 July 2007 killed seven Spanish tourists and two Yemeni tour guides at the Temple of Bilqis (Sheba) in Marib. As the tourists were blown up, Wahayshi, Qaimi, and Quaiti were ghoulishly listening for the blast from a nearby site.

To amplify these and other acts of terror, Al-Qaeda in Yemen began to produce a slick online magazine called *Sada al-Malahim* (*Echo of Battles*) from 13 January 2008 onwards and celebrated the inaugural edition with a dedicated terrorist attack on 18 January when two Belgian tourists and four Yemenis were shot dead in northern Hadramaut, near the historic centre of Shibam. In the next edition of *Sada al-Malahim*, on 13 March 2008, Wahayshi announced a formal name change for his movement, which would thereafter be known as Al-Qaeda in the Arabian Peninsula (AQAP), confirming that Wahayshi was claiming responsibility over operations not only in Yemen but also in Saudi Arabia, the site of Islam's holiest shrines at Makkah and Medina. By January 2009, Wahayshi had fully consolidated control over the Al-Qaeda network in Yemen and issued a video message where all his contemporaries backed his formation of a unified regional franchise of Al-Qaeda.

Wahayshi's plan for AQAP was not merely to make a new branch of Al-Qaeda but to *improve* upon the original. Al-Qaeda had been built by older 'first generation' jihadists like Bin Laden and Ayman al-Zawahiri who had, respectively, fought the Soviets and the Egyptian government since the 1980s. Wahayshi was a leading light of the 'second generation', those who had grown up as fighters in post-Soviet Afghanistan, Chechnya and Bosnia in the 1990s. He sought to incorporate the lessons of Al-Qaeda's failures in Yemen in 2002–4 – and its global reverses since the 9/11 attacks – as he built up AQAP. To prevent another decapitation strike, such as the one that robbed Al-Qaeda of its Yemeni leadership in 2002, Wahayshi adopted Bin Laden's doctrine of decentralised leadership and started an apprenticing system whereby top- and mid-level commanders trained their own replacements to take over at a moment's notice if US drones removed the leader.

Wahayshi made sure that the globalisation of jihad added to his ranks, instead of depleting them. He encouraged any of his fighters with part-Yemeni heritage or full Yemeni blood to marry into local tribes, to create more durable networks of hospitality and mutual protection. (The caste-conscious and xenophobic rural tribes of Yemen would not usually allow their daughters to marry foreign fighters without Yemeni parentage.) From the outset, Wahayshi was careful to maintain collegial and supportive ties to Al-Qaeda branches in Iraq, Libya and Somalia, while at the same time subtly guiding Yemeni fighters towards the jihad in their own country, keeping his best talent at home. If Wahayshi took in fighters from abroad, he preferred Saudis, who would blend in and would have tribal connections.

Even with headline-grabbing local terrorist attacks, AQAP might not have attracted global attention if it had focused on killing Westerners and locals only in Yemen. But Wahayshi proved to be just as committed to spectacular international terrorist attacks as his mentor Bin Laden. AQAP presented an increasingly urgent challenge to global law enforcement in two key dimensions. Wahayshi commanded a potent bomb-making capability through the innovative efforts of Ibrahim al-Asiri, who sent his own brother Abdullah to assassinate Saudi Arabia's top counter-terrorism official on 28 August 2009, concealing the bomb inside his brother's rectum. (In this case, Ibrahim failed; the device only killed Abdulluah as his body contained most of the blast.) Undeterred, Asiri continued his obsession with man-carried suicide bombs, sending Umar Farouk Abdalmutallab, a 23-year-old Nigerian volunteer, onto Northwest Airlines flight 253 on Christmas Day in December 2009 with the intent of killing the 289 passengers and crew over Chicago with a liquid explosives device built into his underwear. Again, the plot failed but Asiri kept trying: in September and October 2010, he couriered bombs built around the high-explosive known as PETN inside printer cartridges, destroying one freight aircraft and narrowly failing to destroy two others on the eve of the US elections in 2010. By 2011, AQAP was experimenting with the use of the lethal poison ricin in its explosive devices.

In addition to the bomb-maker Asiri, AQAP had another unique capability – an American-Yemeni cleric called Anwar al-Awlaki, who had brought the 'underwear bomber' Umar Farouk Abdalmutallab to AQAP's training camps and linked him up with Asiri. In 2010, the New Mexico-born and Colorado-educated Awlaki focused his efforts on recruitment in the West, launching an English-language online radicalisation magazine called *Inspire* in January 2010 and drawing tens of Westerners to Yemen to be trained as terrorists. Awlaki had an insider's understanding of US society and angled AQAP's external operations to strike at American fears and weaknesses – for instance, stoking fear of attacks at shopping malls and other US locations where terrorism was not normally a major concern. He sought out so-called 'lone wolves' to use any weapons available to mount improvised terrorist attacks inside Western countries, with the hope that enough small blows would 'haemorrhage' the US economy by imposing security costs and reducing economic activity. His greatest success at the time was the mobilisation of US Army psychologist Major Nidal Malik Hassan who, after communicating with Awlaki, shot dead 13 people at Fort Hood, Texas, on 5 November 2009. By the end of 2010, every Western intelligence agency was loudly proclaiming that AQAP was the most urgent and rapidly evolving terrorist threat in the world.

Al-Qaeda during Yemen's Arab Spring

It is typically the case that by the time the world has recognised a new development in Yemen, things have already moved on to a new phase on the ground. Just as a fleet of US drones was turning to face AQAP in Yemen's mountains, the country itself was being shaken to pieces by the powerful reverberations of the Arab Spring. By early 2011, President Ali Abdullah Saleh had been running Yemen for 33 years and most of the country's young population could hardly remember a time before his rule. Alongside Yemen's widespread poverty and 25 per cent youth unemployment, Saleh's long and turbulent rule had made him hated by a coalition of youth protestors and his many competitors within his Sanhan tribe of the dominant Hashid tribal confederation.

By the time of the Arab Spring in 2011, Saleh had perilously narrowed his power base to his own Afaash clan (of the Sanhan tribe of the Hashid confederation) and its close confederates. The pendulum swung against him as young protestors sought to bring him down, the only president they had known in their lifetime. The combination of the Hashid confederation and urban protestors conspired to remove Saleh with the support of military forces under Yemen's leading general Ali Mohsen al-Qadhi al-Ahmar (from the rival Qadhi clan of the Sanhan tribe). With Ali Mohsen in the wings, Yemen fell under the rule of a new acting president, Vice President Abd-Rabo Mansour al-Hadi, also a former general.

Never a strong or centralised state in the first place, Yemen was shattered back into its component parts by the Arab Spring. The country reverted not to two countries, north and south, as it had been from the 1960s to the early 1990s, but to a patchwork of much smaller territorial enclaves that felt more like the northern Imamate and the many coastal and eastern sultanates of the early 20th century (see map, p. 10). President Hadi and Ali Mohsen sought to hold the republic together in partnership with most of the international community, parts of Saleh's old party (the General People's Congress, GPC), and Islah. In the north-west, the Houthi rebels were seeking to exploit Iranian military aid to consolidate power.

This was the set-up for the civil war that was to follow: the Hadi government and Ali Mohsen's coterie of Al Islah-linked generals versus the Iran-backed Houthis that the military had fought in six vicious internal wars between 2004 and 2010. To the south, separatists from the 1967–90 People's Democratic Republic of Yemen (PDRY) saw an opportunity to reverse unification and avenge the south's defeat by Saleh and Ali Mohsen in the 1994 civil war, the last time the southern factions tried to break away. To the east, former sultanates like Shabwa, Hadramaut and Mahra were intent on recovering some of their autonomy. A fragile UN-backed national dialogue was just about holding Yemen together.

Into this mix AQAP brought ambitions of its own. As counter-terrorism researcher Ido Levy noted in his 2021 book *Soldiers of End-Times*, nearly every jihadist terrorist group tries to form a conventional military and create a territorial caliphate as soon as they are able to do so – often unsuccessfully and at great cost to the groups. Though a controversial step that requires some deliberation, the effort to consolidate power over populations and resources was both a political necessity and a religious obligation for Al-Qaeda. It had attempted this in Iraq from 2006 onwards and then tried in Syria and Yemen as the Arab Spring unfolded after January 2011. AQAP's leadership was united in sensing that the time was right to seize geographic control from a weakened central government in Yemen. Wahayshi, Raimi and the movement's senior sharia law official Adil al-Abab sought but failed to receive backing for the formation of a caliphate from the Al-Qaeda core leaders in the Afghanistan-Pakistan theatre, who were still recovering from the killing of Osama bin Laden in Abbottabad, Pakistan on 2 May 2011. In a sign of Wahayshi's growing stature, he pushed ahead anyway.

The key military commander of AQAP remained Qassem al-Raimi, also known by his *kunya* Abu Hurayra al-Sanaani. After attending religious schools in Yemen, Raimi was brought into Al-Qaeda by his father, who arranged for him to join Bin Laden's Al-Farouq training camp in Darwanta, Afghanistan in the late 1990s. Raimi and his brothers lived brutal lives: one younger brother, Ali, was detained in Guantanamo and another younger brother, Faris, was killed in Yemen for not answering the call to rejoin the armed struggle in 2007. Methodical and somewhat dull, Raimi organised AQAP's training efforts and set up its military committee and its subordinate governorate and district levels of command. Raimi had a lot of Yemeni blood on his hands: he oversaw a remarkable assassination and intimidation campaign against Yemeni intelligence and military officials from 2009 to 2011 that averaged around 20 operations a month, largely motorbike-mounted shootings and grenade attacks. Striking officials from the defence minister and governors all the way down to local intelligence and police chiefs, such 'shaping' (or preparatory) operations were a prelude to prison breaks and finally the week-long takeovers of southern towns such as Lawdar and Huta in August and September 2010 respectively.

The social effects of Raimi's bloody campaign were amplified by strategists and ideologues such as Wahayshi and Adab. They added smart messaging campaigns that magnified the psychological impact and popular appeal of AQAP military operations during the Arab Spring. Adab seems to have pioneered the adoption of the name 'Ansar al-Sharia' for AQAP-directed military operations from April 2011 onwards. This name (and later the 'Sons of Abyan' nomenclature) distanced Wahayshi and Raimi's post-Arab Spring campaign from the brand of Al-Qaeda, a foreign-linked terrorist movement of declining global impact. Such name changes instead linked AQAP's operations to the popular need for local reimposition of law and order (i.e. sharia law) in Yemen's hour of crisis. AQAP undertook experimental attempts at providing local services – for instance, running small rural schoolhouses. Most important, under Wahayshi's guidance, AQAP made public shows of leniency by releasing government soldiers it had captured, earning approval from their parent tribes. The powerful AQAP online propaganda machine exploited collateral damage caused by Yemeni government retaliatory operations and by US drone strikes. Perversely, a terrorist organisation that repeatedly sought to murder hundreds of airline passengers was seizing the moral high ground from Yemen's tottering government.

The Emirate of Waqar

Al-Qaeda's attempts to exploit the Arab Spring culminated in its announcement of the short-lived Emirate of Waqar (*waqar* means 'dignity'). On 28 March 2011, as Saleh's government was shooting Arab Spring protestors in the squares of the capital, an armed group that included AQAP fighters overran and looted the '7th of October' munitions factory in Jaar, a small town of around 25,000 people. The takeover of Jaar by Ansar al-Sharia and its renaming as Waqar was reported on the town's captured radio station a day later on 29 March. This small city of textile and military workshops was known as one of the areas in which Ali Mohsen and his northern Islah generals had settled Arab-Afghan returnees and other Yemeni mujaheddin who aided the north in the 1994 civil war.

The main leader of the takeover was a prominent young tribal leader from the local Maraqasha tribe called Jalal al-Baleidi al-Maraqashi, also known as Abu Hamza, who claimed the title of Emir of Waqar. In the following weeks, the tiny emirate of 12 square kilometres expanded, spilling 20 km down the R6214 highway to encompass the 15,000-person town of Al-Kawd. Then in late May 2011, as pro- and anti-Saleh military units were exchanging fire in Sanaa and the country teetered on the brink of full-scale civil war, Ansar al-Sharia used the opportunity to assault the largest city in Abyan, the governorate capital of Zinjibar. With just 300 fighters, Ansar al-Sharia defeated three 1,000-man Yemeni army brigades in May and June 2011, pushing the 119th Infantry Brigade and 201st Mechanised Brigade away to the south, and bottling up the local-based 25th Mechanised Brigade in its small camp on the south-eastern outskirts of Zinjibar city.

Months earlier, the AQAP religious sheikh Adil al-Abab had mused about Aden, Yemen's second-largest city: 'It is only a lack of money that has stopped us from entering Aden. Allah knows we were only a few days away from taking power there. But it will fall, first Zinjibar, and then Aden.' By the end of May 2011, money was no longer a problem: the government bank in Zinjibar was looted and £950,000 (300 million Yemeni rials) was removed. Within days, almost the whole of Abyan had fallen completely out of government control, encompassing nearly half a million Yemenis in the cities of Zinjibar, Jaar, Al-Kawd, Shuqra and Lawdar. Wahayshi could now drive nearly 300 km on highways monitored by Ansar al-Sharia checkpoints. In May 2011, the Emirate of Waqar was the largest area controlled by a terrorist group and an unprecedented step forward for an Al-Qaeda franchise. Ansar al-Sharia would soon be able to field not 300 fighters but around 3,000 as recruits flocked to their successful ranks to be hired and given a new AK-47, a car and a pay cheque worth five times that of a government fighter. The English-language *Inspire* magazine gloated that 'the country is falling apart and our brothers are busy picking up the pieces. It's like walking into an orchard of ripe fruit that is falling off the branches and all you have to do is walk through with a basket on your head.'

Abyan, which had never really been fully controlled by any Yemeni government, was now Al-Qaeda's to lose. The very name – the Emirate of Waqar – was an implicit promise: a return to dignity for Abyan's poor tribes. But Al-Qaeda was over-promising: this was a gift mostly beyond anyone's capacity to deliver. Ansar al-Sharia was expected to provide services, including law and order for the year that it ran Abyan. Although Western media coverage was fascinated by the idea of an efficient self-governing Al-Qaeda emirate, this was mostly a mirage fed by the Waqar emirate's own Madad News Agency. Yes, some water and municipal projects were undertaken, as they had even been by the decrepit Yemeni government, but not enough to change life in Abyan appreciably in just a few months of Al-Qaeda rule.

Nor did Ansar al-Sharia strike the right balance in its approach to law and order, an aspect of local life which *was* wholly within its control. Though Abyan residents wanted stronger law and social order, and though they were used to conservative Islamic practices, Al-Qaeda still went too far by rapidly applying sharia law to the minutiae of daily life. This included partial bans on smoking and *qat* chews; limits on financial services and fee collection; changes to educational curricula; stricter gender segregation; and corporal punishment for minor crimes. Ansar al-Sharia made these changes deliberately, with a view that the main contribution they could make to Yemeni society was the strict imposition of rules, law and order. As one field commander in Jaar noted in an April 2011 interview: 'The state has fallen here. If we didn't take over, others will take over. We have tried secular rule and we have tried Socialist rule. Now we need to try Islamic rule because we have no hope but through the Quran and the Prophet's teachings.' The so-called Emir of Waqar, the fine-featured Jalal al-Baleidi al-Maraqashi, was equally open, saying: 'Our goal is to apply the Islamic model like the Taliban did in Afghanistan.'

Neither the US government nor the newly appointed President Hadi was willing to let a Taliban-type state form in Yemen. The US Air Force and Saudi Arabia kept the encircled 25th Mechanised Brigade resupplied with air-dropped pallets of food, fuel and medical supplies throughout the latter half of 2011. Then in early 2012, with the Arab Spring protestors temporarily mollified by the change of president, the Yemeni military and various Popular Committees formed of tribal fighters went on the counter-offensive. Twelve Yemeni National Army (YNA) brigades and one of Hadi's Presidential Guard units were sent to

Abyan in Operation Golden Swords from April to June 2012. In the north, Lawdar was assaulted by four brigades of government troops and a mass of Awadhil tribal fighters in a week-long fight in mid-May 2012 that destroyed part of the town and the area's power station. From 3 June to 12 June, seven Yemeni brigades (most of them armoured or mechanised forces) concentrically squeezed Zinjibar, Al-Kawd and Jaar until Ansar al-Sharia abandoned the fight. As each major area was cleared by government forces, Ansar al-Sharia would throw painful counter-attacks at the advancing troops, sending suicide car bombs as parting gifts. The pursuit moved east, freeing Shuqra on 15 June and Azzan, far away in Shabwa province, by 23 June. Yemeni strike aircraft and attack helicopters began to bombard mountain villages into which Ansar al-Sharia was presumed to have escaped.

The devastation was widespread, especially in Zinjibar, where UN surveys showed that 285 major structures were destroyed or severely damaged in the battle and as many as 3,000 land mines lifted from the defensive minefields laid by Ansar al-Sharia. No one will ever accurately count the dead from the war against the Emirate of Waqar but a conservative estimate would be around 500–700 government troops and Popular Committee fighters killed, plus an unknown number of civilians and Ansar al-Sharia fighters. The lesson to everyone watching was clear: Al-Qaeda must never again be allowed to take control of major cities in Yemen.

II

RETURN OF THE BLACK BANNERS

AQAP had arguably missed a golden opportunity in the Arab Spring and had paid the price through the fall of the Emirate of Waqar, yet Wahayshi was not fazed. His fortunes continued to rise, being appointed the 'general manager' of Al-Qaeda world-wide in August 2013, making him the second-in-command to Bin Laden's successor Ayman al-Zawahiri. Wahayshi immediately began to codify the lessons learned from his failed emirate and then to communicate them to other aspiring caliphs in the Al-Qaeda franchises in North Africa and Pakistan. In an intercepted letter dated 26 August 2012, Wahayshi warned Al-Qaeda in the Islamic Maghreb's leader Abdal Malik Droukdel of the dangers of declaring an emirate before developing the plans and organisational capacity to fulfil the role of a state. Wahayshi had clearly not given up on the idea of an AQAP-controlled territorial enclave but he had learned a lot from the experience of 2011–12. Any AQAP takeovers had to be more genuinely local in nature; cosmetically adopting names such as Ansar al-Sharia or Sons of Abyan was not enough. Every area in Yemen was different and needed a uniquely local approach. Most important, the imposition of sharia law had to be gradual and any changes would need to be liberally greased with cash handouts to the tribes.

Getting this right was increasingly a matter of survival for AQAP because there was now a peer competitor on the scene

– the self-styled Islamic State of Iraq and Syria (ISIS). An even more violent evolution of the Al-Qaeda franchise, ISIS threw off Al-Qaeda's leadership in Iraq and Syria, seizing Raqqa (a Syrian city of 550,000 peacetime residents) in March 2013 and then Fallujah in Iraq (with 350,000 residents). In June 2014, ISIS seized the city of Mosul and around a third of Iraq. Along with its Syrian holdings, the Islamic State ruled a caliphate with up to 8 million inhabitants. ISIS renamed itself the Islamic State in June 2014 and announced its intention to impose its authority as a self-proclaimed worldwide caliphate over other jihadist groups.

This was unacceptable to Al-Qaeda leaders such as Zawahiri and Wahayshi. The first defections to ISIS were appearing in their movements, and the Islamic State was growing much faster than they were. The warning shot emerged in Yemen in July 2014 as the first handful of pro-AQAP preachers in Yemen began to pledge allegiance to the Islamic State. Always sensitive to competition that could leach away his resources, Wahayshi had to act fast. With the United States distracted by the sudden explosion of the Islamic State, Zawahiri and Wahayshi may have felt that they could get away with their own territorial project in Yemen. AQAP announced almost immediately after the Islamic State's formation that Al-Qaeda was also planning to develop a new Islamic emirate in eastern Yemen.

Al-Qaeda and the Yemeni civil war

In fact, not everyone was distracted by the war against the Islamic State in Iraq, Syria and Libya. Someone other than the Americans *was* watching what AQAP was doing in Yemen's east. In the summer of 2014, Brigadier General Musallam R. was marking his first anniversary as the leader of the Special Operations

Command (SOC) of the United Arab Emirates (UAE). He had been born just before the UAE federation was formed in 1971 through the voluntary union of the seven emirates: Abu Dhabi (the capital), Dubai, Sharjah, Ajman, Umm Al-Quwain, Ras Al-Khaimah and Fujairah. With 1.4 million Emirati citizens and 7.8 million non-citizen guests, the UAE was a young nation and a busy one. In the course of Musallam's life, the UAE had grown rapidly into a bustling global centre of investment, tourism and logistics. Relying on these outward-facing industries to build the nation's future, the UAE had been keenly interested in regional stability, freedom of navigation and the prevention of terrorism. As important, the UAE was also one of the world's most successful and generous Muslim nations. That meant the UAE took seriously its responsibility to ensure that extremists did not hijack the Islamic faith and damage its image as a religion of peace. This was the remit that Musallam had been given by the UAE's military commander, Lieutenant General Mohammed bin Zayed Al-Nahyan (hereafter MBZ), then the Crown Prince of Abu Dhabi and Deputy Supreme Commander of the UAE Armed Forces.

In the summer of 2014, Musallam saw the different strands of his special operations and counter-terrorism missions coming together in Yemen. As the head of SOC, Musallam was leading the UAE force that would be the first to act, if and when Yemen collapsed into full civil war, as seemed increasingly likely. President Hadi's internationally backed government grew weaker every day, while the Iran-backed Houthi rebels and the ousted dictator Ali Abdullah Saleh were gathering strength for a combined takeover. It would be Musallam's guys, the SOC close protection team in the UAE embassy in Sanaa, who would be the tip of the spear when it came to safely evacuating Emirati diplomats and other citizens. Even before the emerging 2014–15

HOUTHI AND AL-QAEDA EXPANSION 2011–2015

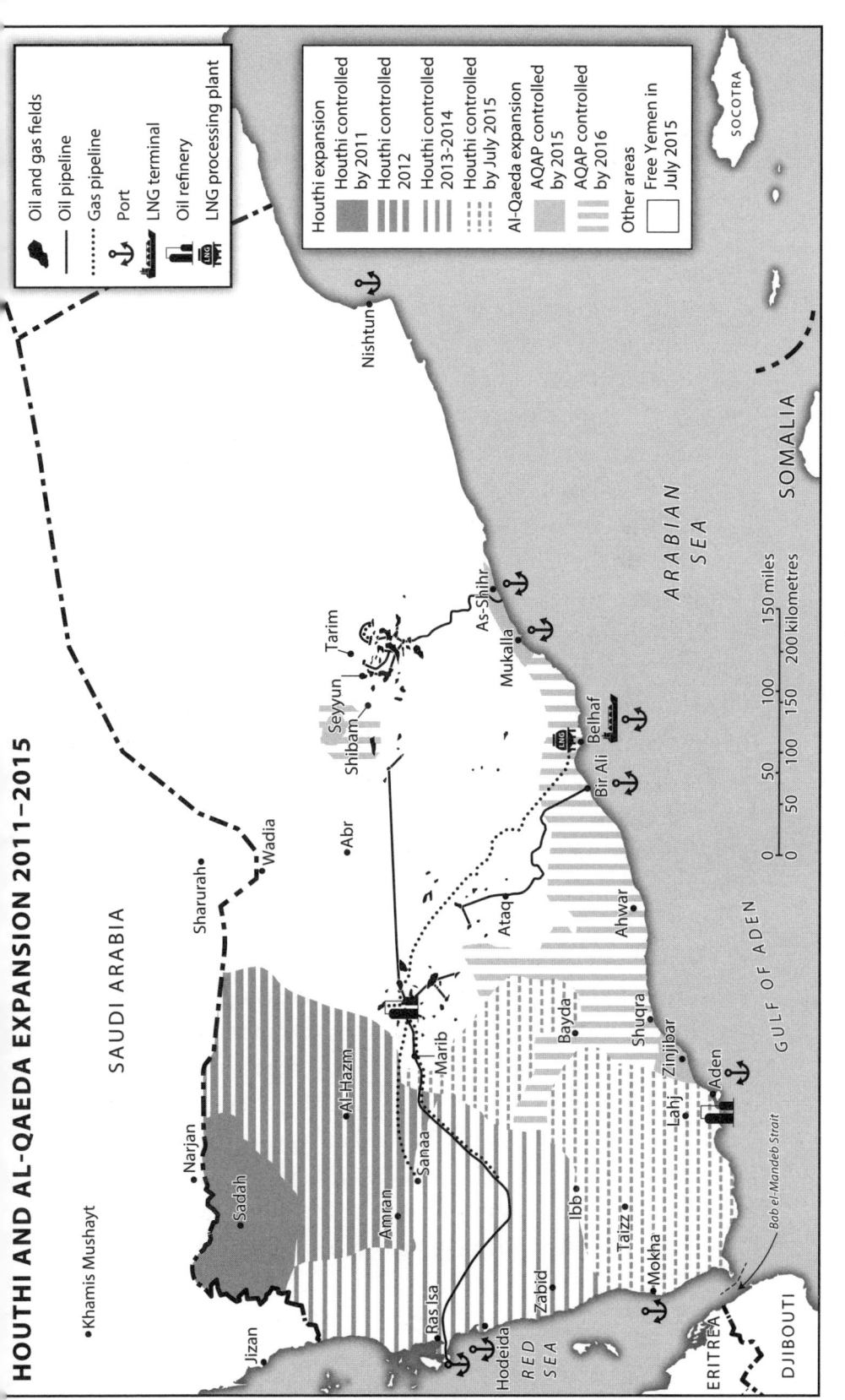

crisis, Musallam had other reasons for keeping an especially close eye on Yemen. It was AQAP that had tried to send explosives-packed printer cartridges through UAE cargo airports in 2010; stopping Asiri's bomb plots had long been a top priority for the Emirates.

The UAE military had been at war with Al-Qaeda for a long time. Almost every SOC trooper and many other soldiers of the UAE Presidential Guard had served alongside US and NATO units in the 12-year deployment of UAE forces to Afghanistan that was still ongoing in 2014. Fourteen SOC task forces eventually rotated through the mission, giving well over a dozen officers an experience of leading such groups. Musallam had personally commanded the SOC task force in Afghanistan's Helmand province in 2005–6. Al-Qaeda and the Taliban had tried many times to kill UAE personnel at the force headquarters in Bagram airbase (where they made up a small part of the broader multinational force) and at the forward bases in Helmand and Kandahar (where they were sometimes directly targeted while on patrols). As the head of SOC, Musallam had a tight connection to the US Joint Special Operations Command (JSOC) and was eyeing opportunities to collaborate with the United States against AQAP in eastern Yemen. If Yemen really was on the verge of collapse, Musallam sensed an opportunity to directly target Al-Qaeda with on-the-ground special operations, as the UAE and NATO had done in Afghanistan, and as the global coalition was now doing in Iraq and Syria against the Islamic State.

Forming the Caliphate, Redux

As Musallam's intelligence officers monitored Yemen, a clear pattern was forming. AQAP was also readying itself for the chaos of civil war, and seemingly learning the lessons of the missed opportunity of the Arab Spring. AQAP's military emir Qassem al-Raimi returned to his tried-and-tested playbook – one that had worked in Yemen in 2009–10 and which was also delivering success to ISIS in Iraq in 2012–14. Raimi began a steadily escalating series of assassination and intimidation attacks on the security and intelligence officials and Popular Committee leaders who had brought about the downfall of the Emirate of Waqar. In the first such attack, one of Raimi's suicide bombers shook the hand of Major General Salem Ali al-Qatan, the commander of Operation Golden Swords, the operation to smash the Emirate of Waqar in the summer of 2012. The suicide attacker pulled Qatan close before detonating his suicide belt and killing the officer on 18 June 2012.

The tribes of Abyan and Shabwa that had fought Al-Qaeda had been effectively abandoned after the offensive, with Hadi's weak Yemeni government reneging on its offers of funding and military support to the Popular Committees. The case of Sheikh Abdal Latif al-Sayyed of Jaar vividly illustrated the blood feud that was pursued by Raimi and his captains in the two years after the emirate fell. Sheikh Abdal Latif al-Sayyed had been the highest profile defector from Ansar a-Sharia to the Popular Committees during Operation Golden Swords in 2012. AQAP killed more than a dozen of Abdal Latif al-Sayyed's brothers and close cousins, tried five times to kill the sheikh himself, and put a bounty of 7 million Yemeni rials on his head. Raimi's men had even left the beheaded corpses of six of Abdal Latif al-Sayyed's relatives on the main street of his home town of Jaar. Raimi's videotaped show trials and executions of government inform-ants was publicised as the Harvest of Spies campaign. (As a sad historical footnote, Abdal Latif al-Sayyed was eventually killed by AQAP in a suicide vest attack on 10 August 2023, more than ten years after they had marked him for death.)

Following this 'shaping' of the battlefield, Raimi's tactics began to turn towards the overrun of government bases, a typical intermediary step taken by Al-Qaeda commanders before they attempted the seizure of terrain. On 30 September 2013, Raimi sent a suicide car bomb to the gates of the headquarters of the 2nd Military Regional Command (MRC) in the southern port of Mukalla, wiping away the gate guards so that an assault team of AQAP veterans could seize and hold the headquarters for three days before they were bloodily wiped out by Yemeni commandos in room-to-room fighting where no quarter was asked and none given. On 5 December, the same tactics were used to overrun the Ministry of Defence hospital in Sanaa and then the 4th MRC headquarters in Taizz on 2 April 2014. On 26 June 2014, days after the Islamic State seized Mosul, Raimi launched a triple attack in northern Hadramaut, overrunning the 1st MRC headquarters in Seyyun, the control tower of Seyyun airport, and the PSO base and prison. As Sanaa fell to a Houthi–Saleh coup in September 2014, the Yemeni military across the country began to collapse, with individual commanders and bases reassessing whether their interests lay with the government-in-exile in Aden, or with the Houthi–Saleh putschists, or even with Al-Qaeda.

With the fall of Sanaa to the Houthi–Saleh forces in September 2014, Saudi Arabia and its Arab partners were now on a road to war. The fundamental issue was that in partnership with Saleh, the Houthi rebels of northern Yemen stood a good chance of overrunning the whole country. They were no ordinary tribal rebels: drawn from a Hashemite elite (known as sadah) that could claim to trace their lineage directly to the Prophet, the group's leaders had been carefully groomed since the 1980s by the Islamic Revolutionary Guard Corps (IRGC) of Iran. The Houthis – formally called Ansar Allah (Partisans of

Allah) – are a family and caste-based leadership group that grew from the movement's founder, religious scholar Badr al-Din al-Houthi, who married five times and who fathered thirteen sons who lived to adulthood. In addition to being a charismatic preacher, Badr al-Din (and most of the key Houthi leaders until today) were known collectively as the Ahl al-Bayt (the descendants of the Prophet), seeing themselves as superior to other Yemenis and the only caste fit for leadership. Badr al-Din and his sons were members of the Jarudi sect of the Zaydi branch of Islam (a sect of Islam that deviates from mainstream Sunnism by venerating Ali as the legitimate heir to the Prophet). Jarudis are also the only sect in Yemen to belong to the prevalent 'Twelver' strand of Shiism dominant in Iran, Iraq and Lebanon. (Jarudis and other Twelvers believe that the proper line of descent from Prophet Muhammad runs via one descendent (the fifth imam, Mohammed al-Baqir) to a messianic 12th imam, while the non-Jarudi majority of Yemen's Zaydis ('Fivers') believe in a different line of descent and method of succession branching from their preferred fifth imam.)

What this meant in geopolitical terms was that Badr al-Din and his sons were warmly welcomed and supported by the fledgling Islamic Republic of Iran after the 1979 Islamic Revolution there, especially because Badr al-Din was a fervent believer in the export of the same revolutionary model as Lebanon's via the Hezbollah movement and eventually to Yemen. Badr al-Din used a Zaydi revivalist movement called Believing/Faithful Youth, which he modelled on the mechanisms of post-revolutionary Iran and Hezbollah – summer camps, youth indoctrination, social programmes and a political party. Throughout the 1990s, Badr al-Din and his sons sent 800 religious students to train in Iran, some of whom (based on similar treatment of Lebanese, Saudi and Bahraini students) were groomed by the Islamic Revolutionary Guard Corps (IRGC) with paramilitary training. In 1999–2000, Badr al-Din's most senior son Husayn spent a year undertaking religious studies in Khartoum at a time when Sudan was the most active IRGC and Iranian Ministry of Intelligence and Security outstation on the Red Sea. Husayn then went from Sudan to Iran, and when he returned from this retreat in 2001, he introduced the now infamous slogan that supercharged the Houthi movement, 'the scream' (*al-shiar*): 'Death to America, Death to Israel, a Curse upon the Jews, Victory to Islam.' Though Husayn died in 2004, this remains the Houthi slogan today, and has been stencilled on Houthi missiles fired both at Israel and at US vessels and international shipping in the Gaza war of 2023–24.

Riyadh reassured all the Arab states that Iran would not be allowed to engineer a takeover of an Arab nation, just a stone's throw away from Islam's two holiest cities, Makkah and Madina, and astride the world's busiest maritime trade routes in the Indian Ocean, Red Sea and Suez Canal. Saudi Arabia had fought a bruising short war against the Houthis in 2010 on its south-western border and had been preparing for a rematch ever since. If war came, Riyadh was clearly going to take the lead on the efforts to de-fang the Houthi–Saleh war machine with aerial strikes and to contain the enemy in northern Yemen.

This left room for the UAE to contribute to any future military campaign in the places where the Houthi–Saleh forces were *not* yet present and where Saudi Arabia was not focused, such as the southern port city of Aden and eastern Yemen's oilfields and coastline. This division of labour suited the UAE, which was an expeditionary power, well suited to longer-range operations, with a growing navy and well-practised fleet of C-17A Globemaster III heavy airlift aircraft and brand-new Airbus A330 Multi Role Tanker Transport air-to-air refuelling aircraft.

Most important, the UAE had the confidence to lead a stand-alone effort in southern and eastern Yemen because its armed forces had spent the last two decades undertaking expeditionary operations alongside Western militaries in coalition operations in Somalia, Lebanon, Kosovo, Albania, Afghanistan and Libya.

Filling the vacuum in the east

To Musallam, it was clear that the creeping coup launched by Houthi–Saleh forces needed to be contained before it spread to Yemen's government-controlled areas in the south and east. But equally clearly, the SOC had an important counter-terrorism job to do in those areas, because any vacuum in state authority would be exploited by Al-Qaeda, as had been the case during the Arab Spring in Abyan. From this overlap of objectives, Musallam began to develop an idea that would grow into a concept of operations: that the UAE needed to be ready to go where the Houthis had not yet reached, and to prepare the local Yemenis to defend their areas against any and all invaders who might exploit the government collapse.

In the UAE military, the placement of senior officers like Musallam was typically not random: they were often in exactly the right role to suit the needs of the moment. In Musallam's case, he had a special interest in eastern Yemen – the former sultanates spread across the modern-day governorates of Shabwa, Hadramaut and Mahra. Like a lot of Emiratis, Musallam's family had deep ties to the so-called Empty Quarter, encompassing huge swathes of southern Saudi Arabia and UAE, the western Omani territories of Dhofar, and Hadramaut and Mahra, the eastern corner of Yemen. As was the case with many Emirati families, some of his ancestors had left Yemen to settle in Al-Ain hundreds of years ago, and other descendants had come out of the deep deserts at that tri-border area in 1950 and drifted towards the Gulf over time. Rather more uniquely, the famous explorer Wilfred Thesiger had dedicated his 1959 book on the Empty Quarter, *Arabian Sands*, to Musallam's paternal uncle Salem bin Ghabaisha, who had guided Thesiger and protected him throughout his journeys. Musallam had grown up hearing the tales of eastern Yemen; of spies and smugglers, vendettas and raids. As Musallam proudly told me: 'Our tribe, we knew no boundary. No Sykes–Picot or Westphalia, no lines on a map. They were wolves of the desert, good fighters, and they did what they had to do to put food on the table. They worked with all the devils.'

Even in 2014, Musallam's family had a fingertip feel for what was happening in eastern Yemen. Musallam's contacts regularly travelled to Hadramaut for business and he could see plainly that trouble was brewing. Al-Qaeda was already probing and attempting takeovers in coastal towns like Ghayl Ba Wazir, a famous seat of Islamic learning and tobacco cultivation, halfway between the port city of Mukalla and the oil export terminals at As-Shihr. Well-informed Yemenis whispered that AQAP was already the power behind the throne in Mukalla city itself, partway through a kind of shadow takeover and emptying private banks at will. By the start of 2015, the international oil companies, always a good bellwether of the real level of risk on the ground, were making preparations for an emergency evacuation of the Hadramaut oilfields and As-Shihr on an hour's notice. On-the-ground contacts were reporting that a lot of money was changing hands in Hadramaut, which is often a leading indicator that military plans are in motion in Yemen. It meant that officials were getting ready to switch sides, and it also meant that Al-Qaeda was not acting alone: practised money-movers from Ali Abdullah Saleh's networks and his Islahi-supported generals were in on the scheme, deliberately engineering the handover of government-controlled military bases to Al-Qaeda in order to weaken the Hadi government.

Musallam's SOC worked closely with their American counterparts and so the UAE had a clear understanding of the extant 'over-the-horizon' US counter-terrorism policy in 2014. This meant that Americans were not present on the front line in Yemen but instead operated a secure site in Al-Anad airbase, just north of Aden, or else were offshore in Djibouti, Saudi Arabia or on board naval vessels in the Indian Ocean. If the presence of the United States could be felt, it was mainly in the form of drones that constantly orbited over three main clusters of Al-Qaeda leadership activity, in Marib, Abyan and Shabwa. US policy was unlikely to change any time soon, especially with so much effort now focusing on the new war against the Islamic State in Iraq and Syria. According to the SOC's analysis, the United States would not be capable of filling the vacuum in eastern Yemen before Al-Qaeda and other violent extremists could take advantage.

A lack of 'over-the-horizon' lethality was not the Americans' problem. There was no doubt that the United States had unrivalled ability to detect electronic signals, track objects moving on the surface of the earth, and then precisely attack them. With AQAP identified as the fastest-growing terrorist threat to the United States since 2009, there were no shortage of intelligence, surveillance and reconnaissance (ISR) assets allocated to Yemen. Some of the US capabilities (which will only be briefly described here using publicly available information, in order to protect their future utility) were simply breathtaking. According to a 2012 leaked document, the United States had established 225 'named areas of interest' in Yemen. To find and 'fix' (track) the targets, these areas were covered around the clock by a large fleet of 11 MQ-1 Predator drones and a combined force of 12 P-3MS, U-28 and MC-12 propeller-driven ISR aircraft, plus an unknown number of satellites and CIA drones and aircraft. Mind-blowing US signals intelligence and cyber intelligence capabilities were also focused on Yemen, capturing vast quantities of electronic data. This information was then processed by powerful artificial intelligence-driven translation and analysis processes. In the creepy lexicon of the US war on terrorism, this provided 'persistent stare with no blinking', as one publicly leaked 2012 report noted. The 'finish' function – i.e. killing people, in most cases – was mainly undertaken by CIA drones and the US Air Force's five MQ-9 Reapers and eight F-15E Strike Eagles allocated specifically to the mission.

These efforts ensured a steady stream of remote killings of self-confessed terrorists, but also caused the deaths of a far wider circle of people who made the mistake of closely associating with them. Each known or suspected terrorist would be code-worded: to use one publicised example, a man called Saleh al-Anjaf al-Harithi became 'Objective Rhodes' throughout the hunt that ended with his death by drone strike. Each 'objective' would be given a 'baseball card', referring to the collectible cards that were once included with packets of bubble gum bought by American children. 'Positive identification' (PID) of those targets might be ascertained by an overlap of intercepted content and voice recognition, collocation with communications devices, and live unbroken tracking with high-definition video or airborne radar systems. In September 2010, a US strike killed Najar al-Qahtan, the editor of the *Sada al-Malahim* (*Echo of Battles*) online journal. In September 2011, a US drone strike killed the men behind the English-language *Inspire* magazine, American-Yemeni Anwar al-Awlaki and his deputy Samir Khan.

Over-the-horizon US counter-terrorism in Yemen

With a green light from Hadi, the US drone campaign had gone into overdrive. US drone strikes began reaching down into lower levels of AQAP in 2012, with an unprecedented 14 strikes in the first half of the year, roughly double the rate seen since 2009. The newly installed President Hadi even called on 5 May 2012 to purge AQAP from 'every district, village and place'. On 6 May 2012, a US drone killed Fahd al-Quso, the most senior of half a dozen terrorists hunted to their deaths after participating in the Yemen-based maritime attack cell that attacked the USS *Cole* and other maritime targets. AQAP struck back immediately, killing 101 Yemeni soldiers and wounding 220 others in a bloodbath – a suicide bombing during a parade rehearsal in Sanaa the day before the annual Unity Day commemoration on 22 May 2012.

It might seem logical that this uptick in strikes would require greater use for local human intelligence derived from Yemeni informants. In fact, human intelligence was not the driver. Without an on-the-ground presence, and disconnected to the local culture, the United States had never had much faith in the tip-offs provided by Yemenis, which were often assessed as inaccurate or driven by tribal vendettas. Instead the surge of strikes throughout 2013 was achieved through the relaxation of positive identification and a reliance on what are known as 'signature' strikes. In these, a strike was authorised on a target (whose name might never be known) because their behaviour – or their 'pattern of life' – strongly suggested membership of AQAP and related networks. A technique first used in Afghanistan and Pakistan in 2008, signature strikes certainly allowed pressure to be maintained on terrorist foes from a distance.

Yet, in the UAE's view, there were also a lot of problems with this 'over-the-horizon' approach, especially if the objective was to build friendly alliances with Yemeni forces in the country's east. First, and most important, signature strikes – and over-the-horizon counter-terrorism generally – failed to take into account the complexity of Al-Qaeda's interaction with local communities, especially those in Yemen. Tribal groups constantly oscillated closer towards or further away from AQAP, depending on their shared interests. As a result, many tribal leaders ticked a lot of the boxes required to trigger a signature strike. An attack on one member of a major tribe could alienate huge swathes of rural Yemen for years to come. This occurred most famously in May 2010 when a US drone strike killed the deputy governor of Marib governorate, Jabir al-Shabwani, whose brother Ayad was an AQAP member and who may have been mediating defections from Al-Qaeda at the time – and thus ticking almost all the boxes needed to trigger a signature strike, merely because they did regularly meet with and talk with AQAP members from their tribe. Al-Qaeda had for years propagandised the heavy-handed collective punishment used by the Yemeni government against cities like Zinjibar and Jaar, and also exploited civilian deaths caused by US airstrikes. In December 2013, for instance, signature targeting resulted in four Hellfire missiles striking a wedding procession in Radaa, killing 12 and wounding 15, and requiring over $1 million (in US dollars) 'blood money' payments to the families. The UAE thought there had to be a better way to reduce the threat of Al-Qaeda in Yemen.

The pitch: on-the-ground operations in the east

By January 2015, Musallam was advocating a completely different but complementary approach to the US campaign. The Yemeni counter-terrorism units built by the Americans before

2011 had either collapsed since the Arab Spring or stayed close to their ousted patron, Ali Abdullah Saleh, and now sided with the Houthis. The new Popular Committees and the remainder of the Yemeni military needed help – and quickly, before they lost heart completely. Fighting Al-Qaeda in Yemen required more than over-the-horizon strikes: it needed boots on the ground. In Musallam's view, the UAE Special Operations Command was the best fit for the job.

To get sign-off for this mission, to get a toehold in Yemen on the eve of civil war, he would need the approval of the highest authorities in the Emirates. That meant his first 'pitch' of the concept had to be rock solid, which required detailed professional planning activity. Ten years earlier, Musallam would have struggled to map out the processes and sequences required to outline and test his plan for a clandestine military operation in an active war zone. But in the intervening years, Musallam had attended the US Marine Corps School of Advanced Warfighting in Quantico, Virginia, a 30-minute drive away from the Federal Bureau of Investigation (FBI) campus. As for many young world-famous UAE officers, a period of military education in the United States post-9/11 was not Musallam's first choice – being that American visa and customs processes felt hostile to Middle Easterners – but the Americans turned out to be good hosts and the experience forever changed him as a military professional.

Musallam was the first Arab Muslim graduate of the programme and it taught him, from start to finish, how to undertake robust mission planning and campaign design. His tutors were US officers just returned from years of combat experience in Iraq and Afghanistan. Musallam immediately put the theory into practice in the lead of the UAE task force in Helmand, Afghanistan. He had a tidy mind and he enjoyed the structure of planning: the real war in Afghanistan took him to the next level of planning in a live conflict, where he found the environment to be 'really murky, ambiguous'. Musallam recalled: 'I learned more in my first year of real war than I did until then in my whole career in the military.'

As the commander of SOC and a sharp thinker, Musallam was expected to put new ideas to the UAE military leadership, including the commander-in-chief MBZ. The UAE's military commander and the SOC chief agreed on the strong probability of an imminent civil war in Yemen. Iran would use the conflict as a proxy war with the Arab Gulf States. The war would offer opportunities to Al-Qaeda and other extremists, not least because such terrorists would present themselves and any new emirate they formed as the 'protectors' of Yemen's Sunnis against the Iran-backed Houthis. Since the Houthis' takeover in Sanaa in September 2014, the UAE military had been practising its rudimentary Crisis Action Plan that would allow the country to go onto a war footing within 36 hours. The crisis was drawing ever closer. Musallam now introduced the idea of helping Yemeni tribes to develop a Hadramaut Protection Force to defend against all comers. MBZ was interested and directed that Musallam put some more meat on the bones of his concept. When they next met in early February 2015, alongside deputy chief of staff of the UAE Armed Forces, Lieutenant General Issa M., the idea was compelling enough for MBZ to request a formal briefing on the issue of undertaking an initial fact-finding reconnaissance into Yemen. On 7 February 2015, six weeks before the Yemen war broke out fully, Musallam briefed the mission to MBZ, Lieutenant General Issa, and the UAE Presidential Guard commander, 'Major General Mike' (hereafter MGM). 'Let's take a peek,' MBZ had agreed, 'look at the social mosaic and the tribal system. Get the ground truth.' The reconnaissance was provisionally given the green light, with the objective of studying the feasibility of building up the defensive capacity of local tribes; establishing training bases; and establishing ways to disrupt AQAP's activities. Musallam visited the Saudi Arabian military leadership and UAE leaders met with US counter-terrorism agencies to liaise and coordinate on the potential operation.

The Yemen war begins

As Musallam was readying his reconnaissance, the dominoes began to fall in what would become Yemen's most destructive war and the world's worst humanitarian crisis. In early March 2015, Ali Abdullah Saleh had said publicly that he would 'drive Hadi into the sea', and in mid-March, fighting broke out in Aden between Saleh loyalists and Hadi's internally exiled government. On 21 March, the Houthi Revolutionary Command Committee declared a 'state of general mobilisation' against 'terrorist forces' in southern and eastern Yemen. Heavily armed Houthi–Saleh columns began streaming southwards and eastwards to link up with pro-Saleh commanders in the major cities of Ibb, Taizz, Bab el-Mandeb, Aden and Abyan. Al-Anad, the US counter-terrorism base in Yemen, was evacuated hastily.

On the eve of the war, on 24 March 2015, Musallam received the order he had long anticipated: to evacuate diplomats and any remaining UAE civilians. Into Yemen went the pre-alerted SOC company. On 25 March, a fleeing President Hadi was en route to Riyadh from Oman after being evicted from Aden by heavy fighting, and was bundled onto a yacht by SOC troopers who got him safely away. Invoking Article 51 (self-defence) of the UN Charter and the Arab League and Joint Arab Defence Treaty, he officially requested urgent military assistance from the

UN Security Council to authorise 'willing countries that wish to help Yemen to provide immediate support for the legitimate authority by all means and measures to protect Yemen and deter the Houthi aggression'. Hadi sent the same message to the Arab League.

The Gulf Arabs had drawn a line in the sand and had been readying for war even since the Houthi–Saleh putschists had overrun the capital Sanaa in September 2014. Yemen would not be surrendered to Iran without a fight. Even if the United States was too busy or too distracted to help, a Gulf coalition led by Saudi Arabia would act to stop Iran from gaining a foothold on the Arabian Peninsula, home to Islam's holiest sites, Makkah and Madina, and to the world's greatest concentration of oil reserves. That defensive action – codenamed Operation Decisive Storm – began in the early hours of 26 March 2015.

III

TASK FORCE EAST

The major air campaign unleashed by the Saudi-led Gulf coalition in the early hours of 26 March 2015 came as a shock
to many observers, who didn't expect a handful of Gulf countries to be able to do what only the United States had done
before. The Gulf coalition proved that it could suddenly
execute a classic 72-hour Air Tasking Order (ATO) – the enormously complex opening move of every modern air campaign
in which three days' worth of pre-surveyed military targets
are methodically struck. The task was undertaken by a fleet
of 170 strike aircraft: 100 aircraft from Saudi Arabia, 30 from
the UAE, and a composite force of 40 aircraft from Bahrain,
Jordan, Kuwait, Morocco and Sudan. In the first three days, the
Gulf coalition destroyed almost all of the remaining MiG-29s,
Su-22s, F-5Es and L-39 armed trainer aircraft under the control
of the Houthi–Saleh forces. All identified SA-2 and SA-3
surface-to-air missile sites and associated radars were destroyed.
The coalition then struck as many Houthi-held ammunition
depots and surface-to-surface missile sites as they could, with
the obvious intent of disarming the Houthi–Saleh conspiracy
of as much military materiel as possible. Then the air campaign
moved beyond the ATO into continuous targeting undertaken
on a rolling basis. At this stage of the air campaign, the aerial
bombardment looked very similar to the kinds of precise but

definitely not perfect air campaigns the United States had fought against Iraq and Serbia from 1991 to 1999. Only much later, as collateral damage mounted from risky coalition strikes on Houthi leaders in key cities, did the air campaign become synonymous with civilian deaths.

For Musallam and his SOC planners, the onset of war gave them a wave of different missions to execute, of which eastern Yemen was now only one of many. As March 2015 ended, the SOC was tasked by MBZ with aiding the Yemeni resistance fighters in the port city of Aden, which was under heavy assault by the Houthis, who were streaming south to link up with Ali Abdullah Saleh's loyalists inside the city's security forces. (For those readers interested in this fascinating battle, the full account is given in my previous book, *25 Days to Aden: The Unknown Story of Arabian Elite Forces at War*.) For some weeks, Musallam found most of his attention drawn south-westwards towards that desperate fight to save Yemen's second-largest city.

The SOC mission in eastern Yemen was provisionally called Task Force East and given a separate planning team to the Aden operation. Continuing to work off the 7 February green light given by the chain of command, SOC put the finishing touches on a reconnaissance into eastern Yemen. It would be a quick 'in and out' mission, a proof of concept in many ways. A team of around a dozen SOC troopers would drive for 23 hours on the highways between the UAE and Saudi Arabia, and then turn south across the Empty Quarter, using remote tracks to drop out of sight during the course of a gruelling 17-hour marathon of dune-bashing and deep-desert night-driving. They would mingle into the stream of civilian traffic entering eastern Yemen from Saudi Arabia's Empty Quarter. The objective was to covertly meet an anti-Saleh sheikh called Amr bin Habraish and secure his support to learn about the environment and the players, and to develop a secure base inside Yemen where tribes could receive military training and resupply.

The team would operate in an unacknowledged way, dressed as civilians and working at the edge of acceptable risk. They would be largely on their own as there was simply no time to set up the ideal Combat Search and Rescue package (CSAR, pronounced 'see-sar'). If they got into trouble, UAE F-16s could be scrambled from Taif, Saudi Arabia, or slow AT-802 armed turboprop aircraft could be launched from Jizan, also in Saudi. But even using after-burners to reach maximum speeds the F-16s would take nearly an hour to get to the reconnaissance (abbreviated to recce or recon) team and would not be able to stay for long. The AT-802s had the opposite problem, being able to loiter for many hours but being so slow that the Yemeni locals called them 'the bicycle'. If they were to be of any help, their support would have to be perfectly arranged and already on-station when a crisis unfolded.

The mission would be led by Lieutenant Colonel Azzan T., an energetic officer with 21 years in the SOC. Azzan was an intense and serious-looking fellow, with a tight jaw and a habit of always meeting a man's eye. Afghanistan had been his academy: he first went as a young lieutenant in 2004 and by the time he left in 2010, he had undertaken five tours (almost back to back) and was a senior major in charge of a SOC task force in Helmand. He was well suited to the mission he was now given, having conducted well over a hundred 'key leader engagement' meetings with Afghan tribes – military jargon for negotiations and relationship-building with local civilian or military leaders. He was also familiar with how to stay alive in high-threat environments, having lived in the badlands of Helmand and hunted some of the Taliban's most notorious warlords and bomb-makers – men who tended to hunt you back.

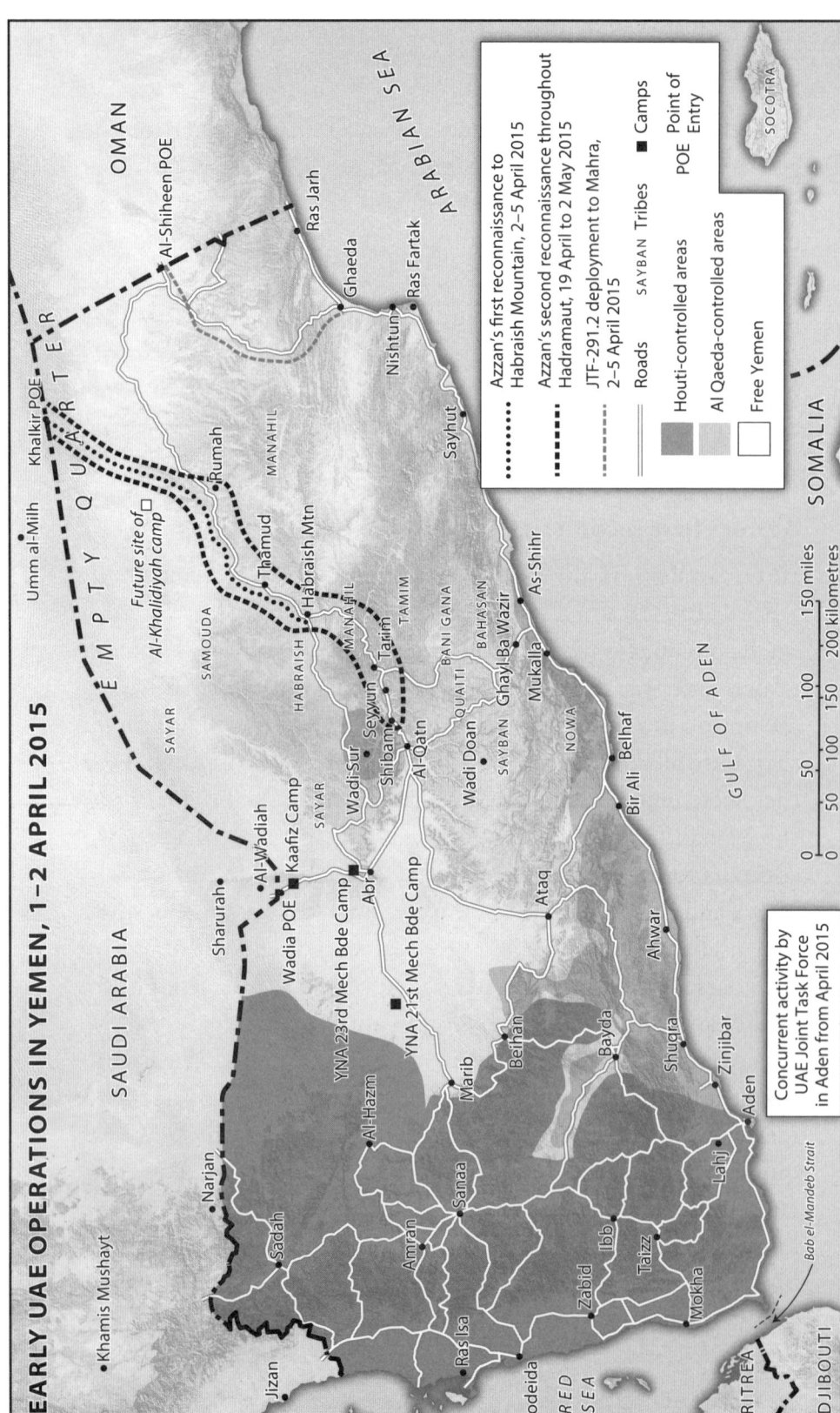

EARLY UAE OPERATIONS IN YEMEN, 1–2 APRIL 2015

Legend:

- Azzan's first reconnaissance to Habraish Mountain, 2–5 April 2015
- Azzan's second reconnaissance throughout Hadramaut, 19 April to 2 May 2015
- JTF-291.2 deployment to Mahra, 2–5 April 2015
- Roads
- SAYBAN Tribes
- Houti-controlled areas
- Al Qaeda-controlled areas
- Free Yemen
- ■ Camps
- POE Point of Entry

Concurrent activity by UAE Joint Task Force in Aden from April 2015

Scale: 0 50 100 150 miles / 0 50 100 150 200 kilometres

Places and labels:

OMAN
SAUDI ARABIA
ARABIAN SEA
EMPTY QUARTER
GULF OF ADEN
RED SEA
SOMALIA
SOCOTRA
ERITREA
DJIBOUTI
Bab el-Mandeb Strait

Khamis Mushayt
Jizan
Hodeida
Sharurah
Umm al-Milh
Al-Shiheen POE
Ras Jarh
Ghaeda
Ras Fartak
Nishtun
Sayhut
As-Shihr
Mukalla
Belhaf
Bir Ali
Ahwar
Zinjibar
Shuqra
Aden
Lahj
Taizz
Mokha
Ibb
Zabid
Ras Isa
Sanaa
Amran
Sadah
Narjan
Al-Hazm
Marib
Ataq
Bayda
Beihan
Khalkir POE
Rumah
Thamud
Habraish Mtn
Tarim
Seyyun
Shibam
Al-Qatn
Wadi-Sur
Wadi Doan
Ghayl Ba Wazir
Future site of Al-Khalidiyah camp
Kaafiz Camp
Wadia POE
Al-Wadiah
Abr
YNA 23rd Mech Bde Camp
YNA 21st Mech Bde Camp

Region labels:

MANAHIL
SAMOUDA
SAYAR
HABRAISH
MANAHIL
TAMIM
BANI GANA
BAHASAN
QUAITI
SAYBAN
NOWA

Before leaving for Yemen, he had been reminded of the golden rules by MGM, who had done his fair share of tribal engagements too. 'Don't make or break promises. Be direct and clear. Be humble and listen to everyone,' MGM had cautioned. And then, most important: 'Remember, *zero* mistakes.' Getting tribal engagement wrong could be deadly. MGM knew that Azzan took this to heart. He was 'tactically smart and careful', MGM recalled, and that meant he could be trusted with this dangerous mission and the lives of the men under his command.

Azzan's first reconnaissance into Yemen

After two days on the road, Azzan's team drove into Yemen on 2 April 2015. To a casual observer, they would have looked like a small convoy of eight civilian vehicles, maybe from an NGO or a trader. Entering Yemen through the tiny border post of Kharkir, about 400 km east of the major Saudi border town of Sharurah, they were already bleary-eyed from 40 hours of driving. There they were met inside Yemen by sun-blackened tribesmen from the Manahil tribe, one of the six major units of the Hamoum confederation (the others being the Habraish, Tamim, Sayban, Nowa and Bani Ghana). These were the same kind of tribesmen as Musallam's ancestors: trackers who could read the desert by the coarseness of the sand, its colour, and the presence of tiny bushes and camel droppings. Azzan and his men could feel the tension radiating from their hosts; only later would he realise that the Hamoum tribesmen always had this edgy feel, no matter what the circumstances. They were ready to fight and quick to anger, but they were here on a job and it was to protect and guide the Emiratis. About 300 km inside Yemen, at a place known as Habraish Mountain, they were met by Sheikh Amr bin Habraish. He had been chosen by the UAE's intelligence services because his uncle, Sheikh Saad bin Habraish, had been the leading voice pushing for the Hamoum tribes to unite, leading Saleh's assassins to murder him in December 2013. So Sheikh Amr was presumably someone who could be trusted, a man who would probably not sell the Emiratis to Saleh or his Houthi friends.

In Yemen, sometimes the exact course of the meeting is less important than the fact that the meeting is happening at all. This was the case when the Emiratis met Sheikh Amr on 5 April 2015. What mattered was that Azzan and his men came when they said they would come. Sheikh Amr pledged that he would not betray the Emiratis and would fight alongside them, and Azzan reciprocated. The partnership between Azzan and the Hamoum tribes had started, but it was only the first step of a long odyssey, and that journey nearly ended as soon as it had begun.

As Azzan and the team 'extracted' themselves from Yemen through the desert towards Kharkir in the early hours of 7 April, a Saudi F-15 was watching them from far above. A tribal contact in Yemen had reported to the Saudis that eight unknown vehicles were driving northwards to the Saudi border. In a war this large, not every piece of the system knew what every other unit was doing – in part to protect operational security. At the Combined Air Operations Centre (CAOC) in Riyadh, a controller had previously told the Saudi F-15 pilot: 'We have some business for you – go and clear this target.' As the powerful aircraft covered the great distances in just a few minutes, the Saudi CAOC director was asked for approval to destroy the convoy, which might have been Al-Qaeda terrorists or drug smugglers trying to enter the kingdom in a time of war. The director was cautious. 'If there is no urgent threat and if we still have minutes, let me go and pray and then I'll give you my decision,' he said.

In those minutes, the Saudis checked around to see if any coalition forces might be in the area. Twenty-five thousand feet above the convoy, Azzan could not have heard the F-15 even if the convoy had been stopped and had their engines silenced. 'They're ours!', a frantic UAE liaison officer called out to the CAOC controllers and the F-15 was vectored away into the night sky. 'Let them know they were nearly dead,' Musallam instructed the SOC staff. When Azzan heard what had almost happened, he felt cold and was surprised to be shivering slightly, an unfamiliar experience for this veteran soldier. That was really close, he thought to himself. He had been under enemy fire many times but this was different. In Afghanistan, he had seen what the weapons carried under the wings of the massive F-15s could do to a convoy or a group of men. They just ceased to exist and there was often nothing to bury. He shuddered to imagine being on the wrong side of that kind of firepower.

The fall of Mukalla

The urgency of mounting a mission in the east had increased greatly by the time Azzan returned to back-brief the results of his reconnaissance. While he had been away, an event had unfolded that brought into sharp focus all the fears that had motivated the formation of Task Force East. On the night of 1–2 April, the port city of Mukalla and its half a million residents had fallen to an armed takeover by factions connected to both AQAP and to Ali Abdullah Saleh. It was no surprise that the city was thoroughly honeycombed by Al-Qaeda and Saleh sympathisers but that still wasn't as shocking as a military overthrow that wiped away any vestiges of control by the internationally recognised Hadi government. A major port and its bustling economy was suddenly under the control of previously unknown anti-government forces who called themselves 'the Sons of Hadramaut'.

The military takeover had unfolded in just a few hours. Late in the evening on 1 April about 20 beaten-up Hiluxes and Land Cruisers had gathered at Al-Aroud Square, a park on the coastline at the western edge of Mukalla's urban sprawl. Video later released by AQAP showed the assembly of the force, which was around 120-strong and divided into six 20-man strike groups. Some of the Hiluxes were 'gun trucks' that carried rudimentary heavier weapons: a Russian-made 23-mm ZSU (pronounced 'shoe') anti-aircraft cannon; an improvised multiple rocket launcher with five tubes welded on the flatbed and loaded with 107-mm Katyusha artillery rockets; and an Improvised Rocket-Assisted Mortar (IRAM) that lobbed cooking gas canisters full of explosives at a high angle. They had come to fight, if push came to shove, but they clearly benefited from some kind of inside intelligence. Just over a hundred fighters cannot take over a city of half a million, including thousands of security forces, if there is organised resistance. Some of the Sons of Hadramaut wore face masks but many were locals, unmasked precisely to show that they were from the local tribes of Mukalla. None of the black flags of Ansar al-Sharia or AQAP were on show that night as the city fell. Wahayshi was applying the lessons he had learned last time when the Emirate of Waqar failed. This time, Al-Qaeda would work even harder to present itself as an uprising of Yemeni tribesmen.

Shortly after midnight the convoy entered Mukalla via the coastal corniche (Sixteen Street) and thus avoided the main government checkpoint on the Aden to Mukalla M100 highway and other guard posts overlooking the highway near the presidential and governor's palaces. Once inside the city, the six teams spread out to seize their tactical objectives. One blocking force pushed

AL-QAEDA TEAMS CAPTURE MUKALLA ON APRIL 1–2 APRIL 2015

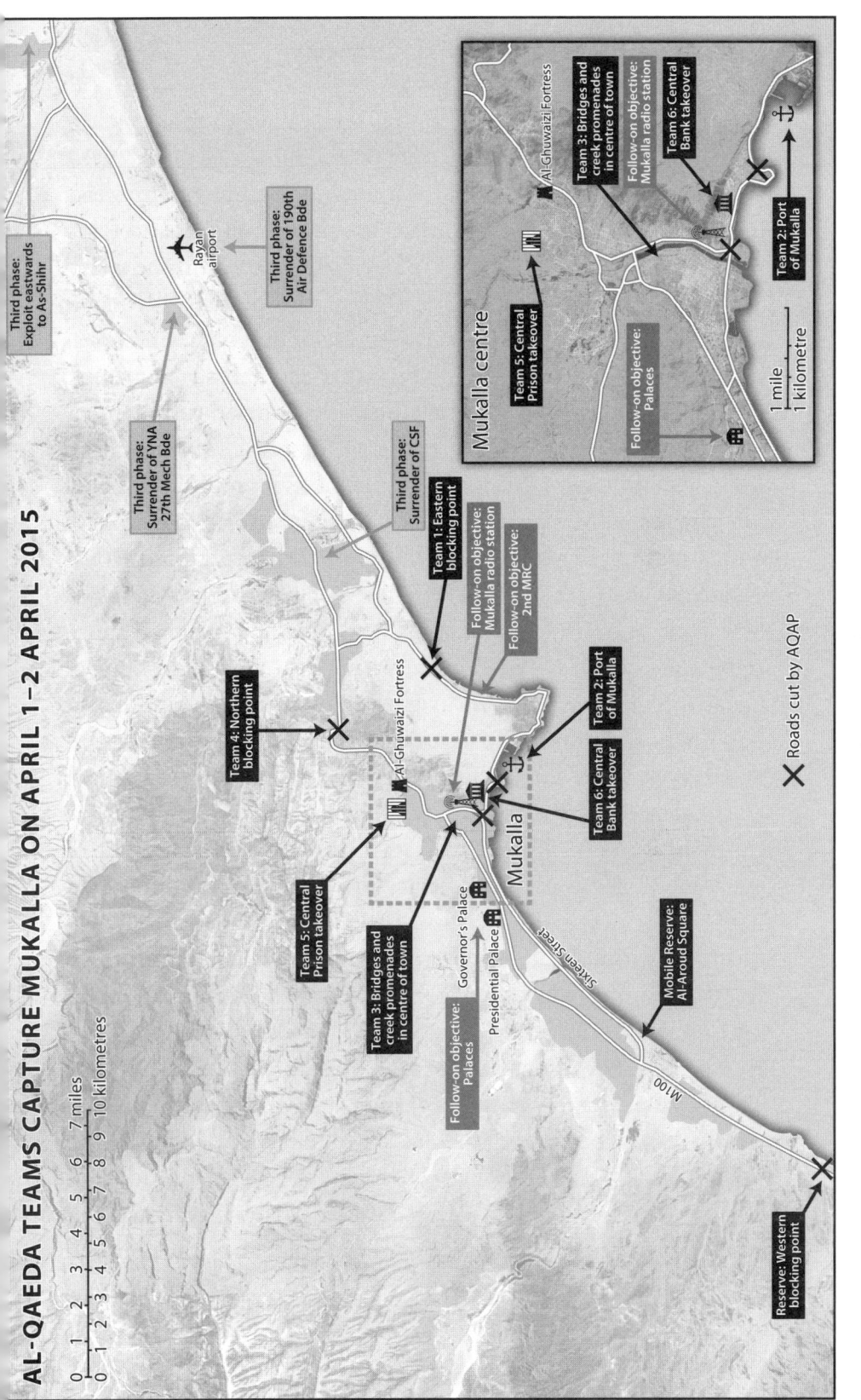

0 1 2 3 4 5 6 7 miles
0 1 2 3 4 5 6 7 8 9 10 kilometres

Third phase: Exploit eastwards to As-Shihr

Third phase: Surrender of 190th Air Defence Bde

Rayan airport

Third phase: Surrender of YNA 27th Mech Bde

Third phase: Surrender of CSF

Team 1: Eastern blocking point

Follow-on objective: Mukalla radio station

Follow-on objective: 2nd MRC

Team 4: Northern blocking point

Al-Ghuwaizi Fortress

Team 5: Central Prison takeover

Team 3: Bridges and creek promenades in centre of town

Team 2: Port of Mukalla

Team 6: Central Bank takeover

Follow-on objective: Palaces

Governor's Palace

Presidential Palace

Mukalla

Sixteen Street

Mobile Reserve: Al-Aroud Square

M100

Reserve: Western blocking point

✕ Roads cut by AQAP

Mukalla centre

Al-Ghuwaizi Fortress

Team 5: Central Prison takeover

Team 3: Bridges and creek promenades in centre of town

Follow-on objective: Mukalla radio station

Team 6: Central Bank takeover

Follow-on objective: Palaces

Team 2: Port of Mukalla

1 mile
1 kilometre

east, hugging the coast as the chasses (pick-up trucks) sped through the night. A 20-man unit pulled up at the outer gates of the 2nd Military Regional Command, which AQAP had suicide-bombed and then overrun for three days back in September 2013. The force formed a blocking point on the coastal highway facing east. A second unit drove into the main port and seized the harbourmaster. Two other strike groups fanned out to the north, one to control the *khawr* or creek area at the heart of the city, and one to seize the northern entry to the city at the ancient Al-Ghuwaizi fort (probably the most photographed and iconic building in Mukalla because of its dramatic construction on a huge sloping slab of rock). The final two assault groups went straight at the most important objectives for the takeover: Mukalla's Central Bank and its high-security prison. A reserve force controlled the rear at Al-Aroud Square on the western approaches, completely sealing off the city.

The residents of Mukalla became more and more anxious at the sounds of booming 23-mm cannon fire in the night, which echoed back onto the city multiple times from the mountains ranged all around. Any sounds – thunder, explosions – are thus amplified in Mukalla and this gave the sense of heavy fighting. If fact, resistance was limited. At the prison, half a dozen AQAP vehicles wound their way up the dirt tracks towards the squat cylindrical gatehouse. Most of the guards had already left after the forewarned warden and the head of security told them not to resist the attackers. A single Rocket-Propelled Grenade (RPG) fired into the gatehouse finished the job and over 400 prisoners were released from the overcrowded prison, including as many as 150 suspected Al-Qaeda fighters. In an instant, the AQAP attack force doubled in size.

The guard force initially resisted at the Central Bank, in the heart of the old city's elite quarter. A 23-mm ZSU was used by the attackers to shoot directly at the bank, each tracer round arcing lazily into the night as the Hilux rocked and squeaked on its suspension. The comical-looking IRAM was also fired, with a cartoonish iridescent fuse lit on each gas cylinder before the tubby bomb was launched in a whoosh of sparks. The guards' sole BMP-1 (a squat Soviet infantry fighting vehicle with a stubby 73-mm cannon mounted in its flat turret) was knocked out with an RPG and burned fiercely. The Central Bank guards called for reinforcements from the governor's palace to the west and the nearby Central Security Force (CSF) base to the east. When a CSF patrol tried to reinforce the bank, it was ambushed and two troopers were killed, and the Ministry of Interior troops fell back on their base and never came out again. The attackers' RPG teams had proven highly effective: video showed fighters bringing armfuls of plastic-wrapped RPG warheads to firing positions, where the clean and dry warheads would be mated up with the launcher carried by each gunner. On both sides of the creek, police cars were burning in the night and one police station after another was falling to the attackers.

By dawn on 2 April, the attackers had moved on to their next targets. A group of newly released prisoners led by a released AQAP fighter called Khalid al-Batarfi went straight for the palaces. The Islahi governor's mansion fell without a shot being fired and the governor was found to have fled as the fighting began. The presidential palace, held by a Hadi loyalist called Khalid al-Kazimi, needed a little more persuasion. Kazimi and his palace guards surrendered only after a car was packed with explosives and detonated remotely at the palace gate. Mukalla's radio station, next door to the Central Bank, was seized. The capture of a radio station seems almost quaint in the internet age, a throwback to the classic coups of the past when control of a radio or television station could make or break a takeover.

But in Mukalla, people still listened to the radio and now it was broadcasting calming messages from the Sons of Hadramaut.

Most of the attackers then moved to the east. The troops in the 2nd MRC headquarters were given three choices: leave your weapons and go home; join the Sons of Hadramaut; or fight and be killed. They gave up. Almost the same deals were made in the other military bases: the CSF surrendered, and many of their men joined the Sons of Hadramaut, whose salaries (99,000 Yemeni rials, equivalent to £312 per month) were roughly three times their government salaries. The 27th YNA Mechanised Brigade in Rayan, 20 km to the north-east of Mukalla, would not leave its base, even when local tribesmen themselves tried to 'rescue' the army from the small band of fighters outside its gates! A further 20 km to the east, the 190th Air Defence Brigade got the best deal of the day: even if they didn't join the Sons of Hadramaut, they could leave with a month's salary, their AK-47s and 120 bullets (a chest-rig of four magazines) each. In As-Shihr, the eastern limit of the attackers' ambitions, the city and energy sites fell with limited resistance. There, the Sons of Hadramaut drove straight into the oil and gas sites and produced a detailed list of the Western employees and demanded their handover. But thankfully the foreigners were long gone, removed by the Pakistan Navy in a non-combatant evacuation operation (NEO) in the opening days of the war in late March.

Mukalla: Seat of a new caliphate

While Azzan had been moving around Hadramaut, the shock of the takeover of Mukalla had been settling in across the Middle East and as far afield as the CIA headquarters in Langley, Virginia. The takeover of Mukalla had been a disconcertingly smooth operation, requiring surprisingly little military force.

Even taking into account the shock effect of the takeover, the government security forces and the citizenry could have squashed the tiny Sons of Hadramaut column like a bug if they had been led effectively. Instead, the Saleh-appointed commanders of the province, its security forces and its prisons had simply handed the city and its arsenals over with almost no resistance. After three days of non-stop hammering, blow-torching and exploding the doors off the Central Bank vaults, the Sons of Hadramaut could now hire anyone and everyone with their windfall of 50 billion Yemeni rials (£157 million). Their force had swollen overnight to become a new Mukalla security force of around 3,000 men.

In the week between the takeover and the next Friday prayers on 8 April 2015, a new governing structure had arisen fully formed in Mukalla – the Hadramaut Dialogue Council (HDC). The local coup had clearly been pre-planned in coordination with local Salafi and Islahi leaders. Installed in the abandoned governor's office, the HDC was led by Omar Saleh bin al-Shakl al-Juaydi and Abdal-Hakim bin Mahfouz. The former, Omar al-Juaydi, was a famous Islahi leader who had introduced the Islah Party into Hadramaut after unification in 1990, and who had led mujaheddin fighters against southern secessionists in the 1994 civil war. Abdal-Hakim bin Mahfouz was a Salafist who led the Al-Hikma al-Yamaniyah religious charity. The HDC immediately identified a local Salafi committee – the Council of Sunni Scholars (CSS) – as its sole legal reference, rejecting Yemen's constitution and civil law in favour of a clerical jurisprudent council headed by the brother-in-law of Abdal-Hakim bin Mahfouz. It was clear who ran the show: the Sons of Hadramaut gave the HDC the princely sum of 1 billion Yemeni rial (£3.2 million) to run Mukalla, while keeping the other 49 billion Yemeni rials for itself.

In Riyadh, Abu Dhabi and Washington, DC, the instantaneous emergence of the HDC looked like a breathtakingly cynical joint venture between Ali Abdullah Saleh and radical Islahi and Salafist militants who were willing to work with AQAP. In Aden, Saleh had tried to seize the city using his sleeper cells but that effort looked to be stalling. In Mukalla his approach was more pragmatic: if Saleh couldn't have Mukalla, neither would Hadi and his international partners – even if that meant that Al-Qaeda got a foothold.

The HDC nominally ran the civilian government in Mukalla but a Sons of Hadramaut militiaman shadowed each director general and department head as they went about their business. Some of the Sons walked around Mukalla unmasked, showing that they were from the area's families and tribes. AQAP was behind this charade, and they were employing an even softer touch than during the Arab Spring, dispensing with their original façade, Ansar al-Sharia.

But one person did not appear to have got Wahayshi's message. After languishing in government prisons for four years, the 36-year-old Khalid Saeed al-Batarfi – another Saudi with a Yemeni father – did not feel like going back into the shadows. He wanted to see how the big shots lived. The mid-level AQAP commander became a YouTube sensation in the days after the takeover of Mukalla, when he had done precisely the opposite of keeping a low profile by posing for pictures in the presidential palace, reclining on ornamental furniture with gilded fluffy pillows, goofing around with a telephone, and wiping his feet on the Yemeni flag. Born in Riyadh to a father from Mukalla, Batarfi (known by a local *kunya* as Abu Miqdad al-Kindi) became the face of the Sons of Hadramaut, who were given exclusive authority over policing and security by the HDC. At Friday prayers on 8 May 2015, the new regime announced via loudspeakers that they had taken over to ensure that Mukalla would not fall to the Houthis. In the race for Mukalla, Al-Qaeda had got a vital head start.

The need to act

Even against the backdrop of frantic concurrent activity in Aden, the general war and other UAE operations worldwide, the fall of Mukalla drew the attention of the full chain of command. In 2011, Ansar al-Sharia had been allowed to dig in for nearly a year in Abyan and the cost was the wholesale destruction of Zinjibar as the city was cleansed of Al-Qaeda. At the moment that Mukalla fell, nearly 20 major cities in Iraq and Syria had been under Islamic State control for between 11 and 24 months. A generation of young Muslim men were being forced into the service of perverse terrorist caliphates. There was no time to waste. Planning for Yemen operations was now being undertaken at the Presidential Guard headquarters. The Presidential Guard commander MGM had been appointed the ground component commander for all UAE forces in Yemen by MBZ on 5 April, while the air component remained under the control of Major General Ibrahim A., the commander of the UAE Air Force and Air Defence. The new Presidential Guard's interim joint operations centre was working around the clock to service the different operations in Yemen, with the most senior commanders sleeping in their offices on makeshift cots and bedding gathered by the officers' wives.

On 6 April, MGM issued the first written guidance for the eastern Yemen theatre of war. The commander's intent was to 'stymie' Houthi–Saleh expansion into eastern Yemen and to 'degrade AQAP' in order 'to restore the legitimate government of Yemen and remove potential threats to Gulf Cooperation

Council countries'. Flowing from this, the guidance authorised 'clandestine ground-based operations within eastern Yemen (Hadramaut) in order to defeat the AQAP and Houthi threats in the region'. Operational objectives included (reproduced in the original order from the directive):

- To degrade AQAP capabilities in Yemen, specifically in Hadramaut
- To prevent the Houthis getting a foothold in eastern Yemen
- To prevent Ali Abdullah Saleh-affiliated eastern brigades from supporting the Houthis in the east.

On 7 April, the joint headquarters authorised the establishment of a new Joint Special Operations Task Force called Joint Task Force (JTF)-291, led by Musallam R. and his deputy Colonel Mohammed S. The JTF would be split into three parts. JTF-291.1 would be led by Azzan T. and would focus on building tribal forces in Hadramaut. JTF-291.2 would be led by Major Ahmed A. and would focus on Mahra governorate, where another clandestine reconnaissance had been undertaken to prepare for action against Houthi smuggling networks that were bringing in advanced weaponry from Iran. Until combat operations began, Lieutenant Colonel Faisal T. would run JTF-291.3, which would prepare to undertake major combat operations in the east from its new wartime base in Sharurah, Saudi Arabia, which was located at the main trade crossing between Saudi Arabia and Yemen, at the western edge of the Empty Quarter.

JTF-291 would thus be hosted by Saudi Arabia and the next big job was to secure full Saudi buy-in for the mission. Clandestine week-long reconnaissance missions into Hadramaut and Mahra were one thing; an ongoing cross-border special operations campaign and all its support requirements was another. The Emiratis were asking to formally establish the JTF-291 head-quarters in Sharurah and to base the CSAR package there: armed AT-802 turboprops, AH-64 Apache attack helicopters, and a SOC quick-reaction force mounted in CH-47 Chinook twin-rotor transport choppers. The initial UAE hope for a start to operations at Sharurah on 10 April came and went as they waited for host nation permissions. Musallam and his deputy Mohammed S. had met with the Saudi Arabian chief of staff and Riyadh's Yemen theatre commander, plus the General Intelligence Directorate, but all were waiting on a political decision from above. There was an understandable Saudi reticence to let the mission proceed: UAE forces in Aden was one thing, but in Hadramaut? Eastern Yemen was Saudi Arabia's backyard, the ancestral homeland of its largest business families. This needed top-level resolution and the leaders got down to business. MBZ was visiting Riyadh on 12 April and he began to finesse a solution. On 14 April, the Saudis proposed the secondment of ten Saudi Arabia special operators to JTF-291.1, and on 18 April the mission was approved by a Saudi royal decree.

IV

AZZAN AND THE TRIBES
OF HADRAMAUT

On 19 April 2015, Azzan's second reconnaissance set off into the dune seas of Yemen from the Kharkir crossing point – known for many years to spies and smugglers as 'the secret gate to Yemen'. His force this time was not much larger than on his previous trip – just 15 SOC operators and six Saudis – but it could count on much better coordination with Saudi air power and they might even be rescued if they got into a bad scrape. Higher headquarters would leave Azzan largely to himself: the Presidential Guard staff and even Musallam at SOC were busy supporting the main effort at Aden, where a growing team of UAE special operators and Al-Forsan rangers were locked in an increasingly brutal block-by-block struggle to save the city from invading Houthi–Saleh forces. In April, May and early June, that meant Azzan had the best of all worlds: a classic special operations mission, sufficient resources to achieve it, and not too much micromanagement from the bosses. It was a soldier's dream and he recalled the next 15 days as a golden moment in his military career.

The next 14 days between 19 April and 2 May would see Azzan's team undertake a 1,000-km round trip into central Hadramaut and back again. The reconnaissance started in the deep deserts of the north, where the UAE already had good ties to the remote tribes. Then Azzan headed down to the ancient cities of Wadi Hadramaut, where certain tribal leaders said they were opposed to both Ali Abdullah Saleh and AQAP. In between these places, Azzan did his main business, with the tough hill tribes of the Hamoum confederation. They visited 32 villages and provided aid to over 500 families. When needed, they provided medical care, solar power generators, tents, water pumps and piping, all of which could make a huge difference to tribal life.

The team lived rough, sleeping in desert camps under the stars to keep their exact location hidden between meetings. Before the deployment, Saudi officers had tried to impress upon the Emiratis the risks of betrayal by Yemeni tribes, warning 'they will sell you for fish'. The Saudis were not wrong, and word of the Emirati mission spread quickly as the Yemeni tribes gossiped. As a result, AQAP had learned almost immediately that the task force was out and about in Hadramaut, referring to them as 'the Emirati tourists'. Al-Qaeda formed a 'hunter-killer' team and sent spies to listen out for news of their passing. Yet Azzan got his team in and out without a scratch, forming what he termed 'the first tribal coalition' of his operation.

The first tribal coalition

This set of trusted relationships with the Hamoum tribes would be the basis for everything that JTF-291.1 would achieve in eastern Yemen. First, Azzan listened to every Yemeni, very closely. Each had an important story to tell and no matter how many times Azzan had heard such tales, he gave each man his full attention. He could see that the tribal system had eroded, in part due to deliberate splintering techniques practised by Ali Abdullah Saleh as he danced on the heads of snakes. Good leaders like Sheikh Saad bin Habraish were assassinated by Saleh's government-protected mafia in Hadramaut, which was made up of newly empowered junior sheikhs and Islahi generals and clerics. One eastern Yemeni recalled: 'Saleh and his generals assassinated [Hadramis] as if they were at war with them – like thugs.' The coastal southerners who ran the local government in Hadramaut saw the northern tribes as strange outsiders with a different brutal culture. 'In the north, if you do not get weapons and fight, you do not put food on the table. They are different from us.'

The eastern tribes were desperate for rules-based leadership that they could finally respect, which seemed to have been largely absent since the days of the sultanates, before the Communists came in the 1960s and then Saleh's northerners came after unification in 1990. Hamoum confederation leaders like Sheikh Saad had been liquidated by the Communists of the People's Democratic Republic of Yemen (PDRY) and, since the 1994 civil war, by Saleh's Political Security Organisation. To Azzan, what these governments had done was ghastly, especially the manner in which Saleh had taught the tribes that the only way to get the government's attention and respect was to make problems – a road blocked here, a pipeline blown there, or a kidnapping just to drive home the point. Under these circumstances, Azzan recalled: 'AQAP were just another bunch of bandits, no better or worse than any of the other outsiders to invade from the south or the north.' This was a key insight that no amount of signature targeting data could reveal. You had to be there, on the ground, listening to these men tell their stories.

It took patience and a cool head to work with people twisted by the layering of Saleh's divide-and-rule tactics on top of an already hot-blooded and insular tribal society. One night in May 2015, an older Hamoum tribal leader felt neglected and anxious to have his say during a long tribal discussion. He decided to get Azzan's attention by suddenly striking like a snake and pinching Azzan's windpipe, just as if he was handling a farm animal, his fingernails digging into Azzan's throat and drawing blood. It took supreme self-control to take the blow and not return it, but that was the kind of man that the UAE had sent to undertake this mission. 'No mistakes,' MGM had said, and this order echoed in Azzan's mind at such times.

Instead of nursing his own pride, Azzan practised graciousness as often as he could. With great apparent interest, he would view the lands of the tribes, which were their greatest pride, and listen to their stories. Before he got the green light to deploy into Yemen, he had passed many of the long evenings in March and April reading the book *Arabia and the Isles,* by British political officer Harold Ingrams, which was about Hadramaut in the 1930s and the negotiation of a tribal compact that became known as 'Ingrams's Peace'. Before each meeting with a tribal leader, Azzan would enquire with his local guides and with UAE intelligence officers about the history of the tribe – the heroes and myths of their fathers and grandfathers. When it was Azzan's turn to speak, he would often delight the man opposite him by fixing him in the eye and saying: 'Of course I know about your tribe, you are famous,' and then following up the statement with an obscure detail from the exploits of that group. Anyone who has done this kind of work knows that exact moment and the warm welcome it unlocks. This was a masterclass in tribal engagement.

Now, on the ground in Yemen in May, there was no point making grand promises to the Hadramis even if Azzan had been inclined to do so. The tribal leaders for entirely understandable reasons had no trust in any outsider. The UAE had a great reputation in Hadramaut, both as the nation of Sheikh Zayed

Al-Nahyan (who had built great works of philanthropy in Yemen such as the new Marib Dam) and as an example of development that Hadramis aspired to. But even the offer of a better future for Hadramaut would have rung hollow in those early days. Trust was the precursor to everything else, and it could only be built day by day, by starting small and keeping any promises that were made. First, Azzan made sure to hire his Yemeni security detail equally from the tribes of the Hamoum confederation, with one chasse of fighters provided by each. The psychology was two-fold: 'If anyone attacks me,' he recalled, 'they attacked *all* the tribes. And if I was attacked, then the tribes had failed, and none wanted to look weak before the others.'

Azzan returned this loyalty. In May, a guard called Zayd fell from his chasse and was badly injured during a bumpy mountain drive through an area that the tribes described as controlled by Al-Qaeda. Azzan overrode all the rules by calling in a UAE helicopter to evacuate the man to the modern hospital in Sharurah. It was undoubtedly the right thing to do. Feeling the bone-shaking vibration of a Chinook helicopter as it landed, with an escort of two menacing Apache gunships that hovered like angry metal wasps, every tribesmen could literally feel the power of the UAE *on their side*. 'That day, we made ourselves look strong and Al-Qaeda look weak in their own valley. The tribes knew we could protect them,' Azzan recalled.

Building the Hadramaut Elite Forces

Next, Azzan extended his tribal force in early May 2015 to include a 250-man battalion from each of the Hamoum tribes who took turns training and guarding the shutdown oilfields and pipelines in northern Hadramaut. This served a dual purpose: first, it protected the critical infrastructure that was the lifeblood of

Hadramaut (and which the Hamoum had long sought to get government contracts to guard). Secondly, the force also created a kind of 'tripwire' at the mountain choke points between the Hamoum areas and the AQAP hub in Mukalla. No one would surprise Azzan or reach his training camps without some warning reaching him.

By 9 May, Azzan took the next step of directly arming the Hamoum tribes by para-dropping supplies into the Hadramaut desert. To reduce the risk of discovery, a pitch-black night with no moonlight had been chosen. The UAE C-17 was somewhere above the cloud but audible in the otherwise silent desert as the loadmaster and his team rolled 28 pallets of arms, ammunition and humanitarian supplies off the huge back ramp. Waiting in the dark, the UAE and Yemeni fighters suddenly started to hear ominous stamping sounds 'like a giant bird stomping its feet around them in the dark', as one soldier wrote in his diary. Distant explosions rumbled across the desert. Azzan ran to his car, thinking all the time of the phrase 'zero mistakes'. If a Yemeni was squashed by a pallet, it would spark a feud and that would be the end of his fragile tribal coalition. 'Everyone! Out of the vehicles! Spread out!' he blasted over the airwaves. Seconds later a pallet crashed through a boxy white and red Hilux close to Azzan – K-RUNNCH – flattening it and sending packets of Kalashnikov cartridges scattering for tens of metres in every direction. A wheel rolled past. Of the 28 loads, 16 were recovered after a careful search across a massive search area that spanned 25 km by 15 km. Twelve loads were fully intact and four were damaged, like the one that had flattened the Hilux. Eight munitions pallets, mainly anti-tank and mortar ammunition, had exploded upon landing. Four pallets simply disappeared and were never found – except perhaps by Bedouin who could not believe their luck as they made off with this gift from above.

Azzan had some explaining to do but he was up to the job. 'Where are our supplies?' tribal leaders would ask him. 'How come those guys got theirs and we're still waiting?' Azzan had answers for these: sometimes flattery ('You're so much richer and stronger than them, that's why they got theirs first') and sometimes tribal logic ('It's like when we enter the Majlis and we shake hands from the right of the room to the left. We wait our turn out of respect, not disrespect'). He made a high-quality dirt airstrip and began landing transport aircraft there from mid-May for greater reliability.

From June onwards, Azzan's ability to provide services for the local tribes was also on the rise. He could now drill water wells for the locals, which they had sought for years from the Yemeni government but never received. Local clinics were established and decked out with life-saving and life-changing medicines. It wasn't all good news, and Azzan, his deputy Major Faisal K. and the rest of the team quickly learned some hard lessons about corruption in Yemen. In mid-July 2015, for instance, Azzan heard about a Yemeni man who had bled to death from a leg injury during the Eid al-Fitr celebration, even though he had made his way to a UAE-supported clinic in a remote tribal area. Undertaking a snap inspection of the clinic, Azzan found it almost abandoned, used as a stable for goats and sheep, with medicines spoiled on the ground. The hospital manager had taken the UAE-provided ambulance as his personal car. The discovery of such callous corruption hit Azzan hard. Speaking to the author in 2023, Azzan's voice cracked a little when he said the incident was 'still stuck in my heart, eight years later. The corruption in Yemen was ten times as bad as in Afghanistan.' Azzan charged characteristically hard at the problem and got the clinic cleaned, fixed up, painted, staffed with five doctors and a midwife, and operational, all within 24 hours. And this time, Azzan ensured

1. It is impossible not to love and admire the Yemenis, who are photogenic, charismatic, self-assured and individualistic. These men are smoking a cigarette after sipping their steaming hot cups of chai, then it will be time for *qat* as they drive on to their destination in northern Hadramaut. The curved dagger (the *jambiya*), the keys to their *chassis*, and an AK-type assault rifle are close at hand at all times.

2. *Qat* is shared out between friends in the afternoon. In Yemen, the war never prevented *qat* being delivered to every corner of active battlefronts, even when ammunition, medical supplies, food and water were not. At the UAE training camps, the Hadramaut Elite Forces were told no chewing would be allowed on training days. Recruits were shamed with the question: 'Your grandfathers did not need *qat*, so why do you?' This reflected the way that chewing *qat*, a northern habit, had gradually penetrated southern and eastern Yemen by the 2010s.

3. On 6 October 2002, the oil tanker MV *Limburg* was struck by an Al-Qaeda suicide bomb originally intended for a US Navy warship. The attack was set in motion by Al-Qaeda's maritime attack planner Abdulrahim Mohammed al-Nashiri, who had previously overseen the 12 October 2000 suicide attack on the USS *Cole* in Aden harbour, which killed 17 US sailors. The *Limburg* was hit just offshore at As-Shihr, Hadramaut, by a boat-bomb with a shaped-charge munition at its prow, specially designed to penetrate a single-hulled vessel like a US Navy destroyer. The double-hulled *Limburg* survived the attack but one Bulgarian crew member was killed and 12 French and Bulgarian sailors were wounded. Ninety thousand barrels of oil were spilled into the Gulf of Aden. Immediately after the attack the UAE helped US authorities to detain al-Nashiri, and he remains in US custody.

4. A Yemeni government 'wanted' poster for Qassem al-Raimi, also known by his *kunya* (nom-de-guerre) Abu Hurayra al-Sanaani. Qassem was brought into Al-Qaeda by his father, who arranged for him to join Osama bin Laden's famous Al-Farouq training camp in Darwanta, Afghanistan in the late 1990s. In February 2006, Raimi escaped from the Sanaa prison cell with other core AQAP leaders. Methodical and ruthless, he oversaw the assassination and intimidation campaign against Yemeni intelligence and military officials and later took over AQAP when the group's leader Nasir al-Wahayshi was killed in a US drone strike in Mukalla in June 2015. A blunt instrument, Qassem al-Raimi undid much of al-Wahayshi's smart handling of AQAP-occupied Mukalla, terrorising the city with public executions.

5. In this 25 January 2012 photograph, members of AQAP, under the moniker Ansar al-Sharia, stand guard at a facility in Jaar, the capital of the Emirate of Waqar. Most of them have their faces uncovered, suggesting they are probably local confederates with limited long-term connection to AQAP, but the masked man at the front may be a different case. Non-local AQAP garrison members often kept their faces covered, in part because they feared that local Yemenis might sell them out to the Americans or the government. AQAP's leader Nasir al-Wahayshi learned hard lessons from the collapse of the 2012 emirate. He imparted these lessons to Al-Qaeda franchises across the world and used the lessons to shape his 2014–15 takeover of Mukalla.

6. A BM-21 multiple rocket launcher fires a 122-mm 'Grad' unguided rocket at an AQAP-held village in Mayfaa, Shabwah on 4 May 2014. Yemeni government tactics had never been subtle, whether negotiating hostage releases with tribes or fighting Al-Qaeda. Bombardment tactics using unguided weapons like these Grad rockets caused significant civilian casualties in the 2012 and 2014 government campaigns to contain AQAP. By killing civilians, the government tied the affected tribes closer to Al-Qaeda. Stand-off collective punishment would not solve the problem of AQAP. Someone needed to take them on surgically, unlike the Yemeni government, and on the ground, unlike the Americans.

7. Yemeni army Shibl-2 armoured personnel carriers take part in a counter-terrorism advance near Lawdar, Abyan, on 30 April 2012. This was part of Operation Golden Swords, the indiscriminate but temporally effective operation by 13 army brigades and local tribal fighters to smash AQAP's Emirate of Waqar in the middle months of 2012. However, as this stunning photograph underlines, road-based armies would always struggle to truly dominate mountainous areas like inland Abyan. Whenever the government retook the cities, AQAP simply melted back into the mountains and waited for government forces to disperse. This pendulum-type dynamic would continue until such time as agile counter-terrorism forces could effectively pursue AQAP into remote rural areas.

8. When Operation Golden Swords ended in mid-2012, the 'hold forces' left to control the former Emirate of Waqar were the local tribal Popular Committees, but these never received the financial backing, equipment or training needed to keep AQAP under control. This December 2011 image from Zinjibar shows a very typical scene from the life of an anti-AQAP fighter: provided with practically no equipment, ammunition or life support, this outpost is isolated and destitute, with no cover even from the elements, let alone the enemy. With only a nice view, the fresh sea breeze, and a cheek full of *qat* to sustain them, men like these were easily worn down by an AQAP assassination campaign over several years.

9. Huge explosions issue from caves in the Jebel Attan military complex in Sanaa on 20 April 2015 after a Saudi airstrike early in the war. The initial strike seems to have caused even larger secondary explosions, which is consistent with the detonation of rocket fuel and warheads from the Scud-B, Tochka and surface-to-air missiles hidden away inside the mountain's tunnels. The Yemeni 5th and 6th Missile Brigades had used the site for decades, but had also dispersed an unknown number of missiles by the time the war started. At least two of these missiles – the very accurate OTR-21 Tochka-U (codenamed SS-21 Scarab-B by NATO) – were hidden south of Sanaa and used to deadly effect against the coalition base at Safer on 4 September 2015.

10. In this November 2014 picture, a Houthi fighter mans his 14.5-mm 'Dushka' heavy machine gun, which has the Houthi motto, al-shiar (the 'scream'), on its ammunition can. It reads: 'God is Great, Death to America, Death to Israel, a Curse upon the Jews, Victory to Islam'. In the background, Al-Qaeda murals are painted onto the rocks of this mountain pass in Rada, the most south-easterly point the Houthis reached as they pushed beyond Sanaa into Al Bayda governorate. The Houthis and Al-Qaeda did fight, but mainly they used the threat of each other as a recruiting tool. In fact, one of the Houthi leaders Abdul-Malik al-Houthi's biggest influences as an anti-Western militant was Osama bin Laden, the founder of Al-Qaeda.

11. Mukalla waterfront in the Hayy as-Salaam area – the old city. In the background can be seen one of the line of Quaiti sultanate forts on the escarpment. The city retains its fundamental appearance: a shelf of densely packed, ancient whitewashed buildings that fills all the flat spaces below the almond-brown cliffs. Brightly coloured fishing skiffs bob in the harbour. The openness of Mukalla to the sea was an overwhelming concern for the Al-Qaeda occupiers and an opportunity for the coalition liberators in 2016. To Al-Qaeda, the town's fishing fleet was a threat, a way for spies to enter and leave Mukalla. After a US drone strike killed Nasir al-Wahayshi, a fisherman was executed as a warning to others. Meanwhile the coalition closely patrolled the coast to prevent Al-Qaeda leaders escaping by sea. A rapid UAE planning effort created an amphibious landing option as a fallback in case the attacks by land failed.

12. One of the most iconic buildings in Yemen – the Al-Ghuwaizi Fort, which guarded the northern road entrance to Mukalla from the mountains. Although the fort was not used by either side in the 2015–16 fighting, the neighbourhood of Al-Ghuwaizi was seized by Al-Qaeda (with the other road entrances) to seal Mukalla off during their April 2015 takeover. Such entrances were then fortified as points where citizens could be checked in and out of the city, and made to explain any lengthy absences. Trucks and oil tankers were searched and taxed by Al-Qaeda near the fort. Eventually, Lt. Col Saeed S.'s western axis of the Mukalla liberation smashed their way into Mukalla through this route after over 30 hours of threading their way through near impassable goat tracks. As Saeed reached the city, he felt a wave of relief: 'Until we had the city, the worry was like a mountain on my head. But here we were, all my friends were alive, the target was secure, and there were happy people celebrating. It was wonderful.'

13. The creek (or *khawr*) at the centre of modern Mukalla town. The picture was taken at twilight, looking north towards the mountains of the interior. Two blue pedestrian bridges cross the creek, which has promenades on each side. Road bridges cross at the coastal end (behind the cameraman) and at the inland origin of the creek (the Chinese Bridge). In April 2015, Al-Qaeda invaders skirmished towards the Chinese Bridge down both sides of the creek, with rocket-propelled grenade teams hunting police cars along the way. Under the occupation by Al-Qaeda, the Chinese Bridge became a site for public executions, with bodies left hanging from the bridge in the hot sun.

14. When Mukalla Central Prison was overrun by Al-Qaeda on 2 April 2015, one group of released fighters led by a local prisoner called Khalid al-Batarfi headed straight for the governor's mansion. Batarfi became a YouTube sensation due to his antics in Mukalla's palaces, where he posed for pictures, reclining on ornamental furniture with gilded fluffy pillows, goofing around with a telephone, and wiping his feet on the Yemeni flag. A spokesman for Al-Qaeda throughout the occupation of Mukalla, he somehow ended up leading the organisation when American drones wiped out most of his superiors.

15. Tribesmen from As-Shihr seize YNA tanks from local barracks as the military flees in the face of Al-Qaeda's takeover of next-door Mukalla on 4 April 2015. In combat such tanks often only had two men abroad: a driver and one man in the turret, doing all the loading, traversing and aiming. The tribes at the eastern edge of Mukalla City and in the neighbouring oil port of As-Shihr actually put up more resistance than the Yemeni military in April 2015. Army units had often been influenced by the ousted former president Ali Abdullah Saleh to hand over their arms to Al-Qaeda and a number of surrenders were negotiated as Al-Qaeda marched east from Mukalla.

16. Typical Marib battle terrain. The Yemeni counter-offensive advanced across the sandy desert between dark brown or red volcanic mounts, often edged with so-called 'volcanic tongues' created around two million years ago as molten lava flows spread out and solidified. The Houthis found the soft rock veins in the basalt mounds and dug shelters into them. Their tactics involved laying landmines in the soft sand build-ups at the edges of volcanic mounts and in the wadis that gave cover from anti-tank fire. Short-range ambushes caused constant attrition to Yemeni attack forces.

17. The main barrage of the Ancient Marib Dam, perhaps the most famous and oldest archaeological wonder in the Arab world, created around 2,300 years before the birth of the Prophet Muhammad. Six hundred metres long and 13 metres high, it included numerous sluices and channels that distribute water across the Marib Oasis. The final collapse of the Sabean civilization – through their inability to maintain the dam – saw 50,000 tribespeople disperse across the Arabian Peninsula, including to Al Ain, today part of the United Arab Emirates. Marib was, therefore, the birthplace of the Arabs. From the late 1970s at enormous expense, the UAE ruler Sheikh Zayed built a modern dam in Marib, which was completed in December 1986. For UAE soldiers, liberation of both the ancient and the new dams held huge significance.

18. The first and most determined defenders of Marib were the local tribes. In this 19 January 2015 image, a local tribal leader called Sheikh Hamad bin Waheed poses for a press photographer with his bodyguards. At this stage, the Houthis were trying to probe whether Maribis might let them take over, as the Houthis had done in the capital Sanaa in September 2014. The answer was a firm no: many Maribi militias had fought against the Houthis in the six anti-Houthi wars in northern Yemen in 2004–10, and, as important, they rejected any foreign invader who was not invited. As Marib-based soldiers loyal to the former president Ali Abdullah Saleh travelled west to join Saleh and his new Houthi friends, the tribes had relieved them of many of their weapons as the price of passage, including even 23-mm anti-aircraft cannons and anti-tank weapons.

19. Another January 2015 picture of Marib tribal fighters, in this case operating a medium mortar. After decades of internal warfare and oil-funded military spending, huge amounts of heavy weaponry and ammunition could be taken by the tribes following the 2011 Arab Spring. A sprinkling of former soldiers in each militia would be minimally proficient in heavy weapons such as mortars – though not proficient enough to level the baseplate of this weapon and thus achieve a modicum of accuracy. The Yemeni instinct for marksmanship did not seem to extend to indirect fire weapons. Yemenis are also generally not natural 'diggers' and tend to build defences up from ground level, in this case a revetment of improvised sandbags. Anti-Houthi fighters had an almost mystical awe of the way Houthi fighters dug down into the earth to make trenches below ground level, which was viewed as an advanced military skill.

20. The Marib counter-attack force was drawn from a pool of Yemeni National Army recruits who were organised into four battalion-sized units called Saqrs (Falcons). This July 2015 picture shows the recruits, a mixture of older former soldiers and raw recruits in Saudi-provided uniforms. The older fighters were too wise to the ways of war to fight enthusiastically; the younger ones had too little experience to endure the initial shock of battle. The Saqrs melted away during the Marib battle, replaced by local tribal fighters who increasingly made up the attacking forces. Eventually, very few Saudi-provided uniforms were to be seen and tribal dress dominated the Saqrs.

21. In this 14 September 2015 photograph, a blend of Saudi equipment, Emirati *ghurta* (head scarves), and civilian tribal attire is beginning to show. In the background, a UAE advisory team's vehicle can be seen – an Oshkosh Mine-Resistant Ambush-Protected All-Terrain Vehicle (known as M-ATV). The Remote Weapon Station on the vehicle – operated safely from inside via a video screen and joystick – marks this out as a UAE vehicle. The pristine desert sand all around – and the lack of volcanic rock – suggests the image is taken at the Al-Tadaween tactical assembly area to the north-east of Marib city, where late-arriving elements of the Saqrs were organised and fed into the front line.

22. 'Standing-to' at dusk. The photograph is taken in Marib at the start of the war in May 2015, and it shows the kind of mobile outpost that could be deployed by bringing together an all-terrain flatbed truck (a *chassis* in Yemeni parlance) and a heavy machine gun – in this case an American-made M2 – the 12.7-mm 'Ma Deuce'. Such weapons were often used to dominate open ground and warn the enemy against advancing. Unless maintained properly in the gritty terrain, they devolved into single-shot weapons that needed clearing after each round or short burst. Even so, an experienced old gunner like the gentleman in the vehicle could undertake intimidating 'heavy sniping' on enemy positions using these long-barrelled weapons and the fingertip feel he would have developed for the fall of shot over long distances.

23. At a Houthi military parade held in Sanaa on 25 September 2023, about a month before the Houthis started launching ballistic missiles, cruise missiles and drones at Israeli and US targets during the 2023–24 Gaza war, the Houthis displayed two OTR-21 Tochka-U missiles (SS-21 Scarab-B) missiles. On them was stencilled the date 4 September 2015 – the day the Houthis struck the coalition base at Safer with two Tochkas. In the Safer attack, the eventual coalition death toll was 67 (52 UAE, 12 Saudi and 3 Bahraini), with 209 wounded (162 UAE, 31 Saudi and 16 Bahraini). Eight years later, the Houthis were clearly very proud of this result.

COMPARATIVE ACCURACY OF SCUD-B AND TOCHKA MISSILE SYSTEMS

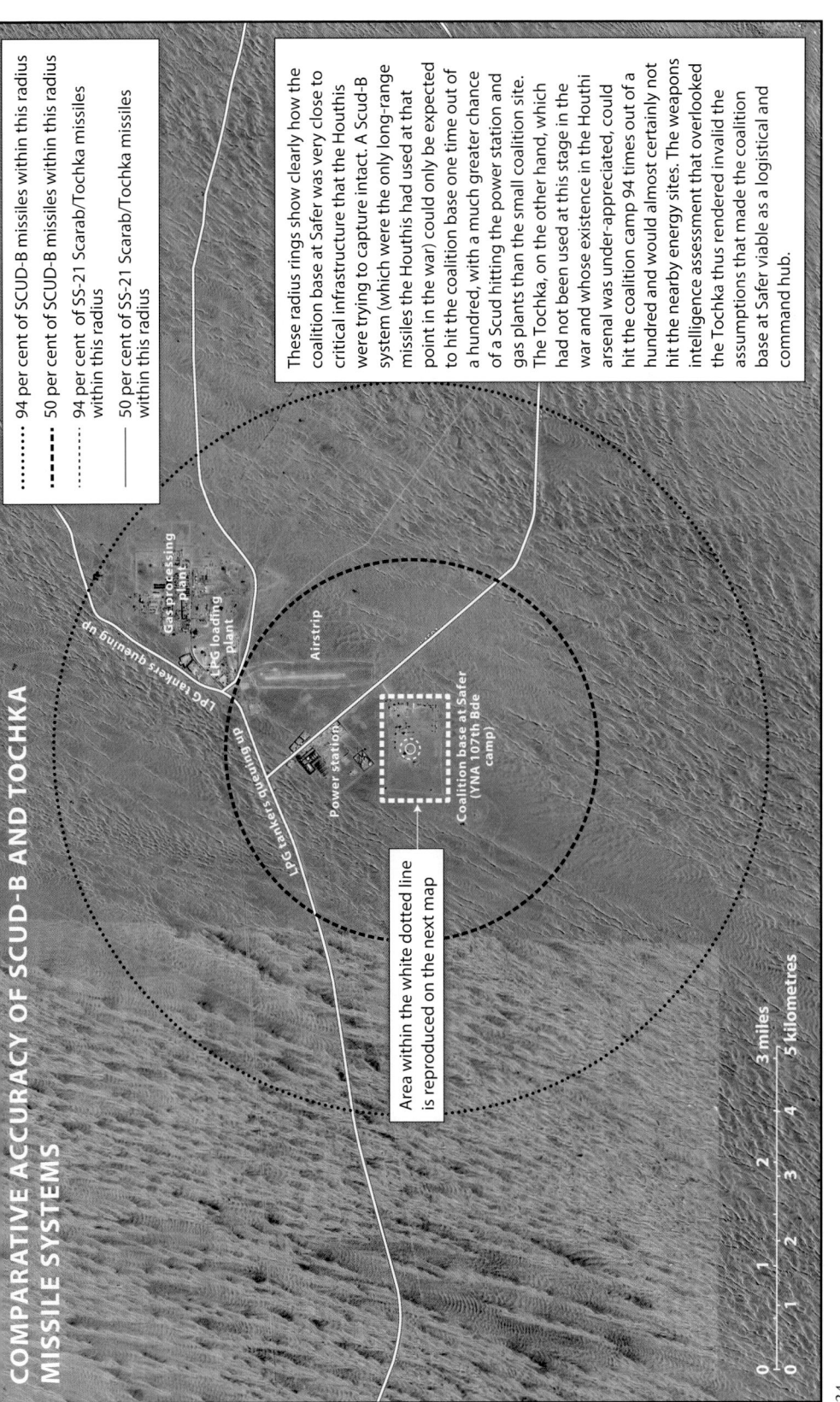

94 per cent of SCUD-B missiles within this radius

50 per cent of SCUD-B missiles within this radius

94 per cent of SS-21 Scarab/Tochka missiles within this radius

50 per cent of SS-21 Scarab/Tochka missiles within this radius

These radius rings show clearly how the coalition base at Safer was very close to critical infrastructure that the Houthis were trying to capture intact. A Scud-B system (which were the only long-range missiles the Houthis had used at that point in the war) could only be expected to hit the coalition base one time out of a hundred, with a much greater chance of a Scud hitting the power station and gas plants than the small coalition site. The Tochka, on the other hand, which had not been used at this stage in the war and whose existence in the Houthi arsenal was under-appreciated, could hit the coalition camp 94 times out of a hundred and would almost certainly not hit the nearby energy sites. The weapons intelligence assessment that overlooked the Tochka thus rendered invalid the assumptions that made the coalition base at Safer viable as a logistical and command hub.

Gas processing plant

LPG loading plant

LPG tankers queuing up

Airstrip

Power station

Coalition base at Safer (YNA 107th Bde camp)

Area within the white dotted line is reproduced on the next map

0   1   2   3 miles

0   1   2   3   4   5 kilometres

IMAGE OF THE COALITION AND YEMENI SIDES OF THE SAFER CAMP COMPLEX

.... 94 per cent of SS-21 Scarab/Tochka missiles within this radius

——— 50 per cent of SS-21 Scarab/Tochka missiles within this radius

Gatehouse

Coalition side of base

Parade ground at the centre of the YNA side of the camp

YNA motor pool

| 0 | 100 | 200 | 300 | 400 | 500 yards |
| 0 | 100 | 200 | 300 | 400 | 500 metres |

POST-STRIKE GOOGLE EARTH IMAGERY OF THE COALITION BASE AT SAFER

- - - - - - The primary blast and fragmentation zones

⊕ The two Tochka detonation points

Medical personnel at the clinic were themselves wounded by the detonations

There were multiple fragmentation fatalities even as far out as the Ops Centre

Musallam's room faced the blast, which raked the western side of the YNA headquarters with shrapnel, even though it was well outside the primary fragmentation zones

Most of the fatalities were suffered in the two UAE personnel tents directly under one blast

Ops Centre (Zayed Control)

Medical clinic

YNA 107th Bde Commander's quarters

Saudi forces accommodation

Bahrain forces accommodation

105-mm ammunition hauler

Concentration of burned vehicles

Mess Hall and kitchens

Animal enclosure (burned)

YNA motor pool

0   20   40   60   80   100 yards
0   20   40   60   80   100 metres

26

27. Materiel recovered from the burned vehicles and personnel tents at Safer. After the 4 September missile strikes, the destroyed materiel was separated from human remains and stored. In late 2015, a detailed accounting process was undertaken to ensure all the destroyed military equipment was accounted for. The heavy charring of these M4 carbines – each the personal weapon of a single soldier – is indicative of the fierce heat generated in vehicle and tent fires.

28. Another UAE-operated Oshkosh M-ATV shown here in the Tadawin tactical assembly area north-east of Marib city in September 2015. A gunner is seen jumping down after adjusting the Remote Weapon Station on the roof, a sweat-towel visible around his head. The UAE had just made successful use of a hundred M-ATVs in the liberation of Aden in late July, and the Marib task force was employing newer variants with the Remote Weapon Station – a life-saver in an environment saturated with Houthi snipers.

he had eyes and ears in the clinic to make sure it did not fail again.

Azzan and Faisal K. had both done multiple tours of Afghanistan and they were once again at the top of their game as tribal relations deepened throughout the summer. The tribes learned that negative attention-seeking was no longer required: Azzan and Faisal were available from six in the morning until three the next morning. They grew impressive beards. Most of all, the Yemenis were suitably impressed when Al-Qaeda put a bounty on Azzan's head, which really boosted his reputation. To the Hadramis, Azzan was like a tribal sheikh, one of the good ones, spending much of his spare time pondering how to fix someone's problem and even mediating disputes and helping to broker marriages.

The plan for Eastern Yemen

Back in Abu Dhabi, the plan for JTF-291 was becoming better defined. The task force was given three lines of effort. The first was Azzan's mobilisation of the eastern tribes, a classic special forces 'train and equip' effort. The second line was the much less promising job of creating an inventory of what remained of Hadi's military in the east to assess whether, in fact, they did still take orders from the president of Yemen. The third line of effort was the direct targeting of AQAP, which was coordinated loosely with the Americans. The CIA and the US Joint Special Operations Command were now fully offshore, having lost their only local base at Al-Anad when Aden had fallen to the Iran-backed Houthis in March 2015. Now the Americans were intrigued to see what the Emiratis could achieve on the ground and what they could learn about the enemy.

The UAE was already learning quite a lot, but these insights had a distinctly Yemeni outlook and definitely did not fit into the neat classifications that Western counter-terrorism agencies preferred. Al-Qaeda's relations with eastern Yemeni tribes were uneven. They had little reach into the deep desert tribes on the Hadramaut border of Saudi Arabia and as yet limited traction with the relatively cosmopolitan coastal communities of Hadramaut and Mahra. The Wadi Hadramaut communities were frequently more open to Al-Qaeda, in part because of their closeness to adjacent religious movements such as Islah and its military offshoots in the 1st Military Regional Command (MRC). Al-Qaeda's strongest ties in the east were to the hill tribes of Shabwa and Hadramaut, including parts of the same Hamoum confederation being courted by the Emiratis.

This was a key insight that the Emiratis would never be able to fully convey to some of the Americans: Al-Qaeda never captured a whole tribe and it never lost a whole tribe. It only ever controlled tiny splinters of each tribe, sub-tribe clan, family and house.

This is why pattern of life 'signature targeting' used sometimes by the Americans resulted in so many civilian deaths: the enemy was threaded intimately – if perhaps temporarily – into Yemeni society. At least until you dropped a bomb on their family and made that tribe an enemy of the United States for the foreseeable future.

Azzan's team could see that AQAP was trying to become more deeply enmeshed in Yemeni society, mainly through marriage, or through youth-based recruitment that began with simple paid-for temporary work without an oath of loyalty. As a Yemeni resistance leader explained: 'Frankly, we are mixed [with Al-Qaeda]. We are one fabric. We are not with their ideology, we want work. You will leave and we'll be here with them. Our youth has nothing to do and they need a salary, any salary.'

Yemenis were so used to bad, corrupt leaders that there was no sense trying to impose Azzan's own moral revulsion of Al-Qaeda onto the Hadramis. In fact, there was little or no anger towards Al-Qaeda in many areas. One tribal leader told an Emirati intelligence officer: 'We treat Al-Qaeda as a tribe. We respect them, they seem to respect us. We need to keep peace with them.' Many tribes felt they had a good rationale for siding temporarily with AQAP, but they would take a better option if it was offered to them and proved to be enduring. Azzan had learned an important lesson: 'There is no point saying to them that Al-Qaeda is bad. That's not self-evident to the tribes. To them, Al-Qaeda are the same as all the others.' It was clear to Azzan that neither hate nor fear would ever motivate the Hadramis to fight Al-Qaeda. In the marketplace of loyalty, Azzan and the UAE had to provide something *better* than Al-Qaeda could. Only a positive vision could forge the Hadramis into a successful fighting force.

Azzan knew that the Hadramis could only be loyal to their *local* cause – that of a more functional, prosperous and semi-independent Hadramaut. In Azzan's experience, the Hadramis disliked the Republic of Yemen *and* the old PDRY; they distrusted northerners *and* southerners. The Hadrami council being formed by Sheikh Saad bin Habraish at the time of his death in 2013 was seeking special, autonomous status for Hadramaut in any future Yemeni state. In addition to being focused on Hadrami interests, the easterners seemed to hark back to a better time when they had a system they could understand, with rules and stability.

Azzan and his trainers had heard on many occasions the older locals speak with pride about the last time Hadramis had an army worth a damn. The old Quaiti sultanate had a uniformed army (called the Mukalla Regular Army, or the Askari) and a constabulary of freed slaves based in Mukalla city, plus tribal irregulars known as 'the shoeless army' who would muster upon need at Al-Lijoun castle, about 100 km north of Mukalla. By the 1950s, the last good decade that Hadramis could remember, the force had evolved into the Hadrami Bedouin Legion (HBL), a force mounted in snappy black Land Rovers with red livery and smart khaki uniforms with red head scarves (*kafiyahs*). Hadramis missed the system that existed until the British departure: one of soldiers with paybooks and pensions, recruited locally for the sole purpose of protecting Hadramaut. Azzan had the concept he needed to build the force: it would be *Hadrami* and its professionalism would make it feel like an *elite force*. 'We will be the new British,' he had enthused. 'We will make a new Hadrami Elite Force.'

Preparing the train and equip effort

By the time Azzan hit upon the right approach in July 2015, the nuts and bolts of setting up a train and equip programme were well advanced. In May, at the outset of JTF-291.1 operations, a site had been chosen for the main training base inside Yemen. It would be called Al-Khalidiyah, named after the tribal leader who owned the land, Sheikh Khalid al-Manahil. It was located around 150 km south-west of Kharkir in the remote foothills that rise up from the dune seas of the Empty Quarter. This site was a quick 'bug-out' (escape) to Saudi Arabia in an emergency and it was much more remote than Wadi Hadramaut, which Al-Qaeda and Saleh loyalists were always watching. By 2 June, an anti-vehicle trench surrounded the first half-kilometre-square version of Al-Khalidiyah camp, which later would expand and change shape constantly. Tribes were given stretches of the perimeter to guard, with their tribe's honour and reputation on the line. As mentioned, Azzan built his airstrip here for direct resupply from Shrurah or even from Abu Dhabi.

The first trainers joined Azzan there on 4 June, building within the month to a ten-man team led by Lieutenant Ali Y., who transferred over from JTF-291.2 in Mahra. The first 250-man intake of future Hadrami Elite Forces arrived as soon as the 30 tents, two generators and a water truck turned up. Each man had been vouched for by his tribe, both as a fighter and someone who could be trusted, via a tribal guarantee that would become known as 'the bond'. These were the first intake out of six groups, who in total numbered 1,500 men drawn from 50 tribes.

Azzan warned the tribesmen that they had to freeze any grievances and blood feuds for the duration of their service. Ali Y. had even more shocking news for the recruits: first, they had to leave their personal weapons and even their curved daggers (*jambiya*) at the gatehouse. If they didn't trust the Emiratis or each other, they could go home. Second, anyone mounting strikes or demonstrations would be sent home, so any wannabe troublemakers were warned to save themselves the time and effort and simply leave straight away. Third, and most radically, the recruits were told that they could chew *qat* on the weekends when they were on leave but never in camp. So, they were advised, anyone needing to chew every day should just go home.

Surprisingly, almost everyone stayed, though some were later expelled for increasingly devious efforts to smuggle *qat* into the base. The rules laid out by Azzan and Ali Y. were the foundation for a mental shift that gradually built in the trainees. At first, they could barely live next to each other due to ancient tribal feuds but Azzan reminded them: 'Mix or you're out.' No one wanted to be sent away, in part due to the shame but also because the 130,000 Yemeni rial (£408) monthly pay cheque, actually paid in Saudi rial, was a fortune – four times an army salary and even more than AQAP was paying in Mukalla. Their families would be angry at them too if they ran away, because tribes who provided fighters were given construction contracts and so-called 'life support payments' for the men's food, cooking gas and vehicle and generator fuel.

The training set-up became more and more elaborate as the summer wore on. Al-Khalidiyah sprouted three satellite camps within eyesight of the main base: Al-Karton (so-named because the men felt like battery hens in the converted chicken farm), Al-Masjeri (an austere camp made up entirely of foxholes, named after an especially lazy trainee who was its first occupant as a punishment), and Khamsa Kilo (where shooting ranges were erected). Two new bases were created closer to Wadi Hadramaut, 25 South and 50 South, named after their distance in kilometres from Al-Khalidiyah. A tightly guarded camp treasury held 60 million Yemeni rials (£215,000).

Backed up by capable Ministry of Defence and Republican Guard instructors who had been gathered together by the Hadi government, the ten-man UAE training team ran the recruits through basic soldiering, including physical exercise, trench-digging and marching. They were formed into platoons, usually homogeneous single-tribe units under a tribal leader. These Hadramaut Elite Forces (HEF) first lieutenants were then put through a platoon leader course that taught the issuance of orders, use of sand tables, and the execution of patrolling, raiding and ambushing tactics. Each platoon also had a trained 'wakil', a warrant officer, reflecting the UAE's own model for units. When the first class of 250 trainees graduated on 5 August after two months of instruction, they were moved forward to the advanced training base at Al-Kahf, which was located at Habraish Mountain, where Azzan had met Sheikh Amr bin Habraish on his first recce, and where Azzan and Faisal K. were now based. As each new 250-man tranche of trainees arrived, they were formed into companies.

The recruits certainly looked pretty, decked out in crisp uniforms, with new weapons, equipment and vehicles. With almost no former military men among them, they had no bad lessons to unlearn and their units had been formed tidily, with exactly the right doctrinal allocations of men, machines and equipment. For Azzan and his team, the perennial question they asked themselves – and were repeatedly asked by others – was: when the moment of decision comes, will the Hadramis fight? In the Aden battle, which ended at the end of July 2015 with the recapture of the city from the Houthi–Saleh forces, the UAE had learned that Yemeni resistance units needed to be supported with heavy firepower and ideally moved forward inside armoured vehicles commanded by Emiratis. This had been the only way to deliver the attack force reliably to their tactical objectives. Understandably, the headquarters staff back in Abu Dhabi could not quite understand what made the Hadramis any different, but Azzan had a good feeling about the men.

The first time Azzan knew for sure that they *would* fight was when a fuel truck at Al-Khalidiyah had caught fire near the storage tank filling point, with the base just seconds away from disaster if the fire had spread to the depot. The UAE had built trenches and walls, and used K-9 bomb-sniffing dogs and biometric security cards, all to keep Al-Qaeda from getting a bomb into the base. But now, as luck would have it, the enemy had played no part as the most flammable and explosive part of the whole site was about to go up in flames. And then, at the moment of peril, a Hadrami driver had got back into the burning truck to drive it away from the fuel tanks, diving out of the moving vehicle just before it blew up on open ground a safe distance away. It was a brave and selfless act.

All peoples have heroes living among them. Why would the Hadramis be any different? The presence of good tactical leaders had become apparent during training and the Hadramis had been surprisingly receptive about discipline and reducing their *qat* use. They *would* fight, Azzan felt in his heart. A better question was: where and when would they first go into action? As the training camps settled down into a rhythm and the first Hadrami Elite Forces graduated, Azzan had expected advanced planning to focus on Mukalla, yet when JTF-291 was first thrown into battle in August 2015, it would not be on Azzan's front but instead in an unexpected fight against a different enemy on a battlefield far from Mukalla.

PART TWO

TEST OF A NATION

V

BUT FIRST, MARIB

Just over two months in, the Gulf coalition's efforts to ensure the survival of the internationally recognised government of Yemen were broadly going well. The results were impressive, especially considering that these states had never mounted a major military operation without US support before. The air campaign's opening moves had removed many of the advanced weapons – aircraft and helicopters, strategic missiles and air defences – that almost no nation in the world would want to fall into the hands of the Houthis, a brutal-minded clone of Lebanese Hezbollah. Saudi Arabia was directly fighting the Houthis on some stretches of the Saudi–Yemen border and supporting local Yemeni forces in other enclaves that backed onto the border.

The UAE had led the effort to check the southwards and easterly advances of the Houthis and their partners in crime, Ali Abdullah Saleh and the remnants of his Republican Guard. From 13 April onwards, UAE special operators from SOC and the Al-Forsan ranger force had been covertly inserted into Aden to bolster the Yemeni resistance fighters in the city. It had been close, but these teams had wrecked Houthi–Saleh tank columns with airstrikes and allowed at least half the city to hold out. The UAE leadership had numerous decision points during the battle where they could either quit or double-down on the mission, but they always chose to persevere.

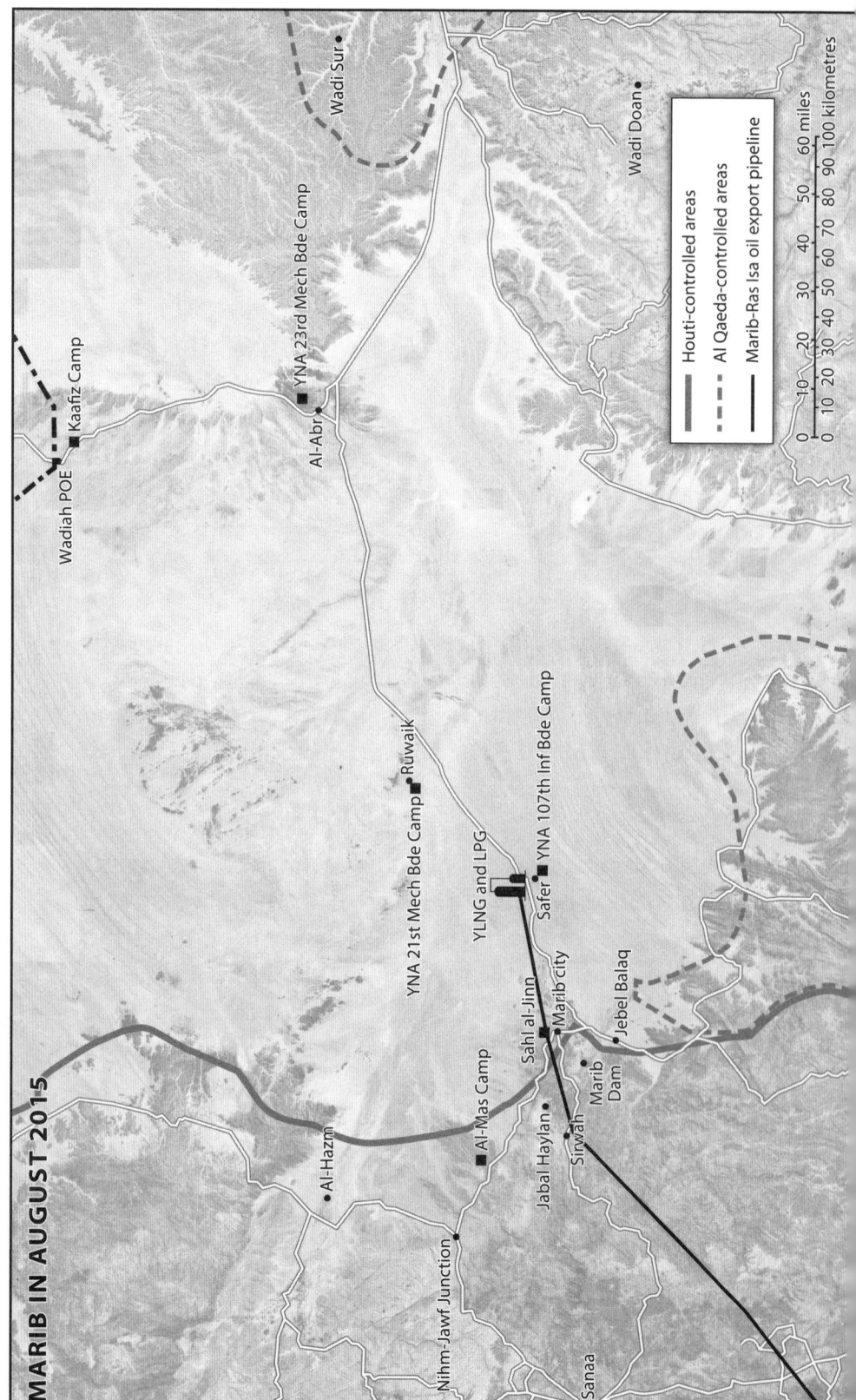

MARIB IN AUGUST 2015

Wadi Sur •

Wadi Doan •

YNA 23rd Mech Bde Camp ■

Kaafiz Camp ■

Al-Abr •

Wadiah POE •

YNA 21st Mech Bde Camp ■ Ruwaik ■

YNA 107th Inf Bde Camp ■

YLNG and LPG

Safer •

Sahl al-Jinn •

Marib City •

Jebel Balaq •

Al-Mas Camp ■

Marib Dam •

Al-Hazm •

Jabal Haylan •

Sirwah •

Nihm-Jawf Junction •

Sanaa ●

Legend

Houti-controlled areas

Al Qaeda-controlled areas

Marib-Ras Isa oil export pipeline

| 0 | 10 | 20 | 30 | 40 | 50 | 60 miles |

| 0 | 10 | 20 | 30 | 40 | 50 | 60 | 70 | 80 | 90 | 100 kilometres |

In June, as JTF-291 prepared for its first combat operations, the UAE task force in Aden (JTF-293) was beginning to wear down the Houthi–Saleh defenders with relentless air, artillery and guided missile strikes, as well as through the efforts of SOC and Al-Forsan snipers. For now, Aden looked like a draw that might turn into a win, but there was no sign yet of a major reversal of the Houthi–Saleh gains. Using captured government arsenals and linking up with defecting army and CSF units, the Houthi–Saleh armoured columns had sloshed like a tidal wave around the Red Sea coast and across much of south-eastern Yemen, including the Bab el-Mandeb Strait, where the Indian Ocean receives the Suez Canal traffic moving in and out of the Red Sea.

In the east, the Houthi–Saleh forces were still advancing on the oil and gas hub of Marib at the start of June 2015. Located 150 km east of Sanaa, Marib looked like low-hanging fruit to the Houthi–Saleh leadership. In early 2015, Marib was by no means a big city, with just about 40,000 residents spread out in a dusty low-rise town of 5 km square – described uncharitably by the *Guardian* newspaper as 'a lump of concrete, rubbish, wire and fumes, set in the middle of pristine sand and mountains'. An oasis town set at the base of a range of small, extinct volcanoes, Marib had definitely seen better days. Under the Sabean kingdom, Marib had been a lush oasis town on the caravan routes of the ancient world, a place where limestone was quarried and aromatic spices, oils and gums were traded. The taxes from these industries had allowed the building and upkeep of one of the wonders of the world, the famous 600-metre-long, 13-metre-high Marib Dam, which had been present in some form as long ago as 1750 BC. The final collapse of the dam around 570 AD saw 50,000 tribespeople disperse across the Arabian Peninsula, including to Al Ain, in today's United Arab Emirates. In the late 1970s, the UAE

Ruler Sheikh Zayed rebuilt a modern dam just upstream from the ancient dam in Marib, at enormous expense, reinvigorating farming there after its completion in December 1986.

Now, in 2015, Marib was growing again as refugees streamed into the city. One reason to care about Marib was its oil and gas resources. Oil production had dipped to 70,000 barrels per day (bpd) by 2015 but potentially there was the capability of exporting a lot more through the 400,000 bpd pipeline that stretched westwards to the Houthi-controlled Red Sea export terminal of Ras Isa. If the Houthis could control this oil they might have a viable state under their control: if not, they would just be in charge of millions of hungry mouths with no income to feed them.

If oil was the reason to care about Marib today, gas was the reason of tomorrow. Also centred on the Safer facility, 50 km east of Marib city, was Yemen's largest foreign investment, a gas project that could generate well over $1 billion a year of liquid natural gas (LNG) exports. This gas, which had to be exported via a special LNG plant in Shabwa, to the south, could be held hostage by the Houthis. Even in the summer of 2015, controlling Marib would give the Houthis ownership of the country's only local source of cooking gas, which was vital to every household in Yemen. From a purely military perspective, the proximity of Marib to Sanaa was a threat to the Houthis and Saleh: on a good day, the capital was a four-hour drive from Marib. It would take longer in an armoured vehicle, but even that meant it was too close for comfort.

Marib resists the Houthis

The Maribi tribes could feel the Houthis probing for weakness, even before the start of the war in March 2015. Ali Abdullah

Saleh had no supporters in Marib, which was instead the main power base of Saleh's rival, Ali Mohsen al-Qadhi al-Ahmar, who had relocated there with hundreds of military officers who fled the Houthi takeover of Sanaa, most importantly the Yemeni military chief of staff, Lieutenant General Mohammed al-Maqdashi. These officers had served under Saleh for decades but were much closer to Ali Mohsen and had abandoned Saleh during the Arab Spring. Saleh's alliance with the Houthis now ensured that these officers would not defect back to the former president: Ali Mohsen's 1st Armoured Division had fought six wars against the Houthis and some had even been part of Yemen's expeditionary force in the Iran–Iraq War, fighting on Saddam Hussein's side. Saleh would not be flipping any forces in Marib.

This did not stop the Houthis themselves from trying to secure defections. At the time, the Houthis were at their most confident, buoyed by years of expansion since 2011. They may have calculated that they had a good chance in Marib, not least because they had just mounted a successful three-year takeover of northern Yemen by expertly wielding sticks and carrots by the tribes, aided by intelligence-gathering techniques learned from Lebanese Hezbollah advisors. The Houthi emissaries visited Marib just before the outset of war in March 2015, calling the locals 'fellow Yemenis' and 'Arab brothers'. They sought a traditional Yemeni tribal assurance of free passage for Houthi–Saleh forces, which entailed a strict promise not to stop in the tribal areas but just to use the roads running through them. But this was not how the Houthis had worked elsewhere; the Maribis knew that everywhere the Houthis had expanded into they had stayed to rule over the tribes.

From the outset, the Maribis largely rejected the Houthis as a foreign organism that had to be resisted. This had not always been their attitude towards the northern Zaydi religious leaders.

In the 1960s civil war, the Maribis had sided *with* the princes of the northern Imamate against the Egyptians and Yemeni Arab socialists. Until the 1960s, the Imamate (which ruled northern Yemen for almost a millennium until 1962) had sent northern soldiers to discipline the Bayda and Marib tribes, tax their farms, and sometimes behead their sheikhs. But at least they had not invited a foreign army into Yemen, as the government did with an Egyptian occupation force. Now, in 2015, it was the Houthis who were inviting in a foreign invader due to their connection to Iran and Lebanese Hezbollah. As Nadwa Dawsari chronicled in a 2018 retrospective, the Maribis still saw the Houthi–Saleh forces as northern invaders and uninvited outsiders. They had recently humiliated the tribes further north in Bayda – blowing up houses and abducting and killing leaders, both of which were serious breaches of tribal law.

But on top of this traditional reaction to outsiders, there was a new sectarian angle. The Marib tribes were mainly Shafei, a school of Islamic jurisprudence based on Sunni practices, whereas the Houthis were aggressively imposing a form of Zaydism (a sect of Islam that deviates from Sunnism by venerating Ali as the legitimate heir to the Prophet) that was doctrinally closest to Fiver Shia Muslims and was shifting ever closer to the Twelver Shiism dominant in Iran, Iraq and Lebanon. Many Marib tribes had sent men to fight the Houthis in the six wars between 2004 and 2010, within the military and in Islahi militias operating in the north.

Tired of waiting for an answer, the Houthi–Saleh camp began launching airstrikes on the Maribi sub-tribes closest to Sanaa in the weeks before Operation Decisive Storm began. Like the terror bombing undertaken by the Yemeni government and its Egyptian allies five decades before, fighter-bomber sorties had lanced out of Sanaa airfields to Marib each day in February 2015. Sukhoi Su-22s screamed overhead and dumped unguided bombs near tribal leaders' houses. Lacking any defence, the tribesmen allowed the Houthis passage via the mountain passes at Nihm and Sirwah but, as expected, the Houthis did not merely pass through – they took over. The choice was now clear to the remaining free tribes of Marib: surrender completely or fight. There was no third way.

Then suddenly there was relief from air attacks. As the war began on 25 March 2015, the Sukhois were largely destroyed and never flew again as the coalition established its air supremacy, meaning that enemy aircraft could not survive in the skies. Now it was a more level playing field. Four of the five main tribes in Marib – the Abida, Murad, Al-Jedaan and the Johim – came together to mobilise. Tribal feuds that had raged for 40 years were (temporarily) put on hold, and the Abida and Murad formed joint units and permitted each other free passage of their lands. Saudi Arabia's intelligence services and Maribi businessmen pulled together funds to buy everything off the shelves of the large arms souks in Marib.

A rough screen of troops was deployed at the western edges of Marib province, guarding the two main roads from Sanaa, via Nihm in the north and Sirwah in the west. At this point, one young tribal fighter explained to journalist Ghaith Abdul-Ahad why he had left the army and joined the rag-tag tribal militia instead.

In the army I couldn't trust my soldiers. The army is divided among the different power centres in Yemen, and this is why when the Houthis came the army split and couldn't stop them. There is a big difference between the tribesman and the soldier. The tribesman will never hand over his weapons: if he surrenders he shames not only himself but his whole tribe and loses his honour. They would prefer to die a hundred times. I know those men around me will never leave – they are my cousins, we are connected by blood and honour.

The Houthi break-in to Marib

But not all the tribes of Marib saw their interests in fighting against the Houthis. The Ashraf were the remaining major tribe, or more accurately a collective of small tribes that acted together, and they had benefited for many decades by sheltering under the wing of the Abida and Al-Jedaan tribes. Secret Houthi entreaties to the Ashraf had been occurring for months. These offers gained a favourable hearing because the Ashraf were not Shafei, but rather Zaydis, like the Houthis themselves. Furthermore, the Ashraf were Hashemites, meaning that they could trace their lineage directly to the Prophet, which was also the defining characteristic of the Houthi leadership cadre. The Ashrafi families had always kept apart from the other tribes due to this strict caste mentality, and they did not marry into non-Hashemi tribes. Their lands spanned farmlands west and south of Marib city, including the Marib oasis, which had once been irrigated by the ancient dam and which now relied on the modern Zayed Dam.

With this single act of treachery, the outpost screen to the west of Marib city was quietly breached in the first weeks of June 2015. Houthi trucks, chasses and trail bikes gradually smuggled in a stream of fighters over a period of weeks, to avoid detection. About 1,000 Houthi troops and pro-Saleh Republican Guard soldiers from the north were assembled in spread-out hide-sites in the Wadi Jufaynah, which lay between the limestone heights of the Jebel al-Balaq al-Qieli and the volcanic Masaria (Hill of the Egyptians). Wadi Jufaynah provided covered access to Marib city and to the Ashrafi farms of the Marib oasis, downstream from the dam. Republican Guard trainers and Houthi ideological officers organised another 400 Ashrafi levies into rough platoons. Houthi Katyusha rocket trucks were concealed within the Ashrafi farms and oriented towards Marib to deliver a surprise opening salvo.

When the attack came on 14 June, the Katyusha barrage came as a complete shock to the defenders. Rockets screamed at a low angle over the city. Panic gripped the refugees in their sprawl of camps, which were splayed out along 2 km of road, about 500 metres to the west of the city hospital. Houthi foot soldiers and Ashrafi levies began moving in groups towards the city, backed up by the odd chassis with a twin-barrelled ZSU-23, which popped off single rounds and short bursts in the rough direction of the city and its military camps. The Houthis were trying to 'roll' the defenders with a show of force and noise, but it did not work. Yes, there was chaos, with Houthis stumbling around the refugee tent city and hospital complex and looking for the Al-Qaeda fighters their Houthi recruiters had told them they were fighting. (Indeed, Houthi foot soldiers were often surprised to learn they were fighting Yemenis or Emiratis, believing the propaganda that they were fighting Al-Qaeda, Americans or even Israelis.) For a while there was no front line to speak of, just troops bumping into enemy forces. But over a period of days, the defence solidified.

The rock on which the attacking wave broke was a cluster of major buildings. One was the governor's office, where Governor Sultan al-Arada's bodyguard – the so-called 'special forces' – held the line. The city hospitals and the Bilqis Hotel became strongpoints, the latter being an elegantly designed semicircular hotel built around a swimming pool made up of three interlocking rings, giving the appearance from overhead of the inner workings of a clock. The 3rd MRC managed to pull together platoon-sized battlegroups of the 14th YNA armoured brigade, with an old T-55 tank here or a BMP-1 there, but these armoured vehicles had almost no main gun ammunition. Elements of the 107th YNA brigade from Safer held a thin outpost line in the sparsely built Al-Jamala neighbourhood, stopping Ashrafi tribes from outflanking the city through the oasis.

But most of the barefooted defenders were tribesmen. Journalist Ghaith Abdal Ahad described them in his first-hand experience as 'high-school kids', the eldest of which was 19 and many much younger, but hardened by the early skirmishes and excited to be 'fighting the Iranians'. Yet the defenders of this half-a-square-kilometre strongpoint served as a breakwater as the Houthis began to bring up more young fighters to attempt human-wave-type assaults delivered at walking pace, reminiscent of the First World War or the Iran–Iraq War. If those waves made it into the city, the Saudi air power overhead would be of no further use. The city would fall, and with it the Safer energy facilities, perhaps collapsing the Yemeni government as well. If the defence was going to hold, it would need help, and quickly.

Taking on the Marib mission

By early June the UAE command centres in the Emirates and Sharurah and Al-Khalidiyah were well connected and holding daily operations video-conferences. For JTF-291, major action still looked to be months away. Ramadan would start on 17 June, and the UAE build-up for the decisive airport liberation in Aden was consuming almost all the attention and resources of the higher command. In Hadramaut, this was a time to conduct training of the Yemeni forces, logistical preparations, and planning for their first major operation in the east.

Opinions differed on where the blow should fall. The JTF-291.3 logistics and planning staff was led by Lieutenant Colonel Faisal T. and his deputy, Lieutenant Colonel Sohail K., and they favoured Mukalla and AQAP as the primary target. Yemeni planners preferred a focus on Ataq, the capital of Shabwa, to secure the southern flank of Marib and block the possible Houthi route into southern Hadramaut. Yemeni's chief of staff Maqdashi wanted all available forces fighting the Houthis, not messing around with Al-Qaeda down in Mukalla. On paper, their plan was sound: push south with the 21st and 23rd YNA Mechanised Brigades from the north; push up from the coast with a surviving naval infantry brigade based at the LNG liquefaction plant at Belhaf; and isolate the provincial capital of Ataq in the middle and seize it. With tribal auxiliaries thrown in, the attack force would number around 5,000 and it would only be occupying ground that the Houth–Saleh forces had not yet entered and where AQAP was apparently not in charge. If the UAE was aiming high with the liberation of Mukalla, the unopposed occupation of Shabwa seemed to be aiming decidedly low.

As the overall leader of the Gulf coalition, the Saudis would have a decisive casting vote on the matter. Yet by 22 June, when the Shabwa concept was being worked up in detail by JTF-291.3, the Saudis suddenly became concerned about Marib, which seemed to be moving up the list of priorities very quickly due to an apparent Houthi–Saleh offensive building in that direction. The JTF-291.3 planning team began to scope how emergency assistance could be provided on the Marib front. From 23 June, Faisal T. and Sohail K. conducted a whirlwind reconnaissance of the potential line of supply and 'forward mounting bases' from which the defence of Marib might be supported. The first stop on this Ramadan tour of eastern Yemen was a new training base established by the Yemeni military at Kaafiz, just 12 km inside

Yemen, south-west of the Al-Wadiah border crossing near Shar-urah. Raw recruits and former soldiers were being put through basic training. Next they visited the army bases at Abr (home of the 23rd YNA Mechanised Brigade) and Ruwaik (21st YNA Mechanised Brigade), where these chronically understrength 1,500-man units were doing little, 'holding' the highway and 'preventing' an impossibly deep Houthi hook behind Marib. The Safer energy facilities and the adjacent 107th YNA Infantry Brigade base were surveyed as a base for ground and air operations. There were clearly no real Yemeni military units in the Houthis' way if they doubled down on their attack, as they seemed to be doing at the start of July.

The Mukalla operation was not going away, Musallam was told, but he might have to 'ride two horses' for a while. By 29 June, it was clear in the UAE headquarters that 'the Marib job' simply had to be done, with the hope that it would take a month or two. On 2 July 2015, King Salman issued a royal decree that established JTF-291 as a force known in the special operations community as a Combined Joint Special Operations Force (CJSOTF) – a multinational and cross-service special operations team. This GCC-CJSOTF (with Saudi, UAE and Bahraini membership) had the mission of 'the liberation of Marib and Al-Jawf' (an adjacent province), thereby effecting a continuous front line all the way up to Saudi-backed forces near the Saudi border, *after which* it then could mount an operation in Mukalla.

The planning of Operation Western Winds

Musallam's task force now got its head down and entered into the twilight world of planning a major operation, which is some of the hardest and most demanding work a headquarters can undertake. With the logistical preparation for the Aden break-out battle reaching fever pitch in early July, sucking up the attention of the Presidential Guard and the Joint Headquarters, the 291 planners could shape the concept of operations without a lot of detailed external input.

The June reconnaissance missions had established the basing infrastructure for the operation, including use of the Safer complex as the main forward operating base, which Musallam personally reconnoitred on 8 July. On the other side of Yemen, the Aden breakout operation on 14 July succeeded magnificently, in part due to the fine efforts of the SOC operators under Musallam's command. Now Musallam and his team started to feel self-imposed pressure building: would their operation succeed like Aden? It was a lot to live up to. In the last ten days of July, the UAE landed a mechanised battlegroup in Aden and undertook a major multi-pronged pursuit operation that pushed the Houthis 150 km north and laid the groundwork for the subsequent liberation of the Bab el-Mandeb Strait.

The first rough-cut lessons of Aden were being absorbed by the 291 planners in real time: they could, and perhaps should, 'go heavy'. At Aden, Leclerc main battle tanks, G-6 motorised howitzers and even Apaches had been used successfully. The Yemeni forces, Aden had taught, needed a lot of bolstering with armoured vehicles and embedded UAE tactical leaders and fire support teams, which were called Operational Mentor and Liaison Teams (OMLTs, pronounced 'omelettes', an Australian and NATO practice from Afghanistan). Aden had shown that the Houthis could be beaten but they could be counted upon to fight very hard, as they had in Aden for the last four months. At the very end of the Aden campaign, the UAE had suffered its first five fatalities of the war, which underlined the deadly seriousness of the fight that was coming in Marib.

Musallam was now leading a team of special operators who were planning what looked increasingly like a brigade-sized mechanised counter-attack on an enemy in difficult terrain. Yet this did not overwhelm Musallam, who enjoyed planning. Nor did Musallam mind 'going heavy': he was cautious and believed in redundancy and over-design: 'if you need a Black Hawk [helicopter],' he'd say, 'bring three. If you bring three, you are sure to have one.' All this would eventually add up to a surprisingly large coalition force package.

When the pursuit operations around Aden ceased on 3 August, JTF-291 was suddenly front and centre of the UAE's war in southern and eastern Yemen. Musallam and the planners were asked to pitch the operation (called Western Winds, or Riyah Al-Gharb) to the UAE chain of command on 5 August. The initial tactical objectives of the operation would be to drive the Houthis back from Marib city to a depth of 25 km on three axes, pushing them out of artillery range of the city and consolidating on tactical objectives that could easily be fortified and taken over by Yemeni forces. The Al-Jawf aspect of the task had been largely removed in planning, as the province was bigger than Marib itself and beyond the immediate scope of the operation. Instead, air power and artillery would provide powerful flank protection across the north-western flank of the coalition counter-offensive along the Marib–Nihm road, which led north to Al-Jawf. The operation would now focus its effort on a set of hills south-west of Marib city, with three brigade-sized Yemeni forces advancing line abreast, each on about 5 km of frontage, with a fourth group in reserve. In theory, it would be a divisional-scale 'deliberate attack', in many ways like something out of the Second World War.

To solidify the Yemeni forces, as had been required in the successful Aden operation, each brigade front would be

MARIB CONCEPT OF OPERATIONS

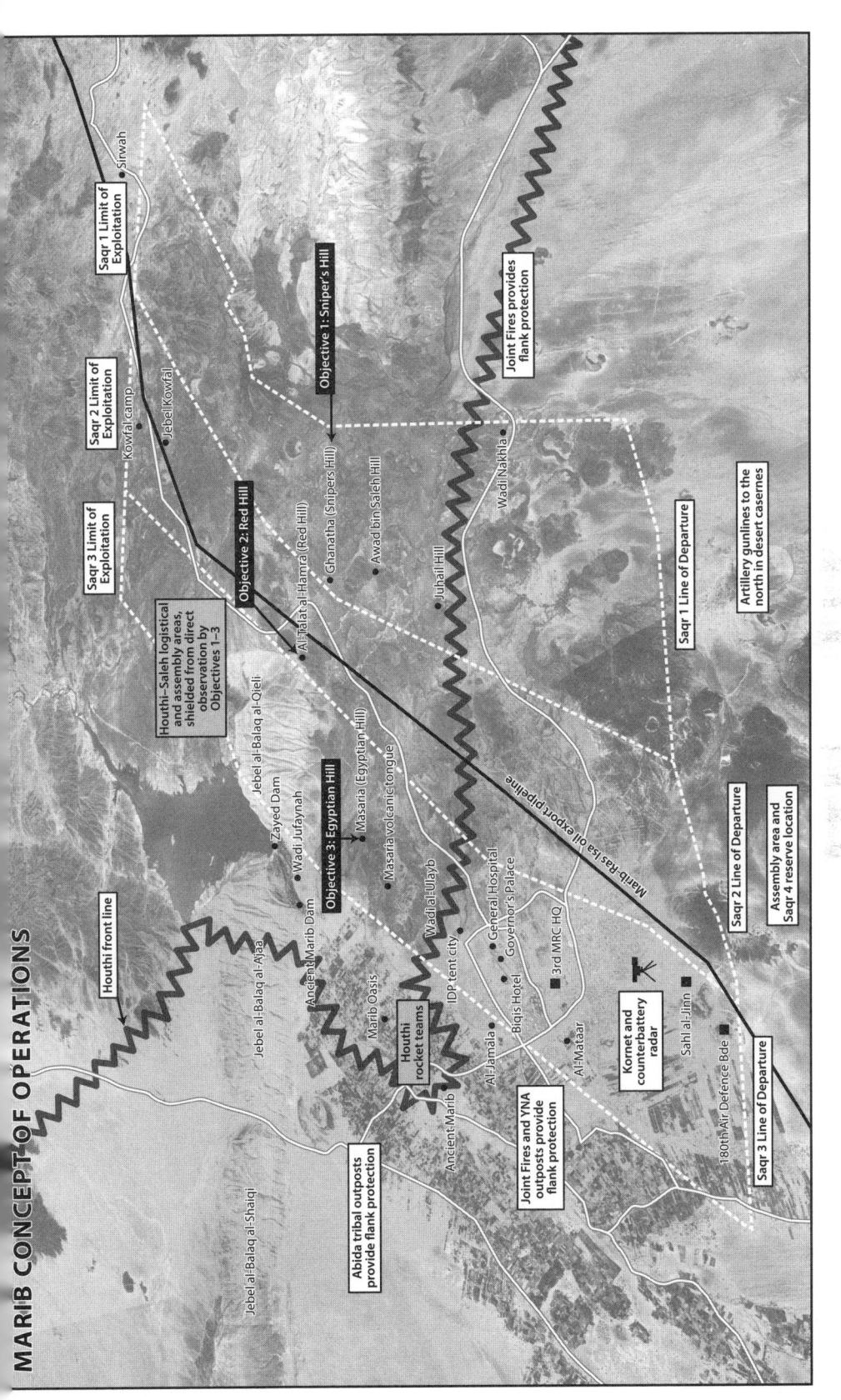

Saqr 1 Limit of Exploitation

Saqr 2 Limit of Exploitation

Saqr 3 Limit of Exploitation

Objective 1: Sniper's Hill

Objective 2: Red Hill

Objective 3: Egyptian Hill

Houthi front line

Houthi-Saleh logistical and assembly areas, shielded from direct observation by Objectives 1–3

Joint Fires provides flank protection

Artillery gunlines to the north in desert casernes

Saqr 1 Line of Departure

Saqr 2 Line of Departure

Saqr 3 Line of Departure

Assembly area and Saqr 4 reserve location

Kornet and counterbattery radar

Abida tribal outposts provide flank protection

Joint Fires and YNA outposts provide flank protection

Houthi rocket teams

Sirwah

Kowfal camp

Jebel Kowfal

Al-Talat al-Hamra (Red Hill)

Ghanatha (Snipers' Hill)

Awad bin Saleh Hill

Wadi Nakhla

Juhall Hill

Masaria (Egyptian Hill)

Masaria volcanic tongue

Jebel al-Balaq al-Qieli

Zayed Dam

Wadi Jufaynah

Ancient Marib Dam

Jebel al-Balaq al-A'jaa

Jebel al-Balaq al-Shaiqi

Marib Oasis

Wadi al-Ulayb

IDP tent city

General Hospital

Governor's Palace

Biqis Hotel

3rd MRC HQ

Al-Jamala

Al-Mataar

Ancient Marib

Sahl al-Jinn

180th Air Defence Bde

Marib-Ras Isa oil export pipeline

accompanied into the fight by a powerful coalition OMLT. The OMLTs and supporting elements would be gathered under the new GCC-CJSOTF. Within this framework, Musallam would make history by being the first foreign officer to be given tactical control of Saudi forces in a war.

Two of the three coalition OMLTs would be provided by a company-sized unit of UAE forces, and one by a reinforced platoon of Saudi Arabian forces. A reinforced platoon of Bahraini special forces would serve as a reserve quick reaction force. In addition, the UAE would provide a mortar company with 12 Agrab 120-mm mortar carriers and a Kornet anti-tank guided missile (ATGM) company with 12 Kornet firing posts that could be tripod- or vehicle-mounted. The Saudis would provide three Milan ATGM posts and three 81-mm mortars for its OMLT.

Going big in Marib

Then it started to get really interesting: both the UAE and Saudi Arabia committed one battery of artillery each, comprising 12 UAE 155-mm G-6 self-propelled howitzers and 12 Saudi 105-mm towed howitzers. The UAE would also station three High Mobility Artillery Rocket Systems (HIMARS), each firing missiles capable of filling an area the size of a football pitch with fragmentation bomblets at ranges of 70 km. In case enemy armour was encountered, as had been the case frequently on all fronts of the anti-Houthi war, Musallam requested a company of ten UAE Leclerc main battle tanks. A forward air base at Safer would host five AH-64 Apache helicopter gunships (three UAE, two Saudi) and three UAE AT-802 light attack and reconnaissance aircraft, plus four utility helicopters. This would enable almost continuous air support to the force, in addition to 'fast air' flying in from air bases in Saudi Arabia or the Horn of

Africa. ('Fast air' is the phase used to describe combat jets that could quickly reach the places they were needed.) To guard this whole force and manage road movements, the UAE would also send a company of infantrymen and military police.

Musallam was clearly 'going big' and this would mean concentrating a large force in the Marib area, something the UAE had only done briefly in Aden at the refinery complex in Little Aden (where they had a platoon-sized force) and later briefly during the landing of the mechanised battlegroup as the coalition began its pursuit of the Houthi–Saleh forces. In recognition of this risk, the 5 August pitch of the concept of operations gave special attention to the issue of the enemy missile and air threat. The Safer forward operating base had been chosen, Musallam briefed, because it was assessed that the Houthis would not risk destroying the very infrastructure they were trying to capture, and their known arsenal of Scud-type missiles was not accurate enough to precisely strike the small 107th YNA camp, at which the forward base was located. (The 107th base was about 4,800 metres away from the gas plant, 3,500 metres from the refinery and 1,500 metres from the power station.) Nevertheless, just to be extra safe, Musallam requested the deployment a Patriot missile defence system that would be capable of intercepting Scud-type missiles.

This was a big ask: Patriot batteries were in short supply and were all committed to protecting the Saudi and UAE homelands. The Houthi–Saleh forces had started firing Scuds into Saudi Arabia in June, launching seven in that month alone. Though no more had been launched yet in July or early August, the coalition was on alert. Saudi aircraft were 'Scud-hunting' across northern Yemen, trying to find enemy launchers on the move. In case Patriots could not be spared by Riyadh or Abu Dhabi, which looked like being the case, Musallam had another way to reduce the risk to the forward mounting base at Safer. He planned for a very rapid and brief concentration of forces near Marib in the days between 21 and 24 August. This would reduce the window of time in which a build-up might be spotted and the base might be targeted. It was an ambitious plan and it would require everything to run smoothly. Overall, 'going heavy' and going soon might reduce the overall risks of the Marib operation and clear the way to hand Marib back to a Saudi lead. The assembled members of the UAE chain of command nodded their ascent and the 5 August meeting was convened. The plan was accepted.

VI

'ZAYED CONTROL IS DOWN'

Just hours after the plan was approved, its first phase was under-way. Musallam sent a SOC team forward into Marib to give him access to local intelligence and to get 'eyes on' the enemy and, as important, on the friendly forces and the terrain. This cell would then 'shape' the enemy forces with strikes that could reduce their effectiveness before the main battle was joined. The night of the 5 August mission briefing, Musallam ordered Sohail K. to go forward with an air and an artillery fire controller, plus a communications specialist and a medic.

His deputy was Major Ahmed H., an air force Mirage 2000 pilot who had qualified as a Joint Terminal Attack Controller (JTAC), which meant he was capable of stacking up air support like an air traffic controller and then directing pilots onto the right targets at the right time. He was a graduate of the first intake of the Presidential Guard's US-accredited JTAC training school – the Joint Fires Initiative – and he got the top score in his class. Ahmed H. had been working in JTF-291.2 in Mahra for the last six months and thought he was going on leave when he was asked to drive up to Al-Khalidiyah. 'No,' he was told. 'You have a new mission, and it starts in two hours.' The next thing he knew, he was loaded into a Black Hawk for Sharurah and then given a hotchpotch of borrowed gear and stuck in a Land Cruiser with Sohail. He was going straight back to Yemen.

Holding the line at Marib

On 7 August, Sohail and his team set out from Sharurah to Al-Wadiah, where they were met by Saudi intelligence agents and two chasses full of Abida tribesmen who drove them all the way to Marib on obscure desert tracks. Dressed in civilian clothing and in an unarmoured Land Cruiser, the team were going into Marib undercover. Stealth would be their best defence. A sole UAE F-16 provided overwatch far above, unheard and out of sight. A risk-taker by nature, Sohail could not have been happier with his mission. They arrived in Marib city in the dead of night at a two-storey family house in the Al-Matar neighbourhood in the east of the city. Sohail's tiny team slipped quietly into the ground floor, so as not to wake the family in the rooms above – local Yemenis who Saudi intelligence had vouched for. The closest Houthis seemed to be about 1,600 metres to the west, which felt near but was in fact almost as far as you could get from the enemy in this close fight for the western edges of Marib city. The team slept in shifts, guarding against betrayal or overrun. Then, in the late morning of 8 August, they got down to business.

The tools of the trade were set out, as they had been in safe houses in Afghanistan, Libya, and Aden beforehand. A tablet loaded with Google Maps and the Offline Map app, iPhones and old Nokias were laid out with their charger leads trailing back to the walls. A Harris radio was placed close at hand. It was time to learn the enemy's locations and his habits – the 'pattern of life', in military parlance. First the local tribes explained where friendly forces were located, and asked some of their outposts to send their coordinates or 'dropped' pins from iPhones. This made a rough 'forward line of own troops' (FLOT). There seemed to be many fewer YNA units than they expected and certainly nowhere near the number of armoured vehicles that they had been told the 3rd MRC was operating. Sohail was appalled.

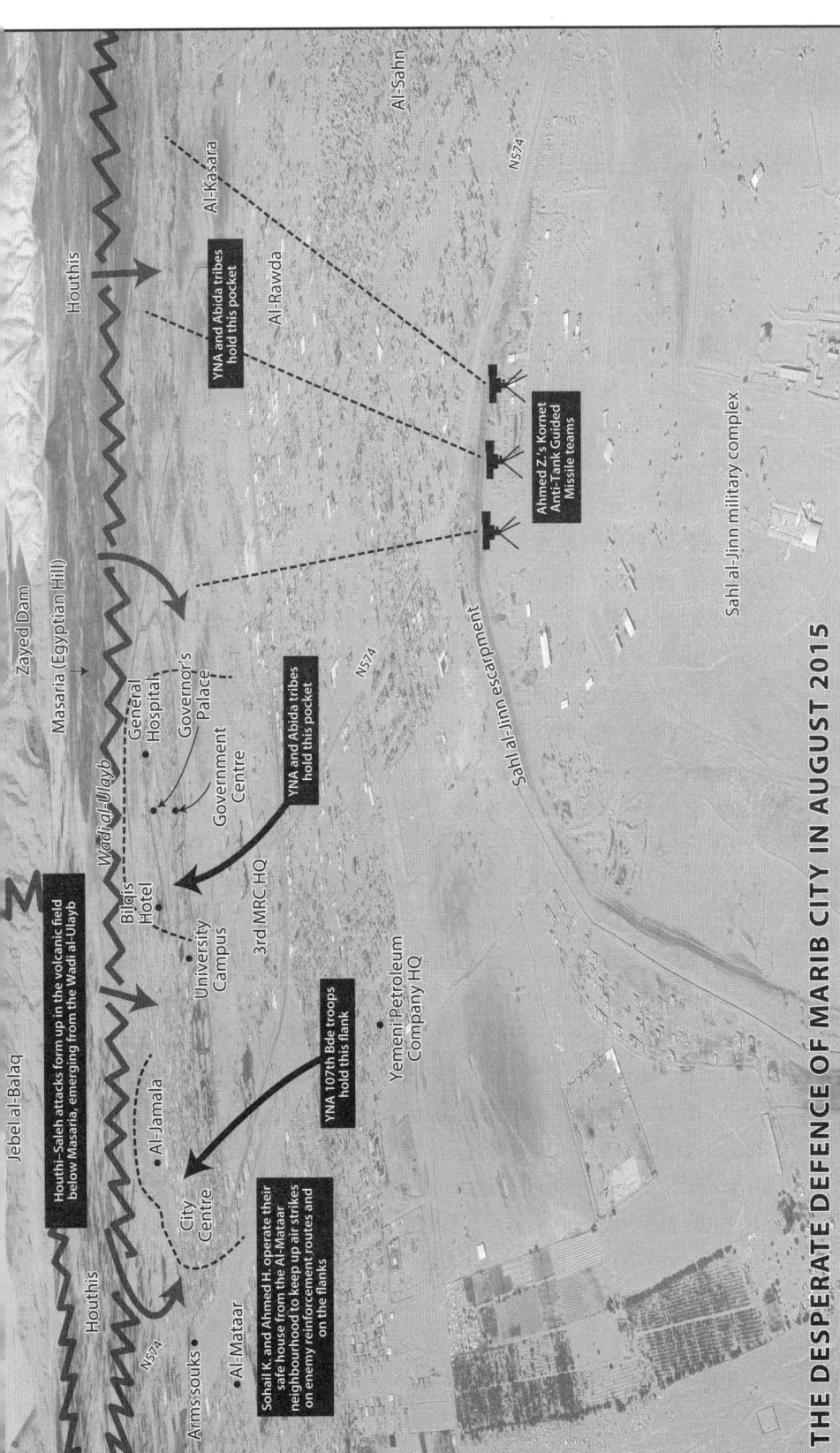

THE DESPERATE DEFENCE OF MARIB CITY IN AUGUST 2015

Jebel al-Balaq

Zayed Dam

Masaria (Egyptian Hill)

Houthis

Al-Sahn

Houthis

Al-Kasara

Al-Rawda

YNA and Abida tribes hold this pocket

Ahmed Z.'s Kornet Anti-Tank Guided Missile teams

N574

Sahl al-Jinn escarpment

Sahl al-Jinn military complex

Houthi–Saleh attacks form up in the volcanic field below Masaria, emerging from the Wadi al-Ulayb

Wadi al-Ulayb

General Hospital

Governor's Palace

Government Centre

YNA and Abida tribes hold this pocket

N574

Bilqis Hotel

University Campus

3rd MRC HQ

Houthis

Al-Jamala

City Centre

Yemeni Petroleum Company HQ

YNA 107th Bde troops hold this flank

N574

Arms souks

Al-Mataar

Sohail K. and Ahmed H. operate their safe house from the Al-Mataar neighbourhood to keep up air strikes on enemy reinforcement routes and on the flanks

There were practically no friendly forces between the Houthis and the city centre. Firepower was going to have to hold the line if the Houthis pushed again, and that meant targets – lots of them.

Now it was time to find the enemy. One thing that puzzled Ahmed was why the United States was not providing any target intelligence. When the US military wanted to, it had an unmatched capability to subject a defined area of the earth's surface to overhead surveillance and signals intelligence, and then produce extraordinarily detailed mapping of potential targets. Although US military briefings said the Houthis were well dug in, they were less forthcoming with grids and details. It was clear that the Americans were under political restrictions. It had not been this way at the start, just four months earlier. Then, President Barack Obama had committed US support, including targeting information, with the White House announcing:

> In support of GCC actions to defend against Houthi violence, President Obama has authorised the provision of logistical and intelligence support to GCC-led military operations. While US forces are not taking direct military action in Yemen in support of this effort, we are establishing a Joint Planning Cell with Saudi Arabia to coordinate US military and intelligence support.

But now, in August, US Congress no longer approved of the Yemen intervention, and US intelligence support had largely been withdrawn.

Sohail and Ahmed H. knew they would have to handle this problem on their own. There were enemy locations already known to the UAE, such as captured YNA camps at Sirwah, Nihm and Al-Mas. Clustering around screens, the Yemenis quickly filled in the blanks regarding the enemy front line. Enemy strongpoints and heavy weapon positions were marked, as were the kind of places where Houthi–Saleh artillery pieces and tanks were seen most often. The roads used by the Houthis to resupply the forward positions were confirmed by local sources, as were some farms where the Houthis gathered newly arrived troops for orientation and advanced training. Every little dot that was added to the Offline Map library – a new potential target – would need to be checked with aerial surveillance but at least now the UAE had an idea of where to look.

As the two officers looked at the Offline Map app, they found it amazing how close the Houthis had got. They were within machine-gun range of the city centre and wrapping around its southern edge, being fed reinforcements through the Ashrafi farms. The enemy held all the high ground west of the city, including the Zayed Dam. That had to change if Marib was to hold.

As mid-August approached, Ahmed H. and his assistant, a joint fires officer trained to direct artillery fires, worked mainly at night, when the Houthi–Saleh forces were most active. At about 18:00 hours, as the sun set, the safe house would start to get busy. All through the night, various intelligence, surveillance and reconnaissance (ISR) assets would pass through the airspace above: Al-Hur drones that could loiter for hours, plus a variety of aircraft using high-acuity infrared pods to identity the heat of engines, weapons and men. More and more Houthi artillery sites were detected, with a mixture of chasse-mounted Katyushas and towed 152-mm howitzers. Beaten-up T-series Russian-made tanks and BMP-1s could be seen scurrying from cover to cover, burying themselves in ruined buildings that they had intentionally 'rubbled' to provide cover and concealment.

Yemeni human intelligence started to trickle in regarding the location of Houthi tactical commanders and inbound vehicles full of reinforcements. As frustrating as it was, these could rarely be validated with other sources and fell short of the requirements of 'positive identification'. Instead, Ahmed H. – using his old call sign 'Caspar' – focused the air power overhead on frontline enemy positions from which fire was originating towards the Yemeni lines – a clear sign of hostile intent. It did not take the Houthis long to realise that something had changed. Now accurate fire was coming down if you fired at the city more than once from the same site, even from covered positions. Before the UAE team arrived, fighter pilots were looking through their targeting pods, which gave a very narrow viewpoint, as if looking through a 'soda straw', to use the US military phrase. Using this approach, finding enemy shooters was a matter of luck in the few minutes before the pilots' fuel ran too low to stick around. Now the strike aircraft were oriented straight onto the right places at the right times. The results were devastating for the Houthi–Saleh units facing Marib city.

Assembling the attack force at Marib

Aside from destructive 'shaping' operations, the other side of the opening phase was the preparation and forward deployment of the Yemeni attack force. The force could be raised by gathering and strengthening existing YNA units or building new brigades from raw recruits, or a combination of the two. It was clear to UAE planners as far back as late April that the existing YNA units were in a pitiable state in the east. The JTF-291.3 chief logistician Faisal T. had begun a database of the Yemeni military units in the east, to encode their assessed loyalty, strength and needs. His job was to ensure that their commanders made the right choices – which meant not siding with the Houthi–Saleh invaders or AQAP, and ideally playing an active part in the fight against these adversaries.

The 1st and 2nd Military Regional Commands had been pretty ramshackle organisations before the Arab Spring and the new civil war, but they were complete wrecks now. The 16,878 men of 2nd MRC were simply gone, demobilised or co-opted by AQAP. The 1st and 3rd MRCs had around 50,000 men on their books but only about 7,000 still in the field on a given day due to chronic absenteeism that had been the norm for decades in a military that was largely a way of employing tribesmen. Of this measly force, only two understrength 500-man battalions of the 23rd YNA Mechanised Brigade were to be released from their bases by the Yemeni military for the Marib battle. They would be mixed in with the 2,000 remaining YNA and Presidential Guard forces spread across the front line. But Faisal knew that army forces were expected by locals to man checkpoints and to guard Marib's open desert flank. That meant that no real reinforcement for combat operations would come from existing military units.

As was the case in Aden, where the YNA played almost no role in the liberation, newly formed units with UAE training, equipment and accompaniment would instead be the core of the attack force. Using the Hadrami Elite Forces being built by Azzan's team at Al-Khalidiyah was not an option: they would fight in Hadramaut only and they were not ready for prime time yet.

That left only two other pools of potential fighters: untrained army recruits who were gathered just south of the Saudi border at Kaafiz, or a new round of recruitment among the Maribi tribes. Kaafiz had been built by the Saudis as a training base for Adenese resistance fighters, but events had overtaken that plan and now it was occupied by around 2,000 Yemeni army recruits, including a mixture of young and older men, Salafis and non-Salafis, some from Marib but most of them displaced persons from Al-Jawf and Shabwa. They were formed by the SOC deputy commander Mohammed S. and Faisal T. into four small battalions, known as Saqr (Arabic for 'falcon'), with Saqrs 1–3 being identical line battalions with four infantry companies, each of three platoons. Each of Saqr 1–3 also had a weapons company with a mortar platoon (four 81-mm mortars), an anti-tank platoon (three 106-mm recoilless rifles mounted on chasses), and a heavy machine-gun platoon (three 14.5-mm machine guns, known as Dushkas). Each battalion had two companies mounted in UAE Oshkosh Mine-Resistant Ambush-Protected (MRAP) vehicles and three unarmoured companies mounted in Saudi-provided Land Cruisers or UAE-provided chasses. The fourth Saqr evolved into a larger reserve force of around 1,000 men, organised broadly similarly to the three line battalions but without heavy weapons, intended to feed men into the front-line Saqrs or reinforce as a unit, as needed.

The Saqr 'brigade' as a whole had a nominal Yemeni commander, Brigadier General Abu Hamza, and also Yemeni colonels to formally lead each Saqr. In practice, the accompanying UAE and Saudi officers would be the driving force behind each battalion, taking tactical control of each Saqr. To bulk up the force and to give it a more local character, referred to by the Emiratis as having 'skin in the game', Musallam reached out to the Maribi tribes for recruits. Around 1,000 Maribis eventually came north to Kaafiz. Discounting around 500 desertions, this eventually gave the Saqrs a combined starting manpower of around 3,500 men when they paraded each payday. How much lower the number would be on battle days was anyone's guess.

Now came the next phase, force assembly near Marib, which proved to be extraordinarily difficult. Musallam's plan relied on rapid movements to reduce the warning that Houthi–Saleh forces would receive of an impending offensive. On 13 August, the JTF-291.3 logistics team arrived at Safer, employing as low a profile as they could, focusing on making the airstrip ready and installing modern firefighting equipment. Coalition units were beginning to stack up in Sharurah but not quickly enough: the pairing-up of UAE and Saudi teams with the Saqr looked likely to fall behind schedule due to the late arrival of combat forces at Sharurah and their inability to get bureaucratic clearance to cross the border into Yemen.

Things were getting tense by 20 August, when Musallam took his command team forward to Safer, bringing the number of UAE troops at the base up to 180. Driving down from Sharurah to the Kaafiz camp and then Safer, he could see, with his planner's brain, that the timeline was slipping. Musallam could still get his supporting elements forward – such as artillery and attack heli-copters – where they could begin the advanced 'shaping' of the enemy while the main attack force linked up with the OMLTs at Kaafiz and then came forward. But this would be a major change to his plan and, particularly, to his efforts to maximise surprise and minimise the exposure of the concentrated attack force at Safer.

Worse yet, the Patriot missile defence system he had requested had not been approved. A stretched-out deployment and no air defence could mean trouble, though the logic still held that the Houthis would not risk hitting the valuable Safer plant with their inaccurate Scud missiles. While the Patriot issue was further debated, the UAE would fly in a Pantsir S-1 air defence missile system, to give the Safer area some protection from the more likely threats of a close-in attack by Katyushas and longer-ranged rocket artillery. Yemeni forces secured a perimeter 5 km out from Safer, to guard against close-range rocket launches and enemy commando attacks.

Friction and delay

By 24 August, the number of UAE troops in Marib had grown to 500. The new additions included a cargo unloaded under conditions of great secrecy on 21 August. Under cover of darkness, UAE transport aircraft unloaded a boxy wheeled container and what looked like two small helicopters. These were UAE-produced Al-Sabr S-100 drones and their control station. The type was so secret that even Musallam did not know about them, and received his first guidance on their capabilities from MBZ, who was a strong advocate of the Sabr and had closely studied its battlefield use in Aden. The Sabr is a rotary-wing drone: it essentially looks like a small, unmanned helicopter, three metres long and shaped like a sturdy fish. In Aden, this drone had been a game-changer, operating close to the front line, from ships and safe houses. A very quiet design that could stealthily watch targets in the dark, the Sabr could stay on-station for four to six hours. Now the strike cell could get close to the enemy at night, even operating below rooftop level or facing caves in the mountainsides.

Also newly arrived was the protection force for Safer and the planned forward artillery firebase closer to the city. Various artillery revetments had been prepared in the desert to the north and east of the city. Some of these were adjacent to the Sahan al-Jinn Republican Guard headquarters complex, which abutted the north-east corner of Marib city and which was elevated enough, and close enough to the front line, to serve as an artillery firebase that could range deep behind the front-line Houthi positions. In the recent battle in Aden, the UAE had benefited enormously from quietly inserting one, and eventually four, G-6 howitzers into the defensive pocket. The forward deployment of G-6s and HIMARS had also initially been the goal in Al-Khalidiyah, both for force protection and to enable so-called 'artillery raids', with the mobile artillery pieces unpredictably moving around in order to 'range' known AQAP targets.

Now this kind of advanced firebase would become a reality and on a hitherto unprecedented scale. In addition to 60 SUVs of Abida tribesmen holding a cordon around these gun lines, on 19 August the UAE next forward-deployed its Kornet ATGM company under the Presidential Guard's Kornet battalion commander, Lieutenant Colonel Ahmed Z. Just a week before, Ahmed had been in the Emirates, unaware that he would soon be at war. Then suddenly he was deployed to Sharurah and now the front line at Marib. His task was meant to be defensive, but the Kornet is such a versatile weapon that he quickly found ways to use the long reach of his missile launchers to hit the Houthis even when they were not attacking. At least four, and sometimes eight, of his 12 Kornet posts were at Sahan al-Jinn. The base's western edge was a 20-metre-high limestone escarpment that towered over the city and its forts provided an ideal line of covered firing points from which Kornet could range all the way out to the Houthi forward positions, 4,000 metres away. A new kind of direct fire was now contributing to the defensive perimeter around the city. The Houthis called it 'silent assassin' because it was so quiet and its back-blast so minimal.

On 27 August, three days later than the initial plan had called for the attack to start, the build-up was still incomplete. The air forces had no problem getting forward due to the prepared airstrip at Safer. Apache helicopter gunships and AT-802 aircraft began to operate from the facility. Also landed on 27 August was one of the UAE's mammoth leased Ilyushin transport aircraft, which brought in a Cobra counter-battery radar system that could track incoming artillery shells and rockets back to their point of origin. Due to Faisal T.'s heroic administrative efforts with the Al-Wadiah border bureaucracy, the huge build-up of coalition vehicles was starting to ease as they began to cross over to Kaafiz and Safer. By 27 August, there were 740 coalition personnel in Marib, including 580 UAE troops, 100 Saudi artillerymen and 60 Bahraini special forces. On 29 August, the UAE G-6 howitzers arrived and were moved forward to the firebases to commence bombardment of the Houthi lines. As August ended, there were 254 coalition vehicles at Safer alone, and well over 800 personnel. On 1 September, the Saqrs were still marrying up with their coalition OMLTs in Kaafiz, a 750-km approach march away, and the likely attack date had slipped to 7 September at the earliest.

Battle preparations

Even with this delay, there was a lot to do in Marib. On the sage advice of MGM, Musallam was methodically rechecking the task force's assumptions and preparations: were the base defence and casualty evacuation plans adequate? Had a reserve force been preserved in case of setbacks? How were the junior leaders performing? What was Musallam's plan when he reached his objectives? Recognising that the task force did not know the foothills terrain well enough, Musallam was planning to take the Yemeni, UAE and Saudi commanders on a forward reconnaissance of each of their attack 'lanes' during the two or three days of battle preparation before D-Day on 7 September. Musallam and his staff were frantically busy. Safer base was a beehive of activity, with 369 vehicles now in Marib and over 1,000 coalition troops on site. On completing their inspection, visiting members of the chain of command asked Musallam what else he needed. Only one thing, he replied: a Patriot battery to complete the layers of protection around the force.

By 1 September, the Houthi–Saleh forces had no illusions that their enemy was coming, and in strength. Apaches were flying over Marib and that meant they had to be forward-based. The Houthis were right: the Apaches were positioned just a 20-minute flight time away from the front line. Though they took indirect routes through the desert from Safer to their 'attack by fire' positions, typically about 4,000 metres east of their targets, it was fairly clear to the Houthis and their spies where they were coming from. Operating exclusively at night, the Apaches soon obliterated a Houthi outflanking effort down the Marib–Nihm highway and began hunting on the Houthi lines of communication just behind the battlefield, where civilian traffic was almost non-existent since the battle had begun. Enemy prisoners later related that the Apache became known among the Houthis as al-Jinia (the witch) or Djinn al-Aswad (the black demon). The Houthi–Saleh forces needed to drive these tormentors away.

The artillery firebases to the north of the city and at Sahan al-Jinn were also to become a huge thorn in the side of the Houthi–Saleh forces. Installed on the high ground of Sahan al-Jinn, the Cobra counter-battery system quickly began to show which Ashraf tribal leaders were allowing the Houthis to use their farms as launch points, giving Musallam valuable evidence to push back on their complaints of unfair treatment when the G-6s sent back pinpoint retaliatory fire. Using the app Offline Map, and the counter-battery radar, the artillery firebase at Sahan al-Jinn controlled by Ahmed H.'s joint fires officer began to bring down rapid fire on enemy positions and movements. Using laser-guided 155-mm munitions, the UAE began to 'plink' individual armoured vehicles precisely, even when they were on the move, with coalition aircraft providing pinpoint laser designation.

By the end of August, a new joint fires room at Safer was ready to complement Sohail's team at the safe house, allowing them some rest after three weeks of nocturnal targeting every night between 18:00 and 05:00 hours. This cell incorporated inputs from other UAE intelligence agencies, such as the Directorate of Military Intelligence and the Presidential Guard's intelligence section, enabling deep strikes such as the HIMARS attack on an Iranian advisor working with Houthi rocket cells in the Ashrafi farms on 31 August. On 2 September, the Emirati targeting cells mounted their first joint 'fire strike', a near-simultaneous engagement of 36 targets using G-6, aircraft and HIMARS. Another 30 targets were hit the following night in another fire strike.

On that evening of 3 September, things finally seemed to be coming together for the coalition forces. Musallam was putting in place the last piece of the puzzle: confirming his good relations with the Marib leadership and their truces with each other before they went into battle together. The chieftains of the tribes slaughtered 50 camels and sheep for a huge feast attended by the acting Yemeni Minister of Defence and chief of staff Maqdashi, the Marib governor Sultan al-Arada, and all the leaders of the Abida, Murad, Al-Jedaan and Johim tribes. Musallam told the Maribi leaders: 'Today we set aside all internal issues. We need to tackle the problem of the Houthis. Will you fight?' 'Yes,' they roared. 'All the way to Sanaa?' 'Yes,' they roared again. Unbeknown to anyone there, a teenager had videoed parts of the feast on his iPhone and naively posted clips of it on YouTube. As 3 September ended, the enemy was fully awake to the threat they now faced.

The fateful blow

In history, to borrow a maxim from the world of intelligence, there are two types of problems: puzzles and mysteries. A puzzle can be solved because all or most of the pieces exist and might be found and clicked into place to form a picture. A mystery may never be solved because the pieces simply do not exist any more. What happened next at Safer is partly a mystery because so many of the participants are now dead, but also because it happened so quickly and because some of those who were there want to forget. Probably no one knows for certain why the Houthi–Saleh forces chose the early hours of 4 September to mount their deadliest ever attack on the coalition forces. Some believe it was the leaked YouTube footage that nudged the enemy into doing what they did next. Quite possibly it was an action that had been planned for some time, perhaps triggered by the increase in fire support in the Marib area in late August or the apparent imminence of a major attack from the Safer assembly area.

What can be said for certain is that the Houthi–Saleh forces were *not* deterred by the proximity of nearby energy sites from launching a missile attack on the Safer forward operating base, which came just before dawn on Friday 4 September. Perhaps this was because the brace of missiles fired were not the inaccurate Scud medium-range ballistic missiles that the Houthi–Saleh forces were known to possess and which they had fired at Saudi Arabia on 6 June. Instead, the enemy used two, much more accurate OTR-21 Tochka-U missiles (codenamed SS-21 Scarab-B by NATO).

This capability had been overlooked in coalition intelligence processes, in part because of over-optimistic coalition assessments of the damage that the air campaign had done to the missile stocks held by Houthi–Saleh forces at the start of the war. The Tochkas were admittedly a reclusive part of the Yemeni arsenal and not as well known as the Scuds. In 1988, somewhere between four and 12 Transporter Erector Launchers (TELs) for the Tochka-U had been purchased from Soviet Russia, along with 115 missiles. Some of these had been used by Saleh in the 1994 civil war and many undoubtedly fell out of service in the two decades since then. Others were probably destroyed in the recent coalition air campaign, but it was unclear how many launchers and missiles remained. Though the Houthi–Saleh alliance had fired Scuds, no Tochkas had been fired before 4 September 2015 (and in fact only another four have been launched in the entire war until the time of writing in 2023). Nevertheless, overlooking the possible use of this accurate weapon was an undoubted intelligence failure that undercut the logic on which the Safer basing decision had been built. In every modern war, tactical headquarters have been struck by accurate missiles: the United States suffered such a strike on its forward brigade headquarters outside Baghdad in April 2003, and Turks, Syrians, Armenians, Russians and Ukrainians have suffered their own disasters in the conflicts since then. All wars and all militaries experience intelligence failures and it is simply a regrettable fact of life that they sometimes occur, despite the best efforts of all those involved.

The Tochka was designed in the 1970s and upgraded in the 1980s to allow Soviet and Warsaw Pact forces to accurately strike NATO tactical headquarters, assembly areas and other 'point targets' of a similar size to the Safer forward operating base. For a Scud-B of the vintage owned by Yemen, hitting the half-kilometre-wide Safer base would have been a 1-in-100 shot, and the energy infrastructure all around the plant would have been more likely to be struck than the base itself. In contrast, the Tochka was extraordinarily accurate. What was a 1-in-100 shot for a Scud-B was a 93-in-100 shot for a Tochka-U, and any 'misses' might still land a useful distance from the intended target. With the Tochka, the Houthi–Saleh leadership could quite comfortably aim at the forward operating base in the secure knowledge that they would almost certainly *not* hit the energy sites a few kilometres away. The first wartime use of these rare and special weapons was clearly of strategic significance and came as a complete surprise to the coalition.

With detailed knowledge of the events that followed, and taking into account the capabilities of this fearsome weapon and how it was used in other conflicts from Yemen to Ukraine, the sequence of events can be portrayed realistically. Two of the precious TELs, carrying Tochka-U missiles, were brought out of caves in which the Houthi–Saleh military had kept them hidden for months, probably in the home areas of Ali Abdullah Saleh's Sanhan clan south of the capital. Somewhere to the west of Marib – probably on the Sanaa–Sirwah highway, around 100 km from Safer – the six-wheeled lizard-like TELs made about an hour's drive. They then stopped and geolocated themselves using GLONASS, the Russian GPS system. The operators quickly fed the coordinates of the launch and impact points into the missile's sophisticated inertial guidance system.

During this stop, the Transporter Erector Launchers would have looked just like any other truck from a distance. They had been designed by the Soviets to be difficult to differentiate, their cargo area opening up and raising their missiles to a horizontal position only in the last 15 seconds before launch. This was a key survival attribute because the coalition air forces had been Scud-hunting every night since the 6 June missile attack on Saudi Arabia, with ISR aircraft on the lookout for TELs on the move or setting up to launch. Whereas the Scuds had to undertake laborious wind and surveying calculations and prepare the liquid-fuel missile engines for flight, the Tochka was built to set up, shoot and scoot within 15 minutes.

When launched at 05:45 hours on the morning of 4 September, the two missiles would have created a bright white burst of light – the 'heat bloom' – as the heavy missiles powered into the air. The TELs would immediately have scattered, knowing that multiple coalition aircraft would have seen the launch and the bright engine-burn of missiles streaking into the sky and arcing towards Marib. Flight time at that range was a mere 55 seconds. Designed to shoot down aircraft, cruise missiles, tactical rockets and drones, the UAE's Pantsir air defence system in Marib stood no chance. The short-range detection radar of the Pantsir detected the missiles just 16 seconds before impact. Coming in at three times the speed of the defensive interceptor missiles, and with 20 times the mass of the Pantsir's SA-22 missiles, the Tochkas would have smashed straight through any interceptor that might have been launched in time.

In the last quarter of a second before impact, the radio sensors in the Tochka nose cones rotated the missiles to produce what warhead designers call 'an angle of meeting' of 90 degrees to the ground, ensuring that the explosive effect would be shaped straight downwards onto the camp. In the last tenth of a second, both warheads detonated 20 metres above the ground. One missile exploded about 110 metres west of the centre point of the Safer camp, and the other 130 metres south-west, broadly mirroring the distances between the two launchers as the missiles took off.

Ground zero at Safer

Subsequent analysis of the debris showed that the Tochkas had both been fitted with 9H123F high-explosive fragmentation warheads. Each was built around cylinders of 162 kilogrammes of high explosive, encased in a metal skin designed to break into 14,500 fragmentation splinters, which raked the Safer base at speeds of 1,500 metres a second – in other words, almost instantaneously. A supply truck that had straggled into Safer late the night before exploded, adding its cargo of 105-mm shells to the blasts.

One moment the base was calm, with many of its 1,100 occupants asleep or breakfasting, and the next it was a disaster zone. The vehicle park in the centre of the camp was full of smoke and small fires, with heavy fragmentation damage to the windscreens and outside fittings and tyres of the Caiman, Oshkosh and Nimr (Tiger in Arabic) MRAPs, as well as to the lighter-armoured Hummers and Mann supply trucks. HESCO barriers – the huge sand-filled wire and canvas bags that made up the walls of the camp – were spilling sand, torn open in places by the tremendous force of the explosions.

The largest personnel tent had been directly hit, and it had partially collapsed and was torn to pieces and burning in places. Many of the UAE soldiers there and in the adjacent Bahraini and Saudi tents were lying still in their sleeping bags, some killed in their sleep and many more unconscious or too stunned and deafened to move. Survivors with total hearing loss were limping around trying to understand what had happened, and personnel from the unaffected parts of the camp were streaming into the blast zone from all directions to help. In these first moments of total chaos, no one could even guess how many coalition soldiers and Yemenis had been killed and injured.

At the outer edge of the fragmentation zone, the front of the command headquarters had been sprayed with shrapnel. This was the dusty headquarters of the 107th YNA Infantry Brigade, a labyrinth of wood-panelled officers' rooms with ornate gold-painted furniture that had seen better days. Musallam's trusty senior non-commissioned officer Warrant Officer Salem S. – known universally as 'the wakil' – had been woken by his window frame being blown inwards by the enormous over-pressure of the blasts. He was partly deafened and, after a few seconds to gather his wits, he looked outside: people were running in all directions, and flames and smoke were spewing from the accommodation areas. The commander was always the wakil's first priority. He knocked loudly on the door of the adjacent room, where Musallam had been sleeping since 03:00 hours, up until which point he had been finalising the battle plan with Mohammed S. and Sohail K.

Now Musallam woke to a burning feeling in his shoulder and the sounds of explosions, which (he pieced together later) were the drumbeat of secondary explosions as burning ammunition 'cooked off'. At the time he ran through the options and actions needed. Were they under attack? Had the order to 'stand to' been given? He felt woozy and dimly heard a knocking on the door. He had to get up and put on his uniform, but as he tried to push a leg into his trousers, blood sprayed from his shoulder across the room. The wakil was suddenly there and used his ghutra (or head scarf) as a tourniquet to stem the bleeding from Musallam's left shoulder. The wound was close to a main artery. The wakil left staff officers in charge and ran down the stairs to get help from the base clinic.

As the trusty wakil left the headquarters building and moved towards the clinic, he began to appreciate the full calamity of what had happened. A veteran of Afghanistan and other missions, he had still never seen anything like this. At the operations centre, 'Zayed Control', multiple wounded were lying on the ground, moaning and rolling back and forth. At least three men there were obviously dead. On his way to the medical tent he helped along a soldier who was limping to the clinic with his helmet clamped to his belly, holding in his intestines. At the clinic itself, the scene was hellish: masses of injured and burned troops were collecting there and the doctors themselves were wounded, albeit still calmly sorting patients into categories. By the rules of triage, there were those who could not be saved and could only be made comfortable; those whose wounds were not imminently life-threatening and could be set aside for later; and those who needed priority stabilisation right now. After the war, the camp doctor was never able to speak to anyone about what he had seen that morning.

Casualties were taken to the airstrip, from which the Apaches and light aircraft had immediately made emergency departures in line with their standing orders. They scattered like birds back to their dispersal locations to the north. Musallam was bundled onto a UAE UH-60 Black Hawk helicopter with the wakil, whose job it was to keep him alive until Musallam got to Sharurah. As the chopper banked over Safer camp, the wakil could see the full panorama of the destruction and also the gaggle of Yemenis in their cars fleeing the power station and gas plant. For 75 minutes the Black Hawk flew low over the desert. The wakil couldn't feel a pulse on Musallam or make proper breathing checks because of the vibration and noise inside the chopper, and the harsh blast of air rushing in from the slipstream outside. But he kept up pressure on the wound. When they arrived, Musallam was as pale as a ghost, but he wasn't dead: he would remember looking out over his ancestral homeland, the beautiful yellow sand dunes of the Empty Quarter in the morning sunlight, and thinking back on his life. At 07:20 hours, Musallam's helicopter touched down at Sharurah.

Back at Safer, command had transferred to the Bahraini component commander, Lieutenant Colonel (Prince) Khalid bin Hamed al-Khalifa, who had bravely stood up and taken command under the worst of circumstances. The word went out to the front-line safe house that Sohail K. would now have to hold the line. No fire support could be organised by the new joint fires cell at Safer: Sohail was back in the hot seat. The secure radio message began with the stunning headline: 'Zayed Control is down'.

VII

A TEST OF CHARACTER

When Musallam had been stabilised and given painkillers, he was told that he was lucky to be alive. The shrapnel had drilled a neat hole in his window, his shoulder and the bed beneath. Just to the left and it would have hit his head; to the right, his heart. But the news was devastating nonetheless: he would have to be medevacked to a real hospital outside the war zone. The Egyptian doctor at the Sharurah clinic had his hands full with the lightly wounded, with helicopters and aircraft coming and going all day to take the more serious cases to hospitals in the Gulf and Europe. Bodies were also arriving at Sharurah, including 45 Emiratis and a number of Saudis, Bahrainis and Yemenis.

Back in the UAE, the growing bad news prompted the Presidential Guard commander MGM to securely message Mohammed bin Zayed and ask the obvious question: should the attack, and in fact the whole UAE operation in Yemen, continue? MGM was pretty sure he knew the answer but needed confirmation. 'Yes,' MBZ immediately replied, giving MGM the signal to keep going. Before Musallam flew out to the UAE, and thereafter to a hospital in Germany, he also spoke to MBZ. Musallam was relieved to hear that the attack would continue as soon as possible. 'How badly are you wounded?' MBZ had asked. 'I can still move my hand,' Musallam said. 'I can be back in three or four days.' And then: 'Please Sir, if I go, bring me back.' MBZ softly reassured Musallam: 'I promise you, you are coming back. You'll drink coffee in Sanaa.' Musallam felt relief: maybe he would return to finish the job. Still weak from blood loss and under local anaesthetic, Musallam was escorted to his plane by the Saudi command team at Sharurah, who were still stunned at the losses suffered at Marib.

'What do you Emiratis intend to do? Will you withdraw?' one asked.

'No,' Musallam managed through the pain. 'That would lose us the war. Our orders are to continue.'

As the crisis unfolded on 4 September, this trial of fire brought out the best in many of the officers present. At Safer, acting commander Prince Khalid bin Hamed was dispersing the forces to open desert areas and evacuating the wounded and the dead. At Sharurah, Faisal T. was handling the logistics of the medical evacuation and the resupply of the Marib force. On the front line, Sohail K. and Ahmed H. were told by their higher headquarters: 'Carry on, don't stop. You'll get all the support you need – just keep them back.' The fear was that the missile strikes had been the opening move of a broader offensive, one of the usual Houthi–Saleh dawn attacks that broke when the rising sun shone directly into the defenders' eyes.

The Riyadh Combined Air Operations Centre surged fast air to map grids – known as 'Kill Boxes' – covering the Nihm and Sirwah roads, to smash enemy reinforcements coming up to the front and to search for TELs. Strike aircraft were stacked up by Ahmed H. over the front line, where he directed strike after strike through the day and the night after. Ten of the 12 G-6 guns were in action most of the day, harassing the known enemy positions. As night fell, they laid down a rolling barrage of parachute illumination rounds to deter any night attacks. Ahmed Z.'s Kornet teams moved all their reserves of missile tubes forward, just in case they became the last line of defence at Marib city.

At the same time back in Abu Dhabi, the military leadership gathered, supported in this dark moment by members and friends of the royal families of the Emirates, by government officials, and by captains of industry. The 4 September meeting was a 'whole-of-government' show of support that reflected the spirit of the nation at the moment when it was most sorely tested. MBZ made the UAE's next steps very clear: they would recover and keep up the offensive in Marib. He directed that the artillery group should be fully replenished within three days and be made ready to support the offensive. The Yemeni Saqr forces should be moved to the front immediately, with no further delay. Strategic infrastructure in Abu Dhabi would be stripped of their missile defence and a Patriot battery sent forward to Safer the following day to counter the newly demonstrated level of threat. The plan was to get the attack back on track by 9 September, just six days after the devastating missile attack.

A show of strength

It is hard for outsiders to appreciate the unprecedented blow that the UAE experienced in Safer and how its effects rippled across UAE society. The citizenry of the UAE is a much smaller and more tightly knit community than larger nations like the United States or the United Kingdom. The deaths of 52 Emiratis – the final death toll at Safer – out of a population of 1.4 million may not seem high by the standard of the annals of warfare, but this proportion of the population is equivalent to 2,392 deaths in the 67 million-strong UK, or a staggering 11,821 deaths out of the 331 million population of the United States (i.e. twice the deaths suffered by the United States in all its military operations in Iraq). Perhaps more important though, the UAE had simply never before suffered a death toll of that size in any single civil or military disaster in its recorded history. The UAE occasionally suffers from flooding, tropical storms and landslides, and even the effects of distant earthquakes in Iran, but it had never suffered a day in which anything close to 52 Emiratis were killed (and 162 wounded) in a single event. The Safer strike was thus the first time the UAE had ever experienced a mass casualty event.

The way that the 'home front' responded to the Safer incident was a crucial inflection point: there could have been a cry for withdrawal or a questioning of why the UAE was risking its sons in Yemen. Eighteen fatalities had prompted the United States to withdraw from its Somali intervention in 1993, the basis for the 2001 film *Black Hawk Down*. Instead the UAE as a nation defiantly rallied around the operation. By the morning of 5 September, the air force and the Joint Aviation Command had done the nation proud by getting most of the martyrs home in record time, in the midst of a crisis. The arrival of 33 caskets at Bateen airbase in Abu Dhabi allowed the commencement of funerals in the cases of proven fatalities. MBZ would eventually visit every family affected in an extraordinary effort to pay condolences to them all. On 6 September, MBZ started this itinerary by visiting six funerals spread across Abu Dhabi and Al Ain, all of them G-6 artillerymen killed at Safer. Presidential Guard commander MGM undertook two extraordinary days of visits on 7 and 8 September, requiring a Super Puma helicopter to shuttle him to gatherings of mourners in all seven Emirates. The 19 bodies too damaged to be recognised initially were also brought home on 12 September, triggering a new round of leadership visits to the families.

These were hard days, where Emirati military leaders visited the homes of the families who had lost fathers, husbands, sons and brothers. They looked directly into the eyes of the bereaved. Yet the main emotions shown in these meetings was defiance towards the enemy. The brother of one martyr sought a visiting general's permission to be transferred from his police role into the military, so he could take his brother's place. A father who lost a son pointed to the other sons, who were ready to join the fight. Though sadness was never far from the surface, they also showed pride at the sacrifice their loved ones had made for the nation. The brother of a martyr called Ali Hussein al-Balooshi told a reporter: 'He died a martyr. I can't express how much pride that instils. To our country's leaders I say, come summer or winter, heat or cold, you command and we will abide.' This was more than anyone could have expected of the families and their example created a national moment of bonding and cohesion. This support could be felt all the way out to the front line, relayed through text messages from the families and friends, and television clips sent from home. And the order was clear: get back on the attack.

Regenerating the attack force

The man sent from Abu Dhabi to stand in for Musallam as the force commander – and to get the attack back on track – was Brigadier General Ali Saif. When Musallam was wounded, MGM had no hesitation in selecting Ali Saif to lead the Marib counter-attack. At the time, Ali Saif was serving as MGM's chief of staff at the Presidential Guard, having accrued enormous experience during one of the longest special operations careers of any Emirati officer. He had been in the first intake of SOC trainees when the unit had formed after the liberation of Kuwait in 1991. If one visits the small military museum at the UAE Officers' Club in Abu Dhabi, a young Ali Saif can be seen in one picture jumping out of a helicopter during one of SOC's early multinational deployments, to Kukes in Albania in 1999. He did two tours in Afghanistan: the first in 2003–4 made him deputy commander of a SOC task force in Zabul and Kandahar, and on the second he led a task force in Helmand in 2008–9. During the year of Arab Spring instability he had led SOC's response capabilities, overseeing operations in six countries, including Libya. MGM then polished this diamond with a stint at war college in the United States, followed by a stint as MGM's chief of staff. But above all, MGM knew that Ali Saif was good in a fight, and a fight was exactly what the UAE had on its hands in Marib.

Ali Saif's multiple phones had begun to buzz about the same time as dawn broke in Abu Dhabi on 4 September, and by lunchtime he was told: 'You are going to Yemen to take command – right now.' As he flew out of Bateen airbase he travelled on an aircraft that had been shuttling back and forth non-stop, bringing the martyrs and the wounded back home. He landed at Sharurah at sunset and saw the helicopters still ferrying the wounded out of the country and the aircraft flying them to hospitals in Saudi Arabia and the UAE.

Early on 5 September Ali Saif landed in Safer and got his first look at the wrecked base and at the men there. Most of the forces had dispersed, so the base was much emptier than he had expected. He was also appalled by the level of destruction. Usually a man of few words, Ali Saif had a vivid recollection of his first hours in Safer. 'It was a horrible scene,' he recalled. There was still smoke everywhere and everything was at least a little singed, if not blackened. The tents were ripped and chairs were burned down to their frames. Little scraps of fabric were blowing around. Many vehicles had been burned down to the metal rims of their tyres and were still too hot to touch. A corral of camels and sheep given to the force by the Maribis had caught fire and all the animals had burned to death. The smell was appalling. The HESCO walling and the tents were splashed with blood and human body parts were still being found during the clean-up.

After just a couple of hours in Safer, Ali Saif drove covertly up to Kaafiz to take the measure of the Saqrs and their coalition OMLTs. Until the Yemenis could earn his trust, he was playing by 'Helmand rules' – that meant no forewarning of his arrival, off-road travel in civilian clothes, and well-armed bodyguards with their fingers on the triggers. He sat with the Saqr leaders and the coalition team leaders for a couple of hours and then, as suddenly as he had appeared, he was gone again.

On his first video-conference with higher command that night (5 September), Ali Saif relayed that morale was sur-prisingly good, all things considered. The force had taken a hammering: the final figures showed 67 dead (52 UAE, 12 Saudi and 3 Bahraini) and 209 wounded (162 UAE, 31 Saudi and 16 Bahraini). That meant that one in four men at Safer had been either killed or wounded in the missile attack. The G-6 and HIMARS gunners had been hit especially hard in the main tent and were in deep shock, so he had taken the unusual decision to give them two days' leave back in the UAE to see their families. His instinct – a big gamble – was that they would come back stronger after this show of compassion.

He wanted to get back on the attack as quickly as possible, and had prepared a wish list of replacement personnel and equipment. Top of the list were G-6 and HIMARS gunners, followed by tank and Oshkosh drivers. In terms of materiel, he needed 20 Oshkoshes to replace those knocked out of action, plus rehabilitation packages for damaged MRAPs: that meant tyres, radios and the weapons and external fittings to replace those that had been torn up by the fragmentation damage. On 6–7 September, the replacement equipment was sent forward

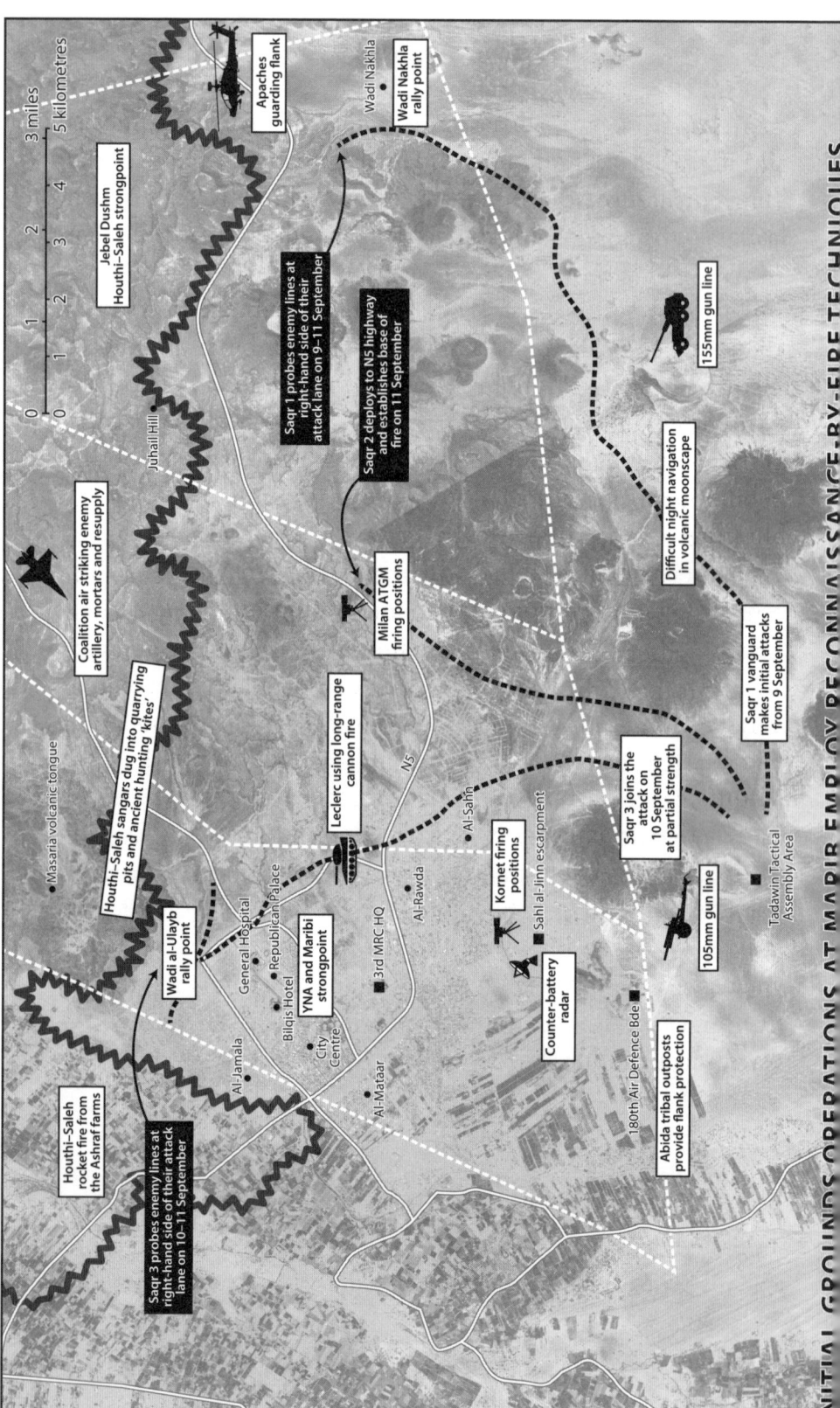

INITIAL GROUND OPERATIONS AT MARIB EMPLOY RECONNAISSANCE-BY-FIRE TECHNIQUES

Apaches guarding flank

Jebel Dushm
Houthi–Saleh strongpoint

Wadi Nakhla

Wadi Nakhla rally point

3 miles

5 kilometres

Saqr 1 probes enemy lines at right-hand side of their attack lane on 9–11 September

Saqr 2 deploys to N5 highway and establishes base of fire on 11 September

155mm gun line

Juhail Hill

Coalition air striking enemy artillery, mortars and resupply

Difficult night navigation in volcanic moonscape

Milan ATGM firing positions

Masana volcanic tongue

Houthi–Saleh sangars dug into quarrying pits and ancient hunting 'kites'

Leclerc using long-range cannon fire

N5

Saqr 1 vanguard makes initial attacks from 9 September

Wadi al-Ulayb rally point

General Hospital

Republican Palace

Bilqis Hotel

City Centre

Al-Jamala

YNA and Maribi strongpoint

3rd MRC HQ

Al-Rawda

Al-Sahn

Saqr 3 joins the attack on 10 September at partial strength

Kornet firing positions

Sahl al-Jinn escarpment

Tadawin Tactical Assembly Area

Houthi–Saleh rocket fire from the Ashraf farms

Al-Mataar

Counter-battery radar

105mm gun line

Saqr 3 probes enemy lines at right-hand side of their attack lane on 10–11 September

180th Air Defence Bde

Abida tribal outposts provide flank protection

expeditiously from Sharurah, with no bureaucracy at Al-Wadiah. These personnel were brought back up to strength via a shuttling of transport aircraft. As Ali Saif had hoped, the artillerists did come back, telling tales to all who would listen of the surge of national determination to fight and to win. He had trusted them and they had repaid his faith in them.

On the evening of 8 September, Ali Saif gathered together Marib dignitaries, the Yemeni Saqr commanders and the coalition staff. He could feel a kind of cold determination steeling the hearts of the leaders. Mohammed S., who would lead Saqr 1, had run into an old friend at Safer days earlier, their first meeting since they had been classmates at military academy. That friend had died instantly as shrapnel struck him in the neck while he slept at Safer. Ahmed Z. had lost six men from his Kornet company alone and he had personally worked to find their burned bodies in the wreckage. In the chaotic hours after the strike, the mother of Joint Fires Controller Ahmed H. had been misinformed by someone in the UAE that he had been killed. It had broken his heart to sense her fear when he phoned her to show he was alive.

The Maribis and Yemeni Saqr commanders looked at their coalition partners differently now: despite their affluence, these Gulf Arabs were not soft at all, they had guts to keep going after such a blow. The dinner was held in the open desert at a site unknown to the Yemenis beforehand and no one was YouTubing this event. As they ate together, none of the Yemenis would have imagined that the recapture of Marib would begin the very next day.

Reconnaissance by fire

Commanders can be outstanding in totally different ways, and there was no doubt that Musallam and Ali Saif were very different men. Musallam was a meticulous detail-oriented planner. None of the forces or materiel or abundant fire support available to Ali Saif would have been in place without Musallam's keen eye for detail and his strong support of the operation. At the same time, Ali Saif was perfectly suited to this moment: an improviser with an instinctive connection to the soldier and his morale, who was quite happy to 'get stuck in' to the enemy in a hasty attack.

That phrase – 'hasty attack' – sounds pejorative to a civilian, but to a military professional it is a term of art. Sometimes there are good reasons for haste and this was one of those times. Both Ali Saif and Musallam's staff were of the same mind on this issue. By coming at the enemy hard and fast, way sooner than might be expected after the Safer strike, Ali Saif intended to shock the Houthi–Saleh forces. He would demonstrate that the losses at Safer had been no impediment to the counter-attack and that they had been immediately replaced. Faisal T. had the same instinct. 'After Safer, we had to show the Houthis that we were not done. We needed to come back at them harder than they could imagine.' The JTF-291 team were on the same page.

Ali Saif's concept was to quickly start probing the Houthi–Saleh forces with short-range advances, using whatever forces were available, building to a broad front as the Saqrs came online, one by one. Coalition artillery and air power would undertake a prepared strike on known targets. Then the Saqr forces would probe until they reached a 'control point', where they would stop, before recovering to a protected tactical assembly area, in effect taking two steps forward and one step back every day. But seizing terrain was not the main purpose of the exercise at this point: the aim was to expose new enemy positions to coalition firepower. This was known as reconnaissance by fire.

To understand the battle of Marib in 2015, you must be able to visualise the panorama as the combatants saw it. Each of the

Saqrs had a 'lane' about 4 km wide that was their axis of advance, extending about 20 km into the distance, on a north-east to south-west bearing. This simple control measure was intended to prevent them from straying into each other's frontages, though this proved difficult in practice because of the confusing volcanic terrain and the profusion of hills that looked similar and had similar names. At this stage, the geographic tactical objectives of the coalition forces were not the priority, so they will mainly be discussed later in this chapter; suffice to say they were a crescent of hills that did not look remarkably different from the others, but upon careful examination of the terrain could not be overlooked from other nearby hills from the enemy direction. The chain of hills thus formed the western edge of the foothills adjacent to Marib city, and a sensible limit of advance on which to consolidate.

Gaining control of the range of hills would also provide observation into the wadis and valleys to the south-west that the Houthis used to reinforce and supply the Marib front, and which were presently masked by this chain of hills. If any one of the objectives could be taken, artillery observers, Leclerc main battle tanks and Kornet teams could place the roads and tracks under direct and observed indirect fire around the clock. Then it would be that much harder for the enemy to hold on to the other parts of the chain. Experience in fighting the Houthi–Saleh forces in Aden suggested that when they sensed that their escape routes were being choked off they often withdrew. This would then achieve Musallam's basic operational objective: to push the Houthi–Saleh forces out of artillery and rocket range of Marib city and seize the highway passes to Marib (and indeed to Sanaa, thinking offensively) at Nihm and Sirwah.

The first axis to get into action on the evening of 9 September would be Mohammed S.'s Saqr 1. This force was ready sooner than the others and it was commanded by an officer whom Ali Saif had fought alongside in the past. This made Ali Saif, a newly arrived commander, especially comfortable with using Saqr 1 as a test case for his concept of reconnaissance by fire. Not all the unit had assembled yet, but they decided to go with what they had, which was around 450 Yemenis supported by Mohammed S.'s OMLT. Numbers were not the key to this kind of operation. After the Safer strike, guidance from higher command stressed the need to stay dispersed and avoid unnecessary exposure of UAE forces that might generate more casualties for no benefit. As a result, Mohammed S.'s OMLT would only bring eight UAE soldiers close to the forward edge of battle in one Oshkosh and one RG-31 Nyala MRAP, with three 120-mm Agrab mortar carriers positioned further back. Agrab means 'scorpion' in Arabic, and these mortars would be the sting in Mohammed S.'s tail.

Mohammed S.'s combat group started out from the main dispersal site for the attack force, which would become known as Tadawin Camp, a stretch of empty desert 8 km north of Sahan al-Jinn. They worked at night, driving with night vision devices, and the 19-km approach march took a torturous three hours. Even with GPS and Maribi guides, the column had to creep forward painstakingly, threading between a dozen small volcanic mounts that ranged from 50 to 200 metres in height.

Mohammed S. approached the N5 highway that cut perpendicularly across the Saqr's axis of advance. Initially the enemy did not seem to be taking the bait, but then sporadic 23-mm cannon fire started to arc towards the vehicles, probably firing towards their engine noise. The Agrabs began to send heavy 120-mm mortar rounds down-range and three Kornet teams began to precisely strike enemy sangars (low fighting positions made out of piled-up rocks) and chasses from their overwatch position to the rear. Overall it was a good night's work and a successful proof of concept: the Kornets had destroyed four newly exposed enemy emplacements and the Agrabs had used up 68 rounds in the precise bracketing of enemy strongpoints.

As Saqr 1 began to withdraw in the pre-dawn period, things got a little hairier. Mohammed S.'s RG-31 would not restart after stalling and enemy fire began to concentrate on the vehicle. With the rising dawn at their back, the enemy rained down mortar shells, B-10 recoilless rifle rounds and Duskha fire on the stranded MRAP. As the rest of the force pulled back 300 metres to their new Wadi Nakhla rallying point, the vehicle was hastily abandoned. When the enemy fire slackened, as it did most mornings after the enemy burned through their on-hand ammunition, two SOC troopers ran forward, got the stubborn MRAP started and drove it home into the wadi.

Next up was Saqr 3 on the other (left-hand) end of the line, led by Ahmed Z. and the capable Yemeni Saqr commander Abu Karim, a brave schoolteacher from Taizz whom the men trusted. Again, most of the Saqr was still in Kaafiz, but some Maribis and some of the punchier original recruits had made it down to Safer and were ready to fight. The terrain facing Saqr 3 was even more dramatic and challenging than Mohammed S.'s front. On the evening of 10 September, the Saqr 3 column threaded from the Tadawin jump-off point through the thinly settled Al-Sahn and Al-Rawda neighbourhoods, and then looked towards the enemy-held foothills that faced the defensive redoubts of the governor's office and the Bilqis Hotel. Standing at their line of departure, the road where the displaced persons camps had been at the start of the battle, the view to the south-west was intimidating: first a wadi cut right across the unit frontage, exactly perpendicular to the line of advance. Then there was about 500–700 metres of bare open desert before the first dark, volcanic foothills.

The Hill of the Egyptians

Three kilometres into those foothills was the 130-metre-high Masaria, the Hill of the Egyptians, so named because it was famous in Marib as a battle site where the Abida tribe had apocryphally killed many Egyptians in the 1962–70 civil war. (Ironically, the Egyptians were then the foreign intervention supporting the government and the Maribis were, in effect, supporting the northern Hashemis who were now, in 2015, led by the Houthis.)

Egyptian Hill was, in fact, a volcano and the 3 km of foothills were what volcanologists called its 'volcanic field', where the once-molten 'lava tongue' had spilled outwards and cooled as its flowed downhill towards what would become the Marib oasis. Far behind Egyptian Hill was the Jebel al-Balaq, a mighty limestone anticline ever taller than Masaria, cut by a noticeable pass, just to the left of the hill from Saqr 3's perspective. This was where the waters of the modern Marib Dam were collected and sent through sluice gates in different directions.

At night, as Saqr 3 began to fan out, this intimidating visage was just a black skyline against a starry night. The Saqr 3 platoons moved forward and down into the 8-metre-deep dried-out watercourse, Wadi al-Ulayb. Though the drivers were quick learners it was still very difficult to manoeuvre the 14-tonne MRAPs in the dark down a sand and rock slope. Thanks to smart procurement by the UAE, they could not have been in a better vehicle for the job: the Oshkosh MRAP All-Terrain Vehicle (M-ATV) had been designed precisely to reduce the number of rollovers suffered by larger MRAPs in Afghanistan, and it was smaller and lower to the ground. An ingenious feature of the Oshkosh M-ATV was that each of its four chunky wheels could independently twist and stretch on its axle by as much as half a metre, which gave the vehicle the ambidextrous agility of a rock climber finding points of hold on a cliff-face with their strong hands and feet.

Even with this advantage, there were half a dozen rollovers and, worse, the sand floor of the wadi had been sown with anti-tank and anti-personnel land mines in anticipation of the attack. Three more Oshkoshes were knocked out by mines, albeit with their purpose-designed V-shaped hulls keeping their occupants safe, if a little rattled. The Yemenis were brave, almost recklessly so, Ahmed Z noted. When one vehicle was taken out by a mine, others would follow to recover the wounded. It was brave, but if they were to survive on this battlefield, they needed more training.

It had been a hard night but the main point of the attack – reconnaissance by fire, and to show strength to the enemy – had been achieved. The 'joint fires' had been very busy on the night of 9–10 September. Fixed-wing strike aircraft had been constantly overhead, stacked up by Ahmed H.'s cell, and were striking all points of enemy movement on the lava foothills of Masaria, where no civilians were present. The kill boxes further back were also busy, trying to choke off what looked to be strong enemy reinforcement of the Marib front line. Five UAE Apaches were now working the front line at night from a dispersed desert air-strip, organised into 'two-ship' pairs, with a spare Apache always back at base to allow helicopters to be rotated and maintained all through the night. AT-802 aircraft were available from dusk until dawn to watch the enemy, and to laser-designate targets for the artillery's 155-mm guided rounds.

All 12 G-6s were shooting, and HIMARS too: the artiller-ists were getting their revenge on the enemy. From hull-down positions on the plateau between the city and Wadi al-Ulayb, the Leclerc main battle tanks had gone into action. In a sta-tionary firing position, employing its super-accurate 120-mm main cannon and night optics, the Leclerc could reliably put a high-explosive round into a cave mouth or sangar. Their ballistic computers accounted for range, wind speed, humidity, temperature, ammunition type, and even how many times the barrel had been used since its last cleaning and maintenance.

The Kornet crews also moved forward to the plateau and hunted targets all night with their excellent long-range thermal scopes. When Anti-Tank Guided Missiles (ATGMs) were first introduced onto battlefields in the 1970s, there was a worry that the guided missile posts would draw attention down onto nearby friendly infantry and tanks, but the reverse proved the case in Marib. It was the Kornet teams – the 'silent assassins' – who learned not to cohabit too closely with the Leclercs, which tended to draw the fire of enemy rockets and mortars with their bright 120-mm main gun muzzle flashes.

The joint fires team could now tally up each night's claimed kills, most confirmed by the full-motion video feeds from the little fleet of drones buzzing overhead. On the night of 10–11 September, no fewer than ten T-series tanks had been knocked out, plus four Russian infantry fighting vehicles (BMPs) and seven chasses carrying troops or 23-mm cannons. Two towed artillery pieces were destroyed as they were being moved in from Sirwah, and two enemy assembly areas were struck by 'fast air'. Four Katyusha cells had been hit by rapid counter-battery fire cued by the Cobra radar at Sahan al-Jinn. Ahmed H. could see no end to the enemy reinforcements coming from Sanaa. Large Houthi–Saleh forces were massing in the wadis behind Masaria.

Three days into the fight, as dawn broke on 11 September, Ali Saif's command had the tiger by the tail – meaning that they had to keep the enemy occupied and there was no backing off. The Houthi–Saleh forces were still massing for an assault, or at least were signalling they would make a tenacious defence of the gateways to Sanaa. With Saqr 2 pushing up between the other axes but only as far as the N5 highway, both the flanks of Saqrs 1 and 3 were floating in mid-air. Fast air and counter-battery artillery were their only flank guards. Saqr 4, the reserve force at Tadawin Camp, was still uncommitted. If the enemy sensed weakness, he might come on strong.

Brigade attack on the Marib escarpment

Ali Saif and the JTF-291.3 command team had taken the offensive and given time for the final companies of the Saqrs and their heavy weapon platoons to move down to Tadawin. While the reconnaissance by fire had been undertaken in Marib, the remaining Saqr forces were shuttled down to Marib with every effort made to hide their movement. What would normally take a day took three because obscure desert tracks were used and the column was protected along its journey by the UAE and Saudi MRAPs spread out along its flanks, like destroyers guarding a convoy from enemy submarines.

At Tadawin, the Yemeni Saqr commanders and the OMLT team leaders gathered on 11 September to meet the new company and platoon commanders and absorb them into their fronts. Even after a few days of fighting, the forward-deployed commanders had the unshaven, tired look of veterans, while the incoming unit leaders were still in clean Saudi-provided 'chocolate chip'-pattern uniforms, with new red berets or Saudi-style flat-topped caps.

The offensive would recommence the following day, 12 September, at 06:00 hours. It would be the first daylight attack by the coalition in Marib. This would be the third phase of the operation, as planned by Musallam and his team in July: an

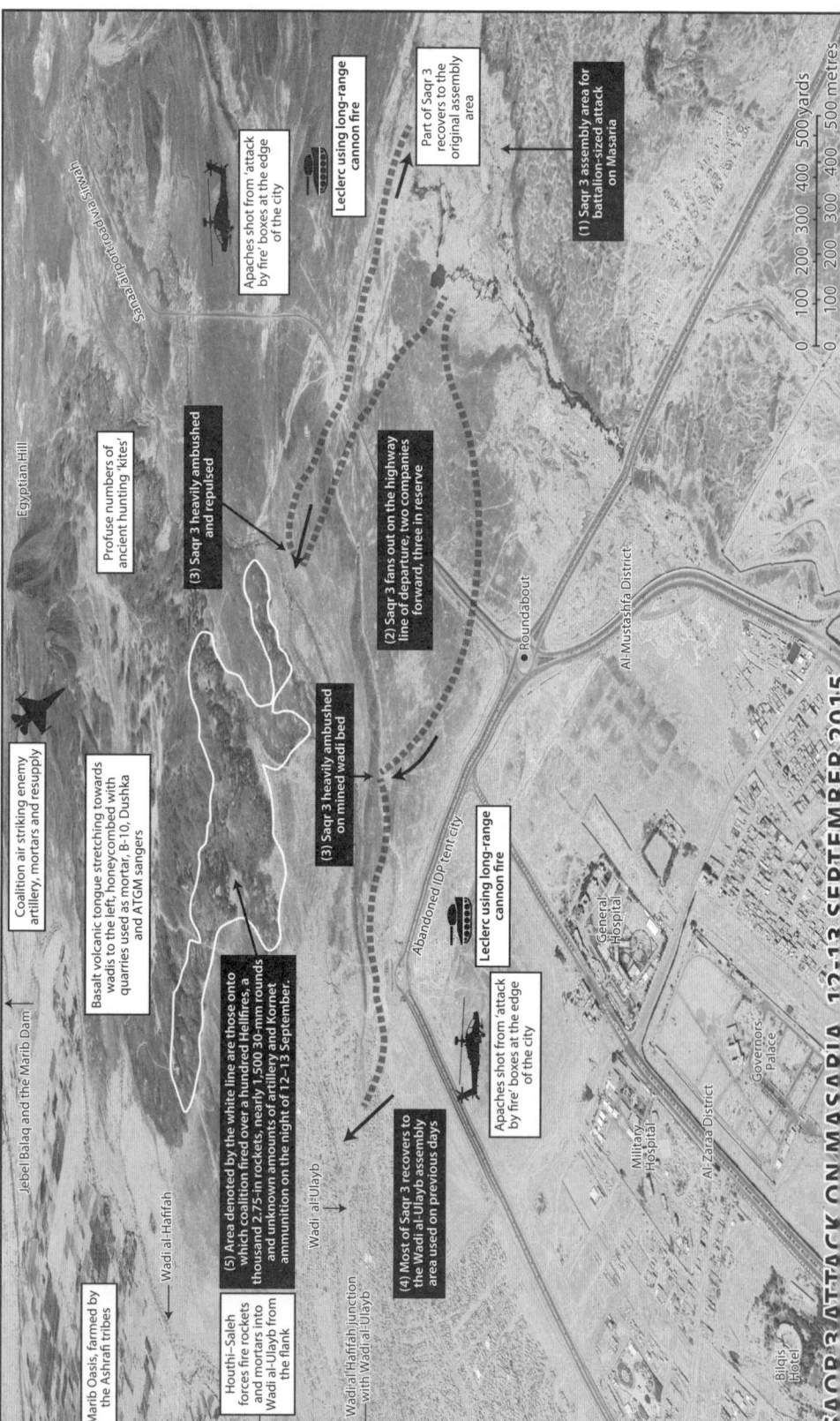

SAQR 3 ATTACK ON MASARIA, 12–13 SEPTEMBER 2015

Coalition air striking enemy artillery, mortars and resupply

Jebel Balaq and the Marib Dam

Marib Oasis, farmed by the Ashraf tribes

Wadi al-Haffah

Basalt volcanic tongue stretching towards wadis to the left, honeycombed with quarries used as mortar, B-10, Dushka and ATGM sangers

Houthi–Saleh forces fire rockets and mortars into Wadi al-Ulayb from the flank

Wadi al-Ulayb

Wadi al-Haffah junction with Wadi al-Ulayb

(5) Area denoted by the white line are those onto which coalition fired over a hundred Hellfires, a thousand 2.75-in rockets, nearly 1,500 30-mm rounds and unknown amounts of artillery and Kornet ammunition on the night of 12–13 September.

(4) Most of Saqr 3 recovers to the Wadi al-Ulayb assembly area used on previous days

Apaches shot from 'attack by fire' boxes at the edge of the city

Leclerc using long-range cannon fire

Abandoned IDP tent city

Bilqis Hotel

Al-Zalaa District

Al-Mustashfa District

Military Hospital

Governor's Palace

General Hospital

Roundabout

Sana'a airport road via Sirwah

Egyptian Hill

Apaches shot from 'attack by fire' boxes at the edge of the city

Leclerc using long-range cannon fire

Profuse numbers of ancient hunting 'kites'

(3) Saqr 3 heavily ambushed and repulsed

(3) Saqr 3 heavily ambushed on mined wadi bed

(2) Saqr 3 fans out on the highway line of departure; two companies forward, three in reserve

Part of Saqr 3 recovers to the original assembly area

(1) Saqr 3 assembly area for battalion-sized attack on Masaria

0   100 200 300 400 500 yards
0   100 200 300 400 500 metres

attack on all three axes at the same time, to shock the enemy and present them with tactical dilemmas. The aim was to push the Houthi–Saleh forces back to the three tactical objectives and thus out of rocket range of Marib city. It would be a hard fight: compared with the early planning assumptions, they now knew that the attacking force would be smaller than hoped for, with the anaemic YNA brigades only good for holding the faraway flanks. Rather than the planned divisional-scale 'deliberate attack', this began to look more like a brigade-strength 'hasty attack', with forces being fed into the front line as they arrived. Instead of thousands of rations sent forward each day, the field kitchens only needed to make 800 meals for each lunch and dinner-time and the requirement for *qat* every afternoon was a fraction of the initial planning estimate. What made the situation worse was that the enemy was even stronger than they had been in July or August, with signals intelligence suggesting that there were around 4,000 mouths to feed each day in the Houthi–Saleh force. Fuel and ammunition requirements suggested there were still around 100 tanks and armoured vehicles and a lot of artillery threaded into the enemy positions. The UAE and Yemeni forces were attacking an entrenched enemy without the benefit of superior numbers, which was decidedly not the 3:1 ratio of attacker to defender recommended by training manuals. JTF-291 would have to do more with less.

In the fight to come, Ali Saif would focus his attention and his reserves on his left flank; the Saqr 3 front at Masaria. The Maribis would take great heart from that hill's liberation because of its history as a symbol of resistance and the fact that it could be seen from the town, unlike the other, less discernible objectives. Masaria was somewhat legendary to the Maribis: that was where tricky Maribis tribes had cut the brake lines on Egyptian trucks and sent them rolling off the mountains to their deaths, at least according to the apocryphal tales of old men. Already the attack force at Masaria had been reinforced once – by part of Sohail K.'s Saqr 4 – and Sohail K. expected the enemy to resist the hardest there, in the maze-like volcanic field. The Saqr 3 axis could be decisive, as the enemy also knew.

Saqr 1 could fend for itself for a few days, fighting its own private war. Ali Saif trusted the Saqr 1 commander Mohammed S. to do his best on the right flank, where the objective about 8 km distant was the black and grey Ghanatha (Sniper's Hill), another 1960s battlefield. But, as important, Ali Saif had no choice but to trust Mohammed S. because no one could make regular battlefield visits out to his front due to the weight of sniper, B-10 and mortar fire hitting anything that moved over there. Mohammed S. planned to switch his forces from the right side of his lane to the left, and would leapfrog from the cover of one hill to another on his way to Sniper's Hill. He knew what he was doing. The Saudi-led axis in the centre could also largely look after itself because it was not the main effort: it would exploit forward movements by its neighbours and edge its way forward towards the furthest away of the three objectives – Hamra (Red Hill), so called because its limestone sides were stained red by iron oxides released from volcanic soil.

As the Saqr 1–3 forces moved towards their objectives, the front line became a mass of dust as hundreds of vehicles began a slow crawl forwards. Platoon-sized lines of MRAPs had been successfully employed by coalition forces in Aden and in the breakout battles that followed, but that had been pretty flat terrain and those had been carefully rehearsed movements with one UAE vehicle commander in each Oshkosh. Now this kind of skirmish line was being attempted on a far larger scale by troops who had never before rehearsed a formation attack with multiple companies. For the first 15 minutes, Saqr 3's movement out of the Wadi al-Ulayb and towards Masaria had been exhilarating. The force fanned out on the right of Ahmed Z.'s Saqr 1 attack lane, aligned on the N574 highway and advanced due south over the open ground to the north of the volcanic field. The huge mass of more than 50 vehicles seemed unstoppable. Then, as the force followed the route down into a wadi, all hell broke loose. Mines in the silt of the wadi bed started to explode under the MRAPs. Five Oshkoshes were knocked out in under a minute. The Saqr recruits panicked and dismounted, running back through a field of anti-personnel mines, with more than a dozen men losing their lives or, at the very least, losing their legs or feet.

Then a line of concealed enemy firing positions began to bombard the trapped force. Enemy prisoners would later relate that the trap had been set by an experienced force of Ali Abdullah Saleh's Republican Guards as well as Houthi veterans. They were dug into shallow quarry pits and holes in the wadi walls where the ornamental stone travertine had once been quarried, or, on the slopes of Masaria, within the mass of Bronze Age 'desert kites', which comprised rows of kite-shaped stone walls used to funnel ibex and gazelle into hunters' pits. Mortar and B-10 fire began to rain down around the knocked-out and reversing MRAPs.

Many of the shots were disconcertingly accurate. The ATGM specialist Ahmed Z. knew exactly what he was looking at: the enemy had brought forward accurate anti-tank guided missiles too. Ahmed Z. later found wire-guided missile control lines strung all over the kill zone. The Houthis had brought up their Konkurs ATGM (codenamed AT5 Spandrel in NATO nomenclature). But these were not old Soviet missiles from Yemeni military stocks: empty launch tubes would show that they were new Iranian-built copies that Russia had licensed Iran to manufacture. Some were from 2015 production runs, making them newer than the Kornet tubes being used by the UAE. Iran had entered the battlefield.

Night of the Apaches

Ahmed Z. rallied the retreating force at Wadi al-Ulayb, about 700 metres back from the ambush. Many of the Saqr had simply disappeared, never to return. Some were dead and wounded, but most had just fled. Most were new recruits and they were not used to this kind of terrain. The right 'fit' between troops and terrain would prove to be an important factor shaping combat morale throughout the Yemen war: hill people liked being in the hills and felt safe there, and city people liked towns and could fight effectively in them. It was always a risk to take Yemeni troops out of their element and put them into terrain in which they felt unfamiliar. Back at Ali Saif's command vehicle, by midday on 12 September it was clear that something had gone badly wrong over on Saqr 3's front. Ali Saif turned to the Saqr 4 OMLT commander Sohail K., who had had more time studying Masaria and its weaknesses than any of the UAE officers in Marib. 'Go now, take one company of Saqr 4 and get us moving again,' he had barked.

Sohail grabbed the Joint Fires Commander Ahmed H. and headed out. By 16:00 hours, Sohail, Ahmed and the reinforcements were in Wadi al-Ulayb at Ahmed Z.'s command post. It was an awful scene. The wadi had offered some protection and was a location known to the Saqr forces, and thus a good rally point, but it had a key weakness. From its left-hand side, the south-west, some parts of the Ashraf farms could see right into the wadi and this allowed a murderous fire to be directed on the rally point with Katyushas and mortars. Clinging to the shadow of their vehicles and small caves, the wounded of Saqr 1 were lying all around, with enemy fire dropping among them.

Each Saqr company had a dedicated Caiman ambulance MRAP with Red Crescent medical markings and no anti-RPG cages to make them visibly less war-like. The ambulances had been constantly shuttling in and out, taking casualties back to the Marib hospitals and the coalition's forward aid post at Sahan al-Jinn, from where serious cases were helicoptered to the field surgical hospital at Safer or even sent for aerial evacuation to Riyadh or Abu Dhabi in rare cases. The Yemenis were begging to get armoured support to head back into the ambush site after dark to recover the wounded and the dead. Grown men were sitting all around crying, which is always a hard and disconcerting thing to see. 'They could see death,' Ahmed H. recounted grimly.

The Joint Fires Commander knew what he had to do. Ahmed prepared to get underneath an Oshkosh MRAP with all his fire control equipment and a Long-Range Thermal Video (LRTV) system, which was about the size and weight of a heavy set of naval binoculars, and which included a cooled thermal imager, colour video camera, integrated laser rangefinder, digital magnetic compass, GPS and laser designator. With fire dropping all around, the MRAP hull and its thick tyres provided Ahmed with the best cover he could get. Even under the vehicle, he could still directly see the targets, allowing him to more easily orient himself and talk the pilots above onto their targets. It was a tight squeeze, about 40 cm between the V-shaped hull and the ground, and he could not fit in with his body armour and helmet, so he stripped them off.

If the Houthi–Saleh forces attacked as night fell, they could collapse the Saqr 3 front and overrun the wadi. That must not happen. Not only would it pave the way for defeat in Marib but it would undoubtedly result in the capture of Sohail, Ahmed H. and other UAE troops. Every Emirati trooper was determined not to be taken captive by the enemy and paraded on television as a hostage. Ahmed brought down the coalition's full power onto the 2,000-metre frontage facing Wadi al-Ulayb. The foothills directly above the wadi from which an attack might come, the volcanic tongue, were pitted with hundreds of impact points that can still be clearly seen, even eight years later. Air-bursting bombs and artillery turned the ground-covering of gravel into deadly shrapnel, amplifying the fragmentation effect of each blast. The Ashrafi farms were hit with accurate counter-battery fire every time the Cobra radar detected a launch. No one in Marib had ever seen such a show of light and sound, even back in the days of the Egyptian invasion. The rooftops of the town were full of civilians watching.

But that evening would be remembered as the 'Apache party' because the attack helicopters provided such ever-present and audible support all through the night. The five UAE and three Saudi Apaches operated from what the Apache crews call an 'attack-by-fire box', a piece of airspace where they can circle without fear of being attacked from the ground below. A two-ship formation of Apaches was always overhead throughout the night, with each pair staying on-station for about an hour and not leaving until relieved by the next shift. Each Apache crew did two or three sorties that night. This was not a moment for conserving ammunition and every two-ship 'came full and left empty', as Ahmed H. remembers.

For about eight hours they pounded the enemy on the front line and just behind it, hitting the roads resupplying Marib and the tracks used to get forces up to Masaria. 'It was non-stop gunning all night,' an Emirati trooper recalled, referring to the 30-mm cannon slung under the belly of the Apache. All enemy movement and fire was met with a squirt of five rounds of high-explosive shells, a rate of fire intended to let the guns cool between bursts, and each Apache fired around 100 bursts in its hourly shift. Below, the wadi was littered with thousands of 11-cm-long brass casings ejected from the helicopters above. Each Apache also shot off its full loads of Hellfire guided missiles and 2.75-inch high-explosive rockets, using them to hit precise targets like rock sangars or to 'ripple fire' rockets onto large areas. No one has an accurate count of the missiles and rockets used that night but it probably included well over 100 Hellfires and over 1,000 rockets. Both the Apaches and the AT-802 lased for the precision artillery shells launched by the G-6s, mainly to accurately strike the modern T-80 and BMP-2 armoured vehicles of Saleh's Republican Guards that had begun to enter the battlefield.

Even when they were not firing, the Apaches could be heard circling and protecting. In the night, the little engine of the AT-802, the slow and loud 'bicycle', was also a source of reassurance to the Saqr forces as the sound echoed around the hills. Come the morning, the enemy had not attacked and Masaria was a smoking death trap. Ahmed H. saw a difference in the men all around. None of them had got much sleep that night but they had witnessed a spectacle of destruction that was all for their protection. It was a demonstration of support that the Maribis would never forget and which restored their morale for another try at the Hill of the Egyptians.

The next push on Masaria

On the night of 13 September, Sohail and Ahmed Z. tried to advance again. Pushing forward, this time up Highway N574, they aimed to skirt north (i.e. to the right) of the Masaria volcanic field that had been pummelled the night before. The force was led by four Leclerc main battle tanks, the most heavily armoured vehicles in the UAE's arsenal. In addition to their standard armour plating, which could defeat a Konkurs or B-10 warhead with ease, they had all sorts of bolt-on armour modules. This made the Leclercs quite a sight: 2.5 metres high, covered in anti-RPG cages and chains, and draped in multi-spectral camouflage cloth that mimicked the skin texture of moths and other nocturnal creatures to reduce the Leclerc's visibility in infrared light.

After wheeling off-road on a south-easterly bearing to encircle the Masaria volcano counter-clockwise, the terrain became broken and almost too tight in places to fit the Leclercs. Their anti-RPG cages were bent and battered. Sharp basalt rocks – one of mankind's first bladed weapons – started to strip the thick rubber treads off the Leclerc tracks, making them slip and slide on the loose gravel. The MRAPs were designed to 'run flat' on punctured tyres but they too were suffering.

Then disaster struck. At 22:15 hours on 13 September, a Houthi fighter fired a B-10 recoilless rifle at the lead Leclerc. There had been occasional pot-shots before, forcing the crews to 'button-up' by closing their hatches, further reducing manoeuvrability and situational awareness. Normally a B-10 recoilless rifle round – which uses a molten jet much like an RPG anti-tank warhead or an ATGM – would not generate even a third of the penetrative power needed to put a hole in the Leclerc. But by freak bad luck, this shell hit the 4-cm high by 8-cm wide vision block used by the tank's driver. Although made of layered armoured glass and polycarbonate, the 22-cm thick vision block could not contain an armour-piercing jet of molten metal designed to cut through 30 cm of steel armour. The driver, Ghalib, was killed instantly, making him the 55th Emirati to be killed in Marib (as two of the wounded from Safer had also died) and the 60th to die in battle during the war. This new death hit the Emiratis hard: they had desperately not wanted to lose any more men after Safer, and this new Emirati fatality brought back all the shock.

Amid minefields and the maze of Masaria, the attack stopped at dawn, with Saqr 3 dropping exhausted into their shallow rock sangars. The Kornet crews would hold the line during the day, each firing post expending their ration of seven rounds, undertaking heavy sniping against any enemy forces moving above ground. The following day, on 14 September, the whole front line witnessed an artillery duel as the Houthis tried to batter the Saqrs back with tens of rockets launched from the backs of chasses that were dashing around in the wadis behind the enemy hills and down in the Ashrafi farms. In the course of this counter-battery dual, an Agrab gunner was killed when a mortar round exploded in the tube, a rare but deadly defect in a fuse that is known by artillerymen around the world as a 'hang-fire'. Now the UAE death toll in Marib was 56 and 61 in Yemen altogether.

As 14 September passed, the Saqrs were undoubtedly in rough shape. At the huge mechanical workshop at Sahan al-Jinn, wrecked MRAPS and chasses lay all around, partially cannibalised to keep others running. Fifty MRAPs had now been knocked out and many more had lost most of their external fittings to artillery fire and to enemy sniping with powerful Iranian-made AM-50 anti-materiel rifles. As the Houthi snipers had shown in Aden months before, and now again in Marib, they were masters at achieving mobility kills on MRAPs and trucks, putting AM-50 rounds through radiators or shooting out multiple tyres. Replacement radiators and tyres were being surged forward from Sharurah for the Oshkoshes and Unimog trucks.

Manpower was also running low. Because of losses and desertions, all the Saqrs were at well under 50 per cent strength and each had been consolidated into one company (not four) per axis, with drivers, bodyguards and messengers also sent to the front. Maribi tribesmen now increasingly made up the main source of replacement manpower in each Saqr, with the chocolate-chip pattern of Saudi-provided uniforms giving way to tribal garb. This meant a lot more *qat* chewing in the afternoons and a dangerous Maribi habit of going out into no-man's land to lift Houthi mines for sale at the arms souks in the city. The shortage of fighters was so desperate that the commanders were even beginning to look with interest at the Somali refugee camps that they passed every day, but the Maribis would absolutely not allow these foreigners to be armed.

Even so, real progress was finally happening by the late hours of 14 September. Sohail and Ahmed Z. got their heads together and developed new tactics: they would break down the Saqr into small infantry squads that would infiltrate forward with Maribi guides who knew the way and who were not afraid of the hills. A vanguard would go ahead, to identify enemy strongpoints and minefields. The tanks would stay back and the mobile Kornet would be man-carried forward to cover each step. By 03:00 hours on 15 September, Saqr 3 forces had broken through the foothills and begun to scale Masaria itself, a smaller version of the US Marines' famous ascent of Mount Suribachi on another volcanic battlefield: that of Iwo Jima in 1945.

As expected, the enemy started to withdraw from Masaria as soon as the Houthis on the crest felt they were being encircled. As Saqr 3's exhausted troops finally looked down the 100-metre 'reverse slope' of Masaria on the morning of 15 September, they could see Saqr 2 conforming to their line on the right, still about 5 km short of the Red Hill. Further away, Saqr 1 was stuck on the chain of hills a few kilometres north of Sniper's Hill. Houthi–Saleh artillery was firing angrily from the wadis and farms that ran behind the line of hills, now directly visible to coalition observers and even Kornet teams. The enemy wasn't budging yet but it might take just one more major blow to crack them. The question was: did the coalition attack force have the strength to continue?

VIII

TURNING THE FLANK AT MARIB DAM

It was at this dramatic moment that Musallam R. came back on the scene. He had been in a German clinic in Munich since 6 September. After a period of initial emergency care and a barrage of tests, he had been told he should commit to a series of operations and a recuperation period of four to six months. 'No,' he answered immediately; he had to get back to the war in a couple of days. The only way that could happen, the doctors told him, was a short-term fix: one operation to screw a temporary titanium plate into his left shoulder to hold it together for a while. But there would be pain, lots of pain, and it was too soon to know what bacteria had entered his body through the wound. It didn't matter, Musallam told them; just do it. He went under the surgeon's knife on 10 September, just as the Apaches were throwing their party in Marib. War is a profession but it is also a vocation, and it would not let go of Musallam. To his credit, Musallam has always been honest about why he risked so much to go back: he wanted revenge for his troops and to finish the job he had been given. Commanders all over the world feel this way. Militaries train their soldiers to be winners, to fight, and to battle through adversity – not to give up. 'Think of an athlete training their whole life for the Olympics,' he told me in 2019. He had to get back to the front line.

The path back to combat command was revealed to

Musallam as he recovered from surgery on 12 September. MBZ called Musallam in Munich to enquire about his health after the operation and how soon he could return to duty. Musallam said he could leave immediately, to help the force get their revenge, and so he could fight again. They talked about MBZ's words of comfort to the families of martyrs the previous day, 11 September, when he had promised them that he would raise a victory flag over Marib Dam. The words had power because everyone in the UAE had heard of the dam that the UAE's founder Sheikh Zayed had built for the Yemenis in 1986, at what was known as 'the birthplace of the Arabs'. Musallam promised to deliver the liberation of the dam. The next day, he left Munich with his trusty wakil, who had been at his bedside for 11 days, and set off to the UAE and Yemen to resume command of the Marib operation. The German doctors begged him to reconsider: four months would allow the wound to recover fully. Instead he left, and would ultimately suffer through five operations and still feel the wound every day on waking for years afterwards. But there was no stopping Musallam: the battlefield called.

In Abu Dhabi on 15 September, Musallam went straight to see MBZ before his flight out to Sharurah. His arm and shoulder were splinted. The idea of a publicised liberation of the dam was growing increasingly attractive. The Houthi–Saleh forces had tried a repeat of the Safer attack on 13 September but a sharp-eyed fighter pilot had successfully destroyed the Tochka on its TEL in the Sirwah area. (The Houthis would try a third time on 10 November 2015, and this time the Patriot air defence system at Safer would intercept the Tochka in mid-air.) The two new fatalities in Marib – the tank driver and the artillerist – had occurred in the short time since Musallam had begun his trip back from Germany. These new fatalities sharpened the need for a tangible sign of progress. Photographs and videos of the dam's liberation would be good for the nation and the coalition's morale. It would show the Arab partners achieving new battle-field victories that the public could recognise. No one at home could appreciate the significance or effort that went into capturing this hill or that hill in Marib's volcanic desert. Civilians could not appreciate their importance as defensive redoubts or artillery observation sites. But Zayed Dam was where the tribes of Marib had sent a lone rider on a white horse to honour Sheikh Zayed and thank him for his generosity and where they allowed him to raise the UAE flag. It was a historic monument to his generosity, vision and connection to Arabs everywhere. Musallam set off for Sharurah having recommitted himself to the liberation of the dam.

The return of the commander

Musallam, his adjutant Lieutenant Colonel Hamad M. and the trusty wakil landed at Sharurah on 15 September and then took a chopper for the final 270 km to Safer early the next day, 16 September. The last time Musallam had made this trip it had also been dawn, but back then his lifeblood had been slowly draining away. Now he was coming home, to his command and to his war. As the helicopter landed he was surprised and even disappointed to be greeted by just one man, a captain sent to pick him up. But that only reflected the frantic pace of operations at Safer. Everyone was at the morning operations briefing with the chain of command back in Abu Dhabi and at Sharurah.

Musallam walked straight into the briefing, and instantly appeared on video-conference screens across the various command centres. He was back. 'I felt eyes looking at me,' he remembered uncomfortably. 'My arm was in a sling and the pain was always with me but I didn't want to show weakness.' After

Musallam received the briefing, he and Ali Saif spoke directly and in private. Ali looked like he had been in combat for a month, but it had been only a week. Musallam also looked grizzled due to pain, constant travel and lack of sleep. As Ali Saif had been promoted to brigadier first, what the military calls 'precedence', and as he had been doing a superb job, many officers in his position would have argued that it was reasonable for him to continue as the task force commander. But Ali Saif gauged the situation correctly and, with huge professionalism, he shook Musallam's hand and completed the change of command.

What followed the next day did great credit to Musallam's professionalism as well. In Sharurah, looking at the maps and the daily reporting, Musallam had been worried by the way the attack force had melted away and the attack had apparently bogged down. But now he was at the forward headquarters, Musallam could see that the battle was raging and that everyone was doing their utmost to keep advancing. Ali Saif had clearly done a heroic job to save the operation after the Safer disaster. The force had been refitted in record time and had been provided with all the joint fires support and missile defence it needed.

Most of all, Ali Saif had been there with the men every step of the way. He had sat with the shattered artillerymen every day after the strike. And now Ali Saif had experienced the pain of seeing UAE soldiers killed since he took over – the tanker and the artillerist who had died in recent days. Musallam knew only too well how that felt. Ali Saif had undertaken 100 km a day of battlefield rotations to visit all the units at the front. As Musallam visited the forward positions on 17 September, he saw the conditions that Ali Saif and the other officers had been living in: sleeping in trenches, not even tents, clinging to scraps of cover, with no fires or lights at night, and no showers or services. On his first day of front-line visits, the bumpy roads to and from the Saqrs caused Musallam fiery bolts of pain as his broken bones rubbed together and his titanium plate pinched nerves. Back at Safer, the command staff spent each night in the sand dunes in sleeping bags, next to the small blacked-out operations tent. With his shoulder burning with pain, Musallam knew he would not be sleeping in foxholes or dunes any time soon.

On their return to Safer, Musallam made a commendable and judicious command decision. He would retain overall command of the task force but Ali Saif would keep tactical control of the Saqrs. The forward headquarters at Safer would be run by Prince Khalid bin Hamad, who had done a fine job since the Safer attack. Meanwhile, Musallam would move to the far-left flank and assume tactical control of a new front to liberate Marib Dam. A wide flanking attack had always been an option in the planning of Operation Western Winds, either towards Nihm using Saqr 4 or against the Jebel al-Balaq and Marib Dam using the Quick Reaction Force made up of Bahraini special operators. The idea of a 'turning' of the flank at Marib Dam now made even more sense: the Houthi–Saleh forces could be levered out of the wadis and the remaining hills if the coalition could wrap fully around and behind them via the towering Jebel al-Balaq. In a masterstroke of improvisation, what could have been a damaging rift between commanders was instead turned into a positive.

Musallam would leave the next day, 18 September, relocating to a tribal leader's house that would become the tactical assembly area for the attack on the dam, the fourth axis. But first he had to do something that could not be put off. In his brief time back in Marib, Musallam had passed through many of the units, giving his condolences on their losses at Safer, and now it was time to visit the artillerymen, those who had been hit the hardest. When they met, there was a strange feeling in the tent, something unspoken, exactly as Musallam had expected. Then one sergeant spoke up: he asked why they had taken so many casualties, why Musallam hadn't protected them better. Musallam's loyal staff were ready to argue for him, but he shushed them. It was his responsibility as the commander to answer the question. 'The men who we lost were not more valuable to you than to me,' he gently told the sergeant. 'I wish that we could all come back home but that is the gamble we take in war. We must take our revenge on the Houthis and not play the blame game.'

Back in the UAE, MBZ had been giving the same message to many of his own commanders since 4 September. Musallam had done a lot of soul-searching in his hospital bed in Munich, and has never stopped thinking about what could have been done differently. His private reminiscences of the battle are full of checking and rechecking his logic, and asking whether he could have done more or known more.

> The troops didn't understand that I had asked for Patriot air defence missiles to defend our FOB [Safer] against Scud missiles but that these were not available. I was not warned about the possibility of hidden, more accurate Tochka missiles. My plan to concentrate my force for four days while close to the oil refinery, which was financially important to the Houthis, carried a low degree of risk. If my plan hadn't been slowed down by events, it would have all worked well.

But, ultimately, he reflected: 'As commander, I know that the events that occur under my command are my responsibility, but that was not the time to assign blame.'

Learning about the enemy

Left in tactical control of Saqrs 1–4, Ali Saif was characteristically energetic. The attack was brought back into action on 18 September. He could be a hard taskmaster and he went right up to the forward edge of battle to give each of the Saqr command teams a strong push. Energetic and confident, he was also strict and often looked angry, and he put each of his Saqr commanders under personal pressure to achieve a breakthrough. On these visits he was now accompanied by the new 3rd Military Regional Command (MRC) commander Brigadier General Abd-Rabu al-Shadadi, a staff college-trained Maribi officer who had impressed the Emirati commanders. Shadadi and his staff kept a tidy headquarters, with professionally marked and updated maps with perfect tactical symbolling. He put his money where his mouth was, literally paying Yemeni resistance troops out of his own pocket, and he walked where the soldiers walked, having survived a couple of mine strikes on his command vehicle.

Indeed, the coalition and Houthi–Saleh forces had never stopped playing a cat-and-mouse game to kill each other's leaders. By this point in the battle, almost the whole enemy force were Houthis, with only a minority of Saleh loyalists left on the battlefield. The Houthi commanders were rarely identified or located because their command-and-control system was highly decentralised. As a result, it was almost impossible to identify anything resembling the enemy's equivalent of the Safer forward headquarters or the Saqr leadership groups and OMLTs. They used messengers on trail bikes, and if they used electronic communications at all, they would almost never emit from their leadership locations but rather from mobile retransmission sites where orders were sent out using low-power Motorola radios.

When the UAE had tried to get an agent to lure the Houthi tactical commanders to one place for a meeting, they were told that the local Ashraf leaders were never allowed to choose the spot and were only brought there blindfolded and without their phones. But despite all the Emiratis' efforts to blend in, the Houthis had identified Ali Saif and commanders like Mohammed S. and Sohail, and had tried to have them killed. On Saqr 1's front, for example, a stranger had been asking around for Mohammed S. one night and had been pointed in the right direction. Then he disappeared. On hearing this, Mohammed S. moved the OMLT team immediately, and just an hour afterwards four heavy 120-mm mortar rounds struck their old campsite. The Yemenis were always regaling the coalition advisors with tales of famous Maribi betrayals – of other tribes, the Egyptians, Saleh, and now the Houthis. In the cut-throat world of Yemen's tribes, a clever piece of treachery was like a work of art to be admired. It was still hard to trust them.

Now, as Ali Saif and Shadadi toured the summit of Masaria, their bodyguards close at hand, they had a chance to see how the Houthis had been living. The volcanic rock on Masaria was of two varieties: hard basalt and a softer type of rock that geologists call lapilli tuff. Making a small sangar involved finding a seam of lapilli and scraping it out a little, ideally with a bit of basalt overhead. Then, if you were industrious, you might pile up some loose rocks on the open side of this shallow shelter, or load gravel into hessian or plastic-weave bags to make sandbags. Each one of these tiny sangars was just big enough for one man and a weapon – a B-10, a machine gun or a sniper rifle. And there were hundreds of them, to allow fighters to duck from one to another all day and night, where they would use the weapon until it ran out of ammunition.

UAE officers readily admitted that the Houthis were a tough enemy: under withering attack by artillery and air, they must have squeezed themselves into their sangar walls. Little scraps of dirty paper with the speeches from the Houthi leader Abdul-Malik were tucked away in each position. Fighters were given nickel-plated Yale-type 'keys to heaven' to wear around their necks, an Iranian custom from the Iran–Iraq War that was said to protect the user from bullets. Deafened and bleeding, they would have survived by drinking little sips of water and taking tablets bearing the image of an ant carrying an elephant. This was the highly addictive amphetamine drug Captagon, produced in Lebanon and brought into Yemen through Iran, Hezbollah and the Houthis. The pills stimulate the central nervous system, increasing alertness and concentration and allowing users to stay awake. Now these tough foes were mostly dead, baking in the sun. These men had been entombed in their defensive positions, surrounded by land mines linked to flat pressure plate triggers under the gravel, and written off to die. In fact, the Houthi commanders seemed to view their foot soldiers as nothing more than human mines, buried in the ground, forgotten, with the hope they might kill a few enemies.

Down in the valley below, the Houthi–Saleh forces had been busily reinforcing the reverse slope of Egyptian Hill, as well as Red Hill and Sniper's Hill. In addition to a smattering of Houthi veterans and the odd Republican Guard platoon who had fully committed to the Houthis, most were illiterate kids from the north-west and from Bayda, some of them sold to the Houthis, who at least promised to feed them. Gathered at hotels on the roads leading back to Sanaa, the recruits would be sent down to Sirwah and then parcelled out for the final leg to a set of farms on trail bikes (carrying the driver plus two fighters). There they would be hastily trained and finally formed into small squads. Team leaders were shown intricate sand tables of the terrain by Arabic-speaking Hezbollah fighters from Lebanon and taught the tactics that worked best on this battlefield. Above all, the

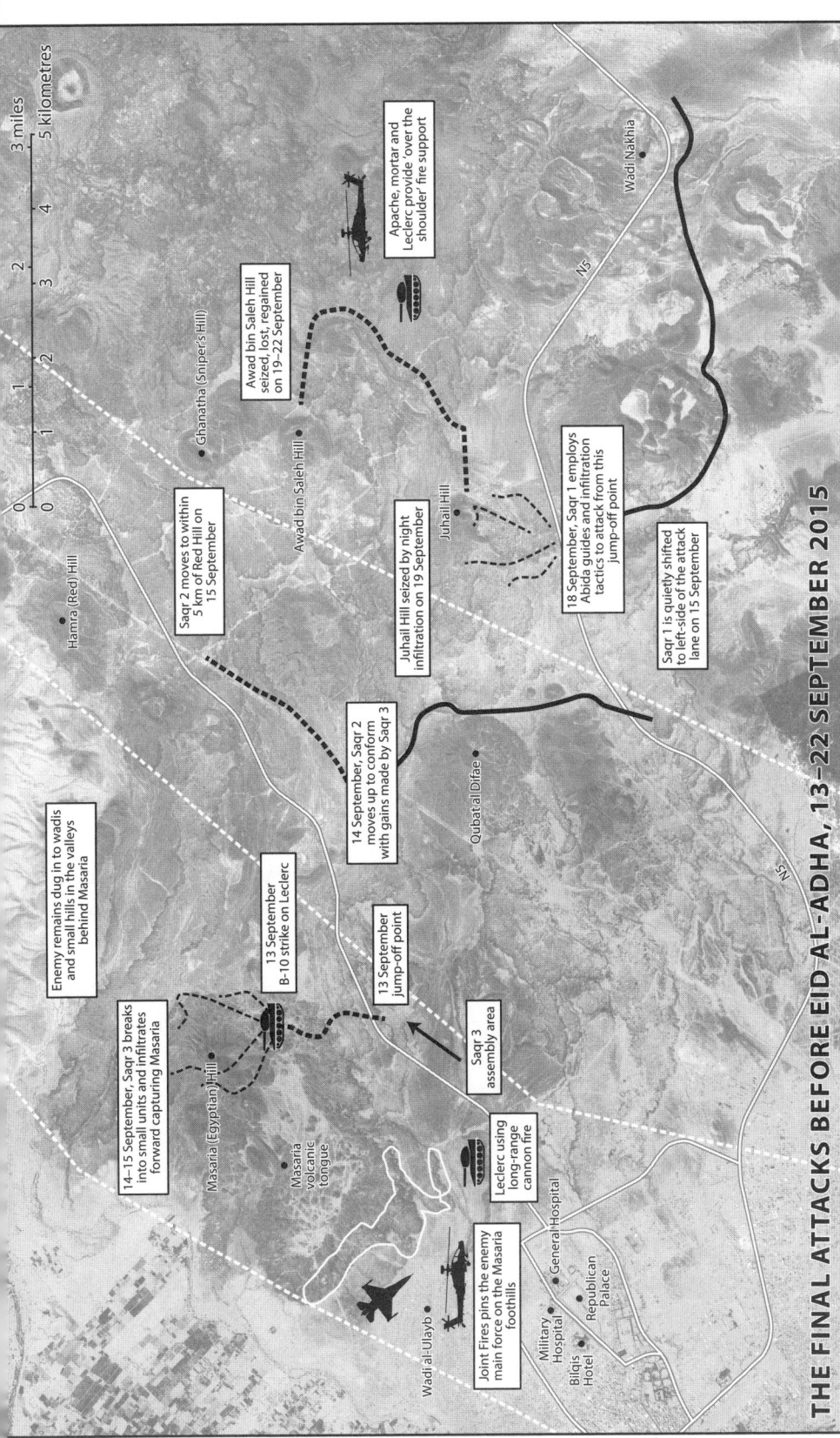

THE FINAL ATTACKS BEFORE EID AL-ADHA, 13–22 SEPTEMBER 2015

Apache, mortar and Leclerc provide 'over the shoulder' fire support

Awad bin Saleh Hill seized, lost, regained on 19–22 September

Saqr 2 moves to within 5 km of Red Hill on 15 September

18 September, Saqr 1 employs Abida guides and infiltration tactics to attack from this jump-off point

Juhail Hill seized by night infiltration on 19 September

Saqr 1 is quietly shifted to left-side of the attack lane on 15 September

14 September, Saqr 2 moves up to conform with gains made by Saqr 3

Enemy remains dug in to wadis and small hills in the valleys behind Masaria

13 September B-10 strike on Leclerc

13 September jump-off point

14–15 September, Saqr 3 breaks into small units and infiltrates forward capturing Masaria

Saqr 3 assembly area

Leclerc using long-range cannon fire

Joint Fires pins the enemy main force on the Masaria foothills

Ghanatha (Sniper's Hill)

Hamra (Red) Hill

Awad bin Saleh Hill

Juhail Hill

Qubat al Difae

Masaria (Egyptian) Hill

Masaria volcanic tongue

Wadi al-Ulayb

General Hospital

Military Hospital

Republican Palace

Bilqis Hotel

Wadi Nakhia

N5

N5

3 miles

5 kilometres

trainers explained the limitations of enemy aircraft, right down to how long each two-ship could stay around and how to count when the different aircraft types had used all their bombs. As a Houthi prisoner later said: 'We know where your jets come from and how many minutes of fuel they have – maximum ten. You make big thunder for us but we can wait you out in our holes, chewing *qat*.'

The last attacks before Eid al-Adha

The new vantage point on top of Egyptian Hill was a fruitful one for the coalition. Now Ahmed H. and his Joint Terminal Attack Controllers (JTACs) could look directly down into the valley below, Wadi al-Jufaynah. A fast air 'fighter jock' himself, Ahmed H. was by now so well known to the pilots that some of them invited him to order custom menus of wing-loads each day, not only allowing him to choose what munitions would be carried but even how they would be fused – for impact, proximity or delay. Along with the air forces and drones above, these observers could profile the enemy reinforcements and resupply runs, by day and by night. In the cold-blooded manner of modern warfare, the joint fires team might watch a vehicle for many kilometres as it moved from a training camp to the front, building 'positive identification' on both the vehicle and every stopping point along the way where a reinforcement would get off the vehicle or a bag of *qat* would be delivered to a foxhole. Through this process it was learned that the enemy used destroyed vehicles as 'dead drops' for ammunition, drugs and water, because they were well-known landmarks that were unlikely to be struck again.

Masaria also provided new firing points for the Kornet teams, which could now see and shoot all the way out to the tops of Jebel al-Balaq to the south-west or the Ashraf farms to the south-east. Running this 'heavy sniping' campaign became ATGM specialist Ahmed Z.'s main role now. Each firing post had its ration of seven Kornet tubes per day, to ensure a good reserve in case of an enemy attack and to guard against unnecessary use. They did their best work at night, when their excellent thermal imaging camera could accurately characterise targets as small as trail bikes, which tried (but failed) to avoid detection by moving with their headlights and brake lights disconnected. But Ahmed Z did not have it all his own way: on some nights, Houthi ATGM teams fired back, causing a spate of near misses. Konkurs couldn't do that at night: looking at missile fragments, Zaabi could see pieces of wreckage from the Dehlavieh, the Iranian copy of the more modern Russian-designed Kornet missile, which also had a thermal night scope. Again, Iran had put its finger on the scale and tried to tip the balance in the Houthis' favour.

The days were counting down before Eid al-Adha (23–26 September), which the Yemenis warned would force the fighting to stop for a couple of days as the troops went home to their families. The UAE had experienced this in Aden, watching their Yemeni partners put down their tools of war and leave the battlefield on the very night of the city's liberation, which happened to be Eid al-Fitr. That night in Aden, six exhausted Emirati OMLT teams had held the line in the half-occupied city as the Yemenis feasted in their homes.

In Marib, the last push to come before the 23 September feast of Eid al-Adha would be on Mohammed S.'s Saqr 1 front line, which had been reinforced with the second-from-last reserve company of Saqr 4. His activities give a sense of a typical 'battle day' – meaning a day in which major attacks were undertaken, in contrast to the in-between days of skirmishing and preparing.

Such days started with Fajr prayers for the Saqr command team and OMLT, who might also be joined by Ali Saif if their front was the main effort that day. On 18 September, Saqr 1 was forming up in a wadi, halfway between the N5 highway and the first of three hills it needed to conquer, a small 40-metre volcanic peak called Juhail. Mohammed S. had slipped his forces to the left-hand side of his lane to put them shoulder to shoulder with Saqr 2, which was making slow but steady progress on Salmi's left.

It was the same old tactic of reconnaissance by fire: little squads of mainly Maribi troops, with hardly any of the original Saqr recruits left, skirmishing forward. They were backed up by four Leclercs, and by the OMLT team with its Agrab mortar carriers and NIMR-mounted Kornets. As soon as any opposition reared its head, it would be pummelled by these fires organic to the Saqr and by Apache firing 'over the shoulder' against targets as close as 100–200 metres from the forward line of troops. In a new twist, the Abida under Mohammed S. had found tribesmen who knew these very hills and who were trackers, allowing them to find the enemy's own resupply and reinforcement routes through the minefields. This allowed Juhail to be taken in a night attack on 19 September, with Apaches and AT-802s smashing a number of attempted ambushes. Next came Awad bin Saleh Hill, a slightly more impressive double-peaked hill about 40 metres high, to which the Abida scouts also found a covered approach.

This was assaulted, lost, assaulted again and lost again, until the enemy finally withdrew on 22 September. The problem was that tribal fighters never thought it was their job to consolidate or garrison territorial gains. In the tribesman's view, that kind of task – to stand around on checkpoints and be on guard – was the army's job, not the job of the fighters. So each day, the Maribis would come back from a bloody, hard-won fight, to go to their afternoon *qat* chews and then their beds, while the Houthis would simply reoccupy the lost terrain by midday. Eventually, Mohammed S. found a solution: the Kornets and OMLTs would hold the line between pushes. Using this method, Mohammed S.'s men had done enough to get the enemy's attention and draw reserves away from the next intended point of attack at Marib Dam.

A council of war

Musallam had left Safer on 18 September to drive the 50 km south-west to the farm of Salem al-Sabran al-Damashqa, an Abida sheikh who owned a lot of land east of the dam. His ranch was remote and well protected on all sides by his guard force. In addition to a 23-mm anti-aircraft cannon, he even had his own artillery – an old Second World War American 75-mm pack howitzer and a handful of shells left over after the gun's use in many tribal feuds over the decades.

The defensibility of the site was important because Musallam was taking a big gamble: he was almost alone at the farm, with only his trusty wakil, his adjutant and his joint fires team, Lieutenant Colonel Mohammed N., a Saudi joint fires officer, and a young Emirati JTAC. In some ways, the team was even more exposed than the one at Sohail K. and Ahmed H.'s safe house in Marib city in the opening days of the battle. The tribal area where Musallam was based could have become a deadly trap if anyone chose to betray him. This was one of the places the CIA watched most carefully – the epicentre of a Named Area of Interest for the US drones overhead – and Al-Qaeda had long hidden their people there. The Houthi and Saleh forces had also put out feelers to local sheikhs to defect to them and thus open the coalition's flank.

But Musallam trusted Sheikh Salem (with his life) for a number of reasons. First, the sheikh had a strong historic connection to the Emiratis. The Abida had gained greatly from the plethora of contracts that the Zayed Dam brought to Marib in the 1980s, and none more so than Sheikh Salem. Secondly, the sheikh had lost two of his sons fighting the Houthis. By taking the calculated risk of putting himself entirely under Sheikh Salem's protection, Musallam was doing him and the Abida more generally a great honour and placing upon them the expectation of strong cooperation. And the farm was just the right distance away from the dam – about 25 km – which would allow Musallam to make the journey to the front line without his shoulder coming to pieces.

Almost as soon as he arrived, Musallam was in the thick of back-to-back tribal meetings. From the Abida there was Salem al-Sabran of the Damashqa and Governor Sultan al-Arada, also from a prominent sub-tribe of the Abida. From the Jebel al-Balaq range there was Abdalwahab al-Kibli and his cousin, a military police brigadier called Dhiyab al-Kibli, whose sub-tribe owned the nearer western end of the dam, the part of the mountain known as Jebel al-Balaq al-Qieli. From the far end of the range, there was Khaled al-Ajda, whose people owned the eastern end, the Jebel al-Balaq al-Ajda. They had all met Musallam before the Safer strike, and to their eyes he struck a heroic figure: his arm in a tight sling, the pain evident whenever he moved. Although the 13 days away from the battlefield had felt like an eternity to Musallam, to them it had been a blink of an eye and he was back already. His bravery, and the great sacrifice made by the coalition at Safer, made the tribes want to show they were brave and could make sacrifices too. He stressed the need for unity and putting old feuds behind them, but he also wanted the tribes racing each other to the dam, so he promised a brand-new Land Cruiser to whoever got there first. Like everything else in this war so far, it would be a race to see who reached the objectives first.

The plan would be simple: the Ajda would go for the east end and the Kibli the west. They would get powerful air, Apache and artillery support that would shift forward to the next objective as soon as friendly forces reached each control point. Musallam had pitched a more sophisticated version of the plan to MGM back in Abu Dhabi on 21 September and got approval. Everyone at the tribal gathering was happy with the plan too. Now for the timing of the attack. In Musallam's view, the best moment would be during Eid al-Adha: momentum had to be kept up and the Houthi–Saleh forces would not expect an attack then. The Yemenis shifted where they sat; things went quiet. This was when Musallam experienced something of the same basalt-like inflexibility that Yemeni partner forces sometimes displayed. In Aden, for instance, they simply would not attack during *qat* time each day and they refused to fight during Eid al-Fitr in July 2015. As 23 September 2015 came around, Musallam too experienced what had happened repeatedly during some of the early efforts to liberate Aden airport: the complete no-show of the Yemeni attack force. Only 40 of the promised 400 turned up. For a commander trying to rebuild his confidence, this was a hard blow for Musallam and a reminder that the tribes would fight this war when and where and how *they* wanted to.

When the rescheduled date for the attack was reached, on 29 September, Musallam feared another humiliating no-show but he quickly realised that he need not have worried. Governor al-Arada had gathered the tribes and Salem al-Sabran reassured Musallam: 'We know Marib; it's not going anywhere and neither are we. We're only doing this *now* for you, Musallam, for your martyrs, for your men.' Sheikh Salem understood loss: in addition to two dead sons, he had just lost a brother, killed by the Houthis in a skirmish on 24 September, during this Eid al-Adha holiday. Instead of a mourning tent at his house, he would accept condolences on the battlefield from the other tribal leaders, a show of resolve and a subtle challenge to them to match his bravery and commitment.

The 450 assembled tribesmen were split about equally between the Ajda and the Kibli. To the Emiratis' eyes, for a force that had been formally equipped by no one, they had a shockingly large number of Dushkas and 23-mm cannons with them. It turned out that many of these weapons had been taken from passing Ali Abdullah Saleh Republican Guard commanders from Marib as they had tried to defect with their weapons to Houthi-controlled Sanaa back in late 2014. The tribes liked heavy weapons and armoured vehicles, and the Emiratis would be careful to establish control points right behind the Forward Line of Own Troops (FLOT) beyond which Yemeni troops were not allowed to take their kit or ammunition home with them. They all wanted an Oshkosh as a war prize, but that was definitely *not* the deal.

Musallam gathered his commanders at around midday on 29 September at a strange hill called Jebel al-Zaman – a farm built inside an extinct volcano, like something a super-villain in a James Bond film would use as his lair. From the edge of the crater, all the commanders viewed their axes of advance through binoculars. The whole force would advance about 3 km on the flat, with the Jebel al-Balaq al-Ajda towering over their left, with flankers on its slopes and also further down on the edges of the Marib oasis, to the right. Khaled al-Ajda's left flank would then begin to climb to the east end of the dam, a 250-metre ascent over about 3 km of travel. The Kibli force, led by Abdalwahab al-Kibli would cross the Marib oasis exactly where the ancient dam was located and try to infiltrate to the western end of the dam via the slopes of the Jebel al-Balaq al-Kibli. With the hills overlooking both ends of the dam seized, Musallam's command group would drive across the Marib oasis and up the switchback access road to the dam, where they would raise flags to create a visible symbol of the impending victory in Marib – something that people in the UAE and across the Arab world could easily grasp as a sign that things were back on the right track after the heavy blow at Safer. Mohammed N.'s JTAC cell in their RG-31 MRAP would carry the long flagpole on which Musallam's UAE 'victory flag' would be raised alongside the Yemeni national flag. Then, after the UAE had taken this honour in the name of Sheikh Zayed, who had built the dam, the Saudi and Bahraini commanders would be escorted to the dam, each by a platoon of their respective special forces, and they too would raise their flags.

The battle for Marib Dam

The Prussian officer, General Helmuth von Moltke, famously said: 'No plan survives first contact with the enemy.' This proved to be true in the battle of Marib Dam. As is often the case, the attack started in good order and everything seemed to be under control. It was 15:00 hours when the wings of the attack separated near the Marib oasis. Thirty minutes of airstrikes opened the attack, with UAE F-16s and Mirage 2000-9s hitting the Houthi trenches identified by overhead reconnaissance and by visual spotting from Egyptian Hill. Then a 40-minute artillery barrage followed. The Ajda tribesmen trudged up the steep hills towards the east end of the dam as Musallam's small convoy, which included Governor Sultan al-Arada and Salem al-Sabran, went towards Marib oasis using the path cleared by the Kibli fighters. Surreally, Musallam's convoy found themselves unexpectedly surrounded by civilians who were coming out of holes in the side of the limestone cliffs. Numerous displaced persons had been living in these quarrying holes in the sides of Jebel al-Balaq al-Ajda, which had been the source of limestone for the great temples of Marib. Up above, the eastern end of the dam was quickly reached by the Ajda tribesmen. So far, so good.

There was no answer from the single Harris handheld radio given to the Kibli forces attacking the crest overlooking the western end of the dam, but Musallam edged his command group forward to begin crossing the oasis to reach the access road. Maybe then the comms would work better or they could get a look at the Jebel al-Balaq al-Kibli. Battle sounds grew closer from the foothills across the oasis to the front. Suddenly a Yemeni appeared out of nowhere and slammed his hands on the front of Musallam's MRAP. 'No! Turn back! You're going to die!' he shouted, in a frenzy. 'Governor Arada, don't go any further!' he said when Arada dismounted to speak to him. Arada looked at Musallam and said to the man: 'Where he [Musallam] goes, I go.' But the man kept begging Arada to let the soldiers go forward, but not Arada himself. The governor spoke to the man, who was clearly in shock: the Kibli had been ambushed and the fighting was intense up ahead. Then carloads of dead, dying and maimed Kiblis started to stream past Musallam's command group. Suddenly, sniper rounds began to chip and splinter the armoured glass windscreen of the command MRAP. The engine block of a chasse was shot through by what must have been an AM-50 anti-materiel rifle. As the wakil recalled, using the common phrase: 'Everyone could see death in each other's eyes.'

Yemenis were also hammering on Mohammed N.'s MRAP. They had two wounded further ahead in the orange groves but they couldn't get to them on foot or in their unarmoured chasse because of the intense sniping and Dushka fire. Mohammed N.

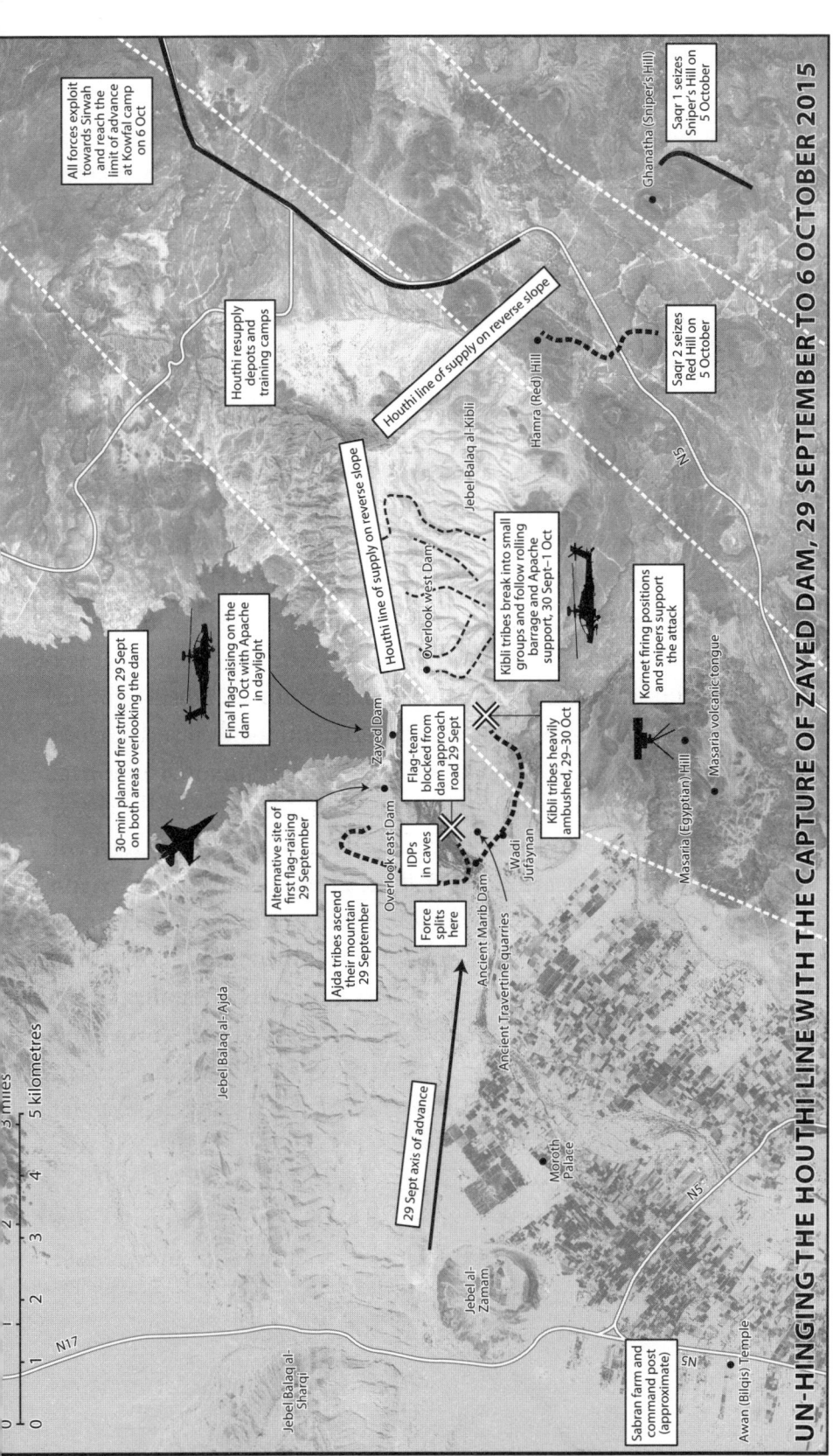

UN-HINGING THE HOUTHI LINE WITH THE CAPTURE OF ZAYED DAM, 29 SEPTEMBER TO 6 OCTOBER 2015

All forces exploit towards Sirwah and reach the limit of advance at Kowfal camp on 6 Oct

Saqr 1 seizes Sniper's Hill on 5 October

Ghanatha (Sniper's Hill)

Houthi resupply depots and training camps

Saqr 2 seizes Red Hill on 5 October

Houthi line of supply on reverse slope

Hamra (Red) Hill

N5

Jebel Balaq al-Kibli

Overlook West Dam

Kibli tribes break into small groups and follow rolling barrage and Apache support, 30 Sept–1 Oct

Final flag-raising on the dam 1 Oct with Apache in daylight

Houthi line of supply on reverse slope

30-min planned fire strike on 29 Sept on both areas overlooking the dam

Kornet firing positions and snipers support the attack

Zayed Dam

Flag-team blocked from dam approach road 29 Sept

Masaria (Egyptian) Hill

Masaria volcanic tongue

Alternative site of first flag-raising 29 September

Overlook east Dam

Kibli tribes heavily ambushed, 29–30 Oct

IDPs in caves

Wadi Jufaynan

Ajda tribes ascend their mountain 29 September

Force splits here

Ancient Marib Dam

Jebel Balaq al-Ajda

Ancient Travertine quarries

29 Sept axis of advance

Jebel al-Zamam

Moroth Palace

N5

Sabran farm and command post (approximate)

N17

Jebel Balaq al-Sharqi

SN

Awan (Bilqis) Temple

3 miles
5 kilometres

0 1 2 3 4 5 kilometres
0   1   2   3 miles

didn't hesitate, directing his driver to go down the sunken farm road towards where the Yemenis said the wounded were sheltering. Soon he was stuck between the lines, with fire criss-crossing past his vehicle from both sides of the firefight. His driver saw a mine on the sunken road, so they started reversing in the tight confines of the sunken track. Then everything went black. His young-looking air force JTAC and the driver thought they were dead. There was oily smoke all around and they were deafened. They had been knocked around by the blast of the land mine but their helmets had prevented their heads from suffering heavy blows. Their stack of radios stowed midway inside the crew compartment were less fortunate and radio comms were down, so Mohammed N. clambered back from the front cab past the metal turret basket and swung open the heavy back door of the vehicle. He waved at his Saudi deputy's Oshkosh behind them, making sure they stayed back. The front windscreen was covered by the buckled engine bonnet, which had been blown open by the mine strike. Mohammed N.'s driver could hear Dushka rounds pounding on it, a metre in front of his face.

Apaches were called in by the other MRAP but there was too much smoke and too many trees to be sure of any target down in the oasis. No one wanted to be accidentally targeted by an Apache; that would be game over. Instead, Mohammed N. and his men climbed down from the rear doorway and carefully worked their way back on foot in the sunken lane, clinging to its edges to avoid stepping on the possibly mined road itself. Mortar and machine-gun fire was dropping all around. As they got off the earthen bank, they were amazed to see the two badly wounded Yemenis under a tree, who they had driven straight past. They picked them up and made their way back to Musallam's command group. The empty RG-31 wasn't going anywhere fast after the mine strike and the Houthis might overrun it at any moment. Standard procedure called for radios and other sensitive equipment on board to be destroyed to avoid capture, so Mohammed N. made the call to put a 500-lb bomb on his vehicle, scattering bits and pieces of it for hundreds of metres – unfortunately including the all-important flagpole.

If the west end of the dam could not be reached by vehicle, Musallam would take the flag up the east side instead. As the sun started to fall behind the great mountains to the west, Musallam and his staff, plus a gaggle of television journalists, started the steep ascent to the dam's eastern end. Salem al-Sabran's body-guard unit fanned out on the path ahead and behind Musallam and his men. They passed Houthi corpses and body parts that the airstrikes had left behind, as well as dangerous unexploded munitions. A maddened Houthi fighter attacked the group from a cave mouth before being gunned down. There were mines sprinkled everywhere.

At a 10–15 per cent gradient it was a moderate hike in the heat, especially for an injured man, but after some hard minutes Musallam began to feel elated as he and the wakil and the tele-vision crews reached the crest and looked down on the dam. The wakil had cut a branch from a tree and shaved it into a rough flagpole and this was raised just before sunset and photo-graphed with the dam as the backdrop. But this was not the visible symbol of liberation that was needed. The photos and videos of the flag-raising on 29 September convey the tenuous foothold that the coalition had developed at only one end of the dam. Posing next to the flag, the officers are shown in the pictures with the unmistakeable stooped posture and strained expression of men under fire. Indeed, bullets were still landing all around, fired by Houthi snipers from the higher western cliffs at the other end of the dam.

The final clearance of Marib Dam

New and more specific orders were quick to arrive. The whole dam must be secured. New pictures of a new flag-raising were needed. A real flagpole needed to be raised at the monument to Sheikh Zayed on the dam itself, where he had stood all those years ago when the dam was completed. Though exhausted, Musallam went back to the Maribis and the coalition commanders in the evening to organise a new attack the following day. The problem, he learned, was simply that the Houthis had put a lot of fighters on top of the Jebel al-Balaq al-Kibli and had dug them in very deeply. The slopes facing the dam and the Marib oasis were pockmarked with ancient quarry workings that provided solid cover from artillery fire arcing in from overhead. There were mines everywhere in the undergrowth. Houthi snipers in caves and trenches had killed 15 Kibli fighters on the first day of the attack and prevented the Kibli fighters from getting to their many wounded, who were bleeding out on the mountainside at that very moment. In the Kibli attack force, not only did the men know each other, but they knew each other's families and were often related. To have 15 killed in a single day was a devastating blow, but they were tough fighters and wanted to continue the attack.

Musallam was a fighter too, and he grasped the situation and began solving the tactical problems one by one. First came the joint fires needed to suppress the enemy snipers and recover the wounded under the cover of darkness. That night, Mohammed N.'s Apaches put cannon and rocket fire into as many of the quarry workings as possible, using the direct fire capabilities of the attack helicopters to get under the rock overhangs of the Houthi firing positions. Little Sabr drones hovered in the dark, lasing the cave mouths for proximity airbursts shot from G-6 artillery pieces. Zaabi's Kornets sent guided missiles into enemy firing positions. All through the night and into the next day, the jebel (Arabic for hill) was bombed and shelled to give the Houthis no rest and no reinforcement.

Next came new tactics. Musallam and Brigadier Dhiyab al-Kibli, the military police general, devised a new scheme: the Kibli would be broken down into little squads like the Houthis themselves were, and later that night infiltrate through the Houthi minefields and lines. Then, on 30 September and the early hours of 1 October, the Kibli tribesmen would clear the western end of the dam. They knew the terrain but it would still be a hell of a fight. As dawn broke, the UAE, Saudi and Bahraini special operations platoons attached to Musallam's flank put all their snipers onto counter-sniping duties. All day long on 30 September, the Kibli fighters worked their way methodically up the mined slopes. An artillery fire-plan covered their ascent, 'lifting' 100 metres further up the slope every 30 minutes, with the fighters following as closely behind the explosive barrage as they dared. At this micro-tactical level, this was not much different from the fighting at Monte Casino in the Second World War: steep slopes, dust, artillery, and the final bayonet charge to end each strongpoint.

As darkness fell on 30 September, the Kibli enjoyed close support that no one at Monte Cassino could have imagined: Apaches putting Hellfire missiles accurately into enemy-occupied quarry workings and trenches. That night they were gunning constantly, as they had done on the evening of 9 September on Masaria, sometimes even hovering below the crest of the jebel to allow them to clear out rock overhangs from beneath with guns and rockets. Only the Apache could get this close to the enemy and safely strike this close to friendly forces, all undertaken in the dark of night.

In the end, though, it came down to what have been known affectionately since the First World War as the Poor Bloody

Infantry. The Kiblis went sangar by sangar, fighting hand to hand. About 100 Houthis had been up on the Jebel al-Balaq al-Kibli at the start of the attack – a huge concentration of forces by their standards. They were split into about a dozen strongpoints, each with snipers, a Kornet, a couple of Dushkas and some infantrymen and runners to distribute the multiple days' worth of ammunition stockpiled on the summit. Firepower seems to have accounted for nearly half of the defenders, with bodies scattered all around; some from the days before, wrapped in blankets, but most forgotten in holes, suspended on rock ledges, or blown into strange shapes by repeated explosions.

About 60 Houthis were still alive when the summit was assaulted. Their pitiful defensive shelters were full of needles and bags of glucose fluids for intravenous injection (to hold off dehydration and malnutrition), plus the elephant pills, *qat* and even a cassette deck to play recordings of Abdul-Malik al-Houthi's sermons. Dirty rags were laid out on the rocks to catch overnight condensation for them to drink. At about 04:00 hours the last resistance ended. Fifty Kiblis lay dead on the hill. There were 20 Houthis left alive – mostly too wounded to fight, or teenagers crying their eyes out.

As the sun came up on 2 October, the UAE, Yemeni, Saudi and Bahraini flags were raised on the dam itself, next to the famous painting of Sheikh Zayed. The television crews got footage of the flags flying and a UAE Apache hovering over the dam in daylight – a first for the nocturnal attack helicopters and thus a powerful demonstration of full control. Finally, having fulfilled his promise to MBZ, it was time for Musallam to take care of his arm. 'What an effort,' MGM reflected. 'He fought the whole battle with his arm half hanging off!' Musallam now asked to return to hospital. In his last act in Marib, he instructed all the Maribi tribes and coalition forces to give Ali Saif their

PURSUIT OPERATIONS BEYOND MARIB AND THE TANTALISING OPTION OF ADVANCING ON SANAA, OCTOBER 2015

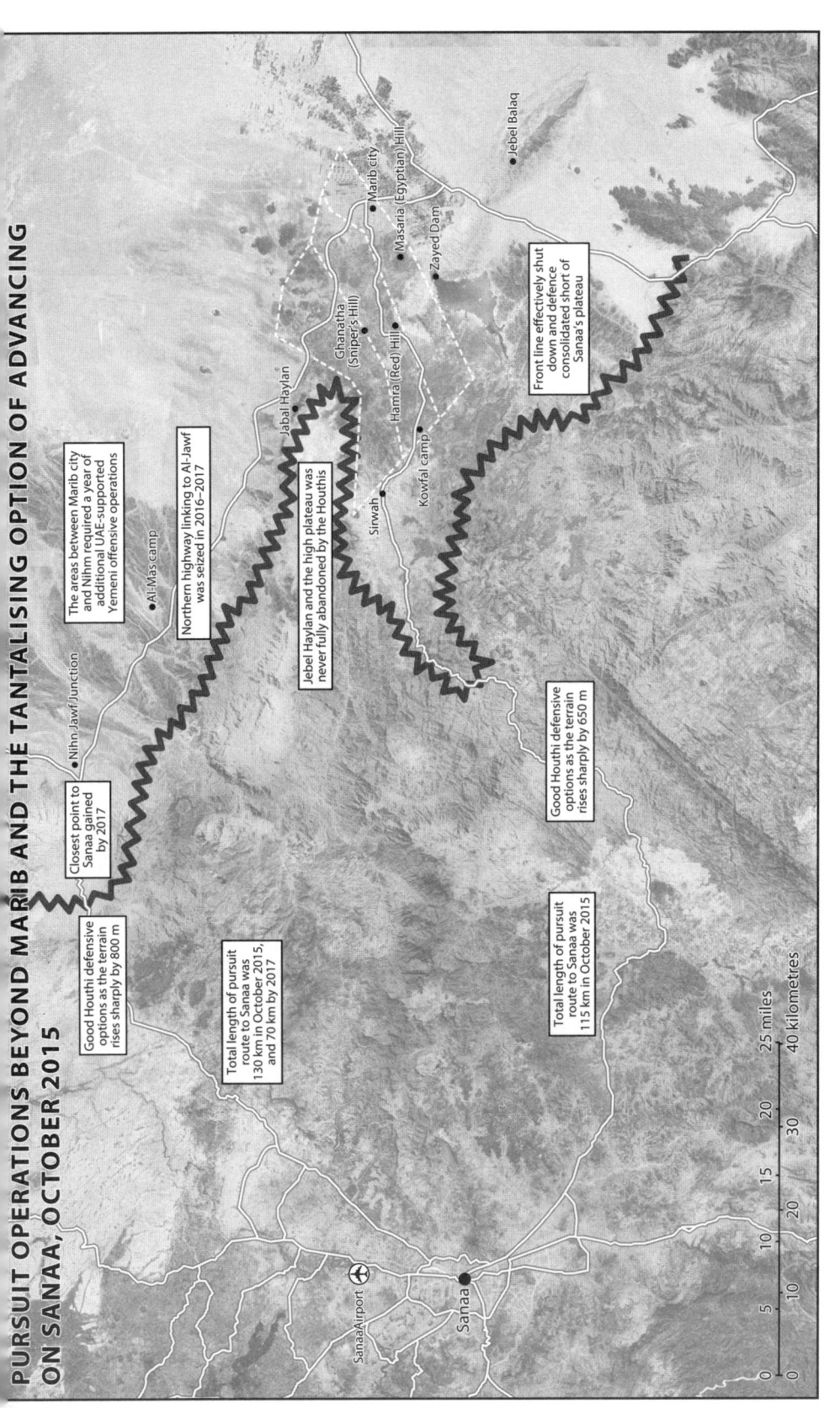

The areas between Marib city and Nihm required a year of additional UAE-supported Yemeni offensive operations

Northern highway linking to Al-Jawf was seized in 2016–2017

Jebel Haylan and the high plateau was never fully abandoned by the Houthis

Front line effectively shut down and defence consolidated short of Sanaa's plateau

Closest point to Sanaa gained by 2017

Good Houthi defensive options as the terrain rises sharply by 800 m

Good Houthi defensive options as the terrain rises sharply by 650 m

Total length of pursuit route to Sanaa was 130 km in October 2015, and 70 km by 2017

Total length of pursuit route to Sanaa was 115 km in October 2015

Jebel Balaq

Marib city

Masana (Egyptian) Hill

Zayed Dam

Ghanatha (Sniper's Hill)

Hamra (Red) Hill

Jabal Haylan

Kowfal camp

Sirwah

Al-Mas camp

Nihn/Jawf Junction

SanaaAirport

Sanaa

25 miles

40 kilometres

0 5 10 15 20

0 10 20 30

full backing to finish the fight. For Musallam, 'those Marib days were the most memorable moments of my life'.

The end of resistance at Marib Dam brought about the hoped-for collapse of Houthi–Saleh resistance along the front line. The Ashrafi tribes, sensing that defeat was imminent, ceased fighting on 2 October and the Marib oasis quieted. The front lines had hardly moved on the Saqr fronts since Eid but now they began to lunge forwards as the Houthi forces fell back and ceased to resupply or reinforce the front. On 5 October, Saqr 2 reached its objective, the Red Hill, and Ali Saif radioed Sohail K. to urge him to take the opportunity to break through the final few hundred metres to Sniper's Hill. 'I'm already done!' he heard back from Sohail, and the headquarters at Safer exploded with cheers. Handguns were fired through the roof of the command tent in a traditional form of celebration. But Sohail had not needed to urge the Yemenis on. When they saw the enemy on the Saqr 2 front collapsing, the Yemenis surged forward on their own into the enemy positions to loot. And it was not only Saqr 1 forces streaming forward. There had been a mysterious force of chasses and fighters loitering at Sohail's rear for weeks. After patient watching and waiting, these professional looters now saw their moment and joined the rush.

The pursuit rolled 50 km west to Sirwah, where the main Houthi–Saleh logistics hub for the battle had been positioned. Here, on 6 October, the Emiratis found a truckload of new Iranian copies of the Kornet and also its RU140TK thermal scope. For many of the officers present in Marib at this moment, the sense of victory was tinged with regret. For them, there will always be a question of whether the Houthis might have kept retreating all the way back to Sanaa and even beyond, if they had been pressed. Something similar was unfolding at that exact moment at the Bab el-Mandeb, where an Emirati armoured bat-tlegroup was rolling up the Red Sea coastal highway.

But this regret should not take away from the achievements of the Marib operation. The UAE bounced back from its greatest national tragedy and was back on the attack in under five days. They had shown for the first time that the Houthi mountain men could be beaten in the hills. The ferocity of the fighting showed itself in the metrics: each artillery tube had fired an average of 125 rounds a day in Marib. About 385 Kornets and 200 laser-guided 155-mm shells had been expended. Averaging various claims and reports, including some by local medical centres, around 400 Yemeni troops and 1,700 Houthi–Saleh fighters were killed in the battle, and also 56 Emiratis, 12 Saudis and three Bahrainis. The coalition had been, as Faisal T. remembered, 'in battle for six weeks of continuous fighting'. It had been a national trial by fire.

For the men returning from Marib, their departure from the battlefield was a jarring transition. With a new UAE task force commander in place to handle the defensive consolidation of Marib by mid-October, Ali Saif was ordered to take leave, begin-ning 17 October, although he would be back in Marib later the same year to continue driving the Houthis into the mountains at Nihm. A trophy for his commander-in-chief, Ali Saif brought out with him a Houthi commander's *jambiya* (dagger), pierced by a bullet, recovered from Masaria. After 45 days of five hours' sleep a night, in the blacked-out battlefield, with no earthlight, his eyes could not adjust to the bright lights at Sharurah and back home in the UAE. Mohammed S. remembered walking around in Dubai, on his return, as if it was a dream. Ahmed H. realised how close he had come to death when his head had nearly been caved in by a mortar shell that struck the car door that he had been dozing against seconds earlier. As he left the war zone, he simply could not believe that he had survived.

PART THREE

THE RACE TO MUKALLA

IX

A WAR OF CHOICE?

As coalition forces broke through in Marib on 5 October, the UAE had won two clear battlefield victories in the war: the liberation of Aden and now the repulse of the Houthi–Saleh forces from Marib city. A third victory was building on the Red Sea coast, where the Aden armoured battlegroup was liberating the Bab el-Mandeb Strait from Houthi–Saleh forces. But then something happened that reminded everyone of the other enemy in Yemen – AQAP and other violent Salafi jihadi groups.

At 06:30 hours on 6 October, three UAE sites in Aden were hit by powerful car bombs. Back in Abu Dhabi, aerial imagery showed plumes of smoke covering the main UAE base at Bir Ahmed, the nearby Al-Qasr Hotel, and a large UAE safe house called the Saleh bin Fareed house near the refinery district of Little Aden. At Bir Ahmed, known as 'the admin area' to UAE soldiers, a car bomb had smashed into the entry checkpoint, killing two nearby Yemenis. The 25-metre-long face of the Saleh bin Fareed house had been torn off by an even bigger car bomb and a wing of the building had burned to the ground, killing seven Yemenis. The mansion had previously been the fondly remembered launchpad for the UAE's liberation of Aden earlier in the summer. Now Al-Qaeda had done what the Houthis never could, wrecking the headquarters from which the UAE had directed the liberation of Aden.

At the Al-Qasr Hotel, a third car bomb made it right through the Yemeni-secured gatehouse and up to the front doors of the hotel, where Vice President and Prime Minister of Yemen Khaled Bahah was based. Like good bodyguards, the six-man UAE protection detail, seconded from the Presidential Special Guard, reacted to secure the entrance and protect their 'principal', Bahah. Four of them were killed instantly by the car bomb as they took aim at it, and a fifth died two days afterwards from his wounds, leaving only one survivor of the unit. Along with seven Yemenis also killed, the final death toll for the day was 20, including five Emiratis. Counter-terrorism was back at the forefront of thinking in UAE military headquarters.

Counter-terrorism within a full-scale war

The UAE's clash with Al-Qaeda in Aden had been building for many months. On 29 June, nearly a month before the liberation of Aden at the end of July, an intelligence fusion and targeting cell had been activated at the Presidential Guard headquarters at Mahawe to prepare for the stabilisation and counter-terrorism phase that would follow the clearance of Houthi–Saleh forces from Aden city. The Presidential Guard knew that AQAP and the Islamic State would feed on post-conflict chaos 'like cancer feeds on sugar', in the words of MGM. Even before the battle of Aden had fully concluded, AQAP was assessed to be the culprit when a bomb was discovered hidden in the room that the Aden task force commander Colonel Ali T. was due to occupy at his new headquarters in the Qasr Hotel – built into his bed, in fact. Other rumours caused a scare that Al-Qaeda was also planning to poison the food being delivered to the Qasr Hotel headquarters. It seemed that Al-Qaeda had also been putting forethought into how to strike hard and strike first.

In August 2015, as Sohail had been directing airstrikes from his Marib city safe house, both the UAE and AQAP were preparing for a showdown in Aden. From the beginning of Aden's Popular Committees, some Al-Qaeda fighters or mujaheddin sympathisers had been present in the resistance forces, but the Adenese had been careful never to let Al-Qaeda commanders run whole committees or whole fronts on their own. Now these Salafi jihadis all flocked to one place, the Sheikh Uthman side of the city near the Qasr Hotel and the UAE's forward operating base. A man known by the *kunya* Abu Salem al-Taizzi (real name Wail Saif Ali al-Muqbal) had begun seizing vacant government buildings as soon as the Houthis evacuated Aden, and he set up checkpoints around them to close off entire streets of Sheikh Uthman, which he claimed as his territory.

As the Emiratis closely watched Abu Salem, they could see a pattern quickly forming. A dozen assassinations of southern separatist leaders took place in the areas near Abu Salem's enclaves, always targeting the local forces who opposed the return of the Hadi-led Yemeni government and Ali Mohsen al-Ahmar's Islahi generals from the north. Eventually 50 such killings would take place, including that of the governor of Aden, Brigadier General Jaafar Mohammed Sayyed, whom the Emiratis held in high esteem for his battlefield efforts in Aden, much as they came to esteem Brigadier General Abd-Rabu al-Shadadi in Marib. Large quantities of explosives were being brought into Abu Salem's enclave by a mystery donor up north. Abu Salem's enforcer and deputy was known by two names, Helmi al-Zengi and Ali al-Kurdi, and he was a mujaheddin who had been fighting to prevent an independent southern Yemen on Ali Mohsen's orders since 1994. The word on the street was that Abu Salem was now apparently also a local leader in the Islamic State in Yemen (IS-Y) – the local branch of the Islamic State group controlling much of Iraq and Syria in 2015. At about the same time as Abu Salem arrived, communiqués started appearing online that declared the 'Wilayat Aden-Abyan' to be a new Islamic State province.

Countering Islamic State and Al-Qaeda efforts to gain a foothold in post-battle Aden, the UAE counter-terrorism forces were also getting into position in the city. The UAE leadership aimed to mount a hard, simultaneous blow against all known AQAP and IS-Y targets as soon as possible. The CIA and US JSOC were keen to get back into their old base at Al-Anad, which had been abandoned since the battle of Aden started in March 2015. Politicians in Washington, DC were much less keen, in case it gave the appearance of US support for the coalition war effort in Yemen against the Houthis, which was viewed negatively in the United States due to collateral damage incidents and the worsening humanitarian conditions in the country.

While the Americans debated among themselves, the UAE established a counter-terrorism fusion cell in Aden city itself on 12 August. It was led by SOC's Lieutenant Colonel Salem D., who had led the first SOC advisors to aid the city's defence in April 2015 and who had been in the city all through the battle against the Houthis. He had returned now to bring together all the key players – the Americans on one side, and the UAE intelligence agencies and their Yemeni partners on the other. In preparation, Salem had been reading US General Stanley McChrystal's 2014 book *My Share of the Task*, which chronicled how JSOC smashed Al-Qaeda in Iraq in 2006–8 with an intense special forces raiding campaign. Salem was aiming to replicate McChrystal's 'continuous targeting cycle' in Aden, in which each raid provides intelligence to launch immediate follow-on actions before terrorist networks could scatter or adapt or destroy valuable intelligence. The cycle required terrorist-hunters to 'find' targets, 'fix' them to a certain time and place, 'finish' them by capturing or killing them, and then 'exploit' new intelligence quickly to restart the cycle. But the 'find' part of the targeting cycle needed good human intelligence and even Salem's most loyal and forthcoming sources were reticent to talk about AQAP or IS-Y. It was Salem who had heard from a trusted Yemeni friend: 'We are mixed. We are one fabric,' and this dilemma would echo constantly throughout the counter-terrorism fight in Yemen. Where did AQAP or IS-Y start and stop? How much did they overlap?

Then suddenly it was not an academic exercise. The bombings on 6 October in Aden and the seven Emirati fatalities required a strong response. The UAE struck back almost immediately. In Aden, the counter-terrorism cell rousted the local police and security forces into cordoning off Abu Salem's enclaves. Though given a chance to leave the city, to avoid an urban battle and civilian casualties, Abu Salem and Helmi al-Zengi chose to fight it out, Mogadishu-style, employing rooftop Rocket-Propelled Grenade (RPG) ambushes to defend their streets. A UAE Apache used precise Hellfire missiles to blow out individual rooms in the government buildings from which machine-gun fire was originating. When Abu Salem and Helmi al-Zengi finally made a run for it, they were allowed to leave and then followed by an Apache. The attack helicopter let their vehicles make it as far as open country, where there was no risk of collateral damage, and then launched Hellfire missiles into the cars, killing all occupants.

To the east, in AQAP's growing emirate, UAE airstrikes then destroyed three known terrorist leadership sites in Zinjibar. Amazingly, AQAP sent back howls of outrage through intermediaries that the suicide attacks in Aden had been IS-Y, not AQAP. Ali Mohsen said the same and asked why the Emiratis were bombing Al-Qaeda. 'Striking us is not your fight, Houthis are your enemy,' AQAP's Khalid al-Batarfi reminded the UAE commander in Aden. Indeed, IS-Y did claim the attacks in Aden, but this mattered little to the Emiratis, who viewed AQAP and IS-Y as the same enemy. 'We saw Afghanistan and how all the groups mixed there. We saw Syria and Iraq, and how Al-Qaeda people turned into [Islamic State] there. In Yemen, they all used the same bomb-makers and money-movers,' one Emirati counter-terrorism official explained. The strikes by UAE aircraft were in a town, Zinjibar, which had been occupied by AQAP for many months. Just months later in Mukalla, the UAE's assessment of overlap between AQAP and IS-Y would prove to be prescient.

Recommitting to the liberation of Mukalla

The war in Yemen had begun in March 2015 and it was now six months later, with no appreciable efforts to roll back Al-Qaeda's gains in Hadramaut, Shabwa, Abyan and Bayda governorates. A patchwork of cities was now controlled by the Sons of Hadramaut, including an Abyan cluster (Zinjibar and Jaar) and a Hadramaut cluster (Mukalla, As-Shihr and Ghayl Ba Wazir). 'Shaping' actions, in the form of Qassem al-Raimi's rolling assassination campaigns of Popular Committee leaders, were unfolding in all the areas separating these two clusters – Shoqra and Ahwar on the coast, and Lawdar, Mahfad, Habban and Azzan in the foothills parallel to the coast. It was already quite easy for AQAP leaders like Wahayshi to move from one end of the emerging 500-km long undeclared emirate to another. Soon, they would probably be able to drive from Zinjibar in the west all the way to As-Shihr in the east, entirely on the blacktop coastal highway. Already the area controlled by the Sons of Hadramaut had a population of around 800,000. And they seemed to be eyeing the oil production areas of Wadi Hadramaut, which were connected to the storage tanks and export terminals at As-Shihr.

For MBZ, and for the Americans, AQAP's expansion was a growing concern. In the six months since Mukalla had been lost to the government, a conservative estimate of the riches gained by the Sons of Hadramaut in Mukalla alone was £235 million, including about £80 million looted from bank vaults, at least £100 million from port operations, and around £55 million from other sources that included extortion of government departments and businesses, plus the sale of oil from the large storage tanks at Dhabba and As-Shihr. A few dozen major trading conglomerates with extensions all over the Islamic world were still based in Mukalla and their operations would continue to be taxed by AQAP. The numerous exchange houses in Mukalla could become a huge 'threat finance' hub for terrorist networks and attacks around the globe. Inside Yemen, money talked: flush with cash, AQAP was already drawing hundreds of new recruits into its training camps, both from the poor hill tribes and the demobilised 2nd MRC units. These recruits came for the money, but might stay for the ideology: given time, these recruits would be indoctrinated. Facing what looked like a small army, the Hamoum and Wadi Hadramaut tribes were laughed at by the Sons of Hadramaut when they had warned the force to leave Mukalla in the summer of 2015. The lesson was clear: any tribal threat to evict AQAP from the port city needed to be backed by strong coalition support.

Among the UAE leadership back in Abu Dhabi, there was growing anger at AQAP's coup in Mukalla. Khalid al-Batarfi was swanning around in fancy cars and living the high life in AQAP propaganda videos. Al-Qaeda was starting to talk of running ministries of interior, finance and Hisba (religious enforcement). They even had smart-looking traffic police. Next would come a call for recognition as a legitimate government. In the opening days of the takeover, the Hadramaut Dialogue Council had sent envoys to President Hadi in Riyadh and the envoys had returned claiming that he had praised their enforcement of 'peace and stability' in the city. The international media seemed tickled by the idea that Mukalla could emerge as a well-run terrorist enclave 'with happy people inside it', as Reuters quoted one unnamed diplomat as speculating. HDC intermediaries started to gently probe Hadi in Riyadh: when might the government reopen the airport? In October 2015 they next tried to negotiate an oil revenue-sharing deal with Hadi, offering 75 per cent of the profits to the government if the government made international oil companies restart production at the Wadi Hadramaut oilfields. As I noted in a 2016 report: 'The government refused, but the offer underlined the stark reality: AQAP was on the verge of developing an emirate at least as resilient and economically viable as anything the Islamic State had managed to build in Iraq, Syria, or Libya.'

At this point, Musallam met once again with MBZ, and this time they talked about Al-Qaeda. It was 11 October 2015 and Musallam's arm was still in a sling from his latest surgery. The new deaths at Aden were on the minds of everyone, especially these two men – the commander-in-chief and his head of special operations and counter-terrorism. The UAE was starting to significantly harden its Yemeni bases with one or two additional layers of checkpoints and other defences. But mostly MBZ wanted to take the initiative and go on the attack. A patient hunter, like his tribal forebears, Musallam was already fully turned back towards the original JTF-291 mission to liberate Mukalla.

The Americans were keen too. Their own political concerns about the broader Yemen war and their force protection restrictions meant that the CIA and JSOC would probably not be getting back on the ground in wartime Yemen any time soon. That just made them more interested in any move the Emiratis could make on the ground to break up the AQAP caliphate before it consolidated its stranglehold on Mukalla. The CIA briefed the UAE leaders on their extraordinary sensor and strike capabilities in Yemen, astounding even the most experienced Emirati counter-terrorism officials. American technical capabilities were undoubtedly impressive, but Musallam knew that this would be a battle of human intelligence and key leader engagement as much as a war of listening posts and drones. He teased the Americans, saying 'our ancestors invented the targeting cycle', and recalling the way that tribal trackers and spies could follow a man for years in order to exact vengeance on a victim who would respect their persistence even as he died. On 6 November, Musallam got the go-ahead to fully develop a Mukalla liberation concept of operations. Azzan got a secure message from Musallam: 'Your turn is next, be ready.'

AQAP's caliphate, one year in

Intelligence Preparation of the Battlefield (IPB) is the systematic process of analysing all mission variables within an area of interest to determine their effect on future operations. For Azzan, whose objective had been Mukalla from day one, that survey of the enemy, terrain and 'human terrain' of southern Hadramaut would be taken to obsessive lengths. Azzan had time, as the months rolled by at his Yemeni camps. He had learned Mukalla's streets like the back of his hand, albeit from a distance, by staring at maps, overhead imagery, photography and video of the city for hundreds of hours. But he needed human voices from inside Mukalla to know more than just the topography and his potential axes of advance. He wanted to know the enemy,

MUKALLA UNDER AQAP CONTROL

Dhabba oil storage tanks

190th Air Def base

190th Air Def HQ

Rayan airport

Rayan

27 Mech Bde HQ

Rayan Roundabout

Controlled by AQAP commander Riyadh Omar al-Shaab (Abu Omar al-Nahdi), a Hamoum tribesman who was the most industrious tactical commander when it came to wiring whole facilities for explosive demolition. He showed pro-Islamic State proclivities during the occupation of Mukalla and later defected to the group

Controlled by AQAP commander Sadiq bin Saydar, who shut down the *qat* markets; taxed the oil trucking businesses; and gender-segregated Hadramaut University

AQAP established coast-watcher observation posts along the coast

Hadramaut University

CSF Camp

Rukub

2 MRC HQ

Ras Khalaf coastal defence HQ

Rabwat Baghshan

Hotel Hadramaut

Central Prison

Courts Complex

Chinese Bridge

Mukalla Main Port

Hadramout Governor's Palace

Al-Aroud Sq

Ibn Sina

Controlled by AQAP commanders Marwan ba Duways, supported by Hisba commanders like Abu bin Taleb al-Katheri (also known as Abu Noura) and Mohammed Saleh al-Ghurabi, a former army officer

Controlled by AQAP bomb-maker, Farih al-Somali who ran the main explosives workshops from around the port

Controlled by AQAP commanders Khaled Salem bin Sabri and Sayram al-Sanani

✳ AQAP major checkpoint

| 0 | 1 | 2 | 3 | 4 | 5 | 6 | 7 | 8 | 9 | 10 miles |

| 0 | 2 | 4 | 6 | 8 | 10 | 12 | 14 | 16 kilometres |

their vulnerabilities, and how to reduce their recruitment and increase defections from their ranks when the liberation battle drew close. He also needed the basics: who were they? What was their pattern of life? That would make them easier to 'find, fix and finish' as the Americans called the process of locating, tracking and killing terrorists.

In theory, it didn't look that hard to get spies in and out of Mukalla. The city had half-emptied when the Sons of Hadramaut took over, but then people had gradually returned from Wadi Hadramaut and Mahra when things seemed to have calmed down in Mukalla. Fishermen still went out to sea every day and truckers came and went just as they had before. There was no travel ban per se. But when UAE intelligence officers had tried to sneak in, they had been turned back by the hill tribes: 'They will smell you coming,' the tribes warned. This was a job for Yemenis only.

Normal people could still come and go relatively freely, and they gave rich accounts of life in occupied Mukalla, but the local tribal leaders whom the UAE wanted to talk to were watched closely. If they were allowed to leave at all, they had to account for the time and were not expected to be gone for long, which made them too nervous to travel all the way to Abu Dhabi or Riyadh for a proper debriefing. Those who made it out were nervous wrecks and always rushed to get back. JTF-291.2 were a good source of smugglers who could get people, communications equipment and weapons in and out, but the risk of exposure and execution was high. And when the Mukalla leaders did come out, they spoke like businessmen: they were not offering something for nothing; they were careful calculators, not glory-hunting freedom fighters.

Azzan's initial 'priority information requirement' was to understand the nature of his enemy and how they were viewed by the local people. Initially, the Sons of Hadramaut had been unexpectedly gentle in their treatment of most of the denizens of Mukalla, changing almost nothing about daily life, as a typical denizen of Mukalla saw it. 'The locals were pleasantly surprised,' as Tawfeek al-Ganad, Mohammed al-Katheri and Gregory D. Johnsen noted in their 2020 report, entitled *387 Days of Power: How Al-Qaeda Seized, Held and Ultimately Lost a Yemeni City.* 'They didn't stop people, including women, from walking in the street,' the report noted. 'They didn't prevent people from watching football matches or listening to music, and they didn't fly their famous black flags.' 'Maybe it was a new form of Al-Qaeda,' a local reporter wrote for the *New York Times.* 'Maybe it wasn't Al-Qaeda at all.'

But AQAP was certainly in the mix, as shown not only by Khalid al-Batarfi's obnoxious antics but also by numerous AQAP online communiqués and by intelligence coming out of the city. For the AQAP emir Wahayshi, this was a do-over, a chance to incorporate all the lessons learned by Al-Qaeda as it had tried and failed to hold on to territory in places like Yemen, Syria and Iraq in previous years. Now, in the summer of 2015, Wahayshi had three golden rules: employ what AQAP called an 'invisible hand' and let locals take the lead; try to improve services; and do not harshly or strictly impose sharia law from the outset. These steps would build tolerance for AQAP's presence, he argued, which in time could be consolidated into active support.

Azzan could already see that the 'invisible hand' approach was working. On 13 April 2015, just over a week after the take-over, the Sons of Hadramaut had committed to a division of labour with the civilian Hadramaut Dialogue Council. The perimeter security of the city would stay with the Sons of Had-ramaut, which meant AQAP, and most Al-Qaeda fighters and almost all the foreign fighters were camped out at the edges of the towns. In the urban area, the state's police stations were shuttered and their role was taken over by the Committee for the Promotion of Virtue and the Prevention of Vice (Hisba) and by sharia courts that processed cases with great efficiency compared with the state system. These law enforcement agencies were staffed by locals and moved around the city unmasked, to show they were Hadramis and to differentiate themselves from non-local AQAP members, who were mostly still masked due to the ongoing US drone campaign.

Most things stayed about the same, because Mukalla was hardly a liberal playground to begin with. The Hadramis, even the urban elites, were conservative by Yemeni coastal standards. Whereas the Communists had brought mixed-gender coeducation, coffee shops, swimming pools and beaches to cosmopolitan Aden, it was very different in Mukalla. Even prior to Al-Qaeda's takeover, there was much less openness in Mukalla to mixed-gender British Council schools, women's gyms and other experiments that had been introduced in Aden. For Al-Qaeda, conservatism was not enough. After taking over in 2015, they also banned urban *qat* markets and group *qat* chews from May 2015 onwards. Then they introduced growing segregation of the sexes in the university, on the streets, and even at picnics or traditional celebrations. Public wedding parades and many other colourful moments disappeared from life in Mukalla.

In civil affairs, the Hadramaut Dialogue Council looked to most people to be in charge in Mukalla, As-Shihr and other towns. Under the surface, AQAP placed one of their men in each ministry branch and major business to oversee the technocrats. Improved provision of services was a focus area for AQAP propaganda. Wahayshi had advised Al-Qaeda's Saharan emir Abdul-Malik Droukdel: 'Try to win the people over through the conveniences of life. It will make them sympathise with us and make them feel that their fate is tied to ours.' Around the world, newspaper editors and think-tanks had instantly fallen in love with the deliciously provocative idea that the people of Mukalla might be better off under Al-Qaeda. There was even some truth in this at first, when the Sons of Hadramaut and the Hadramaut Dialogue Council were still a mystery to Mukalla people and AQAP was showing them its friendliest face – even including an ice-cream-eating festival.

Yet it was all an illusion because most of the achievements were not sustainable and merely helped AQAP to get itself firmly entrenched in what could otherwise have been an ungovernable mess of half a million angry inhabitants. For instance, the HDC could initially pay salaries because it burned through the cash reserves looted from banks. Importers were not taxed, but shippers were, resulting in lower costs for the Mukalla trading elite but the same or higher prices for the street-level consumers in the end. Major businesses were fleeced in a way that probably could not last indefinitely; tax rebates and free electricity were given to the people but that system began to break down after a few months. Small, well-publicised deliveries of aid to hospitals and poor people made the Sons of Hadramaut appear kindly but these were, in reality, a drop in the ocean of what was needed. In a much-publicised success, as the authors of *387 Days of Power* later revealed, AQAP empowered a young engineering student to overhaul the electricity system, repairing weak links and reducing payment tariffs. But again, it was in large part an illusion: electricity supply improved because businesses were cut off from the grid at night to support the curfew and because some of the most prolific users of the grid, the rich, had mostly fled the city. Popular though these steps were, value was only being transferred, not created, and the scheme lived on borrowed time. It was a cheap trick that could not last, especially not after its architect was killed.

Death of the architect

On 9 June 2015, Nasir al-Wahayshi and a small group of associates were caught by the CIA in the open, on the Mukalla corniche, where modern streetlights cast a pleasant soft glow at night and the flotsam and jetsam of plastic bottles and trash lapped up against the rocky shore. Assuming that this super-secret mission used the same approach as most counter-terrorist strikes in Yemen, one CIA MQ-9 Reaper drone watched to ensure civilians were safely distant, and then two others each put a pair of Hellfire missiles into Wahayshi's gathering. The small 45-kg explosive payloads would each have filled a 20-metre-wide area with explosive effect and fragmentation. They were spaced just far enough apart in time to prevent fratricide – explosions that might destroy a following warhead before it reached its assigned detonation point. One ... two ... three ... four. The screens in US headquarters in Langley, Virginia, and in the Middle East would have gone blinding white as the thermal effects overloaded the full-motion video. When the image returned there were a few mangled bodies on the ground. Amazingly, Wahayshi was not killed instantly and survived for three undoubtedly painful days before dying on 12 June and being eulogised by AQAP on 16 June.

The loss of Wahayshi seemed to unbalance AQAP's strategy in Mukalla, with its new emir Qassem al-Raimi adopting increasingly harsh measures with the population. Wahayshi was the seventh senior AQAP leader to be killed by drone strike in Mukalla in the first half of 2015. Three senior sharia officials – Harith bin Ghazi al-Nadhiri, Nasser bin Ali al-Ansi and Ibrahim

Sulayman Mohammed al-Rubaysh – were all dead, as were three AQAP spokesmen, Egyptian Muhannad al-Ghallab (Abu Hafs al-Masri), Mahmoud Abdalhamid and Ghalib al-Quaiti (Abu Hajjar). A bulk cash storage site had also been hit by the United States, burning 10 million Yemeni rial (£35,000). To Al-Qaeda leaders, Mukalla had begun to feel like a death trap, and they displayed growing bitterness towards the population, any of whom might betray their location at any time.

The new AQAP leader Qassem al-Raimi was not nearly as deliberative as his predecessor. While Wahayshi was being carefully groomed and mentored by Bin Laden, Raimi was training foot soldiers in dusty camps. Wahayshi was genuinely liked by those he dealt with, a charming man you could do business with; Raimi was a good tactician, but humourless, hot-headed and confrontational. With no hesitation, Raimi executed two suspected spies on 17 June – Saudi foreign fighters who were described as having been responsible for betraying Wahayshi's location. Raimi had their bodies tied to wooden planks, crucifixion-style, and left them to rot in the sun for three days on Mukalla's busiest bridge, the Chinese Bridge on the creek in the centre of town. Then he sent a message to Mukalla's fishermen, who were subjected to a terrorisation campaign to seek out spies among them, with one suspect executed as an example to the others. The use of cell phones was strictly prohibited and those leaving Mukalla had to designate hostages to be punished if they did not return.

Under Raimi, AQAP became more prominent and crueller in enforcing *hudad* punishments for violating sharia law, such as the amputation of hands, other corporal punishments, and even execution. The Hisba religious police vented their frustration at being disrespected, publicly stoning a woman to death for alleged immorality. Another woman was hanged after an allegation of witchcraft, then left suspended under the Chinese Bridge. A number of men were publicly flogged with whips for smoking hashish and for trading *qat*. For the first time, AQAP started to demolish traditional family shrines or *turba*. Schools and mosques were increasingly taken over – and sometimes renamed – by AQAP.

By October, the first large anti-AQAP youth protests had begun in Mukalla and Al-Qaeda started 'disappearing' journalists and other critics after banners appeared that read 'No Al-Qaeda After Today. Get Out.' Half of the 60 members of the Hadramaut Dialogue Council resigned when their pay cheques stopped coming and thereafter these local leaders started to criticise AQAP, calling for the Sons of Hadramaut to make good on a promise they made in April 2015 to leave the city after a year. If the city notables of Mukalla had thought they controlled AQAP, they had deceived themselves. AQAP and less than half the Hadramaut Dialogue Council now ruled the city. It was AQAP that held all the explosives and weapons looted from the military bases and it was AQAP that still had the vast majority of the money looted from the city. AQAP and its hired henchmen numbered 2,000–3000 fighters at the most, yet they were controlling a densely populated metropolis of more than half a million. They managed this only because they were clearly willing to kill a lot of people to hold on to Mukalla.

The sociology of Al-Qaeda in Mukalla was fascinating. Most of the AQAP fighters appeared to locals to be rural tribesmen, enjoying both the pay cheque and also lording it over the city folk. The AQAP foot soldiery were mostly young and fed up with the tribal gerontocracy, and closer in age to the young AQAP leadership than to the foot soldiers' own leaders. These opportunists were hard to define as Al-Qaeda per se, but for now they served under the black banners.

Then there were the true believers and the handful of dangerous terrorists capable of blowing up an airplane or a mosque, or consigning a city to destruction as they did to many towns in Iraq and Syria. If AQAP tried to defend Mukalla as it had Zinjibar in 2012 – and as the Islamic State was still doing in Ramadi, Manbij, Mosul and Raqqa – the dense city blocks of Mukalla would become a funeral pyre. There were indications that AQAP was developing land-mine and booby-trap factory lines that could mass-produce the explosive devices needed to sow minefields outside the city and undertake urban defence or demolition, block by block. Time was running out.

The need to act

By late 2015, MBZ and Musallam were in agreement that the liberation of Mukalla remained an important objective and that AQAP's momentum had to be checked decisively. Just weeks before the UAE's inaugural Martyrs' Day on 30 November 2015, the Islamic State had killed 130 innocent civilians and wounded 416 in eight bombing and shooting attacks in Paris. The world was at war with terrorism again, from Europe to Iraq and Syria and Yemen. MBZ gave Musallam the nod to work up the concept of operations for Mukalla.

In December, Musallam gathered the JTF-291 planners, now working under Musallam's new deputy, the veteran planner Colonel Abdullah S. After nearly nine months of operations, none of them had expected to be told they had a new mission to plan, but they looked at each other, took a deep breath, and got on with it. Old concepts developed by Azzan were dug out of the archives and the planners got to work, with Musallam turning an office into a miniature Secure Compartmented Intelligence Facility (SCIF) in which he could immerse himself in

29. One of the only high-resolution photographs from the Marib battle in 2015. This 18 September image shows some of Lt. Col. Mohammed S.'s Saqr-1 forces on the right-hand attack lane during the Marib battle. The lack of anti-Rocket Propelled Grenade cages or Remote Weapon Stations on the M-ATVs marks this out as a Yemeni platoon area. A UAE Unimog supply truck in the centre is undertaking daily (sunset) replenishment of this unit with hot food, fuel and ammunition. The forces are readying for a night advance towards Juhail Hill, off to the right of the image. They had just spent a fly-tickled day on this reverse-slope position, sleeping under their vehicles or in small piled-up rock 'sangars' (see following images). The power lines that ran down the middle of Saqr-2's middle attack lane can be seen top left, with the objective of Red Hill in the distance. Saqr-3's attack lane is off to the left of this picture.

30. A small one-man sangar on a limestone hillside in Marib, imaged by the author in 2018 from a few metres away due to the ongoing threat of anti-personnel mines under the gravel between such positions. The sangar is little more than a wall of fitted stones and rubble, potentially offering concealment plus cover from light weapons fire. The word sangar comes from the Persian word for stone, which was passed into Pashto usage in 19th century Afghanistan to describe a stone breastwork built up above ground level due to the difficulty of digging down into mountain terrain.

31. A Houthi sangar in the volcanic plain outside Marib city, photographed in 2015. These look like pyroclastic rocks composed of softer volcanic materials such as ash and lapilli. One lucky Houthi has excavated a snug, full-body bunker in which to shelter from bombardments and the sun. The downside of a bunker made of softer materials than the predominant basalt is its propensity to collapse when artillery shells land nearby.

32. The Houthis made very extensive use of mines in the fighting in Marib, as they did on all their defensive battlefields in Yemen. Ali Abdullah Saleh's Yemen had stockpiled large arsenals of anti-tank and anti-personnel mines that had been purchased by the two Yemens to guard against each other and to block potential approaches from Saudi Arabia and Oman. The Houthis tended to place anti-tank mines in the soft sand that accumulated in wadi beds, interspersed with anti-personnel mines. In mountainous terrain they used smaller anti-personnel mines, sometimes stacked on top of a buried anti-tank mine to create an especially devastating explosion. Marib tribal fighters amazed and infuriated their UAE partners by making night-time sorties into Houthi minefields purely to disarm, lift and steal the mines, to be sold in the arms souks in Marib city.

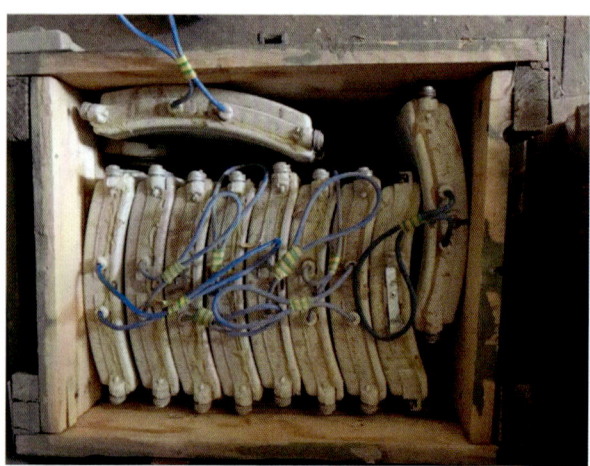

33. 'Claymore'-type anti-personnel mines used by the Houthis on all their battlefields in Yemen. This type of mine, which in US versions has the words 'Front Towards Enemy' embossed over its convex fragmentation panel of ball bearings, was created by the US military in the 1960s. Lebanese Hezbollah and Iran copied and made extensive use of these anti-personnel devices, and the Houthis quickly learned to build them too. The mines were thickly positioned between the Houthi sangars on the defences overlooking the west side of Marib Dam, the Jebel al-Balaq al-Qieli. When Houthi fighters heard pro-government tribesmen infiltrating up between their positions at night, they would detonate the mines, causing heavy casualties among the attackers.

34. The most commonly used Houthi anti-tank weapon: the B-10 recoilless rifle, a 1950s-era Soviet-designed anti-tank weapon that fires an 82-mm shell. Intended to be a towed weapon fired from a stable tripod mount, Yemenis instead tended to use it as a monstrous 70-kg shoulder-fired weapon. Inaccurate at over 400 metres even when being fired from a stable base, it was wildly uncontrollable when fired from the shoulder. Nevertheless, a B-10 shell killed the driver of a UAE Leclerc main battle tank in Marib when it hit the driver's armoured glass vision block in a one-in-a-million fluke of fate.

35. One of the many 'craft-produced' anti-materiel rifles in use with Houthi forces in Marib and on other battlefields. These weapons often reused heavy machine-gun barrels and chambered 12.7-mm, 14.5-mm, and even 20-mm or 23-mm cannon rounds. In Yemen, the art of weapon-smithing whole rifles is still practised by gunmakers in towns and villages. Industrial machine parts may be repurposed and original pieces created from solid or molten metal. Mainly used for anti-personnel sniping, they could also punch small holes through Mine-Resistant Ambush-Protected (MRAP) vehicles and damage the optics and Remote Weapon Stations on even the most heavily armoured UAE vehicles.

36. The mighty Leclerc main battle tank, imaged here in a 2017 photograph by the author. In a stroke of terrible misfortune, a B-10 recoilless rifle round hit the driver's small 4-cm-high by 8-cm-wide vision block, an example of which is visible next to the open hull hatch. Although made of layered armoured glass and polycarbonate, the 22-cm-thick vision block could not contain an armour-piercing jet of molten metal designed to cut through 30-cm of steel armour. The driver, Ghalib, was killed instantly.

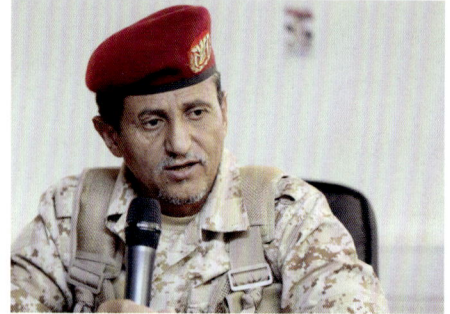

37. The senior Yemeni military officer with active involvement in the Marib battle was the 3rd Military Regional Command (MRC) commander, Brigadier General Abd-Rabu al-Shadadi, a staff college-trained Maribi officer who had impressed the Emirati commanders. Shadadi and his staff kept a tidy headquarters, with professionally marked and updated maps with perfect tactical symbolling. He put his money where his mouth was, literally paying Yemeni resistance troops out of his own pocket, and he walked where the soldiers walked, having survived a couple of mine strikes on his command vehicle. In the left-hand image from May 2015, he is shown fresh-faced at the start of the battle for Marib. The latter two pictures show him after the battle, in early 2016, as he led the pursuit of Houthi forces out of Marib governorate, a much less fresh-faced man after many months of operations. The bottom image shows Shadadi visiting the front line in Marib, where he was killed by a Houthi precision rocket attack on 7 October 2016 along with a number of his command staff. The war saw some outstanding Yemeni commanders prove their quality, but with almost no exceptions their reward was death, either by Houthi drone and rocket strikes, or by Al-Qaeda suicide bombings. Yemen thus lost many of its best and brightest patriots.

38. A mighty 60-ton Leclerc main battle tank returns to a field workshop on 14 September 2015. It has been at the front in Marib and is moving back to the Tadawin tactical assembly area to take on repairs. The UAE operated vehicle workshops at Tadawin and further back at Safer, utilising a blend of UAE maintainers and highly resourceful Yemeni mechanics. The Leclercs took heavy damage, mainly from the environment, with their rubber track-treads torn off by sharp basalt rocks and their cages, aerials and external fixtures battered by cliffs, grit and enemy fire. When the Leclerc could get a clear field of fire, however, it proved to be the ultimate 'heavy sniper', using its 120-mm cannon and linked ballistic computer to take into account wind, temperature, air pressure, and even barrel wear – the number of times the gun had been fired, including since its last cleaning.

39. The classic blend of high- and low-tech in the Yemen war. Here a Yemeni 'headquarters' is supported by a UAE advisor team and their communications station. It is late afternoon and the *qat* chews will have begun. Leader bodyguards are waiting for their bosses to return from their conference. It is almost time to drive out to the front line. Bags of food and *qat* have been stowed, alongside small creature comforts such as the leopard-print fluffy pillow in the nearest *chassis*. These tribesmen, probably of the Abida tribe, became an increasingly important part of the Marib attack force, providing men who intimately knew the goat tracks and volcanic mounts of the battlefield, and who could read the sand and enemy tracks well enough to use Houthi paths between minefields.

40. On 6 October 2015, Yemeni forces regain the 33rd YNA Armoured Brigade base at Kowfal, on the road to Sanaa via Sirwah. This base, also a station on the main oil pipeline from Marib to Ras Isa oil port, was the Houthi logistical hub for the Marib front. The overrun came so rapidly that the coalition forces captured a newly arrived truckload of Iranian copies of the Kornet anti-tank guided missile and RU140TK thermal scopes for Kornet missile posts. For many of the officers present in Marib at this moment, the sense of victory was tinged with regret. For them, there will always be a question of whether the Houthis might have kept retreating all the way back to Sanaa, and even beyond, if they had been pressed.

41. The last al-Quaiti sultans of Mukalla. In the centre is Sultan Awadh bin Saleh al-Quaiti, who is remembered by history books for 'his simplicity, kindness and generosity'. His son and successor Sultan Ghalib bin Awadh al-Quaiti II, a graduate of the Military Cadet School, Al-Zarqa, Jordan, is to the right. The Quaiti palace in the background, with its fine-carved wooden balconies and colonnaded verandas, hints at the Indian connections of the sultan's family. The al-Quaiti sultans had previously served as military officers in Hyderabad, India. In 1967, they tried to avoid being subsumed into Communist Yemen but were handed over to the People's Democratic Republic of Yemen by the withdrawing British. Until forced into exile abroad by the PDRY, the last sultan tried to secure independence for Hadramaut.

42. Al-Khalidiyah camp in 2015. When each 250-man intake arrived, they were grouped in single-tribe platoons, each of which tried to stay far away from the other. Over time, they were forced to mingle and to leave their deep-set suspicions and feuds aside for the duration of the war. As a tangible sign of trust, they had to check all their personal weapons at the front gate upon entry, even their curved dagger (the *jambiya*), and they were not allowed to chew *qat* in camp. Through this process during many months of training, they were stripped of their normal habits and turned into a professional armed force.

43. Al-Khalidiyah camp in 2015. The Hamoum tribal confederation recruits jog off in single file for physical exercise, having received their briefing under the sunshade. The midday sun is undoubtedly hot as they complete their final instruction period of the day, after which the camp will settle down for the night. Usually, this is when many Yemenis would start their *qat* chew but these recruits had to go without, a test of determination and commitment. Instead, they chain-smoked prodigious numbers of Indian cigarettes.

44. An Emirati instructor teaches safe handling of firearms at Al-Khalidiyah in 2016. The UAE instructors processed nearly two dozen intakes of recruits, and used the process to identify a chosen subset of platoons that would make up the Mukalla liberation force, who were sent to advanced training and who were equipped to a higher level. The UAE trainers, backed by capable Yemeni non-commissioned officers, were with the Hadramaut Elite Forces throughout their training and then commanded them in the actual operation, which provided both UAE and Yemeni troops with high levels of confidence in each other.

45. Simple squad tactics being taught at Al-Khalidiyah in 2016. Hadramaut Elite Forces trainees learn how to cover the arcs of fire assigned to them. With most recruits having had no prior military training, they had few bad habits to unlearn. All the recruits are training with weapons assigned to them only for the exercise and without magazines issued. Live firing was undertaken at a satellite site called Khamsa Meel (five miles away, as the name suggests). Every effort was taken to prevent weapons accidents and to prevent Al-Qaeda from getting a terrorist inside the base. There were no 'green-on-green' shootings of either other Yemenis or UAE trainers, in contrast to shooting rampages or bombing attacks at US training bases in Afghanistan and other places.

46. Receiving pre-battle instructions in the days before the Mukalla operation begins. This image shows a Hadramaut Elite Forces platoon, with its mixture of Caiman MRAPs and Nissan and Toyota *chassis*. The vehicles are loaded with the unit's baggage, suggesting that they are making the move up to the jump-off point in the oilfields to the north of Mukalla.

47. The approach march to Mukalla, 24 April 2016. One of very few non-blurry pictures taken during the advance, as most of the cell-phone imagery is unusable due to either camera shake (due to the bumpy journey) or due to dust covered windscreens. The attack axes drove almost non-stop through terrible terrain for (on the shortest route) 17 hours and (on the slowest route) nearly 40 hours. The non-metaled roads were mushy due to previous days' rain, which made for terrifying driving conditions as MRAPs clung to the narrow paths cut out of cliff sides. The landscape above was often so steep that turret gunners could not elevate their heavy machine guns to cover the cliffs and had to use their personal M4 carbines instead.

48. The road to Mukalla, down the switchbacks on Lt. Col. Azzan T.'s central axis. With the break-in fight at Al-Adwas behind them and the coast within sight, Azzan pressed on, despite having been on the attack for over 12 hours. Azzan's route was the only one of three to use a good-quality blacktop road, but it was also the best defended. At the bottom of the slope, Azzan was heavily ambushed by Al-Qaeda, with a powerful suicide car bomb and aggressive teams of veteran jihadis. The older Yemeni army soldiers retreating up the switchbacks blocked the progress of UAE-led reinforcements trying to reach the ambush site.

49. A Caiman Mine-Resistant Ambush-Protected (MRAP) vehicle in the characteristic fern and sand landscape of coastal Mukalla. The Caimans were the largest MRAPs used by the UAE in Mukalla, with the advantage of being able to carry whole squads of Yemeni troops and allowing the gunners of these tall vehicles a long field of fire. It was in such a vehicle that a UAE Land Forces machine-gunner, Corporal Saeed H., hand-cranked his heavy turret around with seconds to spare in a race against time with a suicide bomber. Saeed found the car bomber's smoking number plate wedged in the anti-RPG cages of the Caiman.

50. A post-liberation image from Mukalla's main port. The image provides a good size comparison of the Caiman versus M-ATV vehicles. The M-ATV was a rock climber, low to the ground and equipped with four independently manoeuvrable wheels that could flex and grip like powerful fingers. The Caiman was an older design with a higher centre of gravity and thus a less forgiving tipping point, which resulted in vehicle losses on the heavily sloped western and eastern axes during the liberation.

51. An Al-Qaeda 'torpedo' found in a Mukalla explosives workshop in 2016. The terrorist bomb-makers created a huge variety of improvised explosive devices in Mukalla, perhaps none more strange than this one – a cylinder of explosives attached to outboard motors. Al-Qaeda were aware of an amphibious invasion risk even before a US leak told the world that the Emiratis were coming to Mukalla. They had mined some sections of beach and placed coast-watchers all along the Mukalla seaboard.

52. Al-Dhabba oil loading port, just outside Mukalla, in the post-battle period in 2016. Al-Qaeda had rigged the full oil storage tanks with dozens of explosive charges, turning it into a super-bomb. Nearly every entrance to the site was mined and Al-Qaeda had even placed underwater mines in the small harbour. Some floating mines had also been improvised by putting wired-together explosives inside foam boxes that bobbed around in the little port. UAE Explosive Ordnance Disposal technicians used scuba gear to find and clear these booby-traps from the surface and the bed of the harbour.

53. Yemeni military forces under General Faraj al-Bahsani reoccupy the 3rd Military Regional Command on 25 March 2016. After the fighting was over and the city liberated, the battle needed a Yemeni face and this would be Faraj al-Bahsani, a retired general who after the battle would serve as the Hadramaut governor and eventually as one of the eight-member Presidential Leadership Council of the UN-recognised Yemeni government formed in April 2022. The return to the 3rd MRC headquarters was a symbolic and well-publicised moment, although Al-Qaeda had hardly used the site since its takeover of Mukalla in April 2015, and had instead been steadily stripping all the metals and furnishings from the camp for resale. The ridge in the distance is the 'back way' up to the Rabwat Baghshan mountain that the daring young UAE lieutenant Faisal K. was shown by locals in order to avoid ambushes laid by Al-Qaeda on the roads near the 3rd MRC base.

54. A picture of UAE founder Sheikh Zayed, painted on a wall in liberated Mukalla. Initially locals were afraid that the UAE would suddenly depart, as the British had done 50 years before, leaving them to face Al-Qaeda again alone. But the UAE advisors did not leave, maintaining bases in Mukalla and next-door Shabwah to continue the counter-terrorism fight against Al-Qaeda. At the time of writing, the UAE-Yemeni-US mission continues to diminish Al-Qaeda's presence in Yemen.

55. The fruits of 'sensitive site exploitation'. In this 2018 photograph taken by the author in Mukalla, a haul of documents and devices recovered from Al-Qaeda are being sifted and processed after a counter-terrorism raid. These maps, diaries, data sticks and, most importantly, phones are a vital source of clues that then uncover other targets and trigger follow-on raids. If this is done correctly, new raids unfold before their targets even know the prior cell has been discovered. UAE officers used US General Stanley McChrystal's memoir *My Share of the Task* to deepen their understanding of this 'continuous targeting cycle', which he had used to successfully eviscerate Al-Qaeda in Iraq.

56. UAE-supported Yemeni elite forces (*Nukhba*) undertake a counter-terrorism operation in rural Hadramaut in February 2018. The clearance of Mukalla in 2016 was the opening stage of more than two years of Yemeni-UAE-US 'trilateral' operations against AQAP. In this arrangement, the US still provided high-tech intelligence and drone support, but the UAE provided a new and vital intermediate layer between the US and local Yemeni sources of information on AQAP. This allowed Yemeni intelligence to be used with greater confidence, and UAE-supported Yemeni strike forces to take the fight to AQAP in the remote valleys of Hadramaut and Shabwah.

57. The key operational commanders of the war in eastern Yemen in 2015–16. This 2020 image shows the Emirati leaders who commanded the operations described in this book. To the fore, in Emirati national dress, is the UAE's military commander, Lieutenant General Mohammed bin Zayed Al-Nahyan (MBZ), then the Crown Prince of Abu Dhabi and Deputy Supreme Commander of the UAE Armed Forces. Speaking to 'the boss' is (then) Brigadier General Musallam R. (promoted to head of the UAE's counter-terrorism service). Walking behind is Brigadier General Ali Saif K. (promoted to head of the UAE Special Operations Command), who is talking to Sheikh Hamad bin Mohammed Al-Sharqi, the ruler of Fujairiah Emirate. These two generals had very different personalities and proved to be a potent combination on the battlefields of Marib and Mukalla, and they rose alongside each other to the highest levels of their military profession.

imagery, maps and Azzan's Intelligence Preparation of the Battlefield materials.

The first rough concept of operations was ready for briefing in January 2016. Musallam, Abdullah S. and the other planners had brought all their considerable training and experience into play. Again they had been largely left to themselves due to an intense planning focus in Abu Dhabi to support the Red Sea coast campaign to take the Houthis' ports away from them and land-lock their rebel enclave. The objective of the JTF-291 operation was to liberate Mukalla and degrade AQAP in the process, restoring the city and its neighbouring areas to Yemeni government control. Instead of just killing AQAP leaders, the operation would take a valuable piece of terrain away from Al-Qaeda and show them to be too weak to defend it.

The main attack force would be Azzan's Hadrami Elite Force (HEF), supported by UAE Operational Mentor and Liaison Teams (OMLTs). Phase 1 would be a five-week mobilisation and advance-to-contact with the enemy at Mukalla. Phase 2 would be a two-week assault on Mukalla city itself, while a Saudi-led Yemeni force would pin Al-Qaeda cells to the rear in Wadi Hadramaut, to prevent surprises from that direction. Phase 3 would be 52 weeks of stability operations and follow-up counter-terrorism targeting of AQAP all along the coast. MGM was impressed: the plan was solid and stood up to tough questioning.

MGM took Musallam to pitch the concept of operations to MBZ at the start of February 2016. Musallam remembers being nervous as he walked into MBZ's villa, reading and re-reading his notes. As he briefed the operation, he watched MBZ's face, but it gave nothing away. Finishing the brief, Musallam concluded:

Sir, I need a decision from you. I'm responsible for the fight against Al-Qaeda. It is my core mission. We said we'd fight AQAP, but then the war with the Houthis came and AQAP took Mukalla. Once we free Mukalla, we will take back Shabwa and Abyan. It will be a great step in our long war against Al-Qaeda. This is our real mission, our real enemy. We must get back to it.

Musallam had made a convincing case and immediately received the go-ahead from MBZ to outline the plan to the rest of the military leadership.

When Musallam and his team briefed the operation to the full UAE chain of command, it was 7 January 2016, the first anniversary of the terrorist outrage in Paris that saw 12 people shot dead at the *Charlie Hebdo* magazine offices, an act of terrorism claimed by AQAP. Throughout the autumn and winter of 2015, the urgency of dealing a heavy blow to AQAP continued to grow. Exactly as feared, the Abyan and Hadramaut wings of the emirate had become one contiguous area following the movement's capture of towns such as Azzan, Habban, Mahfad, Shoqra and Ahwar. With the war against the Houthi–Saleh forces still raging across Yemen, Musallam knew that it was a big ask to initiate a new line of operations against another enemy. There was an argument that Mukalla could be left until later, or that the UAE should leave the task to some other nation that was not already fighting a major campaign on the Red Sea coast while simultaneously securing Marib, Aden and Mahra. Why poke the wasp's nest at this time?

But the UAE commander-in-chief knew that every day of delay would make the eventual task of liberating Mukalla harder and more costly, both for the Emiratis and for the people of Mukalla. He gave his view on the need to liberate Mukalla *now*, not later, saying of Al-Qaeda's leader Ayman al-Zawahiri:

> Zawahiri is expanding the franchise, but the franchise
> needs to be killed. We will not be cowards. We are not
> afraid of AQAP. We will not allow them to become
> another monster like Daesh [the Islamic State]. Now it
> takes the whole world to fight Daesh in Mosul. We will
> not let AQAP build up so strong.

Musallam had the go-ahead to free Mukalla and to do it
soon, before AQAP could booby-trap the city for demolition
and indoctrinate a whole new generation, as the Islamic State was
doing in Mosul and Raqqa. But as usual, MBZ also had words of
caution and an expectation. 'Don't start until you can be really
sure you can finish this,' he said, looking at Musallam, 'and I hold
you responsible for any collateral damage. Be accurate, and don't
destroy the city.' The liberation of Mukalla would not be like the
battles of Kobani, Ramadi or Manbij, where the US-led coalition had 'destroyed the city to save the city'. It would all come
down to Azzan and the Hadramis, on the ground, When Musallam securely messaged Azzan to give him the go-ahead to begin
advanced preparations, the mission suddenly got a lot more real
to him for the first time. 'I saw darkness coming towards me,'
Azzan remembered. 'The battle was coming closer.'

X

PLANNING AL-QAEDA'S DOWNFALL

The 291 planners knew that the liberation of Mukalla would not be carried out on the scale of the Marib operation. There was no appetite to get so heavily committed to this ancillary mission, especially not when the UAE was already leading a land and amphibious operation to liberate the strategic Red Sea coast in what might have been a war-winning campaign. The Leclercs and G-6s had been sent back to Abu Dhabi after their heavy wear and tear in Marib, and other heavy equipment had been deployed to the newly liberated Red Sea coast bases at the Bab el-Mandeb and Mokha. JTF-291 would be going back to its roots for the Mukalla operation: a small-footprint operation that would lower UAE exposure, maximise UAE control of the operation, and ensure that the Yemenis got the credit for liberating their own port city from Al-Qaeda.

Completing the attack force

Completion of the HEF had progressed well during the autumn and winter of 2015. By January 2016, it was no exaggeration to say that around 6,000 recruits and 200 company and platoon leaders and wakils had been graduated, a stunning achievement in terms of throughput. But would they fight? Or like the Saqrs, would they come apart and need to be constantly rebuilt, or like the UAE-trained resistance in Aden, would they need six attempts before succeeding? Once, when Azzan asked a cabinet-level Yemeni whether the HEF would fight, the old politician had laughed in his face: 'I will chop my arm off if these guys fight. They are just here for the 2,000 [Saudi rials per month]. They will run away when the bullets start flying. We don't have that warrior mindset; you will face Al-Qaeda alone.' Azzan heard this kind of cynicism more than once from Yemenis but increasingly he knew the Hadramis at the training camps better than the old Yemeni cynics did. Some undoubtedly would not fight, but enough would, Azzan believed.

The tight connection between the UAE trainers and the Hadramis allowed them to view the different components of the Yemeni forces in a clear-eyed manner that was not always obvious to those back in Abu Dhabi or those even further away in Washington. One subtle factor that could easily be missed was that the HEF was not really one force, but three. Of the 6,000 trainees, it was well understood by Azzan that around 2,000 were complete write-offs as actual fighters. Their training was cursory, they had not been given any new equipment, and they were largely employed just to keep tribes happy and to prevent them from turning towards Al-Qaeda.

Of the remaining 4,000, half were garrison forces for central Hadramaut, including three brigades (the Ighaf, Shibam and Kahf forces) dedicated to running checkpoints, oilfield guard forces and the forward defences north of Mukalla. These men had pay, uniforms, a shiny new AK-type assault rifle (to add to their collection or to sell), and some basic training. But the real Mukalla attack force numbered only 2,000 men out of the entire HEF and would become a diamond that the UAE polished and sharpened for a year. For shorthand reference, this increment of the overall force might be thought of as the 'super-HEF', though that was certainly not the name Emiratis used to describe it and, in fact, the force was never given a specific name of its own.

On 22 July 2015, before Marib had fully consumed his attention, Musallam had ordered Azzan to find a tactical assembly and advanced training area closer to Mukalla, where this super-HEF unit could be put into seclusion and perfected. Azzan's choice of site demonstrated how deeply he had already sunk into the Hadrami mindset, becoming 'more Hadrami than the Hadramis', as one HEF commander enthused about him. The tactical assembly area was called Hadramaut Camp by the Emiratis, and it was built at Al-Lijoun castle, the traditional muster point for 'the shoeless army' of the old Quaiti sultanate. With beautiful dam-fed streams even in the summer, the Hadramaut camp was a wonderful setting to complete the development of the hand-picked HEF element that would assault Mukalla.

The senior trainer, Abdullah Y., had built the force from the best recruits out of the 6,000 who had passed through Al-Khalidiyah and the other camps up north. They were all tribesmen who had no previous military service, so he had 'cut them from whole cloth', as the old saying went – meaning that they had no bad habits to correct. As Azzan had predicted, these young Hadramis had a thirst for competent leadership and organisation. 'You gave us a system to use,' said one civilian recruit. 'That's what made us ready to fight.' Now that the green light had been given on 7 February 2016, the HEF were put through six weeks of advanced training alongside the three 23-man Emirati OMLTs they would be paired with. Only here, at the Hadramaut Camp, would they be given full equipment sets, including body armour, and mounted in UAE-provided gun trucks and unarmed chasses. These were the chosen men who would be the Yemeni spearhead of the liberation of Mukalla.

When working 'by, with and through' local partner forces, to use the American phrase, one of the challenges that is talked about least is how to use local forces that foreign commanders have lower confidence in. In this case, these were the 1st Military Regional Command (MRC) units from Wadi Hadramaut and the exiled remnants of the 2nd MRC forces gathered under a Hadrami general called Faraj al-Bahsani. The latter, the 2nd MRC force of 2,250 Yemeni National Army (YNA) soldiers, were gathered at the abandoned 37th YNA armoured brigade base, 40 km west of Hadramaut Camp. Bahsani had needed some convincing to return from retirement in Riyadh to command them, protesting that he was too old and needed a large professional commander's staff, but Musallam told him that it would be a simple operation and that it was important to have soldiers from 2nd MRC in the liberation force. Bahsani's men would be split up among the three axes of attack, sandwiched in the order of march between a vanguard of scouts and HEF, and a larger 1,000-man follow-on force of HEF from Hadramaut Camp that would make up the tail of each column.

In the case of 1st MRC from Wadi Hadramaut, a different solution had to be found. The coastal people of Mukalla would not welcome forces from Wadi Hadramaut with the same openness they might greet the Hamoum tribes of the HEF, who were their closer neighbours. There was a big difference between the people of the faraway northern Hadramaut (the Wadi) and those of the coast (the Sahan), and the hill tribes of the Hamoum were something of a bridge between them. It would be better for the Islahi generals of 1st MRC to tackle a separate mission while the Mukalla operation unfolded. They could play a useful role by pinning down Al-Qaeda reserves in Wadi Sur, a tributary of Wadi Hadramaut. Yemen's 1st MRC commander Major General Abdalrahman al Halili, a canny negotiator, got Musallam to commit to providing weapons, equipment, medical evacuation (to Saudi Arabia and Jordan) and payment for the forces involved in the operation. In return, he would bring around 2,500 YNA troops and tribesmen to Wadi Sur when directed by JTF-291. This would divert Al-Qaeda's attention away from the real target of the operation and provide an alternative explanation for some of the logistical moves taking place in the lead-up to Mukalla's liberation.

The need for speed

As February drew to a close, the guidance from MBZ and the high command shaped the detailed plan for employing the HEF-YNA-UAE columns. The operation should aim to cause serious manpower losses to AQAP, killing as many of the enemy's hard-line cadre as possible to deal them a lasting defeat, as opposed to just pushing them out of the city and having to face them again another day. Musallam's superiors wanted the operation to happen soon, before AQAP really started to entrench themselves in Mukalla. The so-called 'inside resistance' from Mukalla were increasingly worried that AQAP was planning to defend the city block by block and to the last building, as the Islamic State was doing in Iraq and Syria. The example of Zinjibar's destruction in 2012 was foremost in everyone's mind, especially the way AQAP had then laid extensive minefields around and inside the city, and even destroyed and poisoned water wells, preventing resettlement.

In January 2016, AQAP had reached out through tribal intermediaries with a message for the UAE: 'We know you are coming to Mukalla. This is none of your business. Stay away.' Soon after that, AQAP began to prepare its defences. Intelligence was then reaching the UAE that AQAP was accelerating

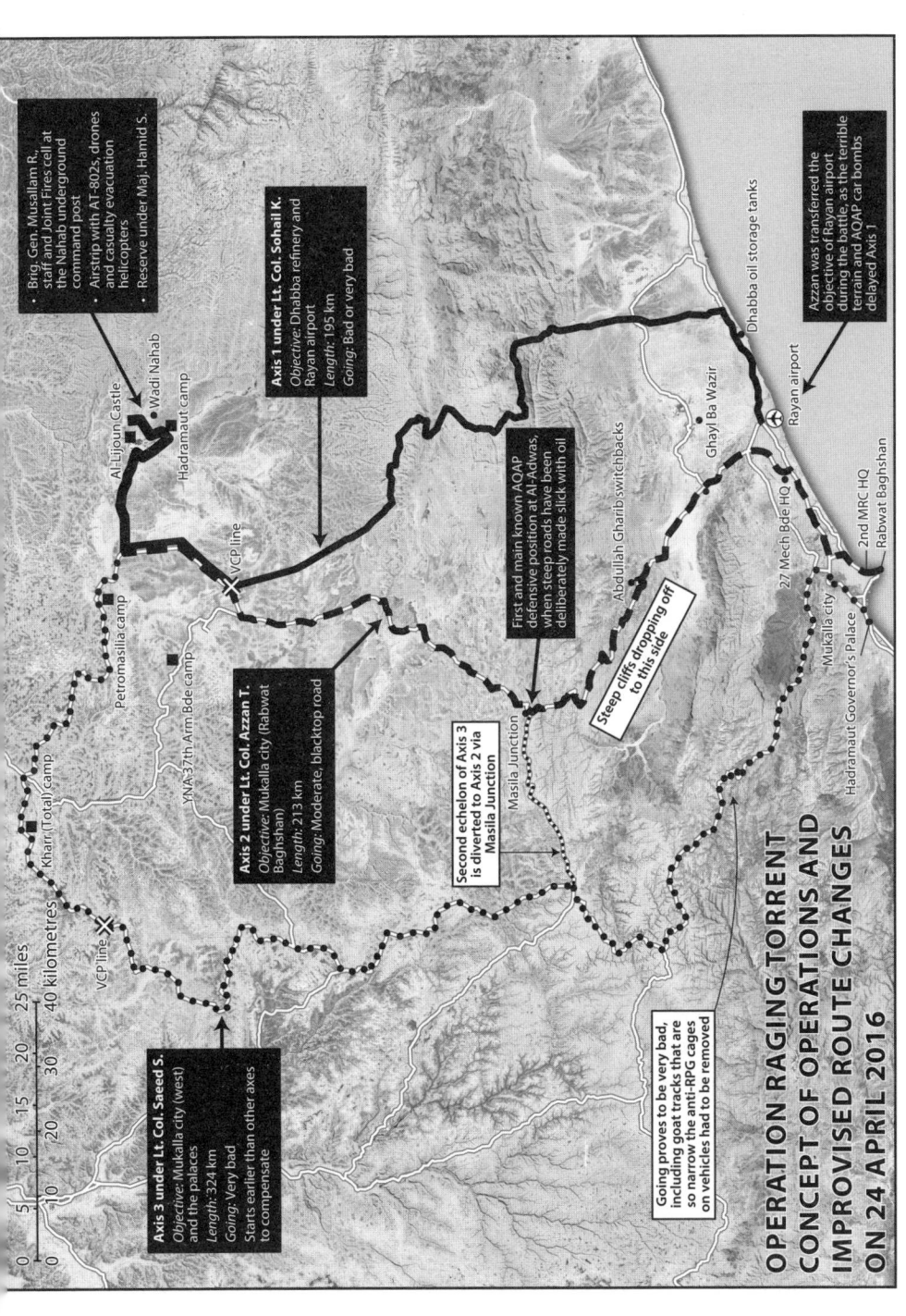

- Brig. Gen Musallam R., staff and Joint Fires cell at the Nahab underground command post
- Airstrip with AT-802s, drones and casualty evacuation helicopters
- Reserve under Maj. Hamid S.

Axis 1 under Lt. Col. Sohail K.
Objective: Dhabba refinery and Rayan airport
Length: 195 km
Going: Bad or very bad

First and main known AQAP defensive position at Al-Adwas, when steep roads have been deliberately made slick with oil

Azzan was transferred the objective of Rayan airport during the battle, as the terrible terrain and AQAP car bombs delayed Axis 1

Dhabba oil storage tanks

Rayan airport

Ghay Ba Wazir

Abdullah Gharib switchbacks

Steep cliffs dropping off to this side

27 Mech Bde HQ

2nd MRC HQ

Rabwat Baghshan

Mukalla city

Hadramaut Governor's Palace

Axis 2 under Lt. Col. Azzan T.
Objective: Mukalla city (Rabwat Baghshan)
Length: 213 km
Going: Moderate, blacktop road

Second echelon of Axis 3 is diverted to Axis 2 via Masila Junction

Masila Junction

Going proves to be very bad, including goat tracks that are so narrow the anti-RPG cages on vehicles had to be removed

Al-Lijoun Castle

Wadi Nahab

Hadramaut camp

VCP line

Petromasila camp

YNA37th Arm Bde camp

Kharr (Total) camp

VCP line

Axis 3 under Lt. Col. Saeed S.
Objective: Mukalla city (west) and the palaces
Length: 324 km
Going: Very bad
Starts earlier than other axes to compensate

0 5 10 15 20 25 miles
0 10 20 30 40 kilometres

OPERATION RAGING TORRENT
CONCEPT OF OPERATIONS AND IMPROVISED ROUTE CHANGES
ON 24 APRIL 2016

production of improved explosive devices (IEDs) and primitive land mines at a factory in Mukalla. The 27th YNA Mechanised Brigade stores and the 190th Air Defence Brigade base had been ransacked for high explosives and detonators, and AQAP's foreign fighters had begun mass production of home-made low explosives suitable for demolitions charges and car bombs.

Some of the same bomb-makers who had rigged houses for demolition at the edges of Zinjibar and Jaar were involved in the effort, most importantly a Somali fighter called Farih. The Dhabba oil storage facility east of the city was being prepared for destruction, in effect a massive incendiary booby-trap that could spill over 2 million barrels of oil into the ocean. Pressure-plate and radio-control detonators and directional anti-vehicle and anti-personnel mines were being mass-manufactured. Wiring was being laid out on some city streets, perhaps to 'daisy-chain' IEDs together and fire them at the same time or in sequence. It was unclear whether Raimi was increasingly listening to the foreign fighters and leaning towards an Islamic State-style defence of Mukalla – or whether he had simply lost control of them. The liberation had to come even earlier than planned, MBZ directed, starting no later than 27 April. And when it happened, it had to be sudden, giving Al-Qaeda less time to deploy an urban defence.

The detailed concept of operations presented to MGM and the Presidential Guard command team on 22 March 2016 was built around a very rapid and hidden concentration of force, as Musallam had planned for Marib also. This time, however, the whole operation was much smaller and entirely in UAE hands. From 28 March to 26 April, the attack columns would quietly at a line of three forward positioned tactical assembly areas more than 100 km from Mukalla, moving to the site in small parcels of troops by back roads and often at night.

Three axes would present the enemy with tactical dilemmas and ensure that even failure on one or two axes would still pierce the AQAP defence. To the east, at Hadramaut Camp, would be Axis 1, which would cut escape routes to the east and capture (and remove explosive demolitions from) the Dhabba refinery. In the centre, at the Petromasila Block 14 oil complex, would be Axis 2, which would lance straight down the best available roads to liberate Mukalla city and Rayan airport. To the west was Axis 3, based at the Total Block 10 oil complex (called Kharir). It would take a long and winding route to block escape routes to the west, reach the coast and then sweep east along the coast road into Mukalla. The overall task force had been allocated eight days to fight their way through to Mukalla on their routes – 195 km on Axis 1, 213 km on Axis 2, and 324 km on Axis 3 – and to seize their objectives in the city. The operation would be called Sail al Arim (Raging Torrent), because the columns would emulate the rain that surged down the wadis to the coast.

The design of the columns was ingenious, and each was a self-contained liberation force. On each axis, the scouts and selected HEF would make up a vanguard. The second echelon (i.e. group or wave) in each column would consist of 1,035 of Bahsani's older soldiers (in reality, each of these forces were each about 350-strong). Bahsani's men would create a close-in perimeter around Mukalla city to catch escaping AQAP fighters and show that the Yemeni government was present in the liberation. Then there was a third echelon of around 500 HEF, mounted in souped-up chasses with gun shields, Dushkas and extra-large ammunition panniers. As each axis advanced, they would 'radio in' whenever they reached the next of a string of 'control points', to let friendly aircraft know that point was secure, and would drop off platoons to create a net of 'denial points' to catch fleeing

AQAP fighters and guard the flanks of the urban battle. A reserve force of 500 HEF under UAE Major Hamad S. would be held back and committed as needed.

One UAE OMLT in an MRAP would accompany each echelon of each axis, with 23 Emiratis per axis, comprising axis commanders, vehicle commanders, drivers, turret gunners, plus specialists spread between the vehicles – JTACs, medics, explosive ordnance disposal technicians, and K-9 dog-handlers and their four-legged partners. Overhead each axis would be one AT-802 light attack and surveillance aircraft and a rotating set of strike aircraft.

'Joint fires' in the Mukalla plan

A major assault on a fortified city would typically begin with an intense air bombardment designed to neutralise defensive commanders and paralyse forces – again, modern euphemisms for blowing them to pieces. This was certainly how it had been in the cities liberated from the Islamic State such as Ramadi and Manbij. For the Mukalla battle, a much lighter touch had been ordered and this effort would be led by Colonel Saif M., a former Mirage 2000-9 and F-16 pilot who had been flying strike aircraft since 2003. An experienced joint fires controller, he would design a targeting approach in the Mukalla battle that was built around restraint and minimal collateral damage at its heart – what MBZ had called 'clean cuts only'.

For planners like Saif, Operation Raging Torrent was a mass of contradictions, but that was normal in modern military operations. Maximum damage had to be inflicted on Al-Qaeda, *but* with minimal collateral damage. The enemy must not escape *but* nor must they be cornered into fighting for every street, the enemy's assessed 'most dangerous course of action' or MD-COA (pronounced 'em-dee-koa') in military jargon. Only one thing was clear: the ground forces had to reach Mukalla and defeat its perimeter defences. Ideally, enemy commanders and reserves inside the city needed to be neutralised or at least disrupted and encouraged not to fight, at least wherever it was feasible to do so without causing collateral damage.

The Joint Target List (JTL) is the instrument by which any air campaign planner pares down the massive universe of potential targets into a refined list of things that need to be struck by joint fires. When Saif started building his JTL, there was precisely one confirmed target on it: a lonely SA-2 surface-to-air missile system and its associated radar, which the United States had kindly told the coalition about, even though its existence was obvious to everyone. No other targets had been provided by Washington, even though Mukalla was one of the cities in the world most closely watched by the Americans in 2015 and 2016. 'We were on our own,' Saif remembered thinking as the targeting process began.

The UAE sent commercial satellites, Al-Hur drones and F-16s over Mukalla each day to photograph the city in great detail and to learn the daily 'pattern of life' of innocent civilian activity – what Saif called 'the rhythm of the city'. Yemeni agents were trained to describe potential targets in a precise manner and to provide their coordinates. To guard against mischievous or lazy human source reporting, every piece of information was carefully tied to its source, and these Yemenis were told: 'It will become known to your tribe and your neighbours if you provide bad intelligence.' This ensured that a degree of accountability was in place. Then Saif set up his overhead surveillance assets over his key Named Areas of Interest and gave the enemy system a prod, destroying the SA-2 and watching how various suspected enemy nodes reacted to the apparent beginning of airstrikes.

AQAP ACTIVITY AND TARGETS IN MUKALLA CITY

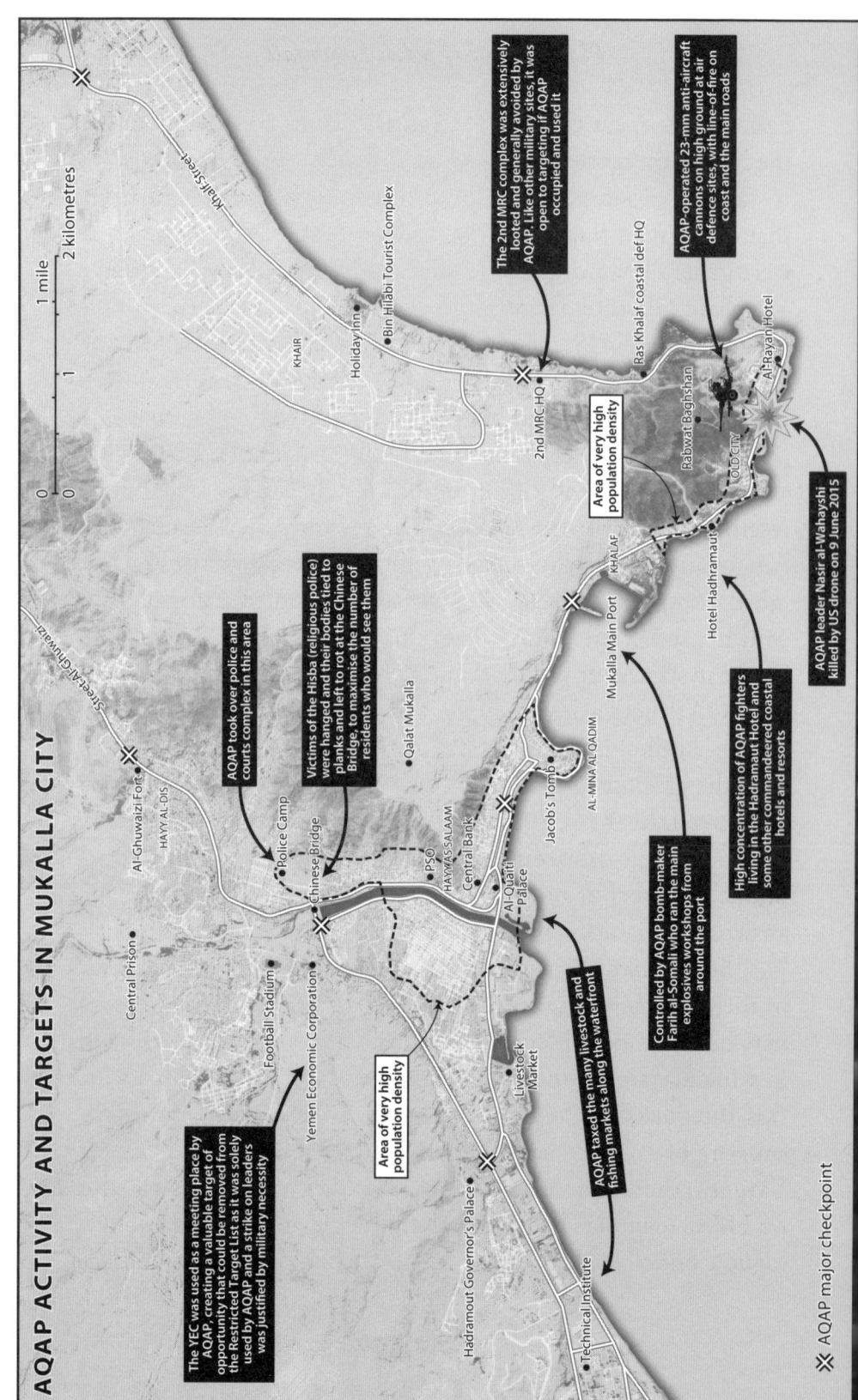

The YEC was used as a meeting place by AQAP, creating a valuable target of opportunity that could be removed from the Restricted Target List as it was solely used by AQAP and a strike on leaders was justified by military necessity

AQAP took over police and courts complex in this area

Victims of the Hisba (religious police) were hanged and their bodies tied to planks and left to rot at the Chinese Bridge, to maximise the number of residents who would see them

The 2nd MRC complex was extensively looted and generally avoided by AQAP. Like other military sites, it was open to targeting if AQAP occupied and used it

AQAP-operated 23-mm anti-aircraft cannons on high ground at air defence sites, with line-of-fire on the coast and the main roads

Controlled by AQAP bomb-maker Farih al-Somali who ran the main explosives workshops from around the port

High concentration of AQAP fighters living in the Hadramaut Hotel and some other commandeered coastal hotels and resorts

AQAP taxed the many livestock and fishing markets along the waterfront

AQAP leader Nasir al-Wahayshi killed by US drone on 9 June 2015

Area of very high population density

Area of very high population density

Khalf Street

Street Al-Ghuwaizi

Central Prison

Al-Ghuwaizi Fort

HAYY AL-DIS

Football Stadium

Yemen Economic Corporation

Police Camp

Chinese Bridge

PSO

Central Bank

HAYY AS SALAAM

Al-Quaiti Palace

Jacob's Tomb

AL-MINA AL QADIM

Livestock Market

Hadramout Governor's Palace

Technical Institute

Qalat Mukalla

Mukalla Main Port

KHALAF

Hotel Hadramaut

Rabwat Baghshan

OLD CITY

Al-Rayyan Hotel

Ras Khalaf coastal def HQ

2nd MRC HQ

KHAIR

Holiday Inn

Bin Hilabi Tourist Complex

2 kilometres

1 mile

0   1   2

0   1

✖ AQAP major checkpoint

Saif would repeat this trick at various points in the lead-up to the liberation battle.

The UAE's target selection process was very different from that of the man-hunters of the CIA and JSOC. The Americans were generally hunting top leaders, and they did this by following chains of interactions and personal intersections. When it worked best, US analysts could achieve astounding feats of detective work, as they did to enable the killing of Osama bin Laden. As often, though, the United States used 'signature targeting' that made regular targeted killings feasible, albeit with a heightened risk of killing innocent people whose activities resembled terrorists too closely. The sort of AQAP leaders the Americans killed frequently were those who communicated the most – spokesmen, religious authorities, and occasionally the emir himself. In the views of Saif and other UAE counter-terrorism analysts, this approach couldn't work for remotely targeting the AQAP tactical leadership in Mukalla. AQAP only used low-power handheld radios and the Americans were needed on or near the ground to pick those obscure signals out of the ether and geo-locate them. The public interacted with AQAP through a number of kiosks around the city where written requests and phone numbers or return addresses could be left to receive an answer to a citizen's entreaty.

The UAE would instead focus on human intelligence sources in the city. Through these the Emiratis and their Yemeni partners built a simple picture of who the key AQAP leaders were in Mukalla and, importantly, who probably did not fall into this category. To the Americans, association with and active support of AQAP made a person a legitimate target. To the Emiratis, there were many shades of grey. More than half of the 60 HDC members had resigned, and even the Hadramaut Dialogue Council leader Omar bin Shakal al-Jaidi and the political

Salafists of the Council of Sunni Scholars did not merit deliberate lethal targeting. The Military and Security Committee set up by AQAP to incorporate many of the Islahi generals and pro-Saleh 2nd MRC leaders was also not targeted, even though it undoubtedly met many of the requirements for 'signature targeting'. The Emiratis wanted to *dismantle* Al-Qaeda networks and pressurise or incentivise Yemenis to detach from the terrorist group, and the time for that would be after the liberation, face to face. Killing everyone who had associated with AQAP simply never occurred to UAE targeteers.

Nor was the UAE willing to go to any lengths to kill the AQAP leaders that it justifiably wanted to 'remove from the battlefield', to use the US euphemism for targeted killings. Collateral damage might be too great and the UAE was going to Mukalla to liberate the city, not level it. In the UAE's view, Raimi, his public mouthpiece Batarfi and their close circle of Egyptian and Sudanese foreign fighter advisors could be left to the Americans, who would no doubt be tracking them throughout any future battle, looking for targeting opportunities. Even though the UAE got brief senses of where these top leaders might be, the locations were always within densely populated neighbourhoods where the ancient four-storey mud-brick buildings practically touched each other, to the extent that neighbours could hand each other foodstuffs between their balconies. Even a 250-lb Small Diameter Bomb (or SDB) might collapse one or more of these houses.

AQAP tactical commanders were more likely targets. The most important was Riyadh Omar al-Shaab (Abu Omar al-Nahdi), a Hamoum tribesman who oversaw the areas east of Mukalla city and who was the most industrious tactical commander when it came to wiring whole facilities for explosive demolition. Marwan ba Duways and Sadiq bin Saydar (the latter of whom tactically led the May 2015 takeover) commanded in the city centre alongside Hisba commanders like Abu bin Taleb al-Katheri (also known as Abu Noura) and Mohammed Saleh al-Ghurabi, a former army officer. The western entrance to Mukalla and the palaces were held by AQAP tactical commanders Khaled Salem bin Sabri and Sayram al-Sanani. At the main port, Farih al-Somali ran the main explosives workshops. But each of these men surrounded themselves with human shields – usually prisoners – and lived right alongside caches of explosives that would level city blocks if detonated by an airstrike.

The initial 300 or so nominated target locations on Saif's first-draft JTL were quickly winnowed down to just 69. Of these, 39 were removed through the review process at the Combined Air Operations Centre in Riyadh because they were either on the No-Strike List (which could not be struck under any circumstances) or the larger Restricted Target List (which might be struck if military necessity required and with additional scrutiny). The remaining 30 targets on the vetted JTL included only three inside the inner city: a courthouse and two police stations in which AQAP had exclusive use and where prisoners were either not present or had been gathered in wings of the buildings a safe distance away from areas of AQAP activity. These three sites and five others towards the edge of the city were subjected to 24/7 monitoring for nearly a month throughout April, to learn what points of the day and night were optimal for a strike with the lowest risk of collateral damage. Modelling from the UAE's Critical Infrastructure Protection Authority was used to calculate how 'explosive effects' could be contained to certain rooms or wings of buildings, and to ensure that nearby structures would be minimally affected. Almost all the final approved targets were at the edges of Mukalla, including AQAP defensive positions, rural ammunition dumps and military and coastguard bases along the coastal highway.

The US role in Mukalla

So as not to distract effort from the anti-Houthi war, the Mukalla operation relied on very few Gulf coalition military assets, but the UAE had expected one external partner to provide some capabilities. The US military and intelligence community had initially been keen for the Emiratis to take on the mission against AQAP in 2015. Now things had changed. In early 2016, US discomfort with the war in Yemen was growing and the United States was unwilling to put even the CIA or JSOC back on the ground. UAE planners had built contingencies to cope with declining US support and their expectations were low. US planning and intelligence support would certainly be appreciated, as would public US endorsement of the specific Mukalla operation against AQAP and post-liberation humanitarian support. No one expected the US military to come ashore openly, and in fact this would complicate life for the Yemenis, who were not comfortable with an overt US role. The UAE wanted full credit to go to Hadrami forces, which would help them as they sought to hunt AQAP remnants, restore order, and stabilise Mukalla over the long term.

If expectations were being raised by anyone, it was often the US military itself, which from the start of 2016 had teased UAE hopes with a variety of options, from 'heavy' (intelligence support, airborne refuelling, maritime interdiction, naval gunfire support and on-the-ground JTACs); to 'medium' ('heavy' but with JTACs afloat); to 'light' (just intelligence support, airborne refuelling and UAE Combat Search and Rescue aboard a US warship off the coast). The UAE was going to do the Mukalla liberation whether the Americans came or not, but US naval assistance would definitely have been helpful because the bulk of the UAE Navy was in the Red Sea, threatening amphibious landings against the Houthi flanks near Hodeida. The UAE would also be pleased to receive US intelligence, surveillance and reconnaissance support, which would only require in-place US drone and intelligence assets to share what they were already seeing in Mukalla and in some cases to redirect their gaze from other parts of Yemen to support the operation.

As the operation was aimed at AQAP, not the Houthis, it seemed as if US cooperation might be forthcoming. After all, on 27 March 2016, the US had badly damaged an AQAP base just west of Mukalla, killing nearly 50 AQAP recruits as they lined up to get lunch. Preventing AQAP from ruling Mukalla – just as the global coalition was rolling back Islamic State control of Iraqi and Syrian cities – would seem to be in the United States' interest. And it felt somewhat wrong to be without the Americans, especially as the UAE had been with them every step of the way on the post-9/11 global war on terrorism. 'Our closest counter-terrorism partner was always the Americans,' the JTF-291 deputy commander Abdullah S. explained. 'We went everywhere with them. We were joined to them. Our [US] liaison officers wanted to help.'

Nevertheless, it had been prudent to guard against a disappointment, so UAE planners began preparing a contingency 'branch plan' on 29 March 2016 in which the UAE would go it alone. It introduced the kind of compromises and risks that no planner wants to accept: less CSAR cover if something went wrong; a much longer casualty evacuation process if no US naval vessels were available; potentially dangerous refuelling over Yemen or less endurance for fast air; plus the re-tasking of the UAE naval force in the Red Sea to support the Mukalla operation instead.

This contingency planning proved very worthwhile when it suddenly became clearer that the Americans were not even going to go 'light' at Mukalla. They were simply not coming at all, and maybe did not even want the operation to take place. On 7 April, the UAE got indications from its Washington diplomatic mission that journalists were asking about a forthcoming operation focused on Mukalla. It looked and smelled like a leak out of the Pentagon, a well-known tactic inside the Washington Beltway when someone in the bureaucracy wanted to kill off US involvement in an operation. But this was not a unilateral US mission that would now be scrapped: it was a mission that was going to happen anyway, but now the enemy had another indication that it was drawing close. In the following days, the UAE drew out of its embarrassed US military partners that there would be no US involvement in Mukalla. The UAE would have to quickly backfill all the maritime interdiction and naval gunfire aspects of Musallam's plan with its own Red Sea flotilla.

Moments like this tended to make the UAE more, not less, determined to get the job done. In early April, MBZ had told his commanders: 'Islam has been hijacked by a small group. Our task is to fix it: it is not the task of the Americans or anyone else, because they are our sons. We need to bring them back to the right way. Islam is our religion and we should correct it.' In Abu Dhabi, Sharurah and Yemen, the determination of the UAE to succeed, entirely on its own, was doubled.

That meant going heavy. On 8 April, senior commanders discussed the option of a fourth axis to the Mukalla operation – a battalion-scale amphibious assault. The fourth axis would re-task the UAE's Red Sea amphibious task force, known as JTF-293.5, which had been planning to mount a similar assault near the Houthi-held port of Hodeida. It was no coincidence that this force was now led by none other than Brigadier Ali Saif, who had led the Saqrs in Marib. Now he had been given another demanding combat mission: to prepare the riskiest amphibious assault since the British retook the Falkland Islands from Argentinian invaders in 1982. His task force would now be diverted to partially fill the maritime gap left by the United States, restoring some naval gunfire support and a minimal CSAR and casualty evacuation capability. If the group also landed its amphibious battalion landing team, the UAE ground involvement in Mukalla would shift from being just a few OMLTs to a battalion-sized unit of nearly 30 BMP-3s, a half dozen Leclercs and a battery of G-6 howitzers.

The back-up plan

Throughout March there had been a question mark in the minds of Presidential Guard and Joint Headquarters commanders about whether the three land axes alone could liberate Mukalla. It was a fair and natural question to ask: in Aden, Yemeni forces with UAE OMLTs had needed six bites at the airport to succeed. In Marib, the Saqrs had disintegrated in less than the eight days allocated to major combat operations in Mukalla. This would be the HEF's debut in combat and thus far they had only impressed in training. Were they really different from all previous efforts to train and equip Yemenis? Or were Musallam and Azzan falling victim to the same understandable phenomenon that all special forces trainers tend to experience, that of becoming so close to their trainees that they lose impartiality? The likely no-show of US naval support had sharpened the reasonable fear that the HEF and YNA columns might underperform. If JTF-293.5 was bringing its maritime intercept forces to close the maritime flank off Mukalla, why not develop an amphibious landing option as well? From 14 to 16 April 2016, planning for an amphibious fourth axis got underway in Abu Dhabi and aboard the ships of JTF-293.5.

Soldiers are trained to follow orders, but they are not robots. For JTF-291, the potential transfer of the main thrust to the amphibious flank was understandably jarring. For a year they had trained for this mission and built the Yemeni forces to accomplish it. Now, about ten days before their new launch date of 25 April, everything was changing and overall command of the operation might move from Musallam's team to a higher headquarters in Abu Dhabi, reflecting the need for overarching coordination across the two task forces led by Musallam and Ali Saif. It came at the worst possible moment. The planners at JTF-291 were at their most tired, in the final stages of their long-awaited operation. The hard-pressed JTF-293.5 planners had been disappointed time and time again by the postponement of their amphibious assault on the Red Sea coast. Now they were suddenly thrust into frantic preparation to assault totally unfamiliar beaches against a different enemy, but at least they might get to do what they had prepared for so long to do – assault an enemy beach and liberate a city. No amount of wargaming or training could prepare these staffs for the extraordinarily high-pressure environment in the UAE military headquarters in late April 2016. This was a true test of military professionalism.

When Musallam spoke to MBZ on 19 April he knew from basic reckoning that the UAE maritime intercept force would be offshore on the planned D-Day, 23 April 2016, but that the amphibious landing team of the force would not be in position to hit the beaches until a few days later. No one was advocating a delay to the planned D-Day so that meant the pressure was still on his land assault to go first. MBZ asked for an update on the plan, which was always evolving. 'How do you propose to take Mukalla?' MBZ asked. Musallam was ready:

Simple, Sir. First, an intense air bombardment. Not slow, like Aden, over three months. They will expect a long bombardment but we will take out all the high-value targets at once, the same night. We will attack and take the city immediately after. If we don't seize the city suddenly, in 24 hours, then we have failed and the amphibious becomes the main effort. But we can succeed with speed and shock. We will swallow the distance.

MBZ ended his review with the question that kept recurring: 'Will the Hadramis fight? How confident are you in your force?' Musallam thought back to what Azzan had said the last time Musallam had asked him the same question. 'These guys will not let us down. I'm sure,' Azzan had said. 'They are the best of the best. They will fight. Nothing will stop them but death.' Then Azzan characteristically added, with his usual clenched jaw, 'and if the Hadramis do run away, then the amphibious forces will find my dead body when they land because I'll try it with my own 20 men,' referring to his OMLT. Musallam put these feelings into his own, more diplomatic language and gave a new pledge to MBZ: 'We will win. The UAE will triumph. You can have faith in us. Just give us 48 hours.' MBZ agreed, but with one proviso: 'OK, but I need the amphibious force just over the horizon in case you're wrong.'

XI

RAGING TORRENT

On 20 April, both Musallam and Ali Saif headed out to join their respective headquarters. Musallam was smuggled into Hadramaut camp under conditions of great secrecy. The nearby Wadi Nahab, a beautiful spot that the Hamoum had used for hundreds of years to gather its sheikhs, became the tactical assembly area for the Mukalla operation. Safely distant from Hadramaut camp, which had been occupied for months, the Nahab camp was new and, Musallam hoped, not yet noticed by anyone with accurate missiles. As further insurance against the Safer-type attack, a fortified underground command bunker had been built and also an airstrip that would base AT-802s, drones and casualty evacuation helicopters. As Musallam arrived, he was given a tour by Azzan's young deputy, Major Faisal K., who had been at Azzan's side throughout the last nine months in Hadramaut. Musallam decided to test the young officer's views and his morale.

'What's the probability of success? Do you trust the HEF?', Musallam asked bluntly.

'We've spent nine months with them every day. We sorted out the good from the bad. They'll fight,' Faisal replied.

'How long will it take?' Musallam asked.

'Two days,' Faisal shot back casually.

'You think it's PlayStation?' Musallam responded with

a sceptical eyebrow. 'This is no video game.' Musallam was a little shocked but also impressed by the confidence of the UAE trainer. Maybe Azzan really had built a force that could go the whole way.

As the land attack force was undertaking final planning, battle preparation and communications checks, the maritime intercept force was assembling over the horizon from Mukalla. The small armada had sailed at 19:00 hours on 20 April and consisted of the faster vessels of JTF-293.5, which could arrive first and which were combat ships that could clear the littoral of enemy fast attack craft – the naval term for armed speedboats with rockets, RPGs or machine guns. *Al-Hesen* (P172) and *Mezyad* (P174) were both powerful UAE Navy Baynunah-class corvettes, new guided-missile ships that came into service just before the war. Alongside the corvettes, the Navy sent two Egab coastal artillery boats (P201 and P205), which were Ghanna-tha-class 24-metre amphibious transport boats, armed with a rapid-firing 120-mm mortar system. These ships were on-station 44 km (24 nautical miles) off Mukalla by 20:00 hours on 23 April. Holding at half that distance from shore – at 22 km (12 nautical miles) – was a ragtag navy of 12 armed fishing trawlers and speedboats piloted by Salafi fishermen, whose job was to blockade Mukalla from the coast to ensure that AQAP leaders could not slip away by boat, as they had done from Zinjibar in 2012. Indeed, to make extra sure the leaders did not escape by speedboat themselves, as the senior Houthi commander had done from Aden in July 2015, the Emiratis had also brought the fastest speedboat in the navy, just in case.

At the other end of the speed range, the command ship *Al-Futaisi* (A82), aboard which Ali Saif and his staff were hastily planning the amphibious landings, would not arrive until late in the day on 25 April. The four landing craft loaded with UAE amphibious forces (L71, L62, L64, and L65) would not even sail until 24 April in preparation for landings from 27 September onwards. They would provide a valuable safety net or back-up plan if the land attack did not achieve an immediate break-through success.

Foreshadowing potential delays on the land axes, Musallam had been forced by weather to postpone the intended H-Hour (launch time) of 00:23 hours on 23 April by a full 24 hours, now becoming 00:23 hours on 24 April. It was a wise move. The advance routes were hardly the best roads to begin with, to put it mildly. Only Azzan's 213-km central axis was mostly blacktop highway, albeit narrow and steeply graded along much of its length, with sand encroaching a metre onto the highway on either side. Sohail's 195-km eastern axis was notionally the shortest route, but consisted of minor dirt roads, some of which approached the maximum trafficable gradient for MRAPs. Saeed's 324-km western axis was the worst by far, threading its way through steep, narrow chasms and even donkey tracks in its final 80 km.

Even under optimal conditions, these routes would be tough but there had been heavy rain in the days leading up to 23 April. That meant that the original intended D-Day of 23 April itself would be a blustery post-storm day, with broken cloud, ground winds and too much humidity for accurate laser designation. Better to let the ground dry out and the humidity steam off for a day, with optimal daytime conditions predicted for 24 April. Rather ironically, Raging Torrent had been postponed by a literal downpour.

Shock and awe

Although the exact H-Hour (launch time) of the assault was

THE UAE'S 'SHOCK AND AWE' STRIKES AT THE OUTSET OF OPERATION RAGING TORRENT AND THROUGHOUT THE OPERATION, 24 APRIL 2016

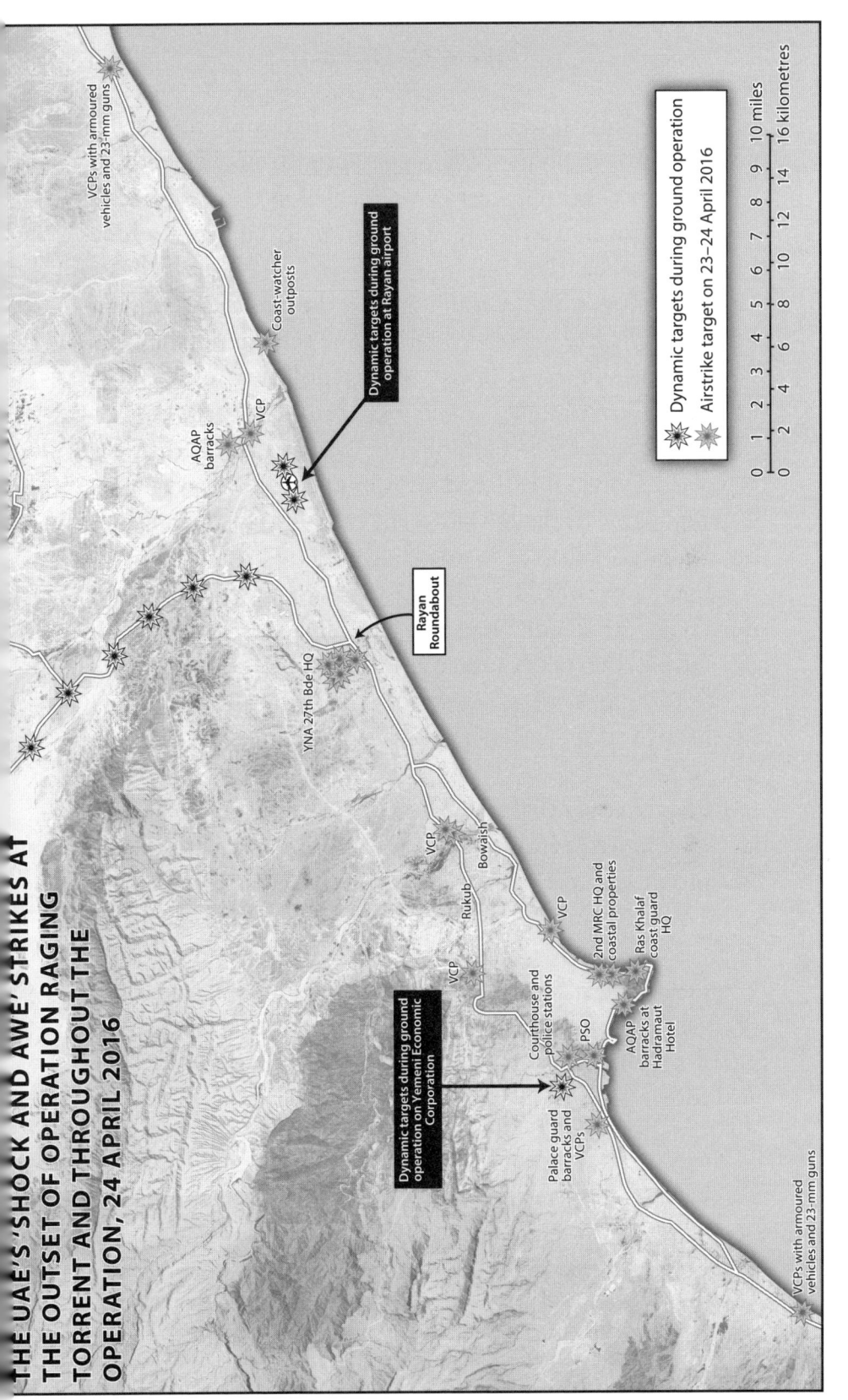

VCPs with armoured vehicles and 23-mm guns

Coast-watcher outposts

VCP

AQAP barracks

Dynamic targets during ground operation at Rayan airport

Rayan Roundabout

YNA 27th Bde HQ

VCP

Rukub

Bowaish

VCP

VCP

2nd MRC HQ and coastal properties

Ras Khalaf coast guard HQ

Courthouse and police stations

PSO

Dynamic targets during ground operation on Yemeni Economic Corporation

Palace guard barracks and VCPs

AQAP barracks at Hadramaut Hotel

VCPs with armoured vehicles and 23-mm guns

Dynamic targets during ground operation
Airstrike target on 23–24 April 2016

✳ Dynamic targets during ground operation
✳ Airstrike target on 23–24 April 2016

0 1 2 3 4 5 6 7 8 9 10 miles
0 2 4 6 8 10 12 14 16 kilometres

carefully guarded, to generate what is called 'tactical surprise', there was no possibility of 'strategic surprise' because Al-Qaeda had known from the start of the year that the Emiratis were coming. Batarfi had messaged this to the UAE back in January 2016. Since then, the Hadramis had kept up a constant dialogue with AQAP about the possibility that the terrorists might evacuate Mukalla city before any fighting began, or at least limit its defence entirely to the outskirts of the urban area. Merchants, clerics and government officials had all tried to convince AQAP to leave. 'You are not fighting the Americans, you are fighting your own people,' Batarfi had heard from local councils of elders. 'Don't destroy Mukalla.' This kind of mediation effort was, by now, commonplace in Yemen since the example of Zinjibar's devastation in 2012. In both Iraq and Syria, tribes made similar deals with the Islamic State to save their villages from destruction, albeit with uneven success.

The Emiratis were in two minds about an evacuation of Mukalla by some or all of the enemy. The most dangerous enemy course of action was an urban last stand, but the assessed most likely course of action (ML-COA, pronounced 'em-el-koa') was a mass exodus of AQAP into the hills of Shabwa and Abyan as soon as they believed a major force was really coming to Mukalla. Inside the UAE chain of command, avoiding mass destruction was foremost in their minds, even if trapping and killing Al-Qaeda's hard-core fighters was also an objective. 'We needed to get them out and then kill them on the outskirts,' one planner remembered. That was, in fact, exactly how the US-led coalition was operating in Iraq and Syria in urban battles against the Islamic State. As the noose closed in on cities like Fallujah and Manbij, the local Iraqi and Syrian security forces offered the Islamic State an escape corridor, to reduce destruction and loss of life. Such deals later happened in Raqqa and Deir ez-Zour in

Syria as well. 'We were not super thrilled about that,' one senior US commander relayed to this author, 'but this is what it meant to have Arabs liberating themselves. They did it their way.' The Emiratis were certainly not going to stop the Yemenis from trying the same trick in Mukalla if it would save the city from a destructive battle.

In the weeks before the liberation was due to begin, the UAE had watched the negotiations with interest. There were plenty of tribal intermediaries who dealt with Al-Qaeda in Aden, Mukalla, Marib and elsewhere. This was how the UAE intelligence services had secured the release in August 2015 of Robert Semple, a British hostage held by AQAP. It was also how the Emiratis had quickly recovered one of the brave Yemeni resistance scouts who had been seized by AQAP tribal auxiliaries in early 2016 as he was undertaking ground reconnaissance of the attack routes into Mukalla.

An effort was made to splinter AQAP down a fault line that the UAE had noticed over the last year: on one side the local AQAP fighters who wanted to spare Mukalla a battle, and on the other side the Yemeni hardliners and foreign fighters who wanted to defend Mukalla to the last bullet. The last effort to split Al-Qaeda unfolded on 22 April 2016 at a clandestine meeting under the Chinese Bridge, where an intermediary told Yemeni agents that AQAP would not evacuate the city. Yes, some local leaders like Batarfi wanted to spare the city and melt away to the redoubts in Shabwa. Raimi wanted to make sure the attack was not a bluff. Others – mainly foreign fighters – wanted to hold on for as long as possible, and some even wanted to 'burn the city' if it could not be held.

Perhaps it was no coincidence that the UAE's local agents received a tip-off later that day that many of the hardliner AQAP fighters would be gathering on the night of 23 April to coordinate the street-by-street defence of the city. The building in question was a large warehouse owned by the Yemeni Economic Corporation (a kind of state-run shopping cooperative) that was positioned about 500 metres west of the Chinese Bridge. The building was not occupied by civilians and had been characterised by persistent surveillance as being used solely by AQAP, but it was on the Restricted Target List because it was a piece of economic infrastructure. As UAE drones watched armed fighters gathering there, Musallam got the target specially cleared by the Combined Air Operations Centre in Riyadh. The curfew was underway for the night in Mukalla, and almost the only vehicles allowed to move were Al-Qaeda. After the arrivals slowed, around 120 fighters were assessed to be inside the warehouse. Overhead, a UAE F-16 released a single 2,000-lb bomb fused to airburst immediately after piercing the roof. It struck dead centre. Almost everyone in the building was killed, judging by the relatively small number of ambulances that came and went in the hour after the strike. It was a shot to the head for the most hard-line AQAP fighters who wanted to defend the city street by street.

Saif's occasional test-strikes had been useful for profiling enemy reactions but also for desensitising Al-Qaeda to things that go bump in the night. As midnight approached, the enemy probably could not tell whether this explosion was one of the occasional American strikes or something else entirely. At 00:01 hours on 24 April, Saif's 'shock and awe' targeting began. Saif had planned an orchestral symphony of strikes to demoralise and disrupt the enemy: as the smoke cleared between rounds of strikes, allowing a clear view and accurate lasing, other 2,000-pounders were hitting empty mountainsides in order to reflect soundwaves back into the city and create a kind of 'rolling thunder' effect. 'The aim was to shock the enemy into surrender or running away, out of the city,' Saif explained. 'My aim was to tell them: "It's over, give up."'

All 30 pre-planned targets were struck in quick succession by UAE Mirage 2000-9s and F-16s, as well as by the mighty Saudi F-15s. The strike occurred as the streets were at their most empty, with Al-Qaeda's curfew in effect by a couple of hours. The first round of strikes hit buildings where AQAP fighters and leaders were known to sleep, and these were struck first to maximise fatalities. The large courthouse was struck at only one aimpoint and with a single 2,000-pounder. The strike was pinpointed to ensure no damage to the prison wing and the large bomb was set with a five-millisecond delay to ensure that it dug deeply into the ground before exploding, to contain its blast effect. The Hadramaut Hotel, taken over as an enemy barracks location, was pummelled at 12 distinct aimpoints with GBU-12 500-lb bombs. The Hisba headquarters, the PSO building, 27th YNA brigade base, the Ras Khalaf coastal defence brigade, and the 190th Air Defence headquarters also received delayed-fuse 2,000-lb strikes. A number of AQAP barracks in checkpoints, warehouses, coastguard facilities and police stations were struck with 500-lb bombs with 2.5-millisecond delay fuses.

All identified tanks, 23-mm anti-aircraft cannons, BMPs and other armoured vehicles at the city's edges were destroyed by 2,000-lb bombs, where it was safe to use them. For some smaller targets, 250-lb Small Diameter Bombs were dropped from F-16s and Mirages piloted by flying officers whom Saif knew to be particularly careful and accurate. Wherever possible, the bombs were launched from as far out as they could be, to give the maximum amount of time for pilots to observe the function of the guidance system and, if necessary, splash an errant bomb into a mountain or the ocean.

Now Saif's focus shifted to supporting the advancing axes, but some of his strike assets kept up a watch on the city's exits – looking for fleeing AQAP convoys – while others sustained the 'rolling thunder' psychological warfare strikes. The two Egab mortar boats would prove useful in keeping up a suppressive fire on coastguard bases, the sea-facing outposts at Rayan airport, and various coastal resorts where AQAP had placed coast-watchers.

Though many tip-offs about AQAP movements began to be reported, it was impossible to satisfy the UAE's rules of engagement regarding positive identification now, in a city full of moving parts, including 'inside resistance' fighters who looked exactly like their AQAP enemies. This is where having US intelligence support would have been so useful, and where having the small Hellfire missiles of UAE Apaches based on a US helicopter carrier would have opened up whole new classes of target to precise observation and attack.

The rule of three

As UAE soldiers always say, if you send three of anything you definitely have one. Most UAE attacks in Yemen used no fewer than three axes of advance, in order to present the enemy with tactical dilemmas – spreading their defences thin – and to give a degree of assurance that even the failure of one or two axes would still result in success. In the case of Mukalla, this was especially significant, because the routes over which the UAE had to advance were so treacherous to navigate and potentially so easy to block by an enemy who knew what they were doing. There was even a real chance that all three axes might be decisively blunted by a strong AQAP defence of the mountain passes, at which point the amphibious landing might have become the main effort and vital insurance policy for success. In the event, the three-axis plan proved as useful as ever, with each route challenged by either heavy opposition or bad roads, but fortunately not both.

The night was dark with no moon showing and smelled of rain as Azzan sent off his vanguard of scouts and HEF with an OMLT led by Lieutenant Ahmed B. It was 00:01 hours on 24 April and this was the moment that Azzan had been awaiting for as long as he could remember. He had been with the Hadramis for a year, and these last three months had seen him get only two or three hours of sleep a night as the operation drew close. 'The only way back to a normal life was *through* the battle,' he remembered thinking.

Azzan's second echelon – Faraj al-Bahsani's command group and a few hundred former soldiers – went next. They passed through the last friendly checkpoint and then into the 70 km of no-man's land before Al-Qaeda territory. The winding road gradually rose upwards towards the distant crest, invisible in the dark, where the first AQAP defences were expected at a place called Masila Junction. At around 02:00 hours, Azzan's RG-31 MRAP, a type of vehicle he superstitiously considered lucky, came to a halt facing the crest, which he surveyed through night-vision goggles. (The RG-31s were also popular with commanders and JTACs because of their large numbers of armoured glass windows: most MRAPs were all armour and tiny little windows, which reduced situational awareness.) This was where the intelligence staff reported that Al-Qaeda had poured slippery fuel oil on the road as it sloped upwards, gaining 50 metres in altitude over the next half-kilometre. The enemy at this blocking point were supposed to be a force of 150 hard-core AQAP fighters led by a mysterious Egyptian deputy of Raimi's, another 'second generation' Al-Qaeda veteran of Afghanistan in the 1990s.

ELEVATION PROFILES OF OPERATION RAGING TORRENT AXES, 24 APRIL 2016

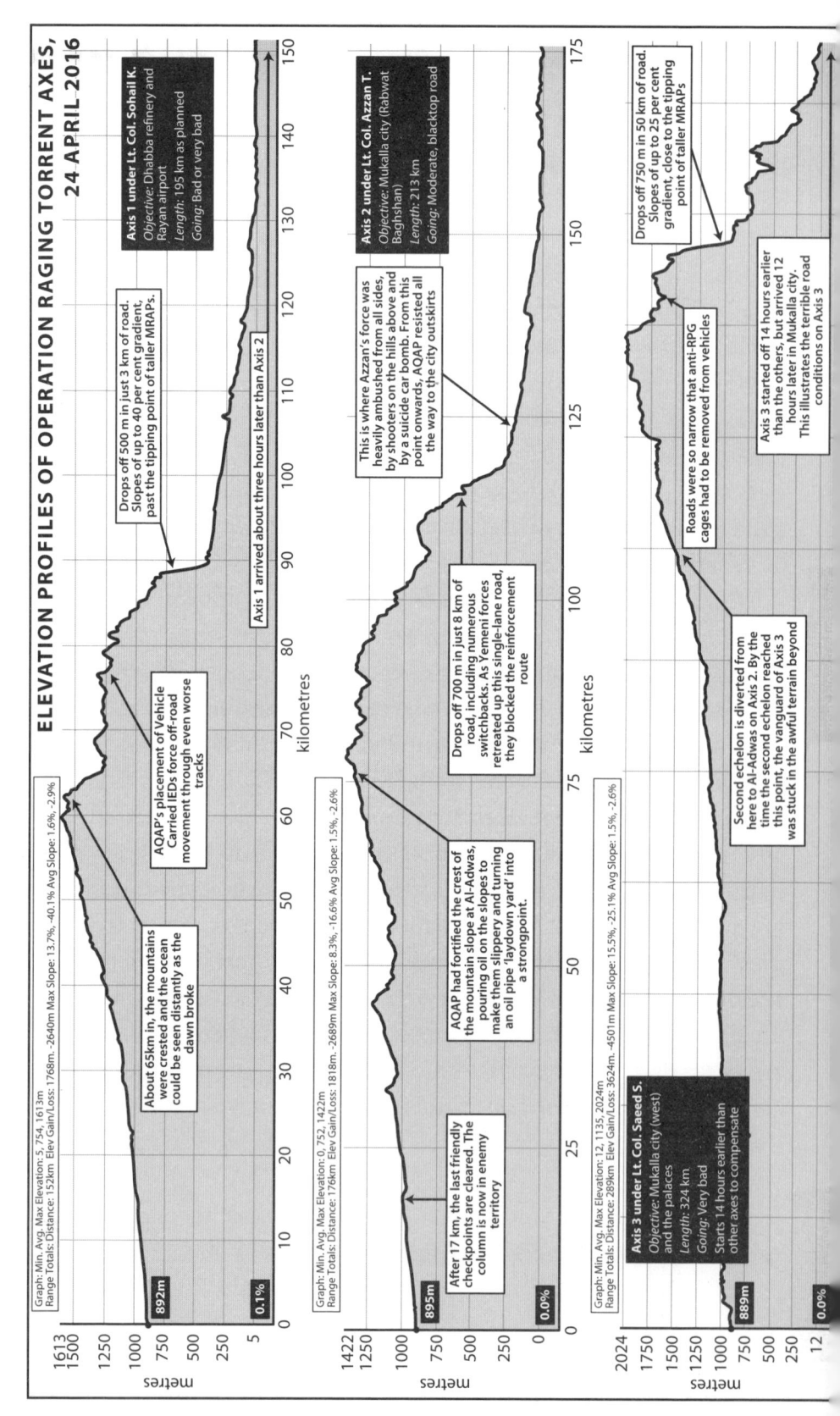

Axis 1 under Lt. Col. Sohail K.
Objective: Dhabba refinery and Rayan airport
Length: 195 km as planned
Going: Bad or very bad

Graph: Min. Avg. Max Elevation: 5, 754, 1613m
Range Totals: Distance: 152km Elev Gain/Loss: 1768m. -2640m Max Slope: 13.7%, -40.1% Avg Slope: 1.6%, -2.9%

Drops off 500 m in just 3 km of road. Slopes of up to 40 per cent gradient, past the tipping point of taller MRAPs.

AQAP's placement of Vehicle Carried IEDs force off-road movement through even worse tracks

About 65km in, the mountains were crested and the ocean could be seen distantly as the dawn broke

Axis 1 arrived about three hours later than Axis 2

Axis 2 under Lt. Col. Azzan T.
Objective: Mukalla city (Rabwat Baghshan)
Length: 213 km
Going: Moderate, blacktop road

Graph: Min. Avg. Max Elevation: 0, 752, 1422m
Range Totals: Distance: 176km Elev Gain/Loss: 1818m. -2689m Max Slope: 8.3%, -16.6% Avg Slope: 1.5%, -2.6%

This is where Azzan's force was heavily ambushed from all sides, by shooters on the hills above and by a suicide car bomb. From this point onwards, AQAP resisted all the way to the city outskirts

Drops off 700 m in just 8 km of road, including numerous switchbacks. As Yemeni forces retreated up this single-lane road, they blocked the reinforcement route

AQAP had fortified the crest of the mountain slope at Al-Adwas, pouring oil on the slopes to make them slippery and turning an oil pipe 'laydown yard' into a strongpoint.

After 17 km, the last friendly checkpoints are cleared. The column is now in enemy territory

Axis 3 under Lt. Col. Saeed S.
Objective: Mukalla city (west) and the palaces
Length: 324 km
Going: Very bad
Starts 14 hours earlier than other axes to compensate

Graph: Min. Avg. Max Elevation: 12, 1135, 2024m
Range Totals: Distance: 289km Elev Gain/Loss: 3624m. -4501m Max Slope: 15.5%, -25.1% Avg Slope: 1.5%, -2.6%

Drops off 750 m in 50 km of road. Slopes of up to 25 per cent gradient, close to the tipping point of taller MRAPs

Roads were so narrow that anti-RPG cages had to be removed from vehicles

Axis 3 started off 14 hours earlier than the others, but arrived 12 hours later in Mukalla city. This illustrates the terrible road conditions on Axis 3

Second echelon is diverted from here to Al-Adwas on Axis 2. By the time the second echelon reached this point, the vanguard of Axis 3 was stuck in the awful terrain beyond

kilometres
metres

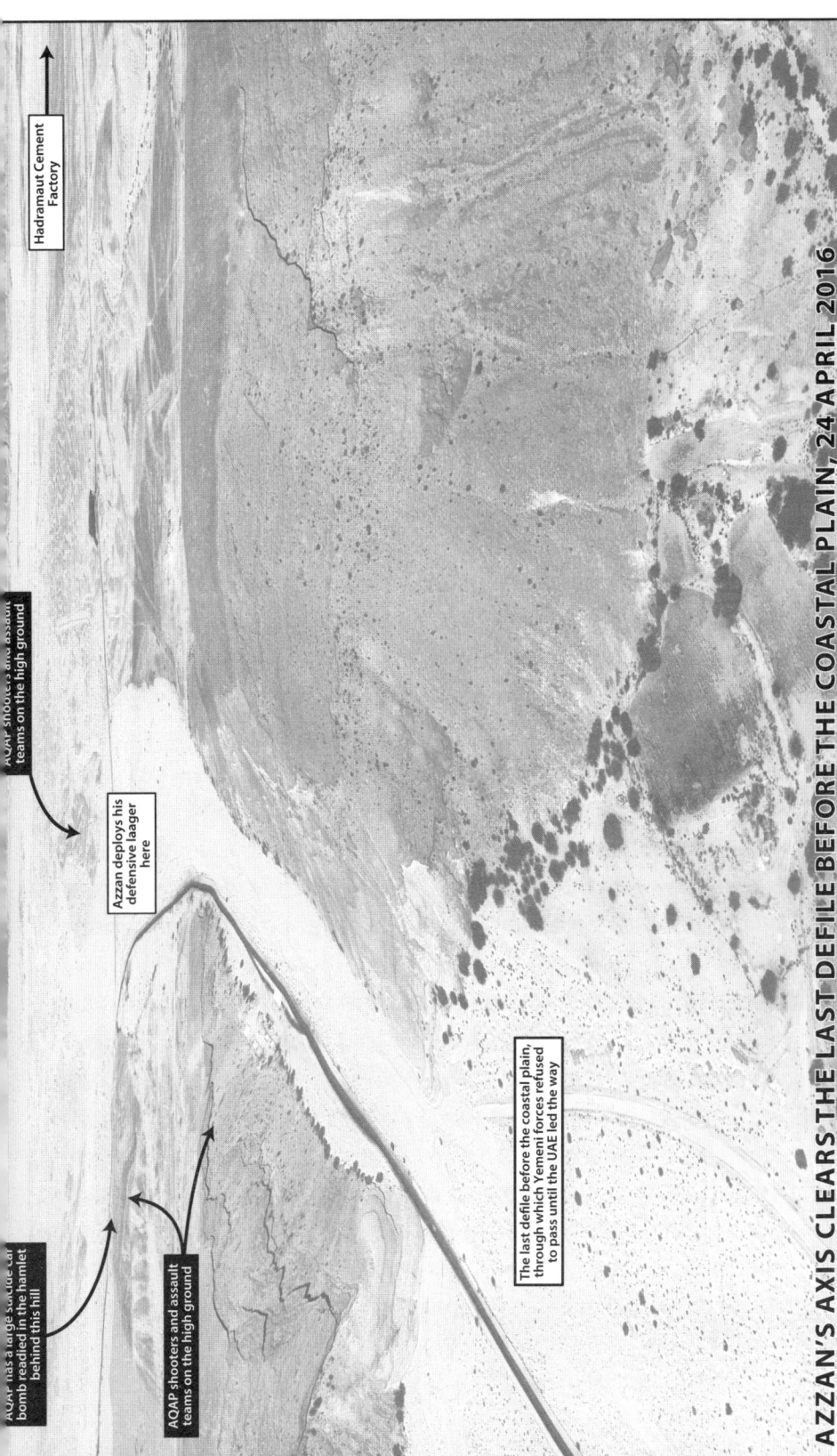

Hadramaut Cement Factory

AQAP shooters and assault teams on the high ground

Azzan deploys his defensive laager here

AQAP has a large suicide car bomb readied in the hamlet behind this hill

AQAP shooters and assault teams on the high ground

The last defile before the coastal plain, through which Yemeni forces refused to pass until the UAE led the way

AZZAN'S AXIS CLEARS THE LAST DEFILE BEFORE THE COASTAL PLAIN, 24 APRIL 2016

Azzan now put the 'break-in' phase of his central axis battle into effect. It was time to go loud. The centre of the defences overlooking the oily road was what is known in the oil industry as a 'pipe laydown yard'. The complex was positioned at the top of the slope at the Masila Junction. Enemy activity at the site had been carefully profiled for weeks, and one building had been identified as the main barracks block. This structure was 'dropped' by a single GBU-12 500-lb bomb in a thunderclap that echoed around the hills. Enemy small arms fire began to punctuate the night. Then, as the column brought up trucks specially loaded with sand to cover the oily road, the enemy complex was watched from the ground and the air, and hit twice more when enemy small arms fire was seen originating from the complex. Ahmed B.'s vanguard moved up onto the crest above and began scouting a path for the column through a belt of daisy-chained roadside bombs, or IEDs packed into culverts where the blacktop passed over little streambeds between ridges.

Watching by drone, Musallam and the joint fires cell could see the Al-Qaeda fighters at Masila Junction falling back in good order to prepare their next defence line in the oil-blackened truck-stop town of Al-Adwas. 'I could see they were well-organised,' Musallam remembered. 'They fought like a conventional army. They used concealment and manoeuvred under the trees.' Ahmed B. watched the same movements from the ground using night-vision goggles and could see that civilians from Al-Adwas were spilling out of their houses and getting caught in the crossfire between his Yemeni fighters and the next Al-Qaeda defence line. He led his OMLT forward in their vehicles, drawing them and the HEF between the civilians and the AQAP defences, to get the people out of the line of fire and allow them to escape. Saif, back in the Nahab underground command cell, directed stacked-up F-16s to mount three GBU-12 strikes to destroy enemy firing points visible through the pilots' infrared targeting pods. Ahmed B. waved Azzan's main attack force through at around 03:00 hours; he would root out the last AQAP and catch up when the third echelon relieved him and garrisoned Al-Adwas.

Azzan's OMLT was now in the lead, with Bahsani's command group and his second echelon of 350 former soldiers immediately behind. They began a meandering six-hour advance over the multiple crests of the mountains, flanked by dramatic 700-metre drop-offs, until reaching the point where the road began to slope consistently downwards towards the coast. As dawn came up, the ground was wet and the mountains were breezy, the way it always was after heavy rain. The rest of the morning saw the column work its way carefully down the switchbacks between the mountaintop and Abdullah Gharib, dropping from 1,400 metres above sea level to just 200 metres in only 40 km. By 10:45 hours, Bahsani and his men felt like this might be a good point to call it a day: they had been going for more than 12 hours now and were tired. So was Azzan, but there was no way he was stopping and making camp when the coastal plain was less than an hour's drive away. The enemy had sniped at them and there had been the odd roadside bomb to avoid, but clearly the attackers had tactical surprise on their side. Any of these switchbacks on the single-lane road would make great defensive choke points if properly held and suspicious chasses were seen in the distance shadowing the column: this was no time to let the enemy recover and plan a counter-attack.

As midday passed, Azzan could feel the pressure building. The other two axes were nowhere near as far forward as he was. That made his effort the best chance to break through on this first day. There was only one more defile between his axis and the coastal plain, then it was just 40 km of flat road to the coastal highway and Mukalla city beyond. But Bahsani and his column were still hesitant, so Azzan took his OMLT and HEF vanguard forward through the final pass to show that it was safe. Here, countless millennia of rainfall had cut a gap 200 metres wide. Passing under 100-metre-high cliffs on the wadi floor, Azzan took his force through, the turret gunners scanning the high ground.

On the other side, he drew up his little force into a triangular laager (a wagon caravan set up for all-round defence), with their guns facing outwards. Azzan's RG-31 and the two of the larger six-wheel Caiman MRAPs were interspersed with three chasses of Hadrami bodyguards and scouts. Just a few hundred metres away was the permanent outer vehicle checkpoint of Mukalla, the large sunshade covering the inbound lane, in the past manned by bored, hot soldiers, but empty now. This place was a symbol: if you held it, you held the door to Mukalla. And the enemy knew that too. Suddenly, from every ridge all around the low, wide bowl in which the force was circled, heavy fire began to smash into Azzan's force.

The ambush at Al-Ayoun

As soon as the ambush had been sprung, Azzan knew he had met the enemy's main line of resistance. A multi-direction attack involving mortars, snipers and heavy machine guns was known as a 'complex attack' in military terminology because it signalled forethought and organisation. Azzan had seen hard fighting against the Taliban and Al-Qaeda in Afghanistan, and he had been wondering if these Yemeni AQAP were made of the same stuff. 'Experience from Afghanistan told me that I was in a kill zone,' Azzan remembered with a shiver, eight years later. The RG-31 was rocking as heavy rounds hit its tyres and windows.

When you are in a bullet-proof vehicle being hit with small arms fire, the sound is oppressive, with repeated sharp cracks on metal and armoured glass making it hard to think. As noted previously, this type of MRAP was popular with Emirati command teams because of its great all-round visibility, which means armoured glass windows all around, and those large windows were now all getting hit. Outside, the Yemenis on the chasses were bailing out and finding cover. Azzan counted four obviously dead already. 'I *have* to manoeuvre, return fire, do *something, anything!*' Azzan had told himself. 'Afghanistan experience told me if I was passive, we'd all be dead.'

The enemy was shooting from high ground, often behind ridges, but those positions would offer no cover if they could be flanked if Azzan's vehicles kept making small movements to get better angles of fire. By moving, Azzan could also draw mortar fire away from the Yemeni wounded lying all around. The Caimans shuffled back and forth to give their 12.7-mm heavy machine guns better angles on enemy shooters. Azzan even 'broke the seal' on his RG-31, opening the door a little way to allow him to lob grenades onto the hills at high angles using an RG-6 six-shot, revolver-type 40-mm grenade launcher. Azzan's door now came under accurate fire, with a milky spider's web of concentric cracks spreading a few centimetres out from each impact point. He watched a Yemeni bodyguard sniped cleanly between his body armour and his chin, right in the throat.

The Emiratis back at Nahab were desperately trying to call the Yemeni general Bahsani's second echelon force of 40 chasses forward through the pass. These old soldiers felt vindicated by the rising sounds of battle and the mortar and grenade explosions up ahead: they had imagined ambushes everywhere and, as the saying goes: 'Even a stopped clock tells the right time twice a day.' Instead of coming forward, their convoy doubled back on itself, driving back up the hills towards Abdallah Gharib. 'These Emiratis are crazy. If they want to die, let them,' one of Bahsani's officers told him. Abdullah B. had been making his way up the column after leaving a garrison at Al-Adwas and tried to get his OMLT to help Azzan, but the single-lane road was now choked with Bahsani's column fleeing back into the mountains. 'Come back . . . use your force,' the Emiratis begged, 'or at least get them off the road.' Azzan and his men were trapped and alone.

At moments like this, air power often comes to the rescue of modern armed forces in a bad tactical situation. But air power had its limitations. In the early afternoon of 24 September, the skies over Azzan's force were temporarily empty. Fast air like the F-16s, Mirages and F-15s could not stick around for long over each axis because of their limited fuel endurance when they are heavily loaded with ordnance and working at long ranges. Again, this was where US refuelling tanker support would have really helped, but the Emiratis would make do with what they had. JTACs referred to this kind of fast air support as 'throw and go' because if you did not have a target for the jets as they arrived, you might miss your chance to use them on that sortie and they would be gone. The real killers in this kind of close fight were the UAE Apaches – but they were sitting on the USS *Boxer*, a US helicopter carrier, not available for use in the battle due to Washington's unwillingness to authorise UAE combat operations against Al-Qaeda from the US vessel. Instead, the UAE had partially filled that gap with slow prop-driven AT-802s, which shadowed the column and might have developed the 'finger-tip feel' for the friendly and enemy positions below that is needed to provide close air support. There had been an AT-802 overhead for most of the first 12 hours of the attack, but now, as luck would have it, one was heading back for refuelling and its back-to-back replacement was delayed.

Maybe Al-Qaeda had sensed that there was no help around because they chose this exact moment to bring in their heaviest weapon – a suicide car bomb. Ahmed B. had shouldered his personal Caiman vehicle through Bahsani's retreating chasses and had reached Azzan's encircled group to add a fourth MRAP to the laager. In the gun turret of Balooshi's vehicle was Corporal Saeed H., then a UAE Land Forces machine-gunner who volunteered to join the Hadramaut OMLTs. Looking due east through the flames and smoke of burning chasses, Corporal Saeed could see a white Nissan Patrol car moving quickly around the base of the hill that hid a little hamlet from his view. An unarmed drone showed the headquarters staff at Nahab that the area seemed to be a gathering point for enemy fighters and it had probably been the 'hide site' and launch point for this car bomb.

But Corporal Saeed was not assuming anything: he had rules of engagement and even in the midst of this firefight, he knew that it could still be a civilian escaping or a resistance vehicle returning to friendly lines. Like a lot of young gunners, Saeed had superb eyesight and as he watched the vehicle's odd progress he could clearly make out the very young man driving the car – probably young because older Yemeni tribal men had usually grown beards. None of this looked right. Then, after seeming to pass by the laager to its rear-left, the driver veered off the road and headed straight towards the OMLT from behind. Clever. Everyone scrambled to realign the laager. Ahmed B. put his MRAP between the suicide bomber and Azzan's RG-31. Corporal Saeed hand-cranked his turret traverse as fast as he could: it would be a close race. With a second to spare, he thumbed off the safety catch of his heavy machine gun and put a precise group of rounds into the driver-side windscreen. He just had time to register the window shattering and a hint of red and then everything went dark.

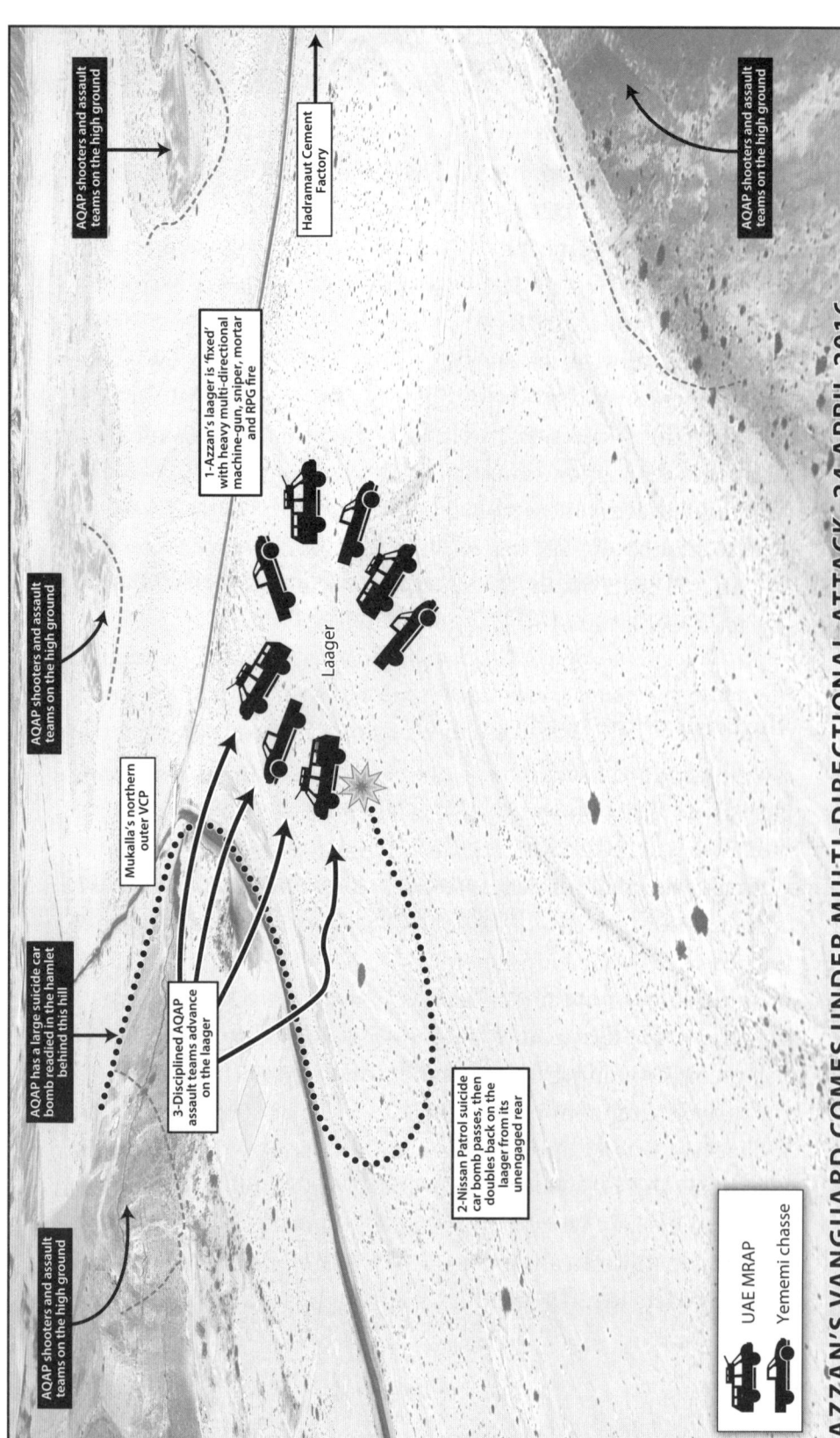

AQAP shooters and assault teams on the high ground

AQAP shooters and assault teams on the high ground

1-Azzan's laager is 'fixed' with heavy multi-directional machine-gun, sniper, mortar and RPG fire

Hadramaut Cement Factory

AQAP shooters and assault teams on the high ground

Laager

Mukalla's northern outer VCP

AQAP has a large suicide car bomb readied in the hamlet behind this hill

3-Disciplined AQAP assault teams advance on the laager

AQAP shooters and assault teams on the high ground

2-Nissan Patrol suicide car bomb passes, then doubles back on the laager from its unengaged rear

UAE MRAP

Yememi chasse

AZZAN'S VANGUARD COMES UNDER MULTI-DIRECTIONAL ATTACK, 24 APRIL 2016

Above, a watching drone recorded the huge explosion and its concussion wave sending a dust wave outwards. The Nissan's engine block had landed 50 metres away.

Azzan couldn't see much as he looked out of the windscreen, which provided a thin strip of forward visibility between the roof, cage armour and the engine cover. Despite the best efforts of the delicate windscreen wipers, the window was covered by a layer of encrusted road dust and its tinting was peeling at the edges, framing the scene in a light blue halo. Remembering ambushes in Afghanistan, he left the radio net clear for those who might need it most, the vehicles close to the blast. There was a tense silence and he waited with his jaw clenched. Nothing. Nothing. Then Ahmed B. called in, barely able to speak from the acrid smoke and unable to hear any reply.

The crisis of the battle

Corporal Saeed looked out from behind his bent and smoking gun shield through the thick black smoke that was rising in a mushroom cloud above the laager. Ten metres from his 27-tonne Caiman was a huge crater. A licence plate was wedged in the anti-RPG cage of his MRAP. A Yemeni resistance chassis had been flipped over by the blast and its Dushka gunner and driver were burning somewhere underneath it, with nothing to be done to save them. He dropped down into the MRAP personnel compartment, crouching on the metal gunner's platform between the driver and commander's seats. Everyone was mouthing 'What happened?' and checking each other for wounds. 'You're bleeding,' Ahmed B. silently gestured to Saeed, and together they sterilised his arm wound and applied a tourniquet. His helmet was ripped up from sharp fragments of the Nissan Patrol but it had saved his life. Then he saw movement not far outside the

MRAP through the damaged windscreen. 'Enemy!' he shouted, and stood up into the turret to begin gunning again.

In the seconds after the suicide car bomb exploded, the AQAP fighters moved swiftly to close the distance on the smoke-shrouded laager. It was a scene of total devastation: three burning chasses, a huge smoking crater, dead Yemenis lying all around, and four MRAPs, their tyres and windows scarred by fragmentation and bullet impacts. Azzan's command RG-31 had multiple bullet impacts in his commander-side window and he did not know how many more hits the ballistic glass between him and the bullets would take. Then, through his spider-web-cracked window, Azzan saw something that took his breath away.

A young Yemeni survivor of the bodyguard unit was standing next to the window, probably in shock, and dazedly looking at Azzan. 'I could see death in his eyes,' Azzan remembered vividly. The Yemeni put a blood-soaked hand on the window, with one finger missing. 'I have to do something for my soldier,' Azzan remembered. 'To me, they were my sons.' He told his gunner to lay down suppressing fire and then clambered over the creaking, clanking non-slip metal floor panels to the rear door of the RG-31, where the incoming fire was less intense. He took a deep breath and shouldered the door open, pointing his M4 carbine in case of enemies close by, then jumped out and slammed the door behind him. He commando-crawled under the RG-31 and pulled the little Yemeni down with him, manhandled him to the rear doors and threw him in. Azzan's face and hands were covered in so much blood when he returned that his crew were sure he had been hit.

Looking out of a window, Azzan could see an older Yemeni HEF fighter with white hair, still firing his rifle. Inside the MRAP, the wounded Yemeni was brave too; he quietly said to Azzan: 'Don't worry. We'll win.' Azzan became strangely calm. When interviewed eight years later, Azzan seemed to be transported back there to those pivotal moments of his life. Remembering those few seconds vividly, he would sum up his mindset as follows. 'We couldn't get far on our tyres and I was not going to retreat anyway. The whole UAE military was behind us and the whole of Mukalla was in front of us. I might be dead, but the UAE would not lose. We might die here, but if we are going to be shot, let it be in the front not the back.' He issued precise final orders: 'Gunners – expend all remaining ammunition. Full rate of fire, 360-degrees. Everyone – get ready for hand-to-hand fighting. Be prepared to dismount and attack.'

As Azzan was readying the final stand, the enemy was 30 metres away, then 15. Via drone, these 30 or so Al-Qaeda veterans could be seen moving and firing towards the MRAPs, using tactical hand signals to communicate despite the noise. Soon they would be pulling on the handles of the MRAP doors. It was almost time to dismount. They were 30 seconds away from the end, Azzan calculated. And then he heard Saif, the joint fires controller, over the radio net. F-16 and AT-802 were overhead, but their laser-guided bombs would land almost on top of Azzan's vehicles because the enemy were right on him. 'Doesn't matter!' he shouted. 'Danger close?' Saif confirmed. Azzan roared 'NOW! SHOOT!'

Explosions rocked the MRAPs on their suspensions, throwing their occupants around. The enemy close to the vehicles were gone in an instant, as if they had never existed. On the hills above, one F-16 was identifying firing points by their thermal signature and lasing them, while another dropped one bomb after another, and then they swapped roles until both had bare wings. The hills echoed with explosions for ten minutes straight as the stacked-up air power decimated the ambushers. It was about 15:00 hours. Now the third echelon would take the lead for the last leg of the assault on Mukalla.

XII

THE LIBERATION OF MUKALLA

One of Musallam's greatest moments of pride during the Mukalla operation was watching the sub-commanders on Azzan's axis passing the baton from one to the other, smoothly and without hesitation. The 'passage of lines' – military terminology for passing one force through another without disordering either of them – was not an easy manoeuvre to pull off, even in peacetime exercises. With these men, Musallam did not need to prompt or prod. They got on with it.

It was now Faisal K.'s turn to be the spearhead. He was the cocky young officer who had told Musallam they would take Mukalla in two days. If he could reach Mukalla today, he'd cut that time frame in half. Faisal had struggled his way forward with his HEF forces through the disintegrating wreckage of Bahsani's former soldiers. Now he was with Azzan, whose MRAP had 14 major 'dings' (bullet impacts) in its armoured glass, as well as cages bent from RPG strikes. Azzan held a quick Istikhara prayer with Faisal for guidance and to prepare them both. (Istikhara is a type of prayer recited by Muslims who are in need of guidance from Allah when facing an important decision in their life.) 'Are you ready to take the lead?' Azzan asked.

Faisal was. But he decided to take only one of his two Caiman MRAPs to the front of the column, with just himself, his driver and JTAC on board. The other members of the OMLT could

LIBERATION OF MUKALLA, 24 APRIL 2016

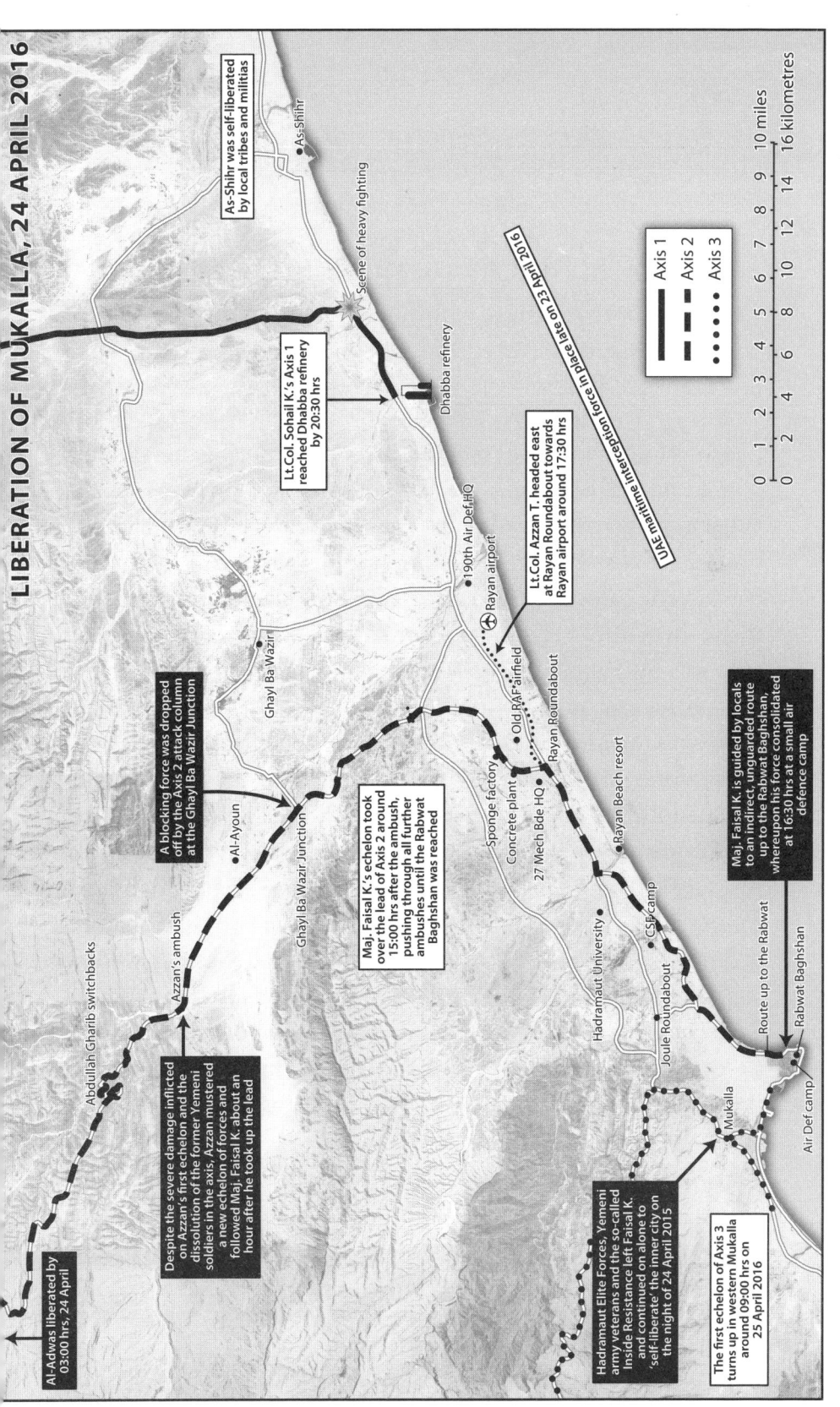

As-Shihr was self-liberated by local tribes and militias

Scene of heavy fighting

Lt.Col. Sohail K.'s Axis 1 reached Dhabba refinery by 20:30 hrs

Dhabba refinery

Lt.Col. Azzan T. headed east at Rayan Roundabout towards Rayan airport around 17:30 hrs

UAE maritime interception force in place late on 23 April 2016

Axis 1
Axis 2
Axis 3

0 1 2 3 4 5 6 7 8 9 10 miles
0 2 4 6 8 10 12 14 16 kilometres

A blocking force was dropped off by the Axis 2 attack column at the Ghayl Ba Wazir Junction

Ghayl Ba Wazir

190th Air Def.HQ

Rayan airport

Old RAF airfield

Rayan Roundabout

Al-Ayoun

Ghayl Ba Wazir Junction

Maj. Faisal K.'s echelon took over the lead of Axis 2 around 15:00 hrs after the ambush, pushing through all further ambushes until the Rabwat Baghshan was reached

Sponge factory

Concrete plant

27 Mech Bde HQ

Rayan Beach resort

Azzan's ambush

Abdullah Gharib switchbacks

Despite the severe damage inflicted on Azzan's first echelon and the dissolution of the former Yemeni soldiers in the axis, Azzan mustered a new echelon of forces and followed Maj. Faisal K. about an hour after he took up the lead

Hadramaut University

CSF camp

Joule Roundabout

Maj. Faisal K. is guided by locals to an indirect, unguarded route up to the Rabwat Baghshan, whereupon his force consolidated at 16:30 hrs at a small air defence camp

Route up to the Rabwat

Rabwat Baghshan

Air Def camp

Al-Adwas liberated by 03:00 hrs, 24 April

Hadramaut Elite Forces, Yemeni army veterans and the so-called Inside Resistance left Faisal K. and continued on alone to 'self-liberate' the inner city on the night of 24 April 2015

Mukalla

The first echelon of Axis 3 turns up in western Mukalla around 09:00 hrs on 25 April 2016 stay further back in the column, so that they could take over if his own team was hit as hard as Azzan's had just been. To protect the Yemenis in the vanguard, they would all be packed into 12 of the big three-metre-tall Caimans – nine Yemenis per vehicle – with 12 chasses full of the HEF hanging further back. And to protect better against ambushes, scouts in civilian vehicles would move further ahead and on the flanks on the more open coastal plain. The Emiratis were learning lessons as they fought and were adjusting their tactics accordingly in the midst of the battle. Azzan's battered echelon would reorganise and follow half an hour later with some reinforcements arriving from the HEF reserve. Bahsani's force was gone for good and was written off.

Faisal's command MRAP ranged up and down the column like a sheepdog keeping a flock together. He had taught the vehicle commanders and drivers to control their speed and maintain even spacing between vehicles and, most important, to always push through any ambush. 'You stop or reverse, I'll ram you off the road,' he warned them. Now, as snipers, machine guns and RPGs harassed the column from the flanks, Faisal simply pressed on past the aggregates plants and shallow quarries. Saif's air cover was now overhead at all times. Enemies firing on the flanks were dealt with by the air force, either the Mirage 2000-9s dropping laser-guided bombs onto firing points or AT-802s firing laser-guided 2.75-inch rocket pods. There were no mountain peaks here to break the laser lock from a guiding aircraft, so the fire support was constant and accurate every time. A huge explosion cleared the way for the column in Al-Ayoun as Mirages destroyed an enemy blocking point that had unwisely been set up next to a petrol station.

A flank guard was dropped off at the junction to the Al-Qaeda stronghold at Ghayl Ba Wazir and then Faisal's force kept going. The reddish earth of the uplands (known as the joul) gave way to the sandy light earth and scrubby trees of the coastal plain. Past the sponge factory, past the concrete plant and beyond the old abandoned British airbase. As they took a right along the coastal highway towards Mukalla city, AQAP fighters in the 27th YNA brigade base began to snipe from the towers and gatehouse, but Faisal again pressed on, his gunners using their machine guns to suppress enemy fire and protect the more vulnerable chasses to the rear. It was around 16:00 hours and the sea was just 1,500 metres to their left, parallel with the coast road. The water looked alluring: grey-green and wave-flecked in the shallows, turning to an unbroken, placid blue as it deepened. They pushed on past the university and the old *qat* market. They took fire from the Central Security Forces base in Bowaish, where the cage on Faisal's MRAP caught and pre-detonated another RPG. Still there was no stopping: just a rolling advance with the gunners raking enemy firing points on their assigned arcs.

Now local expertise showed its value. Mukalla people began to interact with the Yemenis in Faisal's column. They warned about ambushes on the coast road near the 2nd MRC head-quarters and suggested a better way up to Faisal's objective – the small mountain overlooking the city centre, Rabwat Baghshan, with its unfinished Republican Guard base and air defence sites up on the plateau. Faisal had spent so many months poring over satellite imagery of Mukalla that he grasped exactly the back-door approach that his Yemeni guides were recommending.

Inside the city

The column threaded its way up the 80-metre-high hill and found itself looking down over the whole of Mukalla city: the black earth of the hill contrasting with the whitewash of the city and the line of four little Quaiti sultanate forts overlooking the old city and the sultan's palace. Rows of aquamarine fishing boats rolled around on the breezy sea. Then it hit Faisal: he might be the first Emirati commander in Mukalla but that meant he had a city of Al-Qaeda fighters all around him. The local guides were feeding him reports that AQAP was readying a counter-attack on the hill. His force of about 220 Yemenis and Emiratis suddenly felt very small, especially as one in ten of them was wounded.

The Republican Guard base was not a site that could be secured for a force this small: it was triangular, about 1,600 metres per side, and had no real perimeter. Furthermore, it wasn't a military base at all; rather, it was a maze of mounds that had not yet been levelled for building. The lines of fire were short, and sneaking up on his men after the sun set would be very easy. Squatters were living in little shanties all around and the scene was rapidly becoming surreal. Young men on trail bikes were riding around with confetti blowers from wedding parades that ejected shiny foil and paper, which was fluttering everywhere. Mukalla people were coming up to the base to meet the liberators, but so too were Al-Qaeda, Faisal's guides confirmed. He would not be able to tell one from the other and he couldn't count on air power while he was in among all these civilians and their shanties. AQAP had no such restrictions: at around 16:30, 120-mm mortar bombs began to land, walking their way towards his force, suggestive of a preparatory barrage that might precede an Al-Qaeda assault.

Commanders need energy and optimism, and they are rewarded for being aggressive. But the line between confidence and overconfidence is a fine one. Faisal realised that he needed help. Expecting Azzan's second echelon to be 30 minutes behind,

Faisal radioed his commander to get some advice and enquire when he might be arriving to reinforce the lodgement on Rabwat Baghshan. But Azzan had bad news for him: the central axis objective had been switched while Faisal was charging into Mukalla, and Azzan was instead in a nasty close-range fight at Rayan airport, which he had been ordered to take because Sohail's eastern axis was still hours away. Somehow, Faisal had not got the message and was told calmly by Azzan: 'No one can help you right now, you will have to help yourself.'

At that moment, Faisal was again helped by his Yemeni fighters. A local Mukalla man on his force, an old naval officer, suggested they consolidate the defence at a smaller coastal air defence battery site that was halfway down the hill. When they arrived, Faisal agreed that this was the right place to make a stand. It was a much more compact 200-metre-wide site that was unoccupied. Dead Al-Qaeda fighters, destroyed 23-mm cannons and scattered anti-aircraft shells were lying all around after one of Saif's opening airstrikes. Also fluttering around and caught on wire fences and bushes were UAE psychological operations (psyops) leaflets warning civilians to stay away from Al-Qaeda sites and not to put their families in danger by sheltering Al-Qaeda. One image showed shining Dubai; another, a destroyed wartime city. Which did they want?

Faisal took a breath and ordered an inventory of turret gun ammunition: each MRAP and each chasse started out with one 'line' of 4,000 rounds per turret gun, but after gunning all the way from Al-Ayoun and through multiple ambushes, they were mostly down to about 200 rounds per turret. Faisal broke into his reserve, ordering the resupply Unimog truck to issue a new 4,000-round line of ammunition to all guns. Then he jogged around the force and arranged them for all-round defence that night. The UAE's RPG-22s and a tripod-mounted Kornet were readied for anti-tank use, and the Yemenis distributed their older RPG-7s to places where tanks might climb up to the base. And even though the air forces were tied up supporting other forces, Faisal and his men got reassuring fire support from an unexpected angle – Ali Saif's JTF-293.5. Roaring in out of the sea mist at 38 knots (70 km/hour), the two Egab mortar boats began to lay accurate suppressing fire on the assembly areas where Al-Qaeda fighters were gathering below the air defence camp, their fast-firing 120-mm mortars putting six rounds in the air before the first one had even landed.

To the east, Azzan's journey to Rayan airport had been a testament to the resilience of the UAE and Yemeni forces. After staring death in the face, Azzan and his OMLT had simply got on with the mammoth task of changing tyres on their fifteen-tonne RG-31 vehicle with the help of the ever-resourceful Yemeni mechanics. At their improvised field workshop, Azzan had been surprised to see Amr bin Habraish, the Yemeni leader whom he had come to meet way back on the first reconnaissance in the opening days of the war. Sheikh Amr had been at the tail of the column but had driven all the way to the front with his bodyguard because he had heard the fighting was heavy. Azzan's blood-smeared face made a strong impression on all the Yemenis, as did his battle-scarred vehicle. As Azzan's OMLT and Sheikh Amr's bodyguard all mounted up to follow Faisal, the column had picked up a stowaway: the wounded Corporal Saeed was not going to be left behind, so he sneaked into another OMLT's vehicle to make sure he would get a chance to see Mukalla. (It would be a week before he was discovered and sent back to Sharurah to have fragments of the Nissan Patrol removed from his infected wounds.)

On the way back through the ambush site, Azzan tried to free the bodies of the dead Yemeni from the upside-down chasse

– to ensure they could be buried – but Amr bin Habraish and his men held him back. 'Too dangerous', they said. 'It's still red hot and there might be grenades in the vehicle waiting to go off.' Yet, as grim as things were, the men could still cheer up their commander. As they drove away, with Azzan at the wheel of the RG-31, he clipped a Caiman with his front shock absorbers. 'Need some driving lessons, Sir?' his cheeky driver said from the commander's seat next to him. They both smiled. As long as they could make jokes, Azzan thought, morale was still good.

As the column approached the coastal T-junction near the 27th YNA base, Azzan's gunners scanning to the left saw the old wrecked 1960s aircraft scattered all around the former British Royal Air Force base to his left, while those with right-hand arcs carefully watched the AQAP-occupied 27th YNA base. Turning left towards Rayan airport (instead of right towards the city, as Faisal had done), Azzan sped the last 6 km towards the airport, thinking that he was merely following Faisal's cleared path towards the new central axis objective of Rayan. In fact, no friendly force had preceded him and Azzan had actually entered an actively defended strongpoint of the enemy. As his column burst through the airport's perimeter gates, they began to take fire from the main airport buildings and guard posts along the outer wall.

After taking Faisal's distress call, and also a somewhat premature congratulations radio call from headquarters on seizing the airport, Azzan again took stock of the situation. This time, Saif's joint fires were entirely at his disposal. As this was coastal Hadramaut's only real airport, he was careful to cause the minimum of damage. Two points in the airport buildings considered to be non-essential were precisely struck with small 250-lb bombs, and another six targets across the perimeter were quieted with either laser-guided bombs or 120-mm mortar fire from Egab mortar boats just off the coast. At 17:30 hours, the airport was clear of resistance as the enemy scattered in the dusk. At that point a Yemeni brought out an old UAE flag he had been saving for that moment, and handed it to Azzan to raise alongside Yemen's flag. He had not allowed himself a moment all day to stop and think and feel. Emotion, relief and shock suddenly flooded through him and he pushed his face into the flag to hide his feelings and to soak up the tears that came without warning.

Sohail's long mountain trek

Next to arrive was the eastern axis under Lieutenant Colonel Sohail K. After Marib, Sohail had gone through a health scare with leukaemia and had only just returned from getting the all-clear when he was sent back to Yemen. Sohail didn't know the Hadramis well, having only just arrived, but his deputy on the eastern axis was Lieutenant Ali Y., the trainer who had been with the HEF for 84 days at that point. Their objective had been Dhabba oil terminal and Rayan airport, with a second-ary mission of locking down the suburbs east of Mukalla city. They were in two echelons: a scout team and vanguard of HEF led by Sohail, and then Ali Y. with a hefty main body of about 500 HEF, a company of which were mounted in MRAPs. The heavy weapons platoons were mounted in gun-truck chasses with 81-mm mortars and Dushkas. The convoy was followed by fuel tankers and 14 UAE Unimog trucks carrying a second line of ammunition in case the fight was long or the force became isolated. Passing through the final friendly checkpoint in the opening minutes of 24 April, Sohail's vanguard at first moved parallel to Azzan's axis, which was about 10 km to the west, and, like Azzan, Sohail climbed a gently rising road through pitch-black rolling hills.

Unlike on the central axis, Sohail faced no thick outer defensive crust like the one at Al-Adwas. On the eastern axis, AQAP was trickier, rolling out remote-detonated car bombs (known as Vehicle-Carried IEDs, VCIEDS) that were parked on the road to kill enemy scouts, or even deployed when the scouts had gone by, in order to kill commanders in the main force. Sohail's first experience of this was an explosion up ahead at about 02:00 hours, right where his Yemeni guide was checking the route. When Sohail pulled up, a chassis-load of Yemenis were lying around, the dead and dying loaded together. His guide was safe but some local Yemenis trying to help him had been blown up by a VCIED. The ambulance MRAPs behind would look after them; Sohail had to push on.

Quickly a second potential VCIED was spotted on the road ahead in the dark. One of Sohail's Explosive Ordnance Disposal (EOD) techs put on his bomb suit. This was the astronaut-looking suit of armour that the bomb-defusers wore when they made their lonely approach to a suspected bomb, going alone so that the minimum number of persons would have to risk their lives. The EOD man switched on his night-vision goggles and began his long walk in the dark towards the vehicle. The Toyota Corolla was low on its suspension and, getting closer, he could see that it was piled up with artillery rounds and bags of raw explosives. The EOD technician was scared (who wouldn't be?), but also calm. This was what he had trained for and he had been here before – in Afghanistan and other conflict zones. It was hard not to imagine a triggerman watching him at that very second, deciding whether to push the button. But that guy was probably waiting for vehicles to arrive. Could there be anti-handling devices? Or a mine right where he would stand to defuse the device?

Then, in the midst of his professional EOD musings, a classic Yemeni moment occurred. He became aware of people standing next to him, which is not the kind of jump-scare you want when you are next to a bomb and potentially surrounded by the enemy in the darkness of a moonless night. Yemeni HEF fighters had casually strolled up to get a look at what he was doing, and they were standing around him like curious meerkats, peering through the windows of the huge car bomb. The tense, cinematic, professional EOD tech moment was over. It was time to get this crowd – a rather attractive target for a triggerman – far away from the VCIED.

Back at the column, Sohail and his scouts were working on a bypass. This entailed driving off-road and along steeply sloping muddy tracks that ran parallel to the left of the main road blocked by the VCIED. To the Yemenis in their ground-hugging chasses, this kind of road was a fun challenge for 'real men' – the Yemeni equivalent of the macho sport of dune-bashing – but in a tall 14-tonne MRAP, it was a nerve-shredding experience. It was very dark and night-vision goggles were required to differentiate open desert from the sudden cliff edges that dropped off to the left of the track. The MRAPs were slithering around on the muddy rock shale and ripping up their tyres to keep a grip, frequently approaching their tipping points. In each driver's cab, a large spirit-level was bolted to the hard metal dashboard between the driver and commander showing the pitch and yaw of the vehicle and how close it was to tipping over. The 27-tonne Caimans were some of the tallest MRAPs around – three metres plus their turret height. This was great for towering over walls and dominating long lines of fire but it made for a terrifying mountain trek. Eventually, a Caiman turned over and slid down a slope, thankfully with no loss of life. In the pre-dawn, AQAP snipers on ledges above were keeping up an accurate fire on the slow-moving vehicles, spider-webbing their armoured glass windows. F-16s were overhead, scanning the area with their infrared pods, dropping laser-guided bombs onto hotspots from where firing was originating.

About halfway to the coast, Sohail's team crested the 1,600-metre-high mountains and looked down as dawn came up over the sea, about 70 km distant 'as the crow flies'. But it wasn't 70 km away as Sohail would drive – the washing-away of roads in the recent rains meant that they were still many hours away from the wadi-fed agricultural plain below. It took nearly eight hours to descend the 730 metres to the coast, by which time one of Sohail's objectives – Rayan airport – had been transferred to Azzan. Instead, Sohail would secure the outside perimeter of the Dhabba oil storage facility, 10 km east of Rayan.

Passing through the T-junction where the attack axis met the coastal highway, Sohail saw bodies scattered around between the sand dunes, light green bushes and taupe turfs of sea grass. Someone else had fought hard here, but who? He didn't know at the time, but one tribal group of the 'inside resistance' had indeed made a heroic – but doomed – stand against Al-Qaeda at the junction, doing its part to stop AQAP from either reinforcing or escaping. Perhaps no one will ever know the story of this tiny action, which might have been as brave and as brutal as anything that happened on the day of battle. Other tribes were at that moment quite effectively self-liberating As-Shihr to the east. Just as in Marib, Sohail's own Yemenis suddenly went their own way, racing off into Mukalla city to get in on the liberation. When Yemenis got on a roll, there was no stopping them or controlling them. At 20:30 hours, Sohail's OMLT reached Dhabba. He had left in the dark, and now he arrived at his new objective in the dark.

Sohail's exhausted men set up for all-round defence outside the Dhabba plant. It was impossible to relax, even though they had all been on the go for nearly 24 hours now, doing some of the most nerve-wrecking driving of their lives. The oil tanks loomed over them and it was hard to know how far away from them to set up camp. What was a safe distance if 3 million barrels of oil exploded? At moments like this, soldiers tend to have a dark sense of humor. Imagining a toasted kebab as he tried to sleep, Sohail thought: 'If the tanks blow, we're all gonna be shawarma.'

Consolidation

As dawn came up on 25 April the UAE task force had a lot to be proud of and relieved about. It had taken less than a day to get two of the three axes to the coast. Three lodgements had been secured at Rabwat Baghshan, Rayan airport and Dhabba. The Hadramis in the attack force had mainly spread out through the city overnight and seized checkpoints at its outer edges. The 'inside resistance' had grabbed a number of known AQAP leaders, fighters and civilian collaborators.

Lieutenant Colonel Saeed S.'s western axis had started out first, 14 hours before the others, and it would arrive last. He had the longest route, 324 km, and the worst roads. Half of his journey was a huge 180-km hook out to the west before emerging not far from Masila Junction at dawn on 24 September. Thereafter his vanguard had begun the real hard trekking: a steep 2,000-metre descent in just 40 km on washed-out mountain tracks that were so narrow that the anti-RPG cages had to be removed from the MRAPs. The going was so bad that Saeed detached his entire second echelon to follow Azzan down the central axis via Masila Junction and Al-Adwas. Now, as morning came on 25 September, Saeed and his exhausted vanguard seized the palaces, the port, and IED factories in the west of the city and reinforced Faisal K.'s defensive foothold on Rabwat Baghshan.

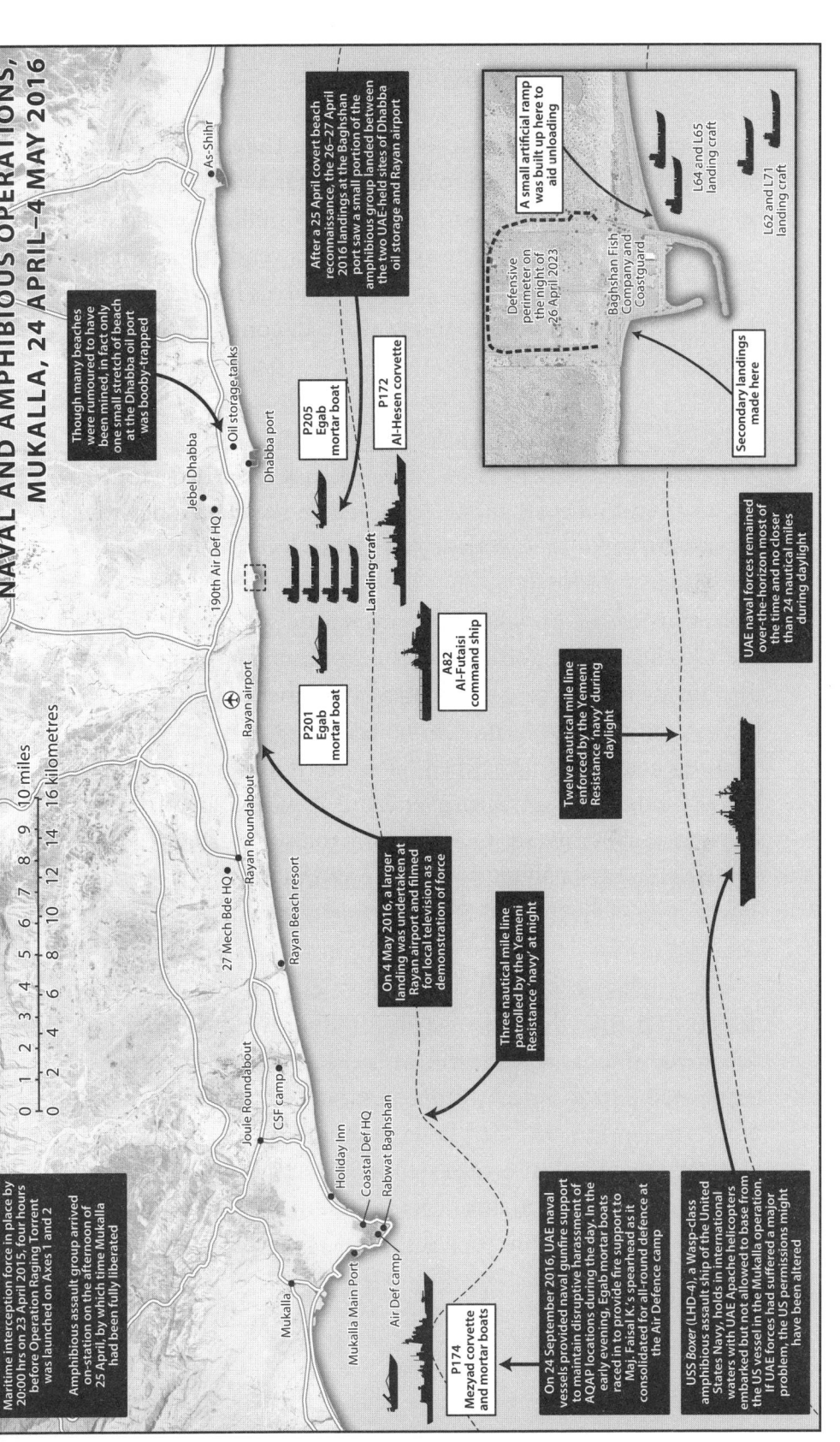

NAVAL AND AMPHIBIOUS OPERATIONS, MUKALLA, 24 APRIL–4 MAY 2016

Though many beaches were rumoured to have been mined, in fact only one small stretch of beach at the Dhabba oil port was booby-trapped

After a 25 April covert beach reconnaissance, the 26–27 April 2016 landings at the Baghshan port saw a small portion of the amphibious group landed between the two UAE-held sites of Dhabba oil storage and Rayan airport

A small artificial ramp was built up here to aid unloading

Defensive perimeter on the night of 26 April 2023

Baghshan Fish Company and Coastguard

L64 and L65 landing craft

L62 and L71 landing craft

Secondary landings made here

P205 Egab mortar boat

P172 Al-Hesen corvette

Oil storage tanks

Dhabba port

Jebel Dhabba

190th Air Def HQ

Landing craft

A82 Al-Futaisi command ship

P201 Egab mortar boat

Rayan airport

On 4 May 2016, a larger landing was undertaken at Rayan airport and filmed for local television as a demonstration of force

Twelve nautical mile line enforced by the Yemeni Resistance 'navy' during daylight

UAE naval forces remained over-the-horizon most of the time and no closer than 24 nautical miles during daylight

Three nautical mile line patrolled by the Yemeni Resistance 'navy' at night

Rayan Roundabout

Rayan Beach resort

27 Mech Bde HQ

Joule Roundabout

CSF camp.

Holiday Inn

Coastal Def HQ

Rabwat Baghshan

Mukalla Main Port

Mukalla

Air Def camp.

P174 Mezyad corvette and mortar boats

On 24 September 2016, UAE naval vessels provided naval gunfire support to maintain disruptive harassment of AQAP locations during the day. In the early evening, Egab mortar boats raced in to provide fire support to Maj. Faisal K.'s spearhead as it consolidated for all-round defence at the Air Defence camp

USS *Boxer* (LHD-4), a Wasp-class amphibious assault ship of the United States Navy, holds in international waters with UAE Apache helicopters embarked but not allowed to base from the US vessel in the Mukalla operation. If UAE forces had suffered a major problem, the US permissions might have been altered

Maritime interception force in place by 20:00 hrs on 23 April 2015, four hours before Operation Raging Torrent was launched on Axes 1 and 2

Amphibious assault group arrived on-station on the afternoon of 25 April, by which time Mukalla had been fully liberated

As-Shihr

0 1 2 3 4 5 6 7 8 9 10 miles
0 2 4 6 8 10 12 14 16 kilometres

The clearance of explosives was now a priority across Mukalla. It was clear from local informants that AQAP had indeed begun to 'wire' the city for demolition, but they had been just too slow – or rather the UAE had been just fast enough. Bases like the 190th Air Defence and 27th YNA brigade headquarters had daisy-chained artillery rounds laid out on their internal approach roads and anti-aircraft stores and ammunition bunkers had been turned into mega-booby-traps. There had been a lot of close calls in the dark: as the sun rose at Dhabba, Sohail and Ali Y. found themselves looking at their own tyre tracks from when they had parked their truck the night before, after they finished their inspection of the defensive perimeter. An anti-tank land mine was sideways-up in their tyre mark, where the edge of their wheel had levered it out of the ground.

Like a lot of Arabs, most of the Emiratis would not describe themselves as 'dog lovers', but they had a lot of respect for their K-9 explosives detection dogs, who had been through the ambushes and bone-shaking drives right alongside them. Two of the three dogs – Shakira and Victor – were still in good enough shape to do the demanding work of clearing Dhabba. (The third dog was so shaken up by the drive and the long confinement that she was medevacked by helicopter back to Sharurah.) The dogs now led the way.

As intelligence had suggested, the eastern-side commander for AQAP, Riyadh Omar al-Shaab (Abu Omar al-Nahdi), had been the most enthusiastic and active tactical leader when it came to rigging Mukalla's infrastructure for demolition. His headquarters at 27th YNA brigade base had contained mapping that showed the extensive preparations underway at the time of the liberation. Also at Abu Omar al-Nahdi's headquarters, the Emiratis found both AQAP and Islamic State flags, underlining what they had long assessed, which was considerable overlap in these two brands of Salafi jihadism. Indeed, in later years Abu Omar al-Nahdi would lead a split in AQAP and draw many of its members to the Islamic State instead.

Inside Dhabba, a team of UAE and Saudi military technicians plus divers, Emirates Red Crescent de-miners, contractors and the K-9 teams would uncover an astounding booby-trapping effort. In daylight, they could see that the main gates had been wired as a huge IED made from anti-tank mines and 152-mm artillery shells, so it was fortunate that Sohail and his men had not tried to enter the night they arrived. The whole perimeter was a minefield made up of webs of wired-together IEDs, mortar bombs and 152-mm shells. The storage tanks themselves were nearly full and had 68 demolitions charges attached to them, wired and ready to blow. On the breakwater and jetty at the loading port, AQAP had installed wired-together bombs inside foam boxes so that they floated on the water. A sunken ship had been filled with explosives and wired as a kind of naval mine in the port's approaches. And there were growing signs that some stretches of beach had been mined against the possibility of an amphibious assault.

The final reinforcements of the Mukalla force would arrive by sea in the week after all fighting had ceased. On 25 April, Ali Saif's JTF-293.5 arrived to witness the beautiful sunset over the mountains that occurred each night. They immediately oversaw a beach reconnaissance that same evening. The amphibious landing would go ahead as a show of force and as a way of exercising the capability ahead of a combat assault on the Red Sea coast. The landing was intended to take place at the small fishing port and coastguard base at Baghshan, which was between secured areas of Rayan airport and Dhabba. Intelligence had previously ascertained that about 20 mines had been planted on a beach somewhere east of Mukalla, but that turned out to be 10 km to the east, at the heavily mined Dhabba oil storage site.

Landing craft full of UAE vehicles and combat troops assembled on the evening of 26 April, just as Azzan's OMLTs were spreading out across the city to lead the hunt for AQAP stay-behinds. After two days of difficult landings, Baghshan fishing port was secured by part of the force. A better beach site was identified right next to Rayan airport and a major landing was broadcast on local television on 4 May as a show of strength to anyone still leaning towards Al-Qaeda. Although the amphibious and airmobile options had not been needed to seize Mukalla, they had provided an important back-up plan if the land advance had been blocked, which was a real possibility. The 'belt and braces' approach to the operation – in which all options are pursued to make sure that something is safe or works properly – was a sign of the professionalism and experience of the UAE planning staff. The many lessons of the Mukalla landings were incorporated into future plans for UAE amphibious assault on the Red Sea coast.

The balance sheet in Mukalla

As the first humanitarian assistance ships arrived at Mukalla's main port, the Emiratis had much to feel relieved and satisfied about. The operation to liberate Mukalla had succeeded beyond most people's expectations. A city of more than half a million people was no longer under Al-Qaeda's control. Some of the hard-won lessons of Safer had made a difference: relying on itself alone, the UAE had concentrated its forces at a new base, well out of sight of all enemies, and then crashed down suddenly with tactical surprise. No Emiratis died in the liberation, which had been achieved with a very light UAE footprint. As Saeed S.

remembered: 'Until we had the city, the worry was like a mountain on my head. But here we were, all my friends were alive, the target was secure, and there were happy people celebrating. It was wonderful.'

Of course there had been a human cost. Forty-five Yemeni fighters had been killed in the battle and 79 wounded. But their losses were much lighter than the hundreds of Iraqi and Syrian fatalities in the clearance of similar-sized cities. As important, unlike in Ramadi, Raqqa or Mosul, the civilians had been spared and their city was liberated entirely intact. Whereas 20,000 structures were destroyed by fighting in Mosul, 11,000 in Raqqa and 3,000 in Ramadi, the number in Mukalla was 31. Of these, 30 were carefully selected targets, most of which were repairable because the damage inflicted on the buildings had been precisely calculated. A post-battle call for compensation would show that only one building suffered unintended damage – a cultural centre that was empty at the time and which was repaired after the battle. Coalition strikes in the Mukalla battle caused zero civilian deaths.

As it would in other Yemeni cities, AQAP melted away when it sensed defeat coming. 'We knew they would run away if we came, but we still had to take it from them,' Azzan remembered. 'AQAP used to sell oil to tankers in the sea. They ran the police. They had ministries. They were a state. Now they were gone, and to see people celebrating made it all worth it.'

The world had a less charitable – and less accurate – explanation for Mukalla's liberation. Knowing next to nothing about the battle, many observers filled the gaps with conspiracies. 'Hardly a shot was fired,' the *New York Times* reporter in Mukalla noted. 'We woke up one day and Al-Qaeda had vanished without a fight.' But there *had* been a fight, as 45 dead Hadrami fighters, nearly 80 wounded men, and dozens of shot-to-hell vehicles could attest. The fight was out at the edges of Al-Qaeda's defence, not in the city. AQAP itself tried to claim credit for leaving the city to protect Mukalla from destruction, but that propaganda effort didn't hold up to scrutiny either. They had a chance to leave and many of them did not. AQAP left because of the coalition advance and they only did not fight harder because their most hard-line fighters were killed in the 23 April warehouse decapitation strike; because their explosive defences were not ready; and because the liberation unfolded too quickly.

Then the Associated Press (AP) got a new scoop: AQAP had been given free passage out of Mukalla along with their weapons, cash and loot. 'Coalition fighter jets and drones were idle,' the AP reported, and there was even a goodbye dinner to bid AQAP farewell. Some AQAP had been allowed to stay in the city and some had joined the coalition-backed security forces, AP reported. 'Awkward questions' had been raised, a *Washington Post* op-ed noted, by the 'graceful exit' that AQAP had made from Mukalla.

There is an old saying that 'first reports are always wrong', and the modern news and analysis cycle is definitely not focused on ensuring the accuracy or the long shelf-life of its statements. This was the case in Mukalla. An idea circulated that AQAP had been given what was long ago called the 'honours of war' – an ancient tradition used to end a siege by allowing the garrison to march back to their own front lines with all their arms and flags. In the case of Mukalla, there was no 'honours of war' offered to AQAP. Such formal truces *had* occurred in Iraqi and Syria, but did not happen in Mukalla. It was true that some AQAP leaders sensed the end coming and got clear: for instance, Qassem al-Raimi had left well before the battle and Khalid al-Batarfi fled the night before. But no deal to surrender the city had been proposed by the UAE and none had been offered by Al-Qaeda.

Instead, they scattered like rats in every direction during the battle. In some places, they had an escape plan, firing 23-mm cannons and Dushkas to draw surveillance away from their escape routes. The foreign fighters tried to flee along the coast, where they would stand out less, but many were intercepted in hotels in Mahra coastal towns. Nine boats were sunk on the night of 24–25 April off Mukalla when they refused orders to stop. The survivors from these interceptions were added to around 40 AQAP captures that night.

If anything could be mistaken for the honours of war, it was a mysterious convoy of 20 vehicles that burst out of Mukalla towards the AQAP strongholds in Shabwa on the night of 24 April. These were no doubt AQAP leaders and family members, but their exit was hardly graceful. The 'inside resistance' saw the convoy but were not very keen to get into a fight with 20 chasses of Al-Qaeda bodyguards and leaders. From above, the UAE's drones ticked off one form of positive identification – these cars could violate the AQAP curfew and drive right through check-points without slowing. That might have been good enough for the United States under its 'signature targeting' rules but not for the UAE. The convoy was followed for 40 minutes as Saif sought additional means of validating the targets, but then it split in all directions and the UAE alone did not have enough drones to follow all the 'squirters' as they were known in counter-terror-ism circles. The US military had watched such columns leave the Iraqi city of Fallujah under the honours of war and had the surveillance assets to parse out the most high-interest vehicles, validate them as targets, and then destroy them selectively after they had driven far away. Perhaps if the United States had helped, this would have been possible against AQAP in Mukalla too.

If the coalition or the Hadramis really did have a truce with Al-Qaeda, as Western media reports suggested, then it was one of the worst truces in history. Two days after the liberation, a stranger asked to eat with a group of eight soldiers at the Hamra checkpoint, at the western edge of Mukalla city. The commander, with his seven-year-old daughter on his lap, welcomed the man, who then got as close as he could and detonated his suicide vest, killing everyone. AQAP defectors to the Islamic State bombed the Presidential Palace, the 2nd MRC and later a recruiting centre in Mukalla, in some cases using follow-on suicide bombings to strike first-responders. Bounties were placed on the heads of Azzan (50 million Yemeni rial), his wakil (25 million YR), and Ali Y. (12 million YR).

The ongoing terrorist threat was illustrated dramatically on 28 April when a televised press conference was held at oil company offices at the edge of the Dhabba complex. As Musallam announced the arrival of humanitarian assistance at Mukalla's ports, there was the sound of gunfire in the distance. AQAP shooters had suppressed the outer checkpoint with heavy close-range fire, allowing a Toyota Camry to jump the anti-vehicle ditch outside Dhabba. The next checkpoint had not fired a shot, leaving it up to the Emiratis at the inner checkpoint to riddle its driver with bullets, bringing the car to a rolling stop 100 metres outside the inner checkpoint. Ali Y. had inspected the corpse, which was shot full of holes but, in a creepy turn of events, was hardly bleeding. When Ali asked the medics why, they pointed to the masses of tranexamic acid tablets the driver had taken to clot his own blood. When Ali asked the Yemeni gunners on the inner checkpoint why they had not fired, they had an instant answer: 'You'll leave and they'll kill us, even years after.'

XIII

EPILOGUE

The Emiratis did not leave, and in fact they brought the Americans into Hadramaut in a way that made sense. Ali Saif had once again received a transfer of command from Musallam, taking over JTF-291 in late 2016. Ali Saif made it clear that the UAE commitment to Al-Qaeda's defeat was enduring, saying: 'The counter-Al-Qaeda operation will remain and we will remain in Yemen until AQAP is broken. We will stay until it is done.' There was no truce with the jihadists and there never would be.

The immediate post-liberation period provided proof that the truce idea had always been nonsense. By the end of April 2016, all available intelligence had been brought together – from prisoners, truckloads full of documents, cell phones, GPS devices and human sources. The continuous targeting cycle then began in earnest. Massive caches of explosives were recovered. In one furniture factory, 1,992 IEDs were secured and later destroyed, further evidence that a Mosul-type defence had been planned and narrowly averted. Twenty-six shipping containers of explosives were emptied from one AQAP base alone. A suicide-vest workshop was uncovered at a house of prostitution in Mukalla. In its pursuit of Al-Qaeda, the UAE applied many of the lessons it had learned while building Yemeni counter-terrorism forces in Aden in 2015 – replicating and improving what worked, and avoiding what didn't – to quickly develop a Yemeni raiding force in Mukalla.

These Hadrami special forces arrested one AQAP recruiter who had sent his own children outside Yemen so that they could be spared, and another tactical commander was brought in wearing a woman's full-body cloak, or abaya. The Hisba commanders who had executed civilians at the Chinese Bridge – Mohammed Soroor Saeed al-Oraibi and Humam al-Nashir – were thrown in jail. Mohammed Saleh al-Ghurabi, a former army officer who had terrorised Mukalla and As-Shihr with the Hisba, was seized in a synchronised operation that, on a single night, took down all eight of the safe houses he used. The raid was led by a 29-year-old team leader who had trained with Ali Y. in the HEF since 2015. 'He was a crazy brave guy who knew every street and rock in Mukalla, the best navigator I ever saw,' Ali remembered proudly. When Mohammed Saleh al-Ghurabi was dragged out of his hiding place, Ali got a close look at his enemy:

> He was shocked, quiet and weak-looking. He had been the ruler of Mukalla's streets. The safe house was full of gold and silver AKs [Kalasknikov rifles]. When he was cuffed, it was the end of his world. He was so shocked that we had got him, in his cousin's house, on a farm, one of a big group of farms he moved between all the time in car, taxis, trail bikes and on foot. But he had set a pattern and we had noticed it.

President Barack Obama had called Yemen a 'model' for counter-terrorism partnerships in 2014, but, soon after, the war knocked the CIA and JSOC base out of their only base in Yemen at Al-Anad. There were limits to what the United States could do from outside a country using over-the-horizon targeting. Khalid al-Batarfi had claimed the *Charlie Hebdo* killings in Paris for AQAP, underlining that the movement could still mount external operations in 2015. In time, if AQAP had been allowed to control an emirate with huge resources, external plots would have intensified again.

AQAP obviously survived the liberation of Mukalla and also the loss of 45 senior leaders killed by US drone strikes in 2016, but these *combined* efforts brought about a near-complete cessation of AQAP external operations and a global diminishment of the movement that Wahayshi had aimed to build. From the liberation of Mukalla in 2016 to the time of writing in 2023, AQAP mounted no major external attacks and failed to provide a successor to Al-Qaeda leader Ayman al-Zawahiri who was killed in July 2022.

The Mukalla campaign was followed by new counter-terrorism campaigns that moved west into AQAP's next closest sanctuaries in Shabwa. The effort would showcase the trilateral formula that should be remembered as the real Yemen model – the US-UAE-Yemeni offensives of 2016–18. In the aftermath of Mukalla's liberation, MBZ had passed a message to the United States that said simply: 'I wish you had not let us go alone but you can still join us.' JSOC did indeed return to Yemen after the liberation of Mukalla, now working protected by a UAE force protection scheme and deploying alongside the Emiratis. As early as 6 May 2016, the US Department of Defense spokesman confirmed that a 'very small' US military detachment was back in Yemen following Mukalla's liberation. Speaking of Mukalla, the spokesman said: 'This is of great interest to us. It does not serve our interests to have a terrorist organisation in charge of a port city, and so we are assisting in that.' With the JSOC cell came all the US intelligence, surveillance and reconnaissance capabilities that would have been so useful weeks beforehand. The captured cell phones, laptops and flash drives were plugged into the incredible US intelligence machinery, triggering four drone strikes in a week in May 2016, which were followed by 125 drone strikes in the 12 months after the liberation.

This effort would become a powerful model for future counter-terrorism efforts in Yemen because it did more than remotely kill the external operations planners and spokespeople that the West had in their cross hairs. Influential critics of drone-led counter-terrorism in Yemen such as Gregory D. Johnsen had, for years, advocated a different approach. The UAE had the same view. 'Taking their leaders out had little impact. They would always make more,' Musallam believed: 'Taking their money, their prestige, their banks and their ports, showing them to be weak in front of the Yemenis, was the real blow.' Between the Yemeni informants and the US drones there was now a transformative middle layer that elevated the effort from over-the-horizon counter-terrorism to on-the-ground counter-insurgency (COIN) that could take terrain back from AQAP and hold it. Sharp observers like Katherine Zimmerman, the long-serving Yemen-watcher at the American Enterprise Institute, had always said that terrorists in Yemen could not be allowed to develop safe havens and that the only way to deny sanctuary permanently was by prosecuting successful counter-insurgency campaigns.

The UAE's ability to deploy task forces with drones, Apaches, special forces and MRAPs meant that the United States was no longer the only show in town when it came to counter-insurgency. The Emiratis brought the COIN mindset to its treatment of the enemy, in part driven by their experiences in multinational counter-insurgency campaigns such as in Afghanistan but also simply because they were more attuned to the local environment. They had listened to Yemenis and heard them when they said: 'We are mixed, we are one fabric.' Although Western newspapers saw coalition recruitment of former Sons of Hadramaut fighters as a 'gotcha' moment – proof of back-door deal-making – this was exactly what US forces had done in Iraq. It was the heart of the COIN playbook. Speaking in 2017, Ali Saif was clear about this:

> Many AQAP fighters were just young men under their control who were coerced or persuaded to take up arms. When we cleared Al-Qaeda out of urban areas, they left behind many of these men and it made sense to recruit them, because it sent a powerful message about the Yemeni commitment to the liberation. Counter-insurgency is primarily a battle for hearts and minds. AQAP were effective recruiters but they did not recruit these men to be terrorists, they recruited them to be soldiers. It's important to recognise the difference in such a complex conflict zone.

Partners in counter-terrorism

The Hadrami Elite Forces were a powerful vindication of the 'advise, assist and accompany' approach to COIN, whereby effective counter-insurgency requires special forces partners to be on the ground with the local troops. 'What really counted was that we sat with them every day and every night, eating, sleeping, talking and training,' Azzan concluded. 'We were together for a year. We knew their families and they knew ours. We would ask each other about them every day.' The Emiratis had learned the Hadrami psychology and history, and had used it to remind them of their own military heritage before Communism, Ali Abdullah Saleh or Al-Qaeda. 'After 50 years', a fighter had told Musallam, 'we have our honour and our dignity back.'

As the UAE transitioned fully to the counter-terrorism targeting phase of the operation on 5 May, it was time for Musallam to get serious about finally fixing his busted shoulder. More than a year ago – even before the Yemen war had started – he had sought out the mission of landing a major blow on AQAP: the winding road to Mukalla had taken him into the battle for Marib and through the hell of Safer. He had raced against time to build forces, to bring them together, to recover from injury, and to liberate Mukalla. But now the race was over and Mukalla was free again.

Musallam had struggled through seven months of pain since the missiles struck Safer, and on 7 May 2016 he reached the end. He could either breath or move, but not both. The titanium plate in his shoulder had broken loose. Colonel Abdullah S. took command of JTF-291 and Musallam was flown out to the USS *Boxer*, the amphibious landing ship on which UAE Apaches had to sit out the battle, far offshore in international waters. The Americans on board had wanted to help the Emiratis, but orders were orders: now his friends in the US Navy, the Marines and JSOC could at least do him one favour. Flanked as ever by his trusty wakil, Musallam walked off the Black Hawk helicopter into a US ceremony to honour the UAE forces he commanded. It was a nice touch from soldiers, sailors and airmen who wished they could have done more to fight their shared terrorist enemy.

Musallam returned to Munich, where multiple operations and 23 screws got him back into action. The scars and the pain of Safer would never leave Musallam: they were part of him now. 'I saw myself in the mirror and I knew I would take this wound with me to the grave. Every night as I slept, if I rolled onto that side it would burn me in my dreams.' A few weeks before the second ever UAE's Martyrs' Day on 30 November 2016, Musallam went to Australian staff college to prepare for a new role leading the counter-terrorism services of the UAE, and he passed command of the Special Operations Command to none other than Ali Saif.

Both these commanders would always remember their days in Marib and Hadramaut as they rose alongside each other to the highest levels of their military profession. And their shared enemy, Al-Qaeda, would always remember them. A letter arrived one day at a house in Abu Dhabi, addressed to Musallam. It wasn't Musallam's house, the location of which would always be a well-guarded secret, but the letter nonetheless did make it into his hands and it was in many ways the best accolade he could have received. It was from AQAP and said simply: 'We do not forget.'

POSTSCRIPT

This book was completed shortly after the Anglo-American air-strikes on the Houthis, which began on 11 January 2024, part of an international effort to deter the Yemeni group from attacking shipping in the Red Sea against the backdrop of the Gaza war.

This new stage of the conflict in Yemen might have been avoidable if the Gulf coalition and Yemeni forces had been allowed to complete their operations to evict the Houthis from the Red Sea coast of Yemen in 2016–18.

This tragic campaign involved an agonising calculation of the risks of action or inaction. Inaction would leave the Houthis in control of the vital sea lane linking Asia and Europe. Action to remove the Houthis might disrupt humanitarian assistance and plunge Yemen into full-scale famine. Either path was fraught with momentous consequences and full of lessons about the contradictions that sometimes sit at the heart of concepts such as humanitarianism and uses of the military instrument.

This story needs telling in the same detailed manner as the campaigns of Aden, Marib and Mukalla. The battles for the Bab el-Mandeb, the Red Sea coast and the all-important container port at Hodeidah make up the final and climactic chapter in the history of Arab elite forces at war in Yemen.

INDEX

Page references in *italics* indicate images.

PICTURE CREDITS

Plate sections

1 Matjaz Krivic/Getty Images; 2 MARWAN NAAMANI/AFP via Getty
Images; 3 AFP via Getty Images; 4 Getty Images; 5 AFP via Getty Images;
6 STR/AFP via Getty Images; 7 AFP/GettyImages; 8 Sudarsan Raghavan/
The Washington Post via Getty Images; 9 REUTERS/Khaled Abdullah; 10
REUTERS/Mohamed al-Sayaghi; 11 Egmont Strigl/Getty Images; 12 Yemen
Tourism Authority/Pictures From History/Universal Images Group via Getty
Images; 13 REDA&CO/Getty Images; 14 Author's collection; 15 REUTERS/
Omer Arm; 16 DeAgostini/Getty Images; 17 Werner Forman/Universal Images
Group/Getty Images; 18 Ali Owimdha/Anadolu Agency/Getty Images; 19
Ali Owimdha/Anadolu Agency/Getty Images; 20 REUTERS/Stringer; 21
REUTERS/Noah Browning; 22 STR/AFP via Getty Images; 23 Author's
collection; 24 Author's collection; 25 Author's collection; 26 Author's collection;
27 UAE Ministry of Defence; 28 REUTERS/Noah Browning

29 STR/AFP via Getty Images; 30 Author's collection; 31 UAE Ministry of
Defence; 32 Author's collection; 33 Author's collection, photo Alex Almeida;
34 Author's collection, photo Alex Almeida; 35 Author's collection; 36 Author's
collection; 37 REUTERS/Stringer - REUTERS/Ali Owidha - REUTERS/Ali
Owidha; 38 REUTERS/Noah Browning; 39 REUTERS/Noah Browning; 40
ABDULLAH AL-QADRY/AFP via Getty Images; 41 Author's own image,
with kind thanks to the al-Quaiti sultanate family for providing the photograph
for use; 42–47 UAE Ministry of Defence; 48 Egmont Strigl/Getty Images;
49 SALEH AL-OBEIDI/AFP via Getty Images; 50 SALEH AL-OBEIDI/
AFP via Getty Images; 51–53 UAE Ministry of Defence; 54 KARIM SAHIB/
AFP via Getty Images; 55 Author's collection, photo Alex Almeida; 56 SALEH
AL-OBEIDI/AFP via Getty Images); 57 UAE Ministry of Defence

ALSO BY MICHAEL KNIGHTS

25 Days to Aden is the story of how in a week in 2015 the Gulf States pulled together a ten-nation coalition and the biggest military operation they ever launched unilaterally. It is an amazing account of Arab militaries doing what America would not, preventing Iran from taking a foothold on the Arabian Peninsula.

The risks for global security were huge: Iran already overshadowed one of the world's greatest maritime straits, at Hormuz, and now it sought to dominate the southern approaches to the Suez Canal as well. Aden had to hold out against the Houthis. The Gulf States were used to America stepping up at such moments, but the White House was partway through negotiating a nuclear deal with Iran. No help would come from Washington. Instead, for the first time, the Gulf States acted alone.

Told by an expert communicator on the region, it is a unique story. If the US is truly a global empire in decline, then the story may hold important pointers for a future of warfare driven by emergent powers in the gap left by the withdrawal of American influence.